GENTLE WARRIORS

GEOFF MAINS

 Knights Press

Stamford, Connecticut

A LeatherLit Book

Cover designed by Chris Karukas©

Published by Knights Press, P.O. Box 454, Pound Ridge, NY 10576

Distributed by Carol Publishing Group, 120 Enterprise Ave., Secaucus, NJ 07094

Library of Congress Cataloging-in-Publication Data

Mains, Geoffrey.
    Gentle warriors / Geoff Mains.
        p. cm.
    ISBN 0-915175-36-3 : $9.50
    I. Title.
PS3563.A3828G46 1989
813'.54—dc19   88-31592
                                      CIP

Typeset by The Designers' Typography Studio, Albuquerque, NM

Printed in the United States of America

This is a LeatherLit Book.

To Robert Chesley

1 *San Francisco, Thursday Evening*

He was on break and he spent it on watch. One didn't maneuvre or expect. One waited and one watched.

This was a way of being that Marc had learned from childhood. Watching for sign. Waiting for death.

Through ever-pressing gloom the world might seem to shimmer with gold. Of autumn tamarack. Of scattered words in the gold parchment of fallen aspen. Of frost-burned sedge. Here and there was dark water, but in that zone between muskeg and swamp forest he had learned to discern not pattern, not difference, but that movement in the stillness of dream, that movement which warned of partner, which spoke of quarry.

Here in this bar in San Francisco, those northern memories were not inconsequential. They were alive and as gold as twenty-five years ago. The training they had accompanied, the mind working of the hunter: these things still lived in Marc. Here was another forest, and in its smoke lurked still further dreams.

Dreaming was no answer to death, Marc knew that. Dreaming was the tool of the hunter, the survival kit of the warrior. It could bring death, but it could not avoid it. Death was the inevitable, unmitigatible purpose of life. Most people's dreams skirted it. A warrior's dreaming addressed it, took it in stride.

2 *Upper Market, San Francisco, Thursday Evening*

Gregg was on his way through the dark night to a tryst. He had confirmed with himself that he would take part. He had made a pact with himself and this disease that gnawed continually at the edges of his reality. It was a difficult, an uneasy pact, but Gregg had to make it. Allan, away at his other meeting, off on his political career, would not be pleased. But then Allan would not have to know about any of it until all had happened and the dead bolt had slammed hard into the carapace that was fate.

If there was one thing that continued to amaze Gregg in this strange, transitional world that he had come to inhabit, it was that the laws of physics seemed as coherent as ever. If his mind often slipped and shifted and lost sense of the firm being it had once held, his motorcycle and his skill at handling it remained solid. He took the sweeping, downward curves of Corbett and then Market with a confidence that had gone from everything else. Guided by the pressure of his thighs, Gregg and his bike took possession of the streets as if all the laws of nature were immutable and on his side.

Yes, he was angry with Allan. But he was more annoyed with time. He'd held this vague hope that once the campaign was finally over, the two would have found the occasion to reconnect, to rebuild what had once been between them. Was this delusion? Gregg had changed, and even should that opportunity come, would he ever be able to love Allan in the same way that had once meant so much?

He remembered those first happenings in gay life, those events that followed on the pains of war and family. He remembered them as some of his most moving experiences. That stroke from a stranger's eyes. That look and touch that made two men lovers for a night and for a lifetime. That almost instant communication that followed on the look. Feel of fingers on nipples. Hands, honest and horny in the crotch. And then the opening up. The Crisco, the smoothness of fingers, the clenched fist filling the emptiness inside the soul. The wholesome spirituality that flowed between two buddies in a form of birth. How Gregg had welcomed those experiences. Drunk from them with an almost narcotic thirst. Gregg had no regrets now, only an incredible sadness. Those times could not come back. Those times would never come back. And even if time would permit it, reality had placed its shadow across the way.

Perhaps his anger came forward because he felt used. He was Allan's lover. He shared Allan's ambitions and notoriety. And Allan's campaign opponent made no little thing of Gregg's condition. Yet why was Gregg complaining? Allan's political race was for a good cause. An *essential* cause. And what right had Gregg to bitch? Sure, one bout of pneumocystis, a year ago. One and a half protracted weeks in Franklin and a recuperation that seemed spectacular. He had watched far worse in the grim deaths of friends. He knew there was no escape, that a similar death was inevitable. Allan, damn him, could have shown just a little more sensitivity, just a little more love.

There were moments when riding this motorcycle was all the joy that still existed in this broken world. All of the confidence that things could be right. Now, he almost hated this intersection of Castro and Market Streets, its memories dim and muffled under quiet fog. How they had hoped and dreamed; now the sidewalks seem to smell of blood.

Gregg's machine purred under him, like a giant cat, its claws retracted, his body riding its spine and taking the curves as if it had always been planned that way. Once, in the marines, once in the despair of that war, he had caressed his gun in the same way. His gun had fired as if it bit off and spat out bits of his own flesh. Shooting those damn things took effort and skill and not a small amount of luck. He had won awards for his precision. He had been lucky, the gun hadn't jammed. He had taken medals as a killer. His gun, his eyes and his body had moved as one, firing repeatedly into the green terror. His gun had sobbed with his heart's despair.

3 Southern Oregon, Thursday Evening

Late supper in a Grant's Pass Sizzler had soothed neither of their tempers.

"Damn it, if we travel we've got to stop. So we end up at places you claim you don't like. All the more reason to get it over with."

Brian responded by slamming the truck door. Noise of a starting engine filled the cab.

"Sam, you know that the food is not what I'm upset about."

"Do you think I don't know that? Come on, trust me, guy."

Sam reached across and stroked Brian's leg in reconciliation. There was no response. Brian continued to sit, rigidly and determined. When he was like this, there was something in his lover that Sam liked. Perhaps it was the way his face and dark beard tightened up so he looked almost mean. When Sam would finally succeed and break through, Brian would release that gorgeous smile of his, a wonderful blend of heat, steam and sunshine. At least that had been the way in Sam's previous experience.

"Sam, listen to me. I trusted you on this whole California thing. Oh sure, I'd always wanted to move to San Francisco. That is, if I was going to be there with you."

Sam let the truck into gear and pulled toward the parking lot exit. Damn it, Brian told himself. I'm giving too much; he doesn't care what I think.

"Brian, we've got to get this trip over. I know you don't think I'm up to it, but believe me, I am."

"Listen Sam! You might be a good doctor when it comes to dealing with others, but when it comes to knowing your own limits — "

"You should talk about limits! Your reputation is solid everywhere in the northwest."

Other times, the two would have relaxed into banter on the arcane details of one another. But Brian was not prepared to be diverted with sexual humor.

"Sam. This is like a second honeymoon for us. It's a new life. And given the fact you're not going to be around a lot longer, I want us to take our time, to enjoy it."

"Listen, Brian. When we get there we will. I promise you."

"What the fuck are you doing this for? We rush our butts off in Portland, getting things packed, loading the truck. We rush around saying good-bye to friends. Then we drive as if we're trying to escape a nuclear attack."

Yeah, it was true. Sam admitted to himself. They were tired. Yeah, he would like to do nothing better than stop

7

and sleep. Curl up with this hairy, angry man and stroke his feelings smooth again. Doze in the warmth of each other's arms.

"So what do we do?" Brian continued. "We go crazy getting out of Portland. We go crazy heading down I-5. And we don't have a single commitment in San Francisco. No jobs to be at. All the time in the world. And you insist on driving straight through."

God, I'd like to stop, Sam thought again. But he couldn't stop, and he couldn't tell Brian anything of the pressing reasons. Brian would just have to accept it. The two had been close enough for long enough; their relationship would survive this one.

Time passed, rushing on with the truck, swirling about them like the waters of a mountain river. Brian softened just a little and put some Vivaldi on the portable CD player. Otherwise, he kept to himself, brooding in the warm darkness of the cab, the frenetic stab of headlights dancing unexpectedly off the lenses of his glasses.

Even with the firmness of the wheel gripped in his hands, even knowing, feeling the response of the truck to the smallest movement of his foot, Sam felt helpless.

In some ways, it was like rafting. He and Brian rafted together, often: rivers like the Deschutes in an Oregon that had been part of Sam's very flesh. Rafting brought exhilaration, conscious joys, as they tipped and dropped and lunged, given to the will of the water, protected from the rock beneath them, against them, by a thin cushion of that same water. But now, although he felt himself swept along, it was quite different. There was none of that joyful release that succeeded each sudden recovery from helplessness.

Why was he doing this, Sam wondered, seeking out the strongest, most giddying parts of the current? Sure, he had been swept into it when he had received the same diagnosis he had so often conferred on his patients. That splotch on Sam's leg was no bruise from the time his ten-speed skidded on gravel in Washington Park. The diagnosis had probably been harder for Brian than it had for him. Brian had been shaken with grief. Sam had collared and restrained his own grief in the way he had learned to with each patient. At least he knew the ultimate end of his own odyssey. Brian would be faced with a more difficult future.

Why hadn't he stayed in Portland, among people he knew and in a community he loved? What better place was there to die? He could have been buried by a cortege of empresses in rhinestones and black crepe. But he had given up his practice, sold his house and set off as if this were the beginning of a new life, to a city where it was once believed that nearly everything could be perfect. Was it that he didn't want his friends and colleagues to see him as he began to wither, his normally reserved facade crumbling slowly about him? Or was he going to Oz to die with his dreams, his greatest passion on the truck seat beside him? Was all this illusion, vanity? The perquisites of facing or fleeing death, or both? And had Brian, dear grief-stricken Brian, fallen for these crazy plans only because of confusion, fear, and devotion to Sam? He must attempt to reach out to Brian. If Sam felt this rush of water about them was uncontrollable, for Brian it must seem intolerable.

There was, of course, the real reason for this lunacy, the reason he couldn't explain to Brian. It entailed a commitment beyond himself, a commitment to justice. Back when Jim had first got sick, Sam had gone down to visit him in San Francisco. They had shared memories of their past, their joys, hopes, and fallen brothers. They talked vaguely of causes, anger, and justice. Then Sam went back to Portland and Jim's health seemed to improve greatly. He even was on AZT for a while, but that knocked the shit of his hematocrit and he was forced to give it up. For about eight months Jim tasted hope, the proffered life held out to him again. And then, suddenly, reality became evident: Jim had succumbed to Kaposi's sarcoma, which was consuming him rapidly, inside and out, the last supper of a sordid virus.

In these last six months other things had happened. A specter had appeared, its lurid rumors dancing surreptitiously in the shadows of Washington bureaucracy, playing first in Fundamentalist and far-right circles, but then growing stronger. No one knew the source of the rumors. No one seemed able to validate them. And no one seemed able to better pinpoint these rumblings, so low in pitch that not even the administration would grant them the credence of acknowledgement. Ironically, the spectre began its dance almost that same week Jim's lesions had broken out. The same week that Sam had come to greet his own fate.

Sam had flown back to the city to support Jim. Even in Portland they called it the city, that sort of white and gold acropolis as Steinbeck had once described it, rising from its hills, whatever this calamity, still as beautiful as ever. Despite the shadow, there still seemed to be hope in San Francisco. It was a city one wanted to live in because its very essence made one want to believe that things which counted were possible. And in these times, all of them counted, more than ever. On that last trip, Sam had fallen in quickly with Jim's planning for justice.

His hands set to the wheel, his mind lashed hard to a future that would not be deflected, Sam drove on. No, he couldn't say anything, as much as his heart cajoled him to let go, to bring his lover into his confidence. God, he wanted to share this with Brian who was so hurt and confused. God, how he wanted to show his ultimate faith in a man who had given Sam the most passionate love. But Sam pushed these thoughts away. He had made promises. These were hard times. He couldn't allow himself the luxury of opening up.

Just out of Medford, Brian began talking again, as

if perhaps he were on to something. He seemed to be angling, searching.

"The more I think about it, the more I personally believe those rumors," he announced.

They had talked for weeks on this topic; it had preoccupied gay conversations.

"There will always be rumors," Sam told him firmly. "The North American spread of the AIDS virus was caused by negligence and greed in the blood-products industry. That's pretty well been established by reputable research."

"But Sam, why do these rumors persist? Several Congress people claim to be on to something."

"I don't believe in conspiracy theories. There's a right-wing crazy out there who would like to take credit for something over which he had no control. Sooner or later he'll be exposed for what he is, you'll see."

It was interesting, Brian noted, that his lover could be so certain in downplaying these rumors. That he chose to be so strongly negative against them.

"Sam, that's not what you said when Ken died."

He had spoken in grief things that he regretted now.

"Well, I've changed my mind. That's possible, you know."

"First time *I've* known it to happen," Brian responded.

But he knew it wasn't true. Besides, he didn't trust Sam on this, he was too defensive.

"Listen," Sam told him. "We'd all like to believe that some particular person or group of persons caused this disease. I sure as hell don't like the idea that what I've got is incurable and I'm gonna die. But it's no use making up crazy theories just to have a sense of getting even."

Damn it, Sam told himself, I'm being too defensive. He'll suspect something.

"What about that blood products research you talked

about?'' Brian persisted. ''Suppose it's all a cover-up?
Suppose the CIA has merely deflected the blame for AIDS to
the blood-products industry? What then?''

''That seems highly unlikely, Brian. The research team
was international, not American. The facts are there. The
AIDS virus was in the general U.S. blood pool long before
it hit us. It got there because the conglomerates bought cheap
blood in Central Africa and distributed plasma products in
America without adequate testing.''

''Then why did gays get hit all of a sudden with this
epidemic? I remember you once saying there were just a few
too many coincidences.''

Sam was quiet for a minute.

''Yes, I remember saying that. But I've changed my
mind on that too.''

''Yes, I know,'' said Brian.

Brian was almost exultant. Sam was up to something
and he thought he knew a little of what it might be about.
Let Sam go ahead and drive straight through. Brian would
get this damn thing out of him before the night was over.

4 *Guerrero Street, San Francisco, Thursday Evening*

Except for parked cars, Guerrero Street was deserted. Gregg
slowed down, and pulled his bike backwards into an open
space between a fire hydrant and a bus zone. A beer can,
crushed by the back wheel of the motorcycle, complained
loudly. Near the curb, broken glass littered the roadway.
Gregg cursed as he ran his gloved hand over the tires,

checking for glass caught in the grooves. Then, as he stepped backwards to the sidewalk, he heard the beer can bang against the curb. Everything he did seemed conspicuous. But then he was probably overreacting.

There were no lights on the main floor of the Victorian and the basement entrance was dark. With gloved hand, he knocked twice. No answer. Gregg knocked three times. He was being silly, he told himself, no one could know about this. Again, there was no answer. Was someone watching him behind the peephole, that tiny black-glistening jewel set in the shadow of the door? He knocked once more, a single rap that completed the preordained signal. The door opened, and Jim's housemate swept him in. The door closed, locking them in darkness.

At the end of a passage they entered a dim room. Candlelight flickered ceremoniously.

"Good going," Jim announced to the rest of them, looking up at Gregg briefly, then back at his notes. "Now we're all here and can get down to work."

Gregg placed himself in a vacant folding chair. Jim might label his arrival good, but Gregg wasn't so certain that he felt so good about what he'd decided to do, although he had tentatively agreed. But the others ignored him for now and went on with their planning.

"His intransigence has certainly helped us," Jim told them.

Jim was referring to statements made by the President to the press, that he would not cancel his trip to the city. That San Francisco, as much as any other place, was part of America. That the President would not adopt the attitude of a sneak thief, but would walk in the door as an upright citizen.

"Can we trust his security to let him do that?" someone asked. "I don't think we should limit our plans, but cover as many entrances as possible."

"That's right," someone else commented. "The man's not to be trusted. He's just as likely to say he'll walk in the front door of Moscone Center but actually come the wrong way up Fourth and go in the side."

Gregg listened, unreacting. His gaze was on the dark rug, on the greasy splotches in it that seemed to come loose and drift upwards towards him. They were like memories, like a signature for these dark times from which he forever seemed to be negotiating his own release. He could say he had done what he had done for honor. He looked across the room to where a solitary chain still hung from an eyebolt fastened to the ceiling beams, its links cast in shadows, the darkness of each, even in candlelight, outlined precisely, tautly against the wall, so that the strength of the chain rested firm. The sling had once hung in that corner under a mirror that was still affixed to the ceiling.

He remembered his first night in this room, almost ten years ago, as he floated in that mirror like a dream. It was shortly after Gregg and Jim had met. What would it seem like now, looking at the video, Gregg wondered? Distantly arcane? No, it would probably seem as fresh and as new and as wonderful as it had been then. Did Jim even still have the video, he wondered? Flying as he had been at that time, he could still recapture in his mind that view outwards from the sling; that view of Gregg's own butt, up there on the little television monitor that had sat on the shelf above Jim's shoulder. Gregg's own butt, packed with Crisco, the zoom moving in as Jim's hand slowly took possession for a communion of fire that no strip of tape or film could ever record with true faith except maybe the wonderful screams of exultation and release.

Gregg's mind lifted back from his memories, through the shadows, to the people in the room. Here was Jim, that same man, his face and half his body covered, like some grotesque tattoo, with purple lesions. He was emaciated and he spoke with pain. He seemed a stoic although bedraggled creature, a man far from the Jim whom Gregg had first known. That Jim had been full of animal energy, with great bearlike limbs. That Jim had been a black-bearded Bunyan whose mountainous hands held the limbs of a brother with the love and respect afforded a fine tree.

God, how the two of them had played together, loved together, as men expressing joy in another man. God, how their play, on and off, had gone on for years, the sweetest ecstasy, the long excruciating lingerings on thresholds of that other world. The kissing, oh God, the most wonderful kissing. Even he and Allan had never kissed as had he and Jim. And now, damn it—now! It hurt Gregg more than the thought of his own death. It hurt to see Jim and to think of that kissing, that loving, all that had flowed so smoothly between them. He could not allow himself to forget.

"No," Jim told them all. "We abandon nothing. All the options we worked out earlier must be dealt with. We've already planned to cover several entrances and we must continue to do just that. A group like ours can only hope to second–guess. But we can maximize our efforts at the front entrance and we should cover that point with our sharpest shooter."

With that statement, Jim glanced briefly at Gregg. Then he looked away. "Can we have an update on the status of our weapons?" he continued. "You were talking to Portland," he said to a man beside him. "I understand our northern mission went well."

"Highly successful," the man answered. "We got exactly what we wanted, had them shipped to Portland, and no one expects anything like this. They're quizzing animal rights groups from Boise to Seattle."

Purposely, Gregg tried to disconnect the identity of each speaker from his words. Suffice to say they were nearly all friends, long-standing friends. Suffice to say they included an ex-lawyer and a stockbroker, a former professor from UC Berkeley, an ex-city cop and several businessmen. But to be successful, this operation had to be as efficient, as machinelike as possible. They, all of them, beyond their friendships, had to be committed to its goals. It was better, Gregg had decided, not to mix personalities with plans. They must attempt to avoid analysis of their motives. Once a course was established, they must act unquestioningly and as a whole. It was enough that all of them had been sworn to secrecy and that they were bound together, whatever they did, to this common fate.

"Sam," the speaker continued, "left Portland with his lover this afternoon. He's bringing the weapons with him."

"There's a bad storm coming in," someone commented. "Will snow in the Siskiyous be a problem?"

"Too early in the year," someone else stated. "Not as high as the Sierra. He should make it all right."

Gregg continued to sit, only his eyes moving in the shadows to which he seemed fused. He looked to his left, where Tom sat. On the edge of his gaunt face, his bristling silver mustache pushed into the light. Another fallen warrior, Gregg pondered. None of them had ever sought to be heroes, but they were, all of them, indeed all of their brothers, living their lives as such. Tom was such a man. A man of bottomless faith, unyielding vision, irrepressible optimism. Tom had been one of the first openly gay cops in San Francisco, and the pride he had carried forward into the force had lit up a lot of lives. He'd got citations for his work, most of it with seniors. He'd also done work with Metropolitan Community Church. And the AIDS Foundation. Until about six weeks ago. That was when he had just started to waste. Non-Hodgkins lymphonoma, and quickly taking control. Suddenly Tom had come face to everything for which he had lived.

Gregg had always looked up to Tom. He was that sort of buddy who touched you where it felt real fine. Yeah, the two of them had played once, years ago. A night at the Hothouse, Gregg recalled, doing stuff that would bring indignant reactions from many but that could nevertheless be labeled safe today. He had tied his brother immobile so that the heat of Tom's soul just sort of oozed out between the criss-crossed rope macrame. Gregg would roll those bits of soul between his fingers, caress them, make Tom feel all sorts of beautiful sensations. Yeah, that was the only time they'd played. Gregg knew that Tom had also played a lot with Allan and Marc.

God, he thought, wouldn't that get the asshole Harrison going? He could see the headlines: CANDIDATE FOR DISTRICT ATTORNEY INTO PERVERTED SEX WITH CITY COP!! No doubt they'd dig it up; they had dug up just about everything else including the details of Gregg's own intimacy with Allan. But that wasn't what Gregg wanted to remember about Tom right now. Instead, he let his mind go back to those turbulent times just before he had settled in with Allan, that period of drifting somewhat, of searching through a stupor of drugs and some bitterness. Gregg had been mixed up, and Tom had been firmly there, and an example of what self-belief could really do. He had reached out and touched Gregg, a firm, guiding touch in that frequent dizziness. Gregg would never forget that touch. Tom was worth everything they were doing here.

"A group of us will be down there when Sam and Brian arrive," someone was saying. "To help them unload."

"Good," Jim affirmed. "There should be enough of us there to help them and so that Gregg doesn't particularly stand out. He shouldn't stand out when you go in. And when you come out it shouldn't seem noticeable that he's not with you."

"Remember," someone else commented. "Once we get out of there, that's it. No coming or going later in the day and especially that evening. The army will likely seal off the whole area until it's over."

Yes, Gregg thought. By that time it would all be over and there would be no escape. There might even be a reason to believe.

Another participant went on to discuss what had been learned of security near the Moscone Center—what was likely and what was unlikely. The group discussed the arrival of people at the rally, local traffic flows, the planned arrival of their own supporters, and the President's travel itself. Timing, signals, and fallbacks were all reviewed. Various possible diversionary tactics were analyzed. Possible security strategies were dissected. Nothing seemed failsafe. Still, they continued. Still, they hoped.

Through all this, Gregg only half-listened. While his role would be crucial, little of this planning would change it. He allowed his gaze to relax into the shadows of the wall behind Jim, into flickering candlelight playing on black paint. A row of votive candles lined the foot of that wall, and on its surface were painted names. Like the tip of his tongue playing on the inside of his teeth, Gregg's conscious thought played with the white letters that were each name:

HOOT GIBSON
ALLAN ESTES

God, he told himself, he needed to believe. Once upon a time he would have claimed just that belief of another god. Once, in his own young self-righteousness, he had been certain of his beliefs.

Life at that time had the inevitability of a fine game of pool to a kid who was perfect with every shot and a show-off as well. Balls had clicked one after the other into their assigned pockets and in preordained fashion. High school. Family. God-fearing faith in country and apple pie. God, he thought, it had felt good then. He'd had looks and brains, but not enough brains to seem strange. If he ever allowed another player to sink a ball it was because he deliberately blew the shot so he'd be thought of as a nice guy. Gregg had grown into this faith blindly, and he had cherished it fervently. There was, it seemed, no match to those stars and stripes.

The group was discussing the counterdemonstration now, as well as timing and communications.

Gregg's eyes were still on the wall.

PAUL CASTRO
RICK WOODBURN

Then there was the war. Gregg had enlisted and gone off to fight as if he were rounding out his pool game. It was to be a spectacular shot. He would send the eight ball into the far corner by means of a pretentious double ricochet. The balls clicked and rebounded exactly as planned, until at the last moment, as it approached the darkness of the pocket, the eight ball exploded.

Gregg's life became a psychotic nightmare. He found death, destruction, and human agony. He watched homes burn, people burn, and money burn holes. He lost faith and his god, and he found some solace in long tokes of aromatic smoke. Time and again he was disgusted with most of his superiors, many of his peers and some of his subordinates. More so, he thought he was disgusted with himself. But he shut his mouth, and reflected, looking for hope in himself and something to believe in. Hoping that when and if he returned stateside, something upbeat would happen to his life.

And here he was today, in another psychotic

nightmare, his buddies dying about him, his dreams stranded on rocks. He had watched slow deaths and decaying flesh and his country's dishonor. They were worse than guns and napalm and they happened to people he really knew. Men he had handled and loved and cared for. Friendships and emotions that were thicker than blood.

Gregg did come back to the States. He went to Berkeley. One morning he woke up and found himself gay. He was more confused than ever, and he wanted to believe passionately in something that was *him*. Maybe this was to be it. But his family couldn't understand and his crackpot sister did her best to exacerbate that. Jo-Lyn tried her damndest to disinherit him, but she failed by a fluke. He didn't believe any the more because of it.

One of the votives flickered out, and a corner of the great wall settled into deep shadow. After the meeting he knew that Jim would add new wax to the candle; they burned day and night, despite the darkness, a statement of belief, of dreams that would never be allowed to die. Despite the shadows, Gregg could still read the names:

RON KRAUS
JAMES MINCEY
RICK GRASSO

He remembered Rick. Gentle man. Sweet, sometimes scared man. They had met and played in the darkest and warmest of places. They had given of each other, and passionately, both of them buddies who had been broken by that war. Rick had always seemed to be running—maybe that was one of the ways they trained us, to fear ourselves. Gregg had cherished Rick all the more for his running. He wanted to touch, to stay him, to keep his hand in Rick's butt forever so that Rick would know he had nothing to fear, only the wonderful feeling of a friend to hold. And then, just when it seemed that Rick might be overdosing a little too much on hot drugs and pleasures, he would show how he really believed in all of them, and in a saner world, and go out and walk precincts for Walter Mondale.

Yeah, it was men like Rick, like Jim, like Hoot, like Tom, like Allan, who had made him believe once again. Gregg had willfully deserted his roots. Gregg had fallen into the hedonistic joys of city life in the midseventies. Pool balls had clicked in joyous confusion about him. He had bounced his soul off those of so many others and so many times that he could have been lost. But there, in the midst of this reverberating and rebounding confusion, Gregg reached deeper. He found things that touched him in inexplicable ways. He found a carnal craft called leather that was also an act of love and he reveled in it. He found himself a part of a reaching out for warmth, a sharing between grand people, between brothers. In the calm of that touching, that being and hoping together, in that newfound confidence, in that cherished sense of identity, blowing like rainbow flags up Market Street, singing like hundreds of helium balloons released skyward on Freedom Day—in those things there had become something to dream, to believe.

GENE FORREST
JON SIMS

The letters on the wall began to blur. No, he was not going to allow himself to cry.

It was the man who had founded the Gay Freedom Day Marching Band. He had been there the day Jon had received his citation from Mayor Feinstein herself. Gregg could hear the band, strutting its stuff as the dream had strutted before them, proclaiming hope, pride, and faith. Gregg looked sideways again at Tom. He must believe in their cause. Never before was so much being demanded of him. Never before had he been so passionately angry and hurt.

21

The city and life in which they believed. The dreams they had come to cherish. The strengths of their very touching. All of those seemed as if they would be blown apart now by this lingering, terrible end.

He felt the attention of the others on him as Jim turned once more to Gregg.

Gregg knew they would ask this thing of him now, once again, and for a final time. He knew that he wasn't the only one who could do it. Others of them had served in the war, had handled arms. But he knew he would go through with it. Once more, he would take a weapon, as once he had done so many times before in that war he had meant to be honorable. Once more, he would cradle a weapon, after years of avowal never to do so again. Ex-marine that he was, Gregg would achieve for his country what was required for its honor and for his fallen brothers.

Gregg could almost smile. His name would never be carved into the black Washington monument, into that marble polished with Vietnam suffering. But his name would be remembered on the memorial of this wall, in this room where the flames of passion would linger forever in testimony to brotherhood.

5 *The Mission, San Francisco, Thursday Evening*

Allan Bennett was on a stage in one of those monotone church halls in the true Mission. He was there and the situation demanded he deal with the politics.

He sensed a certain morbidity in the crowd. Children chattered uneasily as if their parents' silence was too much to bear. This was to be one of his most trying moments in politics. Nothing in those years of exile had given him any preparation for this. No single issue or candidate in the tangle of city politics had generated such antagonism. It was academic to observe some large dignity in Allan's campaign. In reality, he was being ripped apart on his very right to be.

"This man," said his political opponent softly, while pointing at Allan. He paused, with leashed tongue like a dog at his master's feet.

The audience sat poised on their fears.

"This man," Walter Harrison repeated. "Stands for his own destruction."

Again, there was a pause. It would not do for this quiet, black Fundamentalist to knock a largely Catholic crowd with his own peculiarities of faith. He would emphasize themes common to both.

"Don't get me wrong," he said, turning his gaze on Allan as if stating fatherly love. "AIDS is a tragedy that hurts us all. But don't expect me to vote for someone who would not do everything within his power to stop it."

Allan's reaction was one of disbelief. Did the horror of death and dying friends leave them all untouched? It was an insult to their humanity and to their diligent efforts to slow this damned thing — efforts that here in the city at least, appeared finally to have worked. But while Allan's mind registered these emotions, his face was unmoved. He thought of his campaign so far, how reasonable the Bennett case seemed, how success *could* be theirs. And then he speculated once more on the quisling on his own team who was passing information to the other side. Allan didn't know who it was, damn him, but he had suspicions. The thought infuriated him.

"Mr. Bennett would not have us draw the line where it really counts. Mr. Bennett would have us believe that all of this was a matter of rights. We all know about rights."

Harrison paused again. This man campaigned with the pause. It talked more of expectancy, of fear, than any words could. In the pause they were considering the matter of rights. A black man was addressing a largely Hispanic audience. His comment was not lost.

"All of us here believe strongly in the subject of rights. But there must be limits to any rights when they bring hurt to others. My opponent Mr. Bennett would have you believe in rights that are dangerous and discredited. Yes, we know all those allegations about homosexual child molesting are a myth. But AIDS is no myth. AIDS won't just molest you. AIDS kills!"

Damn this man, Allan thought. Had they stood on the firing line for nothing? To be taunted by false innuendo? Allan knew as did most of his audience that they would not catch this disease. He wanted to hit out at Harrison for fear mongering, for spreading deception. But politics demands self-control, even response. He would get his chance later, and he clutched the edge of his seat in self restraint. Passion would be allowed when it served a point. Lies based on fear were the most difficult to refute.

Again, Harrison turned to him from the podium. Again, he spoke Allan's name carefully.

"Don't get me wrong, Mr. Bennett. Don't get me wrong, fellow San Franciscans. We do care. We are all willing to help, to share the mistakes and grief. And we will! But we shall not permit people to continue their life-threatening activities when they effect every one of our lives. When they cost us by the hour. I'm not running for City Treasurer, so I won't hark on costs of the AIDS crisis. I am running for District Attorney, so I will talk about laws and enforcing them."

So bless you Harrison, you bastard, Allan reflected facetiously. You're prepared to share in our grief. Damn these snake-tongued conservatives: when had they ever turned to help? Allan knew of the people who were behind this man. They included some of the key leaders of the new right and nearly every American Fundamentalist group that professed true Christianity today. They had backed Harrison with money and campaign staff and with publicity. He was to be their first inroad into San Francisco, a city known for its liberal voting. Harrison was to be a signal that even this city could fall in line with the rest of America.

Their first moves were to poison, to spread unfounded fear. They divided the electorate into 'them' and 'us', and having divided, manipulated their fears further. As with the politics of the McCarthy era, they were fighting a bitter battle to direct society into the tyranny in which they believed. For tyranny was only tyranny to those who fell from true belief. When these Walter Harrisons took control they would turn to their real prize, the extinguished spirit and its enslavement. In their pattern of things, death was a fine second-rate substitute for their failure to achieve these ends. Almost, Allan wished, there was some truth in those insidious rumors lately out of Washington, some awful weapon he could use against the storm this opposition had come to represent.

"I want you to look carefully at your own lives," Harrison told the audience. "At what your rights mean to you. At what you've fought to accomplish for family and friends. For your children. None of us have had an easy time of it. Then I want you to look at *those* people."

He paused. He had been careful to put it just that way.

"Those people," his opponent repeated. "Those people who demand the same rights as you do, but are ready to kill you with them."

Liar, Allan almost screamed. What of Milk? Moscone? Hillsborough? The AIDS-dead? Their blood still staining the floors of this city? He reached into his pocket. If he had had a gun or a knife, there was a good chance Allan would have used it, and against all his principles.

"Those people," Harrison continued, "Just what have those people done for folks like you and me? Oh, we can recognize some of the fine personal works of Mr. Bennett here. But I'm not talking about Mr. Bennett. I'm talking about those he represents. I'm talking about privileged people whose lives and life-styles never agreed too well with the likes of you and me. I'm talking about privileged people who came to San Francisco from all over this nation just to bum around in an area they thought they could take over and call their own. You know, this whole situation is sort of like an uncomfortable meal, wouldn't you say? Where there's some sort of subtle poison at work in the food and your guts rumble but won't get sick although you just know you've got to."

"Yes, we all know what it's been. Those people coming to us. Okay, you blacks. Okay, you Latinos. We want *our* rights. And you know, here in San Francisco, we were stupid enough to go along with them. But that was the past. And you know what? It's time we took a stand.

It's time we put an end to them pushing in among the legitimate minorities."

So here it was, the bottom line, the hidden message. After nearly a decade of the horror and grief of AIDS. After a rising tide of somber violence directed against his community in their own streets, in their own neighborhoods. These right-wing bigots were determined to make inroads to the very heart of a city that had stood for tolerance, for diversity, for fairness. They were determined to exploit what they could, and consolidate their shadows.

It was interesting, Allan noted, what Harrison chose to emphasize, what he chose to ignore. He didn't mention those who had worked and fought for the rights, for the well-being of all the city's peoples. Sure, there were gays who slummed or A-gays who didn't seem to care. But there were blacks who lived on food stamps and drove Cadillacs. No, he didn't mention the Latino gangs that stalked faggots in Noe Valley or along the frontiers of the Castro. No. It was bottom line now. Harrison and his colleagues would decide who was to be legitimate. They would decide who would be turfed out. They would decide what was to be defined as murder. And they would stack the jury.

"Yes, Mr. Bennett. And I address Mr. Bennett because it's to him I want *our* message to get through. Your message and my message. The time has come to take a stand."

Was Harrison about to take a stand against unprovoked violence? Against assault with the intent to kill? Against murder, which he would never accept as such? It was the knowledge that there were others out there who disagreed with Harrison that kept Allan going. There were people out there who still believed in justice and fairness.

But this crowd did not seem to share these expectations. Some people were silent, coldly silent. Another group was applauding Harrison with all caution abandoned, the sharp slap of hands cracking like bone against concrete. Great chords welling in organ pipes; music playing for the soul.

"Yes, Mr. Bennett. As you may have noticed, I'm no lackey of the liberal press. No Uncle Tom of a cozy establishment. No turncoat conservative who shifts a few ideas to please minority voters. I believe in the laws that Congress passed to deal with this crisis. I believe in the laws our President signed. You know the laws I'm talking about."

They all knew exactly what laws Harrison was talking about. He might be a lawyer, high-sounding at times, but there were no language barriers here. Those laws were the reason that Allan was absolutely convinced he had to win, whatever the obstacles, however bitter the taunting.

"I'm talking about the Quarantine Laws," Harrison continued. "Those special measures that give American cities and counties like San Francisco the real means to control the AIDS threat. And I challenge Mr. Bennett to tell me he will actively work to have those laws proclaimed locally and to prosecute when those laws are broken."

William Harrison taunted because it accentuated fear. He would make a bogeyman of Allan and he would try to demolish him with his past. Harrison made his taunts as if certain of his success. He was determined to win big, and it was all the more reason to taunt.

"Let's just take a look at those laws for a moment," he told the audience, emphasizing a sense of perfect reason. "These are laws which our current city administration irresponsibly refuses to act on. Congress passed those laws in its wisdom because the number of AIDS victims in this great nation had climbed upwards of eighty thousand and the contaminated are everywhere. It passed those laws because the contaminated expect to push their contamination."

Harrison looked at Allan. A silent swipe. He would expand on it later, Allan was certain. God, would he like to get his hands on whoever was divulging the details of his own sexual past.

"And we've heard all about those crazy rumors," Harrison continued. "Claims that our fine government planted the seeds of this disease. Let me tell you, the whole idea is hogwash! Many of those with AIDS brought the thing on themselves, plain and simple. Whether God was a mover behind this disease, I'll leave to your personal convictions. But if you've studied these people as well as I have, you'd understand how this thing got out there and spread from their unclean ways. I see children in this audience so I won't detail some of the filthy things these people do."

He looked toward Allan again.

"The sad thing is that this virus has got loose. And that it threatens us. People in San Francisco have had enough of it. They're scared. If they move into a new apartment, how do they know someone hasn't contaminated the place? People in San Francisco don't want any more. Let me tell you a story about my nephew Rodney. He's eight and a real spunky kid. Goes to school over in the Excelsior. Well the other day Rodney called me. He said 'Uncle Walt, three teachers at my school have AIDS and the school won't do anything about them.' He said 'Uncle Walt, I'm darned scared. The kids are real scared to go to class and their moms and dads don't want them to.' You know folks, there *are* things San Francisco can do if it so chose. There's no reason to continue with this fear."

Allan had heard everything. He was sick of insults. He was already disillusioned from watching the few pleasures of his own life turn into sad memories. Hadn't he spent enough of his life battling the distortions and ignorance of assholes like Harrison? But he couldn't desert a battle he had taken on for friends, for people who had stood forth to be reckoned with on the grounds of their beliefs, and who still stood firm. This was a battle for God's gentle warriors.

"I ask you, the voters," Harrison continued, "to consider once again, this man before you, Mr. Allan Bennett. You know the truth about this man's life. You've heard about his dubious loyalty to this country. And you know that this man's lover (or whatever else you might want to call him) — even this man has the disease. Suppose Mr. Bennett is himself diseased? Can you expect Mr. Bennett to enforce the Quarantine Laws?"

Allan's web of agony snapped, and his soul rebounded free. He was fighting mad, and Mr. William Harrison had better be ready for some hard kicks in his own decrepit balls.

6 Siskiyou Summit, Late Thursday Night

All up the grade Brian pretended to sulk. At a gas station near Medford they had been warned that heavy snow was falling about Shasta and the interstate might be blocked. It was a perfect argument for stopping, and Brian badgered Sam again on the folly of driving through. Sam had been even more belligerent, as if every hour closer to San Francisco drew him more strongly to a purpose. But he gave no meaningful justification for his resolve and Brian purposefully settled into a frosty silence.

If he hadn't been pretending to be hurt, Brian would have dared to chuckle. He liked the way Sam sometimes treated him as naive; somehow it had a certain freshness to it. When it came down to the nub of matters Brian usually felt he had quite enough ways of influencing which way things were to be going. At first he thought Sam was merely applying the semiarrogance of his training to his private life: medics tend at times to think they're more perceptive than others. But that wasn't the case with Sam; he let himself think of Brian as naive by default. He didn't want to be an analytic in his relationships as was demanded by his practice. Besides, when Brian did assert himself, it was wonderful to see. On Brian's part, he enjoyed this sort of myth of his supposed naiveté. It meant he could hold his own beliefs more closely, releasing them only when he wanted to.

Yeah, it was funny, how ever since they'd been together, Brian recalled, they'd sort of followed these patterns. They enjoyed them, let them spill over into play, took on metaphorical dimensions. How many times had he turned the tables on a pushy Sam, who found himself greedily licking boot, while Brian mercilessly coaxed tortured ecstasy from his tits. It was wonderful, and he had a hard-on thinking about Sam that way. AIDS hadn't changed the hungry love he had for this man. God, he wanted to reach out, to grab him, to work him before it was too late. He wanted to grab that face, hold his blond beard between his hands, stare into those piercing blue eyes, and tell him to cough up about this conspiracy.

But Brian didn't. He sat rigidly, waiting, while Sam, almost indifferently, his eyes fixed in the darkness, sent their future on its course. Only the wail of the music moved about them, a bleak sweetness, an ecstasy captured and sent on its way to screw the receptive minds it might encounter in some far time.

Did he, Brian, really want to know Sam's secret? Would he be able to handle it; indeed would their relationship survive it? Would it be better to just trust Sam? And then, on thinking just that, Brian's anger boiled forward. He had given his life to this man. He had gladly left Canada, married Sam's sister to get the appropriate status, and moved to a nation whose leaders killed queers. And here he was, blindly following Sam. Didn't Brian deserve some trust, especially in the face of death? And from a man, who up to now, on every other important issue, had given him trust?

If Brian were to put a date on it, he pondered, the change in Sam had become apparent after that last trip to the city. Something had happened. Sam had begun to act as if he had a secret. Almost as if he had another lover. Brian soon discounted the lover idea, but Sam was still distant. There was a cause of purpose that had come to be important, although he said nothing of it to Brian. Brian had felt himself gently relegated to second place. For Brian, there was some resentment, but he kept it within himself. First he would find out what this commitment was.

All up the grade the compact disk was soaring its way to climax: violin wailing and shrieking over the dull thunder of timpani, polar bears dancing bravely in the face of doom. With perfect timing, the Sibelius achieved a triumphant close as they rolled over Siskiyou Summit. There was only the noise of the truck; snow fell lightly into the cold night.

"California at last," Sam announced with mock exultation.

Brian grunted. He shifted the contrived position in which he feigned sleep. His head seemed intent on the uncomfortable task of cradling his arm. Cabs of U-Haul trucks are not noted for comfort.

"Haven't we wanted this all our lives?" Sam went on blithely. "To live in California? Well, here it is."

Brian grunted again. Damn him, it was Brian who had

always wanted to move to California, Sam to live in Portland. No, he admitted. That wasn't quite true. Both had held mixed feelings at different times.

"Come on, aren't you going to get excited?" Sam badgered him. "Break out the champagne."

Brian said nothing. There was no cause for celebration. For all he knew, California would be the end of their dreams.

Sam tried once again:

"Come on babe, you know how much we used to talk about this."

Damn it, Sam told himself, I hate playing this game with someone I love. If only I could make him understand. If only I could reach out and hold him.

Yes, Brian told himself, we did use to talk about going to San Francisco. That was when our dreams seemed golden. God damn it, asshole. Brian told himself, I got to trust him. But God damn it, asshole, *you* got to trust *me.*

"Okay, asshole, fuck you," Sam told the silence.

Again, no response.

In his despair, Brian wanted to cry. What does this man expect me to do? Jump up and down and scream for joy? I want to slug him. I want to pound some sense into him. I want him to know I'm here, that I care, that he can tell me his secrets. I'm not innocent, and I'm not naive. I'm his lover.

But Brian made no move and Sam made no answer. Only the sound of the truck crawling up tedious hills and hurtling down the cracked roads of Siskiyou County. In the headlights, there were rock and sage and road cuts and steep slopes. The mountains were lost in the same darkness into which these curves swept them forward with a rushing sound. It was is if the vistas about them had regressed to a dark and tortuous tunnel through which passage was inevitable, if never-ending. Even coming into this California was imbued with a sense of awful finality.

With his left hand, Sam pushed inside his shirt to fondle his own nipple. It had gone hard and it poked through the mat of blondish hair and it felt good as he squeezed it, so he squeezed it some more. How much longer is this going to feel good? he wondered.

Fuck, Sam thought, I wish I *could* tell him. I'm almost sure he'd understand. But I can't, so that's that. He's just going to have to think I'm going a little crazy with this disease, that the dementia's setting in.

And with that, Sam switched from disk player to radio on the portable lodged on the dashboard between maps, Kleenex box and the inevitable assortment of items retrieved from kitchen drawers during those last moments of moving. The radio spat out a crackle at him. He turned the dial a little. Where was it? Yreka? Weed? Once, late at night on this stretch of I-5, he'd picked up the incongruity of a classical music station out of Reno. Tonight, Sam thought, all there'll probably be is country and western. So much for my cultivated tastes. Could always go back to the tape.

There was another sputter of noise. Then a woman's voice, somewhere in a news report. Sam's fingers froze on the dial. Something in the tone of voice.

"Tonight, it all came out. The secret behind the rumors that have been circulating for several months. In Baltimore, a CIA agent stepped forward to confirm the rumors are true. Mr. Edward Stevens told a press conference that the AIDS virus was created and then tested by the CIA in Central Africa before being planted in the American homosexual population."

Any antagonism between Brian and Sam dissolved. Here was a common enemy, a common fear that superceded all else. Here too, was a sudden twinge of hope that something positive might be forthcoming. Brian shifted closer to Sam.

"Damn them," Sam stated bluntly, bitterly to himself as a sort of affirmation. They had been right. All their planning had been intensified with the rumors. Even as they had wanted these rumors to be based on fact, they had hoped they were not.

The radio continued with its revelations. "From Baltimore, ABC's Joel Ford reports to us directly."

Ford's voice was nasal, almost acrid. It spoke as if scandal were the issue, the driving force behind all reality. People may have died, yes, but they were inconsequential in the light of the sensational facts. Yet with the reality hitting home, neither Sam nor Brian took notice of this lack of compassion.

"The AIDS epidemic!" Ford intoned, as if speaking of the overture to the real show. "A killer virus out of control and threatening us everywhere. In America, as AIDS has taken a mounting toll, mostly among homosexuals, public fears have mounted. Tonight, there may be some hope at least, for those of us in the general public."

Bitterness was creeping over Sam, rising from the impacts to his own life. The loss of a life's work, the giving up of a practice. The slow draining of self-confidence in himself, knowing that at any moment an opportunistic infection could wipe him out. The slow loss in strength, at first barely noticeable, but then growing. With this, the failing ability to walk mountains and fir forests. Lastly, there were the restrictions on his ability to communicate sensually with brothers he wanted to care about.

This bitterness set about Sam like a black aura, several feet out from his body and shining inwards. Sam was glad he could drive as a reflex, that he could almost unconsciously steer this truck along this difficult road. He was glad to feel Brian reach through the blackness and rub the inside of his leg.

"Tonight we have some answers to those rumors that have buzzed through Washington for some time now. Those rumors suggested that the CIA had something to do with AIDS. Tonight, Mr. Edward Stevens, a twenty-year employee of the agency and an expert on virus-caused diseases, told reporters that indeed they had. Stevens provided reporters with documentation that his agency had engineered and released the HIV virus...."

"Can you believe this?" Brian murmured. His hand, having stopped rubbing the inside of Sam's leg, had come to rest near the midpoint of his inside thigh. It was there that Sam's second lesion had become visible.

"In a second meeting, held late this evening in a Baltimore hotel room, Stevens made the following claims. The CIA, in cooperation with the army operates a classi-fied laboratory near Silver Springs here in Maryland. Mr. Stevens is a senior administrator in that lab. Scientists in that facility engineer and test new disease organisms including retroviruses. Many of these organisms have been tested in highly restricted environments, some of them foreign. The AIDS epidemic is the first controlled, large-scale test of a virus intended for the defense of America."

The bitterness that pervaded Sam's heart, that reached in from its opaque aura to consume him, was not the impending finality of his own life. It was rooted in the frailty of innocent friends. It was in the loss of friends, the slow painful end in which brothers with so much commitment to living, so much vitality for the up-side of life and for help-ing others, had seen their hard-fought dreams wither.

When Sam remembered Ken Walker in Seattle, his bitterness could have shifted to rage. A sweet glorious man. Sam and Ken had first met at Jim's, in San Francisco, at a party held for Ken and his lover. One of those joyous parties, carried off with the ecstatic turbulence that knocked them all together, again and again, brothers of that Olympian Coast from Vancouver to San Francisco. Thus he had met Brian, Ken, too many others to remember in name, although their souls would not be forgotten. Tears were on Sam's face. He could hear it now: he and Jim were coming downstairs with fresh beer, and someone back in the playroom was hollering and screaming as if he had just been born, as if life had finally come to make sense. They met Ken at the door. "That's Canada," Ken had announced, as a sort of understatement, as if the innocence in Brian's discovery of joy were a statement of national proportions.

Then he thought of Ken's dying in Group Health, that slow bewildering death in the foreign bleakness of a hospital room. The growing smudge of lesions, the tired frightened eyes that cannot understand this cruel predicament or escape it, even in sleep. Ken was a brother who took each step of his life as a declaration of its goodness and his own affections for others. To watch Ken die was like granting conscious recognition to a blackness, to an evil that had come to squat among them. It had been on that winter day in a Seattle street, tears pouring down his face, that Sam had resolved to fight. But how?

It seemed to him now that in one part of his mind Sam wanted to annihilate himself and this world, to eradicate the gloating triumph of this blackness. He wanted to slam this truck off the mountainous road and send it bouncing like a fruit crate into the depths of some canyon. He wanted to kill, to claim justice, to excoriate the pain. He wanted to take this man Stevens, this creep who was now speaking to them from some Baltimore hotel room, he wanted to take this creep and show him what kindness really was.

"I want to make it very clear that we carried out our experiments with a great deal of care. We were, you could say, creating God's magic bullet. Contrary to some elements of public opinion, the general American population is not at risk. Innocent Americans will not die from this disease. We chose our target population because it is a major threat to national security, to the moral fabric of American life, and to the ideals of the American Dream."

Ed Steven's voice was raspy. Somewhere from the mid-Atlantic coast. He spoke as if he dreamed of being a senator: calm, authoritative and without remorse.

Brian grasped Sam's hand, clutched the wheel.

"I don't believe this," he said.

"I do," Sam told him in direct contrast to his earlier remarks. "I want to kill that man."

Like this truck, hurtling through the night, Sam had taken control of his rage and bitterness. He wanted to kill, but it would be futile to kill either himself or Brian. There were other and equivalent roads, and he was already well along one. There was a reassurance in knowing that Jim and the others had guessed correctly. Sam would do his part.

"We all want to kill them," Brian told him. "And someone will. None of them will last long now."

Sam was silent. He thought of an oblong package, heavily wrapped and delivered to them yesterday by UPS. The package was jammed upright in the hold of the truck between the sofa and a chest.

"Mr. Stevens," Joel Ford was inquiring for the benefit of the radio audience. "Mr. Stevens, you personally don't seem very apologetic about what appears to have been a great tragedy."

Sam was crying loudly now, and Brian pulled close. He spoke, insistently:

"Better pull over for a while."

"I'm going to be all right," Sam declared, his stubbornness rearing up through his tears.

No, we will not give up, he told himself.

38

Again, a drawling, pompous voice told them that America really cared.

"I do not believe we've done anything wrong," Ed Stevens announced to the world. "We're soldiers in God's great battle: we are warriors in the struggle for virtue. From time to time in this war, some of us are called upon to do things that may be special, that are beyond the regular call of duty. I believe I've been called by the Lord, and I've done proud on just that."

"Mr. Stevens, can we hold out any hope to your victims? Is there a known cure to the AIDS virus? Surely you people wouldn't release a killer virus without knowing a cure?"

They waited, expectantly. This was the least good that could possibly come out of this nightmare.

"A cure," Stevens drawled, as if fielding a misguided question. "Now that's just something about which I can't say. Homos and druggies. They deserve what they get."

"Bastard," Brian screamed at the radio.

7 *Spring Valley, Maryland, Thursday Night*

Jo-Lyn stood in the welcome semidarkness watching Carolyn asleep in the bassinet. Unhidden, the thought came to her that what happened might be a good thing. She felt immediately guilty for even allowing the idea to fly through her mind. Her husband may have embarrassed them both. Shortly after that, her husband may have been arrested. But Jo-Lyn could not bring herself to believe she could be disloyal to Ed, whatever the cause. Nor could she not believe that what he had done or said was of service to their country and its cause of greatness.

She could, in this difficult moment, admit that it had been reassuring, even liberating, to have physically pushed away those reporters. She had slammed the door on them. Outside, some of them were still waiting. She had unplugged the phones and she ignored the doorbell.

No, Jo-Lynn was not afraid to blame Ed. She was just too loving, too loyal. If any blame in the matter was to be laid, it should come squarely to rest on her brother Gregg, thousands of miles away. Gregg was the real reason for any discontents, any evils in her life. Ed may have done certain, out-of-the-ordinary things. But Jo-Lyn knew that she and her husband had deserved better, the both of them. Ed may have sprung his little surprise on the world without forewarning her, and it was an important, valid revelation. She could say that to herself, yes she could. Even with her quaking heart and dying brother.

These seemingly confused yet straightforward facts aside, Jo-Lyn was still not convinced that Ed's publicity seeking was the best means to achieve their joint ends. Deep within the most inaccessible reaches of her brain she considered the possibility that Ed might have cracked. The weight of responsibility sometimes brings down its supports. Yet it all made little difference what she thought. Given the circumstances of Ed's arrest, and it hardly mattered that this was America, Jo-Lyn would probably never know the truth. It could well be that she would never see him again, and his yolk would curdle in an unseen grave.

She adjusted the coverlet over Carolyn, sweet little Carolyn, her hope, her one answer to this screwed-up world.

To Jo-Lyn, life in Washington was no milkshake. The taste was gritty and the straw was stuck. Even with the support of their Fellowship, where social and spiritual recognition sometimes seemed slow coming, life seemed forever stuck on the first mouthful.

Certainly Jo-Lyn could step outwards several hundred paces, beyond the shrubbery and the proud elms, beyond the Secret Service men in their unmarked cars. She could view a magnificent Maryland home whose grandeur far exceeded what had been her most modest dreams. Yes, she could conclude, God had rewarded them with all manner of riches. But no, she also concluded, material possessions, even social stature, were not enough.

What was it that they wanted, she and Ed? What was the sanctity she sought?

Jo-Lyn could go back to her fantasies, of course. Part-time romances of a small California town, its streets lined by matronly Victorians. Like any small American town perhaps, but for the incongruous palms set between the oaks, sycamores, and magnolias. There was something in that life she missed, in its *best* intentions guided by the ripening of apricots and almonds. Its very calm was a historical affirmation of the order placed on the havoc of gold seekers. She yearned for that quietness, that peace, but it was not the sanctity that she sought.

Could it be justice she sought? Even here in Carolyn's room, even here in this room of her sweet child, Jo-Lyn was reminded of the injustices she and Ed had faced. But while she was drawn backwards in some sort of vain hope for retribution, Jo-Lyn knew that even this was not the complete answer.

The answer had to lie in Carolyn. The babe had been a giving of herself, a giving of God through herself. As trite as it might sound, Carolyn had represented the coming of new hope. Carolyn had been the duty of Jo-Lyn and Ed as believers. And as bleakly as their fellow-believers viewed the world, as imminent as was the Final Judgment, Carolyn was to be their new light in this darkness.

Her thoughts turned again to Ed, and again in the end she blamed Gregg. By opening his mouth, by letting loose his secrets, Ed may have jeopardized their little Carolyn. However well-intentioned these actions, Jo-Lyn thought they might be difficult to excuse. But then she was being too hard. She loved Ed. She had sworn loyalty to him.

Then, with the thought that she might not see Ed again, Jo-Lyn began to cry. The CIA were never kind to turn-coats. The interests of national security superceded mere love. And none of this need have happened if things had followed the path God had intended for them. The path they were no longer on because of her brother. She loved her brother as the Lord had meant her to. She wept at the thought of his indiscretions and of the terrible death he would pay for them. She prayed for her brother's soul as much as she hated, in a cold passion, the devil within him, the devil that had cheated her. On her knees and beside the crib, Jo-Lyn began to pray.

8 *Upper Market, San Francisco, Late Thursday Night*

When he at last got home, he was tired, and Gregg made the call from his own room, in near darkness. Allan was still out; in any case, he didn't need to know about this call.

The voice that answered the phone sounded muffled, detached, as if not quite having verified its out-side realities. The time was past midnight and Gregg had felt uncomfortable calling. Need had driven him.

"Sleeping, Eight-ball?" he asked.

"No," Tony answered him. "Crying."

Damn it, Gregg thought. Was it vain to ask for respite, any respite? It was like being back in the war zone again, escape impossible. He could sense the sultry crowns of palms, ominous as cobras, about a stormy horizon. In all directions gunshot spattered like firecrackers in sharp assertive volleys, rising as if the gloom had materialized, then fading back into it. Even the fireflies guarded their show, waiting for a better night.

"Gary?" Gregg inquired. "Chicago?"

"Eleven-thirty last night."

Gregg sat silently, holding the phone as if it were part of his body gone numb. These deaths, repeatedly occurring, only confirmed the irony of his own situation. Somewhere, sometime, this phone would ring. Who would call to tell Allan? Who would phone Tony? In the pall, night was growing, and behind the storm clouds a tropical and livid sun set with an awful certainty. Would they, all of them, be safer in the dark?

"Gregg?"

"I'm sorry, Tony. I know how much he meant to you."

"He would have really liked you, Gregg."

There was something sad about these foreclosings of life's business before one really had a chance. All they could label us, Gregg thought, was promiscuous. But in those touchings between brothers, whether or not Gregg had known much of the superficialities of their lives, there had been a taste of raw honey, a sort of hard and gentle tenderness that stroked our angsts and dreams, our hopes and our humanity. And when another brother died whom he might have touched in a special way, but hadn't, it was as if some wonderful possibility had also died, and the universe gone lacking for it.

43

"I'm real sorry, Tony. From what you told me I'd have really got off on him too."

There was silence again, and then a passionate plea.

"Gregg, why does all this have to keep happening to us?"

Tony said no more. He always seemed uncertain when talking about death with Gregg, even if Gregg had admonished him several times about hiding from what he termed reality.

"You want me to come over and hold you, Eight-ball?"

"That'd be real nice, Gregg. But no. I need to be alone. I need to think about Gary."

"See you tomorrow then?"

Was he pushing to much? Should they even try to mix grief with escape? Almost two weeks ago they had planned to meet and play tomorrow night. Gregg had known, even then, how much he would need it with the events planned for this weekend. This would likely be his last time, and he wanted to spend it with someone special. But he couldn't let Tony know this urgency; whatever Gregg's needs, he must respect Tony's need for grief.

"Yeah, Gregg, I still want to. I think"

"I'm going to need you, Eight-ball. Even if we just hold each other."

Gregg didn't go on to say how much he needed Tony, although he was tempted. He hoped the need showed in his voice. But he also hoped it wasn't enough to threaten Tony's grief-stricken state. Was it unreasonable to wish that friends not suffer this repeated agony?

"I'm scared, Gregg. Just scared, that's all. And shook up. You know how fucked up I get when things like this happen. It's like having to learn again."

"I'm a good teacher, babe. You know that."

"I won't disagree. But maybe it'd be fairer if we waited a few days."

God damn it, Gregg thought. There weren't going to be a few days.

"Come on, you need someone to make you feel good. Someone you can trust. Do it for Gary, Eight-ball."

Again, silence. Was Gregg pushing too much? Were the allusions too intense? Tony had, after all, been given his nickname by Gary years ago.

"Besides," Gregg added. "Saturday I'm going out of town for a while."

"God, Gregg. You know how much I want to love you. Hold you. Gregg, I don't want *you* to die."

"Tony, I'm not going to die. Not yet!"

"Oh, Gregg."

Tony halted, uncertainly. Silence again. Night descending over the swampy jungle. Heat lightening grumbling facetiously over far mountains. Gregg hated these moments under siege. It wasn't the leeches dropping silently from the foliage to attach themselves to one's neck and arms. It wasn't the enemy patrols, slipping unpredictably through the undergrowth. It was the feeling of impending doom. It was the inevitability of no escape.

"Gregg?"

"Uh-huh, Eight-ball?"

Through the jungle his mind reached out and wrapped itself about Tony's hand, feeling its square warmth. He wanted to stroke him; he wanted to rinse away their grief.

"I told you before what Gary wrote me in his last letter."

That had been two weeks ago, before the final dementia laid waste to a spry mind. From behind his respirator, Gary had written his former lover:

"You know, Eight-ball, in all of this agonizing shit, I have no regrets. I believe in what we did and what we said. We were better for it and the world was a better place."

They had said that about the war, Gregg recalled. Some people still say that about the fucking war. But I don't happen to believe them.

"That's what I really want to remember about Gary," Tony added. "His faith in all of us."

9 *Northern California, Very Early Friday*

They had stopped for gas in Yreka, in the heavily falling snow.

"Going south?" the attendant asked them. "Lucky if you get through. They've already closed Sierra passes."

He was burly, with a bushy blond beard. He wore a red flannel shirt and tight 501s that showed his muscular butt. He had keys on his belt. Ten years ago there would have been little doubt he was gay. Today he could be anything: drop-out hippy who had fled to the north state, local country boy and redneck, or Vietnam war vet married with four kids and a raving Fundamentalist.

Sam had eyed the butt and the beard and the swell of biceps under the shirt. Ten years ago Sam might have tried to rope him into a three-way. Tonight he feigned disinterest.

"You a doctor?" the guy asked, reading Sam's credit card.

"Yeah, Portland."

When he came back with the slip to sign he looked at them both as if having made up his mind.

"Pretty crazy news, eh?"

"What news?" Sam asked.

"This crackpot in the CIA says the government set out to kill off queers with AIDS."

"Yeah, we heard that," Sam said. "Think it's true?"

"Might just be," the guy told them. "Whatever, it's pretty sick."

As the truck pulled out of the gas station, Brian commented:

"I wonder what he meant by sick?"

"Take your choice," Sam responded.

They drove into the hurrying snow, saying hardly a word to one another. Sam wondered within himself whether it wasn't time to say something. Brian wrestled with the best way to break his accusations to his lover. The heater roared at full-blast.

The radio crackled with news reports and country and western music. They were too tired to think of changing the station. The radio told them that Ed Stevens had been detained at an airport in Philadelphia. While it was four in the morning in the east, reactions were already forthcoming. A White House press agent commented that the President had been informed, that Mr. Stevens had a highly imaginative and irresponsible mind, and that his accusations were categorically denied. And no, this would not in any way alter the President's imminent trip to San Francisco to meet with NATO leaders.

So that means it's true, Sam thought. Flat denials until the truth comes out. But Sam said nothing.

That was what made this silence between them so difficult to bear, so oppressive. Through that silence he could hear Brian's hurts. More than anything, he wanted to push aside the secrecy and tell Brian, especially now that the CIA plot was coming out. He didn't have much left in this life and he wanted a big part of it to involve Brian. God, how he felt divided. He and Brian had really fought only one time before, back on a hiking weekend near Mount Adams. Sam couldn't even remember what their squabble had been over and it would probably seem stupid now. They'd started fighting the moment they had parked the car. And then, for most of the weekend they walked their trails silently, hardly grunting a word of acknowledgment to one another, the animosity spoiling the views. Finally, the last evening, Sam had thrown his arms about Brian. "Let's forget the whole thing," he said simply. "We've punished each other enough." And forget it they did.

Another news brief from ABC punctuated their broodings. Senator Kennedy had been informed of the affair and was expected to call for a Congressional investigation. Reporters had also clarified yet two other matters. Stevens had been definitively linked to the New Covenant Fellowship, a Fundamentalist sect that held the Last Judgment was imminent. "Stevens may truly have believed as he stated, that he was acting as an agent of God." And reporters had confirmed a massive blood-testing program undertaken by US Public Health Service Officials in Zaire in 1975; many of the professional participants in that program had been defense research staff. The program ostensibly looked at blood protein diversity.

Shit, 4:30 A.M. in the east and they're going hot at it, Sam thought. He saw journalists searching the hieroglyphics of medical journals, struggling with difficult concepts and noting names and affiliations. He could hear phones ringing in offices in Europe and Central Africa. He could imagine the whine of overheating shredders as they finally lived up to their expense. At the CIA, in the defense establishment, there would be no rest now if the truth was to remain buried. It almost seemed hopeful.

REST AREA, NEXT EXIT

Sam turned the truck into the off-ramp, then pulled into the parking lot.

"What's this?" Brian asked him. "Changed your mind about going on?"

"No. Come over here."

"Why?" Brian asked, looking at him suspiciously.

"I said come over here. I want to hug you."

Brian pushed himself along the seat until he was touching Sam.

"Okay," he said.

And they hugged, Sam trying harder than Brian. Sam was almost certain that Brian was only doing it to be nice. He tried to kiss Brian, but Brian buried his cheek in Sam's neck. They rocked back and forth, rubbing, clasping.

"Thank you," Sam said, hiding his disappointment. He felt like crying.

"You still feel good," Brian told him.

Christ, what does he mean by that? Sam wondered. Does he still love me? He pulled the truck back onto the road. The snow was coming down as heavy as ever.

"We're not going to make it," Brian warned as they began climbing the grade to Mount Shasta. "We don't even have chains."

"Get lost," Sam told him.

"I'm entitled to my opinion, buddy."

There was an abrasive silence again, the truck in third gear struggling up a slushy road.

"You know, Sam—that guy Stevens. Suppose he's just some crackpot? Maybe he had a grudge against the CIA?"

"Could be," Sam answered him.

"What do you mean, could be? You believe the CIA was involved, don't you?"

"I don't know what to believe."

"Bullshit, Sam. You've believed something like this

for a long time. But you've been trying damn hard to make sure I don't know."

Sam said nothing. The truck skidded a little as he impatiently tried to give it too much gas. He pulled it back on course with a turn of the wheel. Brian hardly seemed to notice.

"You're up to something," Brian accused Sam. "And I want to know what it's all about."

"I'm not up to anything," Sam told him.

"Listen buddy, don't give me that shit. We're going to get this out right now. You hear me?"

"Yeah," Sam said. He was almost glad now that Brian was being relentless.

"Okay, let's start with the facts. Something happened to you when you went to San Francisco in July and saw Jim. Some new attitude. Something's come between us. As if you've got some secret cause under your belt that can't be shared with me."

"It was a hell of a trip," Sam answered. "Seeing Jim in that terrible shape. You know how much I've always liked Jim."

"You've seen it happen to other men. Sure it's awful, but something changed in you."

"I started thinking about what you'll think of me when I get like that."

"Yeah, I'll probably kick you out of my life. Listen, I happen to know Jim's got pretty strong political feelings. What do you guys talk about on those phone calls you make? All this justice business?"

"Christ, have you been listening to my phone calls?"

"No, but you're my lover, Sam. Okay, don't answer me on that. What about this trip, this frantic timing? More phone calls to Jim. We got to be in San Francisco by Saturday, bags packed and all. Last summer you never wanted

to live in the city. You loved Portland and the Pacific
Northwest too much.''

"So I needed to go somewhere else to die.''

"But why all this rush? You're not terminal yet.
All this crackpot timing, driving through blizzards. Is it to
be in San Francisco when the President also happens to
be there?''

Sam was silent. He had wanted this to happen, but
now that it had, he was unprepared to answer. He wanted
to tell Brian and he wanted to feel his love again. He wanted
the trust back.

Brian, for his part, continued his attack. I'm
not letting up now, he thought. Now that I've got him
by the balls, I'm not going to pull real hard, until he's
screaming.

"And what's this business of a package, arrived just
in time from Boise? Who the fuck do you know in Boise?
What's so special about this package that you rushed out
to take it from UPS and wouldn't let me near it?''

Again, silence. The truck was moving along at
a speed somewhat less than fifteen miles an hour, growling
its way through six inches of wet snow. They had reached
the pass.

"It's all downhill now,'' Sam commented. "If we can
make Dunsmuir we've done it.''

"So what's in that package? A high-power rifle?''

"Okay, Brian. Since you ask, I'll tell you. No, it isn't
a rifle. But that's pretty close.''

Again silence. Brian hadn't expected it so soon. Sam
was at last relieved. Yes, he had been sworn to secrecy. But
with Steven's statement to the press, things were different
now. As gay brothers, they were all into it together. He could
and he would trust Brian.

They pulled through the California produce inspection station with cynical humor to each other about

diseased fruits. They were waved through. Sam pulled the truck to a halt in a corner of the pavement beyond the station.

"Listen, Brian" he said. "I want those hugs and kisses you held back earlier. Then I'll tell you everything."

"Everything?"

"Yeah, I promise babe."

10 *The Ambush, San Francisco, Late Thursday Evening*

Friday night at the bar had started slow. It was not that the Ambush had officially closed, a victim of the yuppie avarice that in the wake of AIDS had parasitized so much of South of Market in taking over or closing gay bars. The Ambush, its greatest and most tragic victim, would never die, mindspace that it was.

If anything, the bar was more protected now, a living dream of the family who touched souls there. The visions in art, appearing out of the shadows of its walls like holy illuminations—whether a visiting artist or the permanent collection. The unpretentious, free-wheeling camraderie of hippy bikers and leathermen (who could also be professionals or businessmen). The warm and friendly flow of piss over the backroom urinal by men sharing smiles and stares at each other's cocks and maybe even touches (Oh God, how intense the longing becomes behind scared eyes). The memories of celebrations, for Solstice and Equinox and Freedom Day and even down-home things like Christmas. The bartenders and owners, people who were always more

community then the outside neighborhood: Norman and
Steven and Fergy and Lynda and Jack and Lou Rudolph, and
the imperturbable genius of it all, Kerry. Owners and
patrons, they all still meet in that magic time when the late
afternoon sun, peeping through a tiny window near the
ceiling, is caught in a prism and sends rainbows dancing
through the bar.

If anything, the Ambush was more invincible now,
continually visited, often busy, unreachable by the straight
yuppie out for an evening's kicks and coke before returning wired to a dangerously inflated life. If anything, the bar
could be more select, in a way that could never be challenged
by state or federal law, because its patrons were also its true
believers, and when wild crazy Wayne let loose with his
howling dog, by the animal and comedy within themselves
other men moved and responded and let loose with a part-
nership of canine grunts and howls; and the men in the bar
would shiver and smile with delight.

If Thursday evening at the Ambush had started slow,
maybe it was because of the gutsy weather that hissed over
the city and threatened rain. But then the bar would have
been a warm and attractive place to be. Perhaps it was an
impending sense of gloom that hung over South of Market,
this growing sense of dishonor that distracted minds,
that marked the imminent and ill-timed Presidential visit.
The crowd picked up somewhat near midnight, but then
dwindled again to a dozen or so.

In a sense, Marc was just as happy to take the evening on the easy side. To pause between customers. To watch
the intense and unjostled progress of a game of pool. Not
to have to struggle in collecting empty bottles and glasses
about the bar.

Bill had wandered in about one-thirty and Marc met
him soon after. Marc immediately liked his eyes. They were
green and filled with both frustration and sadness. Not that

he wasn't hot. A sort of bearded, bushy-haired country man with lots of obstreperous curls pushing out his collar and cuffs.

But it was Bill's eyes that got Marc, that made him reach out and touch his hand, stroke it gently, as he served the beer. The eyes spoke of loss. A people who have lost too many dreams, Marc thought. He knew that look, he had grown up with it up in Canada in the forests of the Peace. He had seen that look in the morning-after faces littering the main street of Fort St. John. He had heard the same futility in his father's voice, many times. As on that frigid morning when they met with the disruptive swath of a new seismic line across one of their most productive traplines. *"Merde,"* his father muttered. *"Ils en mangent tous."*

Was it inevitable that Bill and he would retire together to a nearby friend's house when the bar closed, to spend much of the night talking and holding each other? Nothing was inevitable for Marc except the slow tracking of that other side of reality, the world beyond its seams. This brother had reached across to hold his hand.

One of the first things they talked about was Bill's frustration.

"It's like I'm tied in knots," Bill told Marc. "I live in a sort of tension. I live in Colorado and the city was always a place to get away to, so I could be myself. Let my animal self go."

"Whatever, you're still a hot animal," Marc told him, holding him, rubbing their beards together.

But Bill wasn't ready yet for affection.

"Damn it, Marc. You know what I mean. I come here wanting to let loose like we all used to, to fuck, to wallow in each other. I love sharing with a buddy. But it's hard to do that anymore. The city's changed and I've changed. The city's changed. It's full of yuppies chasing designer dreams in their Acura Legends. It'll never come back. I get so frustrated, so sad.''

''I know how it hurts, Bill. It hurts for the guys that live here. It was a special ability that gay men had, a special way with each other that made life stand out. Yeah, it hurts, all right.''

''I guess what I'm really saying is there'll never be this San Francisco to come to again. Here or anywhere.''

''No, Bill,'' Marc told him. ''The dream that is pure and from the heart never dies. It can slip from our fingers, but it lives with our souls, and the magic in it will regroup and be rediscovered.''

There was that hut, at Kahntah, close by the spruce grove on the little rise at the edge of Reservation land. The dreams of a people linked to that land. His people were Cree Indian and Metis. The Metis were those combination-people, Quebecois and Indian that generations of government, even today, continued to shunt around the open lands, the ''Native'' lands. Marc could see his mother scraping and stretching pelts, as had thousands of women before her. Hunters pursuing the footfall of a moose through those northern swamps as heard in a dream. The fishermen, the hunter, descrying the sign of game, the sparkle and leap of fish, by the monuments of trees and deadfalls and rocks perceived in the shadows of the mind. These images danced about Marc like a special music; like the semi-comic whine of his father's fiddle as it lilted through droll peasant tunes of a long-away France. That the owl would pause in its glide through the night air, that the wolf would freeze in its tracks, both to take note of this melancholy shrieking! These were the wisps of dreams, the bitter struggles of a people meshed to their bodies, heritage and lands. Here were fragments of melody that would never perish, whatever the mammons or ordeals, disease or winter.

Marc had started to play with Bill's tit. He had

slipped the plaid shirt open a few more buttons, pushed his hand into the warm hair and taken hold of the shape of the pec. He had Bill in his lap, his warm hips curled into his crotch. Bill's arm was about Marc's shoulders; he rubbed the muscles of Marc's neck with the palm of his hand.

"It's not that simple, you know," Bill continued. "I've traveled all over America. You know, in that era of the great gay traveler. You ever meet Terry Kotas?"

Marc grunted affirmatively.

"I was like him. I may be a ranch hand but I know people in Dallas and Chicago and Key West. I went to New Orleans for Mardi Gras. I slummed in between operas in New York. But there was no place like San Francisco. It was always home. Of course at times I wanted to move here, but I'm a country boy. I can't live without those wide open spaces."

Bill's fingers felt the outline of Marc's beard, rubbing the skin through the brusque hair. There was a lot of gray in it.

"There was something here in San Francisco," he went on, "in the way men looked and touched. In the dreams that were in their eyes. That made me believe."

Marc had found Bill's nipple. It felt as if it wanted play, the way it sat up hard through the fur. Marc applied pressure carefully, rubbing and caressing. He loved the way that tit play, if done just right, made a buddy melt completely into a scene.

Marc was remembering his own travels, his own dreams of this city. In a few seconds he would open the shirt some more so he could suck on those tits. But for now, he just kept stroking, in long careful sweeps of sensation. Even in his own travels as a student, even before he met Allan, even before coming to the US, San Francisco had risen in his dreams; he had ridden the N-Judah out of the West Portal and into the foggy sunlight; he had seen the houses rising white and gold like oracles on the hills. His first coming here, in the enthusiasm of Allan's return from exile, was merely confirmation, a final mastery of himself over his skill at dream.

Bill had reached behind Marc's neck and was tugging at his ponytail.

"How do you get this damn thing undone?" he asked. "Long hair on a bearded man is hot."

Marc fiddled with the bond, and his hair, touched with silver, cascaded loose like black fire. Bill took the hair between his fingers and pulled the face close.

"Damn it, you're hot," Marc told him as they locked lips together, first in gentle caresses, and then in hungry convulsions.

"You look a little like Jesus," Bill told him.

Oh Christ, Marc thought. He hated to think what this might mean about Bill. Benevolent shepherds hovering over midwest chapels where icy preachers instructed fat women in the crimes of living. Congregations competing in piousness. He hated that kitsch. The church had screwed his own people, had screwed the Quebecois before them, and still screwed them both.

"No, really," Bill said, sensing a hesitancy. "Jesus was soft and hard at the same time. Sad and beautiful all together. I believe Jesus must have been gay to love the way he did."

Marc kissed Bill some more. He sort of liked the compliment now.

"That's why they hate us so much," Bill said. "Gay people are talking about the same brotherhood that Christ did. We have the same dream. But we won't suck up to their power trips. Hey Jesus, kiss me some more."

And their kissing dissolved into passion, the togetherness of two men, the communion between souls, desire shifting through limbs coming awake to one another, hands stroking legs, rubbing crotch and butt and tit and bicep. Then the long pauses, drinking slowly through each other's lips, almost as if in sleep, almost as if transfixed. God, how long I've wanted, needed this, Bill muttered to his own mind, how I want to cry to have found it again, to know the kiss of brotherhood. They broke off for a moment.

"Fuck, that was wonderful," Bill said.

"Oh God, buddy," Marc answered, kissing him again.

"Sorry that I get a bit religious at times," Bill told him.

"That's just fine," Marc responded, "I do too."

Marc didn't go into discussing his religion, but he was sure Bill would understand. He sensed him as a man of open spaces who knew the spirits that lived in mountains, that shattered rock, that nested in the roots of pine and spruce, that whirled and whimpered through the forest night seeking prey or condolence.

"You got a lover?" Bill asked him.

"Sort of," Marc answered. "I live with two guys. Real beautiful men. We were all lovers once. Now we're best friends."

He had opened Bill's jeans and had his hard cock wrapped in his hand. The end trembled under the foreskin as his fingers played with it, pushed it open. Marc seemed to remember dark woods in a November rain, somewhere in Minnesota. Tree boles glistened, rising towards eternity. There was caution and there was waiting. Fear whispered in the wet air. The moment taken to an abstract, invisible line that might mean asylum. Distant sounds of voices, south and north. The distant splash of a turning amber light. How Allan came to him out of those same forests that Marc was always tracking. How the conscience always seeks relief.

Allan had come out of that forest, that fear. Two years later, in the early seventies, he had met Marc in a Vancouver bottle club. He had already exorcised several demons from his life and would tackle several more in meeting Marc. And Marc would hold him, comfort him. Marc would tie up his soul like a cocoon so that it felt secure. Marc would fuck him long and hard. He would turn Allan around again to face the forest, to go hunting the demons that waited at every turn.

Marc had Bill's cock between his fingers and his tongue was probing it, his mouth coating it with spit, his fingers relentless in their attack, Bill's fingers now on Marc's own tits, hardened and thick with centuries of love and abuse, Bill's lips and throat and gut moaning with sobs of exultation. And with one hand Marc had Bill's shirt off so his muscular arms were tight against Marc's shoulders and chest while his mouth and fingers sucked and licked and rubbed and stretched the foreskin open and back and forth over them, almost painfully, before rubbing the cock head some more, and Bill climbing all the higher until he screamed, "No, no, I can't hold it anymore," and let loose with great heaving gobs of cum over his hairy stomach and into his crotch.

And then, it was two brothers, kissing, afloat in warm touches.

"See, baby. You got to believe." Marc told him.

Bill kissed him some more.

"With you Marc, there's no way I can't believe. Even if San Francisco has changed."

"But its magic is still alive."

"Some of it," Bill admitted.

Marc kissed him some more. First a peck and then a long careful embrace.

"You realize where we met?" he asked Bill.

"I've forgotten," Bill said. "But it seems like it was the —"

He stopped in midspeech, incredulous.

"They say the Ambush has been closed for years," Marc told him.

11 *Spring Valley, Maryland, Early Friday Morning*

Jo-Lyn was hopping mad. While she disliked this state of chronic rage that had consumed her, it was an inevitability these days. The more convoluted life became, the more Jo-Lyn would flail at it. And the more she put out against this world, even if it was only in her mind, the more intense her anger became.

In a sense, she should be sympathizing with the current predicament of the President, whom she watched now on television. There was something pathetic in the way he and his wife waved at the gawkers during their early departure for Camp David. (There was something comic in the way the dog tugged at his leash as if striving for press attention that his masters would have gladly avoided.) Who were these obnoxious men and women on the sidelines making shrill and unscheduled demands? "Mr. President, did you know of this plot to release the AIDS virus?" "Mr. President, what of your trip to San Francisco?" The President would sort of wave his hands, as if that were the magic required to dispel this unpleasantness. But the spell failed to work, and the questioners and their questions persisted. For just a moment, the President showed annoyance. He barked some combination of "Everything under control," and "In good time." Then, he and his wife and a protesting dog turned sharply and hurried on, once more all smiles. How dare these interlopers break into the important and pleasurable task of greeting an admiring public?

Jo-Lyn did not sympathize with the vision of a great

leader accosted by outrage. She herself was very angry with him. In fact she was so angry that in tightening her fists she inadvertently switched off the television by way of the remote control clutched in her right hand. The President had no right to evade these questions being asked of him. Her husband had come forward and spoken what he knew to be the honest truth. Her husband had worked for and supported this President. What her husband had done was for his country and under the auspices of his country. It was time for the President to acknowledge devoted work and long years of service. Good work could indeed be controversial, but must be recognized. These shallow politicians, thought Jo-Lyn, were all the same. They were ready to disavow even the Lord's work if it could come out against them. When she thought of the support she and Ed had given the President, their work in his campaign, she hated the man all the more. He was supposed to be *their* President.

Ed had called her late the night before from a telephone booth. He was leaving the country, he said. She had sobbed a lot. She wanted to hug him; he sounded so brave. For a moment, last night, her anger towards Ed had faded. He needed her, and she sensed it. Working for the CIA, he had always seemed a lonely, isolated man. Now he was totally alone, and her heart reached out. Whether or not what he had done was right or wrong, he needed her. He might not have let her in on this secret, or this sudden move to reveal it. (He had never told her very much of anything.) But he was out in the cold and dripping wet. He was like a little boy who had run away from home on a rainy night just needing to know that the world did care and that he could come back to love.

Jo-Lyn hadn't said very much for what could have been their final conversation.

"Please tell me you love me," she asked him. "That you love Carolyn."

"I love you both," he told her. "I did it for my country and I did it for both of you," he added, as if the burden had become too great. "Eventually they'll understand."

And that had made her sob into the phone. How could he put her and little Carolyn through all this? How dare he?

"I've got to go," he had told her. "I'm going to Europe. I'll write and you can come and join me."

But that was probably only a cover. Jo-Lyn sensed that Europeans wouldn't be too sympathetic to her husband's fate. An hour later, news reports had confirmed Ed's arrest while boarding a flight with connections to Brazil. News of the arrest had set her to sobbing again, furiously.

And now, as the President evaded all questions from a guantlet of persistent news people; now, as the White House Chief of Staff told the press that the allegations were scurrilous, that Ed Stevens was a miscalculating liar, Jo-Lyn Stevens, watching it all on television, clutched the arm of her sofa and shook.

Dear God, she thought. Please let me pray. Please give me the peace of prayer. Her back to the television, the machine still blaring incessant reports of the mundane as spectacular, still spewing its essential messages of cornflakes and cars, Jo-Lyn struggled to her knees, leaning her body over the couch, her arms clutching and her head buried in a seat cushion.

The first stages of prayer, Jo-Lyn found, were the most difficult. It was a matter of trying to conceptualize whom she should pray to. Just what did her image of God look like? There was no doubt God was masculine. She had little time for that lunatic fringe that claimed God was feminine. There was a sort of image of her father in Jo-Lyn's mind when she thought of God, but that was an incomplete image. Father had been insulted by Gregg and even though father couldn't avoid his predicament, God himself would never put up with it. Of course, there could be something of Gregg in God, but that was back when the whole family had idolized him. Ed was there in her image too, but she could become angry with Ed, and she had. She could never get angry with God. Then there was something Presidential about God; something in the way she had admired their current leader. But she idolized God; she couldn't do the same for the President. And her Lord was much more than just Presidential. He was reverent and blessed. He was immutable when it came to what was right. Jo-Lyn thought of Pastor Wannamaker. She had admired him at certain times for just those reasons, for his piousness and devotion. But when it came to brimstone, even Pastor Wannamaker could seem cold and unyielding. Jo-Lyn could get angry at that, although she had tried not to let it show to the Fellowship. No, God might be unyielding, but he was warm and passionately unyielding. God stood for everything that she and little Carolyn believed in. God supported her every cause and conflict in an unquestioning and devoted way.

"Oh holy God," she murmured. "Oh holy God."

Sometimes she had difficulty using the word *holy*. It almost seemed too Catholic. But this time she was too impassioned to notice; she was too intent that God would listen and help.

"Oh dear God I know how much I've sinned, how unworthy I am of your never-ending love."

She sobbed at her mention of the word love.

"Oh God, please listen to my prayers, please help this hurting soul that is so devoted to you."

"Oh please holy God, hold me close to you, wrap me in your arms and heal my suffering."

Jo-Lyn cried some more. Oh God, it was so unfair that she, such a devoted servant of the Good Lord should have to suffer so much. All unwanted, unexplained suffering, from the day Gregg had outraged the family to their present trials, all of these troubles seemed directed at Jo-Lyn.

"Holy God, please hold me tight," she beseeched. "Fill me with warm peace."

She clutched the sofa cushion in her arms, squeezing it, hugging it. How she needed to be close to someone who passionately cared for her. No one had ever really loved her that way. Yes, she loved Ed, that was her duty. Sometimes he could be nice to her, although she tried hard to forget about the rough times. But accepting these tribulations was also her duty. Yes, he loved little Carolyn. But usually Ed was distant, miles away from her, shrouded in his secret works, even out of the country. If only he could have been near her more often. If only he could have tried to understand her little anguishes, then maybe it would have worked better than it had. Still, she loved Ed.

"Dear Father who art in heaven. Please protect my husband. Please guide him through these difficulties and steer him from evil."

Jo-Lyn cringed. She didn't trust those men who had detained him, those dark nameless shadows of terror and enforcement. They would relentlessly attempt to pry every secret, every motive out of him. He would be shot full of drugs. Left in solitary. Slapped, kicked, and abused. Cajoled and insulted when he refused to talk. Sweetened when he did. Her own life, her own tribulations and desires would be spread out as his, carrion for them to pick at.

"Oh God, dear God, protect us from them. Please protect my Ed."

And these were *his* colleagues who were doing this to her husband.

Before they had married, he had just been another government worker. After, he had told her a very little of his work. "I live a life of secrets," he said. "I may be away a lot and tell you nothing of it. It's required of my work.

I may seem distant, preoccupied with other things. But darn it, Jo-Lyn, I'll still love you."

She cried some more. If he had cared so much about her, he would never have come to tell these secrets. He would never disobey orders. Then, she thought: maybe he had been told to tell everything, and this was part of it. The arrest was part of the act. Oh, if that were really the case, and he'd soon be free.

But there were other things that were involved. Jo-Lyn had that vision again, the runaway child, self-minded, determined that the world would listen. She had quietly noted this about half a year ago. Ed and she attended the weekly prayer group of the Fellowship. Hands linked, heads bowed and eyes closed, their communion ranged through prayer and intercessions, to words of the heart, to commentaries on sin. "Protect us from the evil forces of Satan, from immorality and homosexuality," one participant stated. "We should not fear," someone else added. "AIDS is God's retribution." And then, quietly, she had heard Ed's voice: "Oh Lord, we give thanks for your inspiration that made AIDS possible and let it be used in your defense. Oh Lord we give thanks for that."

Jo-Lynn had been incredulous. She had never heard anything like this before. Ed was trained in science and probably knew a lot of important things. No one else in the group asked any questions, but that was a principle of the prayer circle where one spoke from the heart in a common and confidential dialogue with God.

"Oh dear Lord, why did he do it?" Jo-Lyn questioned her God again.

And he had. Several weeks later, as if determined to be heard, Ed had spoken out again during the communion of the prayer circle. "Oh Lord, thank you for your great gifts. Thank you for your devoted servants who created the HIV virus to fulfill your ways." Once more, there was a certain disquiet in the room. It was as if at last a fine truth was being told, a truth they could only just begin to appreciate. Again, nothing was said directly on the matter. But outside the prayer circle, first within the Fellowship, and then within the associated Christian movement, elusive rumors began to multiply like the dancing shadows from a candle flame. Jo-Lyn knew only one thing, Ed had a secret and he was determined to let it out. But damn him, Jo-Lyn thought. He never considered what it would do to us.

"Oh dear Lord," she continued, abandoning her prayers for Ed. "Oh dear Lord, protect my little Carolyn."

Carolyn had become her point of contention with the Fellowship. There was no one who could say that Jo-Lyn's devotion to Carolyn lacked in any way. And no one could blame her for this devotion. But she could not believe that her devotion was to be futile.

"Oh Lord, love my little girl like Mommy loved me. Protect her from evil people. Help her to grow up in the Light."

Before Carolyn had been conceived, there had been a certain bleakness in Jo-Lyn's beliefs. The calculated passion of prayer meetings and the almost rigid coldness of Pastor Wannamaker's sermons directed them all on their course in these last battles. They lived, all of them, with the difficult knowledge of being the faithful under siege. There would of course be heaven, sweet heaven, after their tribulations. But thoughts of passage through the Final Battle, the inevitable Holocaust and the Last Judgment hung their pall over Jo-Lyn. God had declared his intentions, said Pastor Wannamaker, and his will would be done. None of them in the Fellowship had needed Pastor Wannamaker to tell them these truths. Most of the time, Jo-Lyn had subsumed herself to her duties, lifted her head bravely, and faced the world with all the piousness she could find for reassurance.

Why couldn't she do that now? These present tribulations would be nothing when the skies opened and the seas boiled with fire.

"Dear Lord, please be a Father for little Carolyn. Please!"

As the seed that became Carolyn turned and took shape inside her, Jo-Lyn became conscious of this new life that was her and not her. Whatever the trials of this world, whatever the deadly fate God had in store for it, she could not believe he would harm little Carolyn or that he would hinder the growth of this little sweetness. New life and new opportunity were truly His way. Carolyn was clearly of the meek and she was destined to inherit her due. Her end could not be the dark future preached by their pastor. Jo-Lyn could never question him openly, but more and more, she had found herself believing differently from those in the Fellowship.

"And dear Lord. Please set our world on a course of peace and good. Please conquer all evil and the work of Satan."

This was something for which no one in the Fellowship prayed. They were committed to the coming Judgment and they prayed for its facilitation. What others saw as a dangerous arms race, they saw as an inevitable incineration of the flesh that would distill pure from evil. The scourges of the horsemen: pain, suffering, famine, and diseases were already among the world's people; pestilence had already begun to descend from their skies. Jo-Lyn perceived a sort of bitter pleasure in the faces of some of her fellow accolytes. With Judgment Day nigh, how could anyone pray for peace? People who did that were hypocrites; they ignored the facts. Peace and goodness were only to be found in heaven and enjoyed by the faithful.

Jo-Lyn flailed her body in emotion. She stopped

GEOFF MAINS

hugging the cushion, and lifting it, struck it several times in frustration against the couch.

God, why had prayer become so difficult for her? Gone was her accepting, unquestioning contentment. Her problems refused to leave her. Even as she attempted to pray, her conflicts came forth like black devils to play a game of tag through her mind.

"Oh, please, please God."

She flailed some more. How she wanted to pray for a quiet life. A blissful, rural life, just she and little Carolyn, on a farm somewhere, the clear morning air, the hot afternoons, the fragrant evenings when all she could hear was bird song and the rustle of leaves and just maybe the sound of a distant passing car. No reporters at her door. No lectures on impending doom. No sneaky city people, government lackeys or twisted politicians. Only Jo-Lyn and sweet Carolyn growing together in a world in which all would be just fine. She had almost had that once.

And then she thought of Gregg. The last time she had seen him. Tall and lanky and self-contented. Full of the devil. How she hated thoughts of that Christmas and the tragedy that followed. How she suffered when she thought of her distraught parents. Oh God, the injustice of the way it all had ended, the devil slapping her father in his own face and getting away with it. Her own sweet Carolyn, denied her rightful heritage.

Attempts at prayer had only aggravated Jo-Lyn's dark mood. She must do something, she thought. I must find peace. Maybe she should go and hold little Carolyn.

12 *Upper Market, San Francisco, Early Friday Morning*

Allan was reading the *Chronicle* as Gregg came into the kitchen. Gregg rustled in the cupboard, poured himself a bowl of cereal and added a cut-up banana.

"So," he told Allan with a certain snideness. "We're actually going to have breakfast together!"

"You know how busy I am right now," Allan answered tersely from behind the paper.

"I know," Gregg said.

If they had just been housemates, maybe this would have been all right. But they were still supposed to be lovers. Gregg was disappointed. Allan's campaign seemed like an excuse, a diversion. Oh sure, it was a good thing for the city. Every one of their many friends encouraged him and thought he should run. It just riled Gregg that Allan, with all his community work, with all his previous caring, couldn't deal with Gregg's having AIDS. However, Gregg realized that this was not the time to raise that issue. They both had too many things happening. Maybe when the election was over, and if he was still free, Gregg could confront Allan on that matter.

"So how're you feeling?" Allan asked, again without putting down the paper.

He asks that every day, Gregg noted. It's as if he occasionally recognizes he's been ignoring me.

"Same as ever," Gregg responded. He didn't mention to Allan that they'd found another lesion on his left leg.

Gregg went on eating his banana and cereal,

alternating with mouthfuls of coffee. Allan went on scanning his newspaper to mouthfuls of toast.

Gregg remembered how they had met. The Balcony, its C not quite fallen, on a glorious Sunday afternoon after the night before. Allan had been at the Trock. Gregg had been at the Catacombs. At the time they were both spacing in the golden reality of being alive. It was that day someone had painted across the billboard on the other side of Market Street, so that incoming commuter traffic was greeted with the fine sight of a tight-assed marine declaring butchly:

MAYBE YOU CAN ~~BE~~ ONE OF US

DO

Being at the Balcony on a Sunday afternoon was like being jostled comfortably in a sort of overcrowded womb where one vibrated with the incessant tribal beat of the music. Allan and Gregg had caught glimpses of each other in the crowd, then lost one another for several hours. They had rediscovered each other about five and that was that. This time each didn't allow the other to get away.

"How'd last night go?" Gregg asked Allan.

Allan put his paper aside for a moment.

Gregg caught his eye. Through all his troubles, Allan's eyes had never changed. They were a warm gray. When you didn't know Allan, they seemed open, unmasked. They invited you in. Yet to Gregg they seemed evasive, deluding, But maybe that was because he thought he knew Allan too well.

"Last night was pretty heavy, but I made it through okay."

So Allan was even going to look at him directly. Shit, Gregg thought. I've got to clear these bitchy feelings out of my mind. There's too much at stake.

"Harrison even mentioned you," he told Gregg.

"What did he say? How he didn't want to knock

someone you cared about but that I was irresponsibly spreading my AIDS all over town?''

God, what do I care what Harrison choses to think, Gregg thought. What's important is you, Allan. I still love you. I still think you're hot. Oh Christ, if it could only be the way it once was, the way it was when we met. All arms and passion and good intentions that both of us wanted, needed. Gregg knew that his condition scared Allan. After facing death in so many friends, here it was in Allan's own home. But being scared should be no excuse to turn and run. Gregg could understand Allan's reactions, but he could not accept it.

"Yeah, he talked about you and AIDS as some sort of liability. He also claimed to know about my past and just what we've done sexually."

"Oh yeah? Bet the crowd loved that."

"If there weren't kids there, I'm sure he would have talked in detail about fisting."

"So they've got someone digging into our past?"

"You know what bothers me, Gregg, is not the publicity. I don't care who knows. They take those things we did in love, even the people I love, and smear them around to look dirty."

Gregg had loved this side of Allan from their first meeting. Allan had a willingness to own up to, to acknowledge his own actions, even when they could seem radical. Damn it, the world needed more people like this guy.

"So how'd you deal with it?"

"I had a lot more to deal with. Personal insults. Attempts at divide and conquer, you know—them and us. Outright lies and innuendo. AIDS hysteria. This guy's pulling out all the stops. And the crowd wasn't easy. It was a Mission crowd, almost antagonistic. Planted with a cheering section for Harrison that comes out to all the meetings. But apart from his supporters, a lot of people just don't trust

Harrison. I don't know what it is, maybe he seems too certain, too pious. Hell, this city's been working on AIDS education, intensely, for years. Everyone knows that, and everyone knows that education has worked. Where was this need for extremism that Harrison talked about? A lot of people suspect there are other motives hidden in Harrison's platform."

"Did you reveal them?"

"That will come. But for now I faced him right on. I said I was disgusted with the way people's lives and deaths, loves and tragedies had become cheap fodder for his campaign. These were real people he was talking about. Real tears and heartbreaks and friends. I said I was sickened by his efforts to spread greater fears and discontents, at a time when love and caring and helping were needed more than anything else. Was Harrison one of those who would round up the dying in the name of compassion and abandon them to death camps, away from friends and neighbors, lovers, and family? The last thing this city needs, I told them, is more divisiveness. We've all worked well together in tackling this tragedy. This man wants to split apart San Francisco's communities after we've worked together for each other for so long."

Gregg felt bitterness again. He knew his lover was devoted to others, was good at his law and his politics. But why had he abandoned him, just when Gregg needed those arms, that support? He wasn't winning anything by pushing the issue of AIDS in his own life to arms length.

Allan turned back to his paper. Gregg attacked his cereal. Most mornings he didn't feel hungry, but he knew he had to push down any little pulses of nausea and force some essential nutrition into his system.

"Seen anything of Marc?" Allan asked him, again turning a page.

"Yesterday afternoon. He's okay."

"Are you sure? I worry about that guy."

"He does okay for himself. He knows how to survive."

"I used to really admire his brains. Now he's caught up in these Ambush delusions."

"Yeah? Who's to say his delusions are any different than anyone else's? You should talk about delusions sometime."

Allan chose not to respond. He crinkled the paper to show annoyance.

"They still haven't got any leads on this Missoula firebombing. There's a picture of the place here. Recognize it?"

Yesterday their breakfast conversation had focused on the fact that Gregg had once worked in this Montana office for two years as a wildlife biologist. That was four years before he had moved to the city.

"Yeah, that's the building." Gregg noted.

"I can't understand it," Allan said. "Sure there are lots of groups against the government. But the Forest Service? They've got to be pretty innocuous."

"Environmentalists can be radical. Protecting wilderness values. But as I said, I still believe it's an animal rights group."

Programs to reduce coyote populations were currently a big issue in the northern mountain states. Ranchers pushed for their removal. Environmentalists fought for coyote survival. The Forest Service had recently joined the Bureau of Land Management in initiating a major coyote reduction program. Besides, Gregg knew that a letter, allegedly from animal rights activists and claiming responsibility, had been mailed from Pocatello to the Missoula press.

"These crazy acts of violence are getting to be a nuisance," Allan commented.

Damn you, Allan, Gregg thought. That's not what you

said the night of the White Riots that followed the jury decision to give leniency to the supervisor who murdered Milk and Moscone. What was it: "The most important statement gay men have ever made?" You castigated the "responsible" gay leaders who tried to disown the act. You're just scared for your own campaign.

The phone rang. Allan went to answer it. There was animated discussion. Gregg ignored their conversation and got up for some more coffee. He considered picking up the paper and burying himself in it as Allan had. He turned over the front section, then froze when he saw the headlines. He didn't need to read the details, only to see the enlarged words and a photo of Ed Stevens to understand what it meant. God's magic bullet, the paper screamed. Why the hell hadn't Jim called him? He must have found out after last night's meeting. Then Gregg remembered: after talking with Tony, he'd unplugged his phone.

Allan came back from his call.

"When did this happen?" Gregg asked him. Gregg was studying the paper intently now. "Why didn't you say something?"

"I thought you knew. It happened late last night. It's all everyone is talking about."

"So those rumors were right. The CIA did it."

Gregg was overcome with a wave of exhilaration and relief. They had been right and Jim's planning was on track. These revelations meant they were dealing with a real, hard reality. It was like those moments that Gregg faced the fact that he had AIDS and would die from it.

"It's ironic," Allen made comment. "You read the account in the paper and they've missed the tragedy. They're so busy wondering who authorized the thing and when. Which President and which CIA Chief? And how much does the current President know?"

"It'll be good for your campaign. A tremendous sympathy vote."

"All I'm afraid of is that some crazy queen will choose this as a time to shoot the President. In that sense it couldn't happen at a worse time."

Gregg was quiet for a moment, deciding whether to say anything. Allan looked at him unexpectedly. Damn it, he couldn't know anything, Gregg thought.

"I wouldn't blame anyone if something happened," Gregg commented. "The President's damn stupid to insist on coming here."

Yes, God's magic bullet, he told himself. Besides, we don't intend to kill him directly.

Allan quizzed Gregg with one of his looks.

"I hope to hell nothing happens," he told his lover.

"Don't look at me like that," Gregg almost shouted, but controlled himself. "I just happen to be one of ten thousand men in this city who have the damn disease."

13 *Jackson Square, San Francisco, Friday Morning*

You're sure one persuasive politician to turn that crowd around the way you did."

The speaker was a woman in her midforties, light charcoal suit and shortish brown hair.

"I mean look at the opposition you were up against. That audience was loaded with people brought in by Harrison."

They were talking about the previous evening's campaign meeting in the Mission.

"It's only the beginning," Allan commented, not wanting to acknowledge too much praise. "But thank you, Chris. I had doubts myself as to whether I'd make it."

It's the human values that keep up our belief in San Francisco, he told himself.

It was 9:30 A.M. and they were meeting in the offices of Bennett, Stein, and Associates. They could have met at the campaign headquarters on Valencia, or at the Bennett, Stein office on Castro, but those locations were too conspicuous and possibly insecure. The type of campaign activities that Allan and his manager were discussing were best kept under wraps.

"Who is it, Christine? Who the hell has been feeding out the dirt?"

Christine McIntyre was a stockbroker. She and Allan had met about a decade earlier through the Golden Gate Business Association. They had worked together on several campaigns.

"Damn it, Allan. You've been out there in the community. You've fucked around. They're going to try to dig, just like we are. I don't think you can finger anyone."

"But they know too much, Chris. They even dug out that lawsuit between Gregg and his sister."

"Legal records are public information. Besides, that case was a rallying point for the Christian right. Made a big noise."

"They know all of the screwy details. The bathhouses I went to. The actual things I did with people. Listen, Christine, it goes beyond that. The last pamphlet we put out a few days ago? We planned it secretly. Only a select group on our campaign team had seen the text. The very same day we released it, Harrison's group mailed the identical text annotated with their criticisms. Someone in our campaign, someone from my past is trying to screw me."

"Okay! Do you have any ideas?"

Christine was being formal. They had talked about this before; Christine had been skeptical.

"Yeah. Michael Fraggi."

"Why?"

"He's close to the center of everything. He knew me back in the days we all partied a lot. He's shifty; he evades me. Acts guilty, as if he's hiding his motives."

"Was he involved in pamphlet production?"

Allan nodded affirmatively. "Yes, did a good deal of the text layout."

"He does strike me as being strange, although I think everyone who works on your team, Fraggi included, believes in you. We try to be inclusive here!"

"Sure. You trust too much."

"Allan, you've got to trust. We can't carry out a witch-hunt among the faithful."

"But someone is trying to screw me over good."

"Fraggi certainly exudes an air of being morally superior, he's almost condescending."

"That's his Mormon background. Tell you some more. I played with him a number of times at the Caldron. He was always into heavy humiliation, punishment of himself. Other guys have had the same experience with Fraggi. As you know, most of us learn to step beyond traumatic memories and come to enjoy cathartic sex for what it is. A magical moment. But Fraggi used it to wallow in self-pity."

Allan added:

"I could just imagine his working for the Mormons the same time he took those nights out at the bathhouses."

Christine was silent. She was wary of S/M activities. Once she had perceived them as running against her feminist convictions. Now that she understood somewhat better what they were really about, she still had to accept it all emotionally. She stood up and refilled her earthenware coffee mug from atop the credenza. She motioned unsuccessfully to Allan with the pot.

"So what do you want to do, Allan?"

"We've been watching Harrison's campaign head-quarters for a month now. No one we can identify has gone near it. There's got to be a middle link. Have Fraggi trailed. Check out where he goes regularly, who lives there and whether they have connections to Harrison."

"Are you sure you want this?"

"Yeah. See if Louise and Cathy will do it. And Bob Bender. They're discreet."

"You're sure this isn't going to backfire on Allan?"

"We takes our chances. No. We've got real honest concerns. Do it, Chris."

"I'll try to meet with them today."

Chris admired Allan. As a black dyke, she'd had enough of the same negative attitudes turned towards her. Some of these would probably have been less virulent if she hadn't been a woman or was white. But the way this guy took the shit the opposition dug up and threw at him, how he came through fighting, defending the right to his life-style, Christine thought he was spunky, a hell of a fighter. He was always proud of himself, stood up for himself.

Allan momentarily reflected. Why did he continue to take on adversaries, devote himself to causes? The anti-war movement. Draft resisters in Canadian exile. Environmental groups. The Gay/Lesbian movement. And now, the miseries of Harrison's invective. Was it the same sort of primal impulse that drove Harvey Milk to martyrdom?

Christine broke the silence to review some of their own recent findings. Two close friends operated out of the basement of a home in the Western Addition. With a telephone, phone books, copies of city records, who's whos, and a slew of Fundamentalist and far-right publications, they methodically checked every identifiable person donating to or associated with Harrison's campaign. Sometimes they made forays down to City Hall, or to the state capitol in Sacramento. Lists of nominators and endorsers, lists of campaign donors, names of supporters on campaign literature. Their sleuthing had paid off.

"It's coming out clear," Christine told him. "We'll have the stats together by late afternoon. They're astounding. He's even more rotten than we thought! Can you believe a black man is being funded by the Klan?"

"Yeah, he's sly all right. But we'll get him yet, Chris. I'll need the details for tomorrow's Chamber of Commerce luncheon. Nobody except you and I should know about them. If we time it right, it'll mean Monday's preelection papers will be full of the story."

"They'll be sealed and delivered to you."

Chris was silent for a moment.

"That poll we're taking," she continued. "Results should be in this afternoon. I think we're at the turning point, although there are still a large number of undecided voters."

"We'll do it, Chris. This city is too liberal to fall to a lizard like Harrison. This is no Salt Lake or Clark County."

Chicago and Salt Lake City had been among the first to pass local implementing measures of the federal AIDS Emergency Quarantine Laws. Whole populations had been tested. Everyone carried with them a plastic identification card; cards for those positive to HIV were striped with a red band across the bottom edge. Thousands of individuals were under partial or strict security, as they euphemistically referred to detainment. Job restrictions were applied to the red-striped. And under pressure from the Catholic church and the Sally Ann, a majority coalition of Chicago City Council had declared that AIDS, homosexuality and evil were one and the same and had no rights except to be discouraged by the strongest means possible. Since then, dozens of cities and counties, mostly in the South and Midwest, had taken similar tacks. Police invariably took every opportunity to inspect the cards of anyone stopped on routine matters. It was no picnic to be stopped in Chicago's Lincoln Park and found with a red stripe under your photo.

Chris had a few final words. "Be careful, Allan. There are other things this city prides itself on, along with its liberal attitudes. And that's support for the underdog."

14 *Near Dunsmuir, California, Early Friday Morning*

They had just passed Dunsmuir, and Brian sat silently. He had questioned little of Sam's revelations, occasionally making an uh huh or a grunt. Sam wasn't pleased with a response that seemed flavored with hostility.

"So you disagree with us?"

"I didn't say that, Sam. It's just that it's such a big thing and you kept it all from me."

"What if you disagreed, Brian? What if you went off and exposed us?"

"For Christ's sake Sam, trust me!"

"I'm sorry," Sam told him, "for all the pain and anguish I've caused you. Not saying anything has hurt me as much as it's hurt you."

"Thanks, babe." Brian told him.

And their hands touched, fingers intertwined in the dark warmth of the cab.

The road south of Dunsmuir, as it sweeps downhill, is a glorious experience of views on a clear day. Castle Crags and other peaks are serrated against the sky, red-orange soils are masked with fir, pine, oak, and manzanita. Then there are long views of Shasta Lake, its exposed red shores like a giant bathtub ring. Driving that road, even at night, even without the views, is like gliding: the downs, downs, downs, in long sweeping curves from Mount Shasta to Redding and into another world.

A little later, Brian asked some more questions.

"Is it really fair, Sam? If the thing were undertaken by a former President? This guy obviously inherited it."

"Likely never even knew what's been happening," Sam answered him. "This is another one of those dark secrets withheld from Congress and even the President's office."

Brian was persistent.

"So it isn't really fair, is it?"

"Sure, it is. The President represents the government. The President is ultimately responsible, even for allowing people to continue this work."

"You know, if another group was planning what you guys are, I'd probably applaud. But since it's us, I'm not so sure."

At least he said us, Sam noted. He's just got cold feet.

"Look at it this way," he told Brian. "We're not out to kill the President. Only to give him the virus. If they have a cure for AIDS it'll sure come out fast enough. If they don't then they're so damn rotten, the President included, they deserve to be dead."

Brian stopped asking questions, and Sam felt a new and possibly affirmative tug on his hand. Brian moved over the seat and leaned his head on Sam's shoulder. Sam thought of Jim and his warnings to tell no one. Could he be absolutely certain that Brian still wasn't upset underneath? That he might not try something? That would be just what Jim had been afraid of.

15 *Vulcan's Stairway, San Francisco, Friday Morning*

$\mathbf{M}$arc arrived home about ten A.M.; both Allan and Gregg had gone out. He decided to walk up Corbett rather than take the 37 bus. It would relax him enough that sleep would be just that much easier.

The fog and scattered rain had blown over, part of the storms that had dumped their early snows in the Siskiyous and Sierra. The sky was an intense, Pacific blue. Against it, buildings glowed white and cream, scattered pastels among them, the foliage about them full of irridescent greens. That there could be a city like this one, where houses perched and squatted one against the other up the slopes of these winding streets, each building with its unique gingerbread and protruding windows and decks or cupolas; each proudly standing out as an individual in a glorious whole. That a city would dare name its streets for ancient gods: Saturn, Mars, and so appropriately here near the Castro, Uranus. And where else would they name streets so that local buses went to Geneva or India? Or name them for sheer whimsey? Marc turned into Vulcan's Stairway, most of it so steep that steps replaced the roadway. This San Francisco had an audacity in its soul, a freshness, that made it magical.

Marc's room was on the third floor of a narrow Victorian. The house was pleasantly silent, with not even a rustle from the adjacent eucalyptus. He dumped his black leather jacket in a chair, pulled off his boots, jeans and T-shirt. He crawled under the quilt. No, he wouldn't eat now, he decided; he'd do that later, when he got up. Maybe he'd go to Orphan Andys or Welcome Home before he went back downtown. He'd laughed to himself about it many times; they'd go crazy the lot of them if they knew his money came through a window in time itself.

Marc rolled over in the bed, shifting from one side to the other. He scratched his pubic hair with his hand, then fondled his balls; they were tight and smooth. He played some with his cock, sliding the foreskin back and forth. He thought of Bill, the man he had taken in magic the night before. He thought of that wonderful hair and beard and thick nipples poking through the fur. He thought of Bill's eyes. He thought of the wonderful touch of Bill's soul. He grunted and turned over again. He thought of being Jesus and he smiled. What a nice attitude that guy had. He laughed cynically about the Mother Church where he had been raised, even if it was in those subarctic lands where wild spirits still seemed to survive. (He knew they were stronger than just that.) He mused cynically about some of the Pope's most recent wisdom: that true Catholics, engaged in politics or making public statements, were forbidden to support any homosexual cause on fear of excommunication.

Despite his earlier climb from Castro to Market, sleep seemed difficult to come by, and Marc's eyes drifted open. They caught on a painting. It was a Thom Hinde, full of plunging forms, none of them fully discernable, but the intent, the force, the rhythm of the acts as precise and real and sensual as the writhing, screaming ecstasy of cocks and fists taking possession of holes and loving them. The colors, the highlights glistening with sweat or grease against the pastel softness of skin. Allan had bought the painting for Marc, from its first exhibition above the Ambush pool table. It was a memorial to innocent days of early marriage. That was before Gregg had joined them, wonderful man that he was in his own right. Marc recalled his days with Allan back then: all that slipping and sliding and the touch of belts and chaffened flesh and rubbing hard into sweaty armpits and yessirs and nosirs muttered respectfully for the sake of love and between long wet kisses in which his lover fed him dribbles, beer or spit. But he remembered far more than that. He recalled a day in the West End, the Pacific blue of a late winter high, the sidewalks thick with fallen cherry blossom. In Vancouver in springtime, it could be said, the streets rained from heaven.

Sure, he'd seen this man before, in the Corral, this serious American with shortish black hair (so different from the long hair of the fading hippy era) and his close-cropped beard, almost to a stubble, the same as today except now filled with gray. Marc had liked Allan's smile, that is, when his seriousness ever broke enough to let him relax. (It was even rumored that Allan's campaign team had given him a course in facial expression.) Marc chuckled. That meeting on the street, when they both knew they were for each other. Those moments with Allan, handcuffed and pigged out with indulgence, would lean back on his haunches, not to beg for more, but to simply beam at Marc.

They had walked and talked that day. Marc worked evenings, as bartender. Allan had taken the day off from his work. He couldn't practice law in Canada, but he helped in organizing the emerging network of legal service clinics. Allan liked his work, but litigation flowed in his blood. Perhaps it was his American roots. There was less opportunity for litigative action in Canada and Marc suspected from the outset of their meeting that when the time was right, Allan would want to go home.

Marc found an attraction in this activist; while his own life at the time seemed in a sort of denouement. With great fanfare he had graduated from UBC, the first Metis with a Masters degree in English. From the forests of the Peace, from the knotted poverty of the Reservation, he had made high time. But there was little work available for graduates in literature, at least here on the Coast. Perhaps he could have become a teacher and gone back to work with his own people. But Marc was gay and wanted to stay in Vancouver. Whatever the lack of work, there seemed some hope in life there. To Allan he was a wonderfully romantic notion, an urbane native who could lay claim to real roots.

But if Allan had fallen in love, then so had Marc: here was a smooth, comfortable American whose life spoke of truth to a cause. An American who escaped through Minnesota woods at the time of the war to Canadian freedom. Allan was proud of that. His wealthy Tiburon parents might have thought otherwise, but Allan was convinced that his had been the honorable course. In Canada, he had worked for draft groups, for civil rights and legal services groups, and for environmentalists. He survived on a shoestring, but he survived for real causes.

Marc grunted again and shifted position. He pulled some more at his dick. Maybe he should jack off, then he'd be sure to sleep. Beside the Thom Hinde painting was one by Jim Leff. A cop looked out of a cruiser door, the window rolled down, the eyes and black mustache and crisp uniform saying everything. There was no doubt he was a cop, there was no doubt the pistol, hidden in the picture behind the car door, was real and loaded. Beneath those eyes, that face, a man cried out to be loved in a way that only men who have openly loved one another can sense. It was as Jack Fritscher wrote: when a man climbed into the sack with another man he knew all of the moves that oil the body-to-body slip and sleaze of man-to-man contact. It mattered nothing whether the cop thought he was straight or closet or gay, his soul called out for the firm and tender authority of another man.

Marc found himself getting hard looking at the cop's

face, and he started to beat off. God, he'd loved these men, these men, these San Francisco men. Ambush men. Mature, happy, comfortable men with busy dicks and open butts and lives full of interesting things. They were all the dreams he had cherished in coming to the city, in making this move that had made him a refugee twice over. But this time, he had come to where a strength seemed spread about him and there was a promise of growing and building. There seemed so much positive self-energy in San Francisco. And it seemed that they really had a chance of doing something with it. Marc had pushed aside any guilt at leaving his northern relatives.

There was that time Allan had brought Gregg home for the first time, and the three of them played all night as if it were forever. And it became forever.

Early memories of Gregg. Marc could feel his butt, even now, warm and wholesome, the grunt of pleasure at being taken. How he had loved fisting Gregg, that man of so many levels, Vietnam vet, biologist, small-time business-man and friend. A man who would give himself until he moaned with the fullness of reality. Gregg was really an epitome of what San Francisco was about. Marc was hard now and pumping. Oh God, how he had loved to play with Allan at the same time as Gregg. Or how he and Gregg would take turns with Allan. Oh, the magic of those moments.

Marc came, and dumped a screwed-up Kleenex on the floor beside the bed. Put it in the garbage later, he thought.

He laughed. That he could have been apprehensive when Gregg and Allan had fallen in love. Was this to be the end of their relationship? Or was part of it that he was also in love with Gregg as well? They had been quite a team. He chuckled at thoughts of a private party at Leather Beach, Gregg's short-lived disco. Allan had put Gregg in a face and body harness. Gregg traveled on all fours at the end of leashes held by Marc and Allan. Shit, Allan's opponents would get a rise out of that one if they could ever find pictures. But Gregg, in his own disco, and at the edge of his limits, had forbidden cameras. Yes, Marc liked that about Allan: this desire to stand up for himself as a whole person and for everything he did as honest statement, whether fun or work.

Marc shifted again. On the other wall was a portrait by Lou Randolph. It was Marc, like an Indian warrior awaiting torture, arms stretched and tied Christ-like to tree branches, cock hard and balls exposed, bound with rope and weighted. Before sketching him, Lou had put hot lube and clamps on Marc's tits. There was no doubt in the picture that he was the halfbreed, the Metis, straining to be free, martyred by his own personality that was also gay. Marc felt guilty again. Only recently had he come up against this part of himself, against his own running. He had fled from Prophet River to Vancouver. He had respected and cared for his people's culture but he had had to get out of that world. His dreams as a Metis could never be realized. In Vancouver he believed in his dreams as a literate person and discovered them as a gay man. The latter held warmth and friends and with Allan, new hope. He had never gone back to that black spruce forest at Kahntah, to the log hut with the sheet metal roof, rusted to warm tones, that was home. He could not romanticize about it; he knew he had fled it. Christmas letters to his mother, still alive, were the only communication. At times, he cried.

When Gregg was diagnosed with AIDS and the sheer, awful reality of it all struck home with such force, Marc turned his thoughts more and more towards the past. It wasn't that he was afraid. He'd stopped playing with either of them several years ago. (That meant nothing of course, he knew he was HIV positive.) He and Gregg and Allan were good friends. But the emotional tension of the crisis made living difficult and dreams nigh impossible. And without dreams, cultures die. Of the three of them, only Allan still had dreams, if his instinctive aspirations for political office could be termed that. So Marc's thinking had turned to the hunting trips taken with his father and with other band members. To their use of dreams.

There was a great strength to be found in that dreaming, a strength that grew from the rock and the aeons of inhabiting the land, that spoke in the images of hilltops and knob-topped spruce and aspen groves and the dark oily waters of tamarack swamp. He came to hear again the cry of the loon, the belligerent foghorn of the moose during rutting season. He came to see again the autumn land bright with yellows and reds from berries and bog birch and kinnikinnick. Allan had ignored Marc's thrust towards mysticism. Gregg had downplayed it. For Marc these were new trails and they were personal ones. His greatest accomplishment was to find a route back into the Ambush. Few would believe him, but he didn't care. What did concern him was his travel. Was he still running, or was he finally going home?

His eyes stayed closed, and he settled into a gentle snore. His mind opened up into another painting, the canvas by Snowflake that had hung for so long on the third floor of the Ambush. It was a forest glade, and in it, naked men with smiles and beards and happy bodies were frolicking and tying each other up and hugging, doing all sorts of delectable things. Many hung from rising balloons so that couples in the midst of reaching orgasm or exhilirating from it drifted through the foliage. Marc's mind focused on the faces. Every one of them was a portrait of an Ambush man, some who still lived and yearned, but many who had died. He could feel the weight of their deaths. They spoke to him firmly, reassuringly. He sensed evil, the damp chill creeping into the foliage. His mindspace looked upwards into a dimming sky. One by one, the balloons, carrying their sweet messages upwards, were popped and blew their skins. He must locate the evil that was doing this. He had always been aware of its presence, but he had never been able to perceive it as he did now. He must be able to talk with the trees. Together, they would find a way to save the sun.

16 *South of Market, San Francisco, Friday Morning*

Gregg geared down his ZL1000 and swung onto Duboce in a continuous arc from Market Street that neatly avoided the manhole covers. This was not a good intersection to turn in the rain. His mind was spinning with news of the day: Ed Stevens (damn that named sounded familiar), secret CIA labs, testing in Africa. The devious means by which the virus was alleged to have reached the New York gay community. Two homo agents who had unknowingly been pumped full of it and sent to pig out at the Mineshaft and the St. Marks Baths in the guise of checking national security.

Gregg rode along under the expressway and up Thirteenth to Harrison. On concrete freeway supports someone had spray-painted shield-shaped decals proclaiming CIAIDS in red and blue. Some of the decals had been there for years; how ironic they seemed now. Gregg gunned his bike into fifth. He was angry. He thought of friends like John Ryan, Wayne Whitcomb, now only names on the Wall. You bastards, he almost shouted at a BMW sedan, like him, turning onto Harrison and blocking the way. But he calmed himself. They had the edge now.

The head office of M2P (or Music Madness Plus) was in a squat building near Harrison and Ninth. As president, Gregg occupied a small corner room with a simple desk, several phones, and a framed poster advertising Folsom Megahood. Let the staff that deal with clients have the fancy offices, he had said. I'm only here a couple of times a week. I don't want to be here more. And in keeping with that philosophy, Gregg rarely overdressed in anything more than jeans and a sportshirt; occasionally he was known to throw on a tie.

Friday mornings were for review of accounts in general. Tuesday afternoons were for reviewing stock and purchasing. Wednesday afternoons discussed sales and advertising. Meetings with counsel were extra. Gregg had a good staff, and he trusted them. Except for one bad apple in the past who had tried to rip M2P off for about ten thousand (and ended up with a two-year prison term), staff responded to his trust accordingly. And here at head office, they were nearly all gay.

Michael Hardy pecked him on the cheek as he met Gregg at the office door. He held a sheaf of papers, statements, checks for review and signature. Michael was a short man with a cute blond mustache and the sort of Castro twinkle in his eyes that belies perpetual youth. Years ago they might have tricked together, but from the beginning of M2P, Gregg had intentionally separated all sex from work.

"God, I hope you keep doing as well as you are, Gregg! You look just fine. What do you think of the news?"

"Shocked. But maybe that means there's a cure caught up in all of it."

"My buddy Frank died Wednesday night." A tear caught in the corner of Michael's eye.

"Sorry to hear it. If you want time off for the memorial service, let me know."

"Thanks Gregg, but it's Saturday."

Michael handed him the papers, explaining how they were grouped. Together they reviewed expenses, payroll costs, money tied up in stock, new investments. They had recently made heavy expansion into the compact disk market; they needed further investment money without the high rates. Sales at the Hayward and Berkeley stores were booming. The Mission store was doing okay. So was Daly City and Guerneville. But the Haight store was down. They had tried a neighborhood approach there: an eclectic mix of punk, space, rock, and metal. Tapes and records sold, but few seemed to want to buy electronics components in the Haight, despite M2P's low prices. Maybe they should cut things back at that store, Gregg pondered, stick with recordings. Next week at the monthly staff meeting they'd review it. Gregg's mind jerked into reality. Damn it, he told himself. They can't. I won't be here.

"Michael, can you arrange a meeting of the executive staff for about one today? We've got some issues to resolve."

"Sure. Everyone's here except Sandy. She's in Hayward at the warehouse."

"See if you can get her back here. I'll review these checks and bank statements and see you in about thirty minutes."

Michael left and closed the door. Gregg reached for the phone. He called LBE. No answer. Dave or Bonnie must have stepped out for coffee.

When Gregg died, M2P would be run by an executive committee drawn from the staff. They would elect a new president from among them and hold 60 percent of the shares. Allan would get the remaining 40 percent. That is, if Jo-Lyn didn't make a second grab for the money. Damn that bitch.

He thought of almonds and apricots. Olive trees. Fruits ripening in long methodical rows that ran down to the valley sloughs. Fruits that had transformed into records and stereo sets, video equipment and compact disk players. But it wasn't the fruit that had made money. It was those tracts under the orchards up in Fair Oaks and Citrus Heights, and inherited by his father. They were sold in the sixties at the height of the boom in Sacramento and for millions. The farm he had grown up on, when sold, brought far less: Yuba County land that was distant from the path of the urban devil. Yeah, his father, however much he had hoped to disinherit Gregg, might have been somewhat pleased, at his son's successful investments. That aside, Gregg could feel nothing towards his father now but cold. Sure, they had been good-intentioned, conservative American parents. They'd encouraged him in some things, stifled him in others. They'd cared for him when he was sick, notably after he came back from the war. He might breathe today on their money but he felt no warmth. After the hatred of the 1975 Christmas week, he could not accept them again.

He dialed LBE once again. Leather Beach Enterprises. Gregg was president and sole owner. His one-time efforts at a successful disco had failed, but what had been the business shell for Leather Beach was now a part-time management front for millions in investments. From the tax-free returns Gregg garnered more than enough to live off of. The rest was recycled. He doubted Allan knew a quarter of its worth. And Allan didn't know that he would inherit about a third of it. Another third would go to Marc who had so consistently assisted him through his hospital stay a year ago. The rest would go to gay charities. Again that is, if Jo-Lyn didn't try to hook it back. He had good lawyers and he paid them well, although that was no guarantee of anything these days.

The LBE phone rang twice. Bonnie answered it. Dave was on the other line. He wanted to talk with Gregg, urgent-ly. He'd call right back.

"I'll be here," Gregg told her.

He started reviewing and signing checks, the big G of his first name looped back on itself, the two terminal g's neat and close together, the last name as precise as the first, the signatures appearing beneath his fingers almost automatically once each check was reviewed against the computerized voucher attached to it. What is in a name? He was a millionaire. So what did it all matter? He owned property he rented in Diamond Heights. He still owned land up in Yuba County. He even owned a small bar in Nevada City. He had been a successful biologist. And now he was going to die. How would it have ended if this disease hadn't happened? Some tired old queen, frail from a life of drugs and sex, descended into bitchiness? Living with two other bitchy old men who washed away the dregs of their lives with alcohol and hapless memories? Fuck, don't be stupid, Gregg told himself. I always admired the older gay men I knew. The men I watch on the streets: trim, self-assured, neat beards and silver mustaches. Seventy-year-old gay men who still went to the gym daily and still tricked out. Men who were not afraid of age, who refused to let themselves become decrepit. Men full of warm maturity. Minds full of interests from opera to Zen, from preserving the heritage of San Francisco houses to climbing San Bruno Mountain with a hope of seeing rare butterflies. They might be well over fifty, far past sixty some of them, but their lives were vital and their youths were still intact. Dreams may have matured or dampened, but living was yet a joy and a hope. God, how Gregg admired these men, people like John Beckham and James Broughton. Gregg might say that he had spent one part of his life mutilating people. But he could also say that he'd spent much more of it in loving and admiring them. It was that latter that really counted. He started to cry.

17 *Washington, DC, Friday, Near Noon*

Jo-Lyn had had a change in mind. She had cried herself to sleep in that horrid, all-hating mood, and she had a remarkably peaceful night. She had awakened with new revelations. She had fed Carolyn, and that had calmed her.

She considered her new thoughts as she drove in along Connecticut Avenue. At K Street she cut across town to New Covenant Hall on the edge of the Adams-Morgan District.

Maybe it had been those comments reported on the news later that previous evening. A black Christian pastor had praised her husband's actions and affirmed that God was on his side. He had been sandwiched between dozens of harping critics of the government and that awful Ted Koppel. But Jo-Lyn had decided that what was really happening was that her husband had been acting according to a plan of duty and that his colleagues were now engaged in protecting him. Those CIA people did care for their staff. Hardened professionals had been seen to cry with the news of Buckley's death in Beirut, Ed had told her that. They were always bargaining hard with the Russians for captive agents. The CIA was holding Ed until it was safe. His pictures had been on TV, in the papers, around the world. It would be crazy to leave a prized agent exposed, only to be shot by some queer.

No, Jo-Lyn was not deluding herself, she emphasized. She had overreacted yesterday. But everything was going to be all right; Ed would not have planned it any other way. Perhaps a new life. Another name and country? At least she didn't have parents to worry about. It'd be fine for little Carolyn.

She could even have been construed as smiling as she pulled the Volvo into the church parking lot. A cloth banner with scarlet letters announced: RUMMAGE SALE AND BAZAAR. She lifted Carolyn from the portable bassinet on the seat beside her and held her close. They googled together. She put Carolyn back into the bassinet. God, it was good to breathe again the fresh air of a regular, wholesome life. Jo-Lyn reached for her purse, conscious again of the power in it. She shuddered; this was so unlike her. She got out of the car and headed towards the church; then things began to happen.

She called out at Ellen Shreiber across the parking lot. Ellen was the pastor's sister and president of the Church Board. Ellen glanced at her, said nothing, and looked away. She went back to her car as if purposefully avoiding Jo-Lyn's walk across the tarmac. Oh dear, Jo-Lyn thought. Maybe she didn't recognize me.

At the door they took her ticket. There was a young woman she had never seen before and Mrs. Lake. This must be her daughter who was away most times at Liberty University in Lynchburg. Mrs. Lake was usually full of gossipy nonsense for all of them, Jo-Lyn included. Today she said nothing, lips pressed firmly together and staring coldly. As soon as Jo-Lyn had passed by, she heard whispered comments behind her. She fled forward.

She found Joanne Smeal beside the soft-drink table. She was middle-aged and almost lasciviously plump. They had an expensive home in McLean, Virginia. Sister Joanne was chief organizer of this event and her hawk eyes darted quickly over every person and every action in rapid judgment.

"So you decided to make an appearance, Sister."

The tone was accusatory. It was not clear whether this disapproval was due to Jo-Lyn's being late or to her mere presence.

"Why, yes," Jo-Lyn told Sister Smeal. "I did promise to serve at one of the tables."

Joanne showed no signs of appreciation. "Quite impossible, Sister," she told her. "We've put Lori Dutra on your table. With all that's been going on, I'm surprised you even dared to show your face today."

"But Sister, I was looking forward to helping at this—"

Sister was not to be placated. Brusquely and coldly she interrupted Jo-Lyn, taking her by the elbow. "Come with me, then. Maybe you can help Lori."

She led her to a table heaped with clothing for young girls. Any semblence of order at the table had been broken by a jostling crowd of women, mostly black and poor, who picked and sorted and turned the items in every direction.

Joanne Smeal departed as quickly as she could, and Jo-Lyn found a place close by the corner for the bassinet. She crammed her purse between the bassinet and the wall. Should she leave it unwatched? In it was Ed's special revolver, taken from its secret cache at home and now, never far from her.

Lori was keeping as busy as possible chatting up prospective customers. It took her a good while to even recognize that Jo-Lyn was at the same table and trying to help.

"All shirts are three dollars," she dryly informed Jo-Lyn. "All blouses are two-fifty. Sweaters are four." Then she turned abruptly to one of the customers. "Isn't that a lovely color? What color is your little one's hair?"

Jo-Lyn hated this feeling. It was if she herself had been accused of deserting the faithful. Then she overheard two women at the next table, both from her prayer circle, and talking about her.

"To think she would dare to show her face here," one of them said. That was Susan MacKillop. She was a snob.

"All those terrible things her husband did." That was Letty Duval. She and her husband hated Ed.

"Don't get me wrong," Susan whispered in loud tones. "It's wonderful our government set out to eliminate the queers. But Ed should never had said anything about it. To think that he's brought all this attention to the Fellowship. Why do you know what Pastor Wannamaker went through with the press today?"

Jo-Lyn waited to hear no more. She grabbed her purse and the bassinet and fled back to her car.

She sat in her car bewildered. Carolyn thankfully, was asleep. How could they? she asked herself. When they should be backing Ed, praising him for fine Christian deeds, they condemned him for putting the church in a difficult position. And it wasn't that they didn't believe in what he did. Why, one brother from a place down in Virginia had his car vandalized several times here in Washington because of a KILL A QUEER FOR CHRIST bumper sticker. They all knew what was right, even though it might be hard to get some of the world to understand. And that's what they should be doing, standing behind their beliefs, not deserting their brethren.

Many of the Fellowship had never liked Ed, never appreciated his full qualities, Jo-Lyn was convinced. Like the time he ran for bishop and lost. Susan MacKillop's husband had been elected; he claimed to be more pious and he made countless testimonials to persuade people of it. "Praise the Lord," he would announce. "I was driving by the White House yesterday and God spoke to me." Jo-Lyn was skeptical. The Good Lord didn't waste his time speaking to clods like MacKillop. He just happened to be a crony of the pastor.

No, Ed never complained when he lost. Ed just took it all in his calm, reserved way. "There'll be other elections," he said. "I done right running in this one."

Secretly, Jo-Lyn wondered if Ed, in speaking out about his secret work, might have done what he did to gain attention in the Fellowship, to make a sort of testimonial of his own. Lord, there was hardly a sermon in which Pastor Wannamaker hadn't something to say about queers and queer supporters and their effects on our children. Ed was only speaking the Word of their God.

Then she had second thoughts. She clutched her purse. Ed had been so kind, so gentle with her. Well, nearly always. How could he deliberately plan to kill people? Including her brother! God knows her brother deserved it as much as any of those homos. She might find it difficult to see Ed as a killer, but this was truly a war against evil, and she couldn't dismiss his role in it. Jo-Lyn had never seen him at work and double agents had many sides. She knew he'd been to Africa. He brought back all those ebony wood elephants for her; they paraded across the mantelpiece. He often worked late at the lab. It could all be true. But was it?

Her thoughts went back to Gregg. Damn it, she thought, hadn't she heard from her cousin Rose something about him having AIDS? Why hadn't she thought of it before? How could she be so stupid? He was going to die and she'd have another chance for the family money.

Jo-Lyn was startled by a rap on the car window. Pastor Wannamaker stood there, looking pale and a little tired.

She wanted to feel hostile towards him. What did he want?

She rolled down the window.

"Good afternoon, pastor," she said as pleasantly as she could.

He smiled a little; his face didn't look so grim.

"Hello, Sister Jo-Lyn."

At least *he* hadn't excommunicated her.

"I'm sorry of course," he told her, "to hear all you've been going through. Your husband is a fine man, fighting a fine cause."

Jo-Lyn smiled. Maybe there was hope.

"But you must know that the whole issue is a highly sensitive one. The Fellowship has been under a lot of pressure from what Ed's done, and we'd prefer as far as possible to avoid the publicity. Mrs. Stevens, I think that perhaps it would be better for both you and the Fellowship if you dropped from sight for a few months. It would give you some of the rest you surely need."

Jo-Lyn was astounded. When was a testimonial to God ever too big or too sensitive? She was almost certain that Wannamaker was hiding other things he didn't want the press to latch on to. His personal investments in the church name, for example. They all knew that MacKillop was tied up in that too. Yeah, the church retreat that also served as his summer home.

"Not even prayer circles?" Jo-Lyn asked him.

"Please," he told her. "Not even prayer circles."

She was shattered.

"Remember, we're not abandoning you. If you'd like company in your home prayer, if you wish spiritual guidance, call me. I'll be happy to come round and be with you in the spirit of God."

18 *Financial District, San Francisco, Friday Morning*

There's something disarming in recent San Francisco politics. It's maybe that people vote the way they feel in some combination of heart and mind, whatever the trends elsewhere. Marin and Berkeley, of course, might also do that but then both have reputations that border on the zany. San Francisco is just plain independent. In 1984 there was no Reagan landslide in the city; in fact Reagan was not elected. (In 1986 the Republicans closed some of their San Francisco offices for lack of support.) And in 1988, San Francisco and seven of the nine Bay Area counties all elected Dukakis, not Bush, by margins that were as large as 70 to 30. Even up in the monied districts of Pacific Heights and Seacliff, the trend has been independent, liberal voting. It's hardly unusual to overhear opera matrons castigating Republican politicos.

But politics in San Francisco is more than being a Democrat. Allan had that credential, although he guarded his distance and freedom from the bosses of the Sacramento machine. He'd got their endorsement only grudgingly, although he was determined not to need it. That was a de facto victory: in many cases the central party parachuted their own candidate into the race to make battle with the fellow Democrat who would not yield to their control. But the Sacramento bosses and their tactics had been rebuked several times in San Francisco elections and maybe they felt uncertain in Allan's case. They were sensitive to the issues perhaps: in no case should Harrison win.

Gentle Warriors

Christine McIntyre pulled her Acura Legend onto Broadway. Allan was in the seat beside her. It was a glorious day, full of intense colors. Chris had grown up in Detroit in neighborhoods that were rundown, firebombed, and inconsolably desolate. Here, neighborhoods tumbled into one another, each not quite the same, each with its special and wonderful views. Chinatown fell into North Beach, which tumbled into Telegraph Hill and Jackson Square. Everywhere in this city, neighborhoods jostled good-naturedly with one another for patches of hillside or hollows or hilltops. And most everywhere, they thrived with new paint and personal aspiration. AIDS may have slowed the handiwork of gay gentrification, but blacks and Chinese and women and Latinos carried on the tradition. It didn't always succeed: developers could be too greedy. Hunters Point and Bayview were still depressed. But for Christine, like Allan, there was no other city like it.

It's too easy to say that this San Francisco is a product of independent people determined to embrace life in patterns of their own choice and making. San Francisco has always had its crazies and radicals, its separatists and its peace movements, from Gelett Burgess and Isadora Duncan and from the City Lights crowd to the flower children in the Summer of Love. Anarchists and ecologists. Poets and sex liberationists. San Francisco has always been a melange of forces that brought color. Yet these groups hardly controlled it. Some of them gained respectability. But for decades, the city rested solidly under the thumb of a monied bourgeois who might from time to time like to flirt with the daring and outrageous while voting conservatively. For years there were no Blacks or Asians on the City Board, and few if any women.

When it occurred in the sixties, the transition, the wrenching of power, was sudden. Many of the middle class had fled to places like Orinda or San Mateo. Neighborhoods, the Castro a prime example, were on the decline. And there was the battle over a massive Yerba Buena project in which a startled establishment were shaken to their core. Developers discovered they had to listen to terms other than their own or those of their cronies. The city had begun to say no. From this new dissension, George Moscone emerged as mayor. Voter registration was pushed, and ethnically and culturally diverse supervisors were elected. Boards and commissions, formerly people with staid interests came to be flavored with Asians and gays, the elderly, Hispanics and community activists, all of whom were to shift the city's direction. Some individuals still see the assassination of Moscone as an attempt to derail that process of change. Whether or not it was, the ploy never worked. The city reacted in outrage and its experiments, started in the previous decade, continued. Whether supervisors were elected in districts, or at large made little difference. They were still diverse and they still courted the city's many interests and communities.

Allan and Chris were on their way to Pier 39 to address an election luncheon of SPUR, also known as the San Francisco Planning and Urban Research Association, and a good example of these politics. SPUR is a sort of moderate lobby for the urban environment: planners, architects, environmental professionals, some neighborhood people, and some big-time developers. In the perpetual motion between developers and neighborhoods, groups like SPUR tread a cautious, sometimes wavering, center road: they believe that the process can work. And on some fronts at least, San Francisco was a demonstration that SPUR's type of politics worked. SPUR also endorsed various ballot propositions, and sometimes candidates; their endorsements carried weight. Allan had sought their endorsement and got it. Barely.

The car turned into Sansome, going west.

"They didn't really want to do it, did they?" Allan commented.

"They're too liberal," Christine offered. "The issue's too sensitive. They can politely reach the conclusion that your candidacy is distinct from urban planning. Then they can claim no official preference on District Attorney."

It was the large Gay/Lesbian contingent in the urban design and planning industry that had spearheaded support for Allan. (Few in SPUR actually favored Harrison.) Getting the matter to the vote had been the issue. Is there really some truth, Christine wondered, in the perception that so many gays are involved in the reconstruction of environments, inside or out, cultural or structural, or urban or wildland? Because of that, some people no doubt, think gay people are subversive.

"SPUR's a funny case," Christine noted. "Environmental groups think they're in the paws of the developers. Developers think the groups are too radical. I've always said that San Francisco politics requires more than excellent balance. Oh, some politicians make it on that. But more often it takes evidence of commitment."

They waited at a stop sign on Lombard Street. Another restored neighborhood: old brick warehouses glowing warmly in the sunlight, even a railroad roundhouse refurbished into public spaces and shops for the designer Californian.

"What's Harrison going to bring up today?" Allan wondered out loud.

"More sordid details of your past to embarrass SPUR. Harrison thinks little about urban planning issues except that planning's probably a bad thing in the first place."

Yeah, Allan thought privately, that time he'd taken Gregg to the Brig, bare-assed and in chaps. The time in an alley outside that he'd handcuffed him to a car door. Thank God no one but Hoot Gibson had seen them in action. How much of Allan's wonderful past had been uncovered by Harrison?

"It won't work with SPUR," Christine told him. "He'll offend their sensibilities for even raising the issue of sex. They'll be even more against him."

The car moved on again. Now they were waiting to turn into the Embarcadero, that angular expanded intersection of ancient and largely unused railway tracks and streets indeterminate in size and direction. On winter days the rain swept over the piers and across this space with a vengeance.

"What about that drunk-driving conviction? I wonder if he's dug that up yet?"

"So what!" Christine answered. "Everyone's allowed a mistake. You largely gave up drinking five years ago."

Finally they pulled onto the Embarcadero, shrouded in the diesel fumes of a tour bus. Tour buses and cablecars were constant reminders that this was also a tourist city.

"This Fraggi business," said Christine.

"I'm not sure," Allan commented. "But he seems the most likely."

"Joan called me at the office just before I picked you up. Said Michael Fraggi had been bugging her to let him get going on the layout for the big pamphlet."

Allan had hinted to the campaign team that something big was being worked up on Harrison.

"Hey," he told Christine. "I've got a great idea. Let's you and I write some chicken feed on Harrison. Something that's total garbage. Strongly insulting. Inaccurate. We'll give it to Fraggi and see how far it gets. Tell him it's highly secret."

"Well, get a load of this," Christine commented. "A parking place outside."

"Well, what about it?" Allan said.

19 *Vulcan's Stairway, San Francisco, Friday Afternoon*

Marc woke from total darkness and a dream in which his uncle accused him of deserting his roots. Accusatory dreams, touched with guilt, haunted Marc in times of uncertainty. It was late afternoon.

He sat up, his back against the wall, his legs in lotus position. He rubbed his tit and squeezed it hard against the ring. He put his hands in his lap.

"Enough recrimination. I've got to stop this nonsense.

Marc focused on his breathing, breaking the focus only with the ostinato of his mantra. He felt muscles relaxing, a warmth creeping up inside him. His vision relaxed into a haziness. Oh God, how good it felt to be himself. Diligently, as if with a tiny broom, he swept away the impetuous wisps of thought that crept into his mind, uprooting them before they could take hold. The stillness intensified. Images of the room began to blur, dissolving into a textured gray. The gray dimmed some more, and for a time he rested there, waiting on a threshold.

The forest he came into was dark and he fast arrived at its edge. He heard the chattering of a light wind in the dead aspen leaves. There was a beaver pond beyond the trees, perfectly still, intensely black. The pond crept up and about the snags trapped behind the dam, up to the mouldy edge of the forest floor. He could feel the chill of the water in an air filled with autumn. Across the pond, now a blur, a tangled stand of black spruce leaned into one another. A single golden tamarack accompanied them, almost ready to shed for winter. It was just visible through the space between the knob-topped spruce, and sunlight was creeping up on it, little by little, until the tree burned with brilliant gold.

He looked into the pond, through the shiny, almost oily surface on which twigs and a few leaves drifted like little boats. There seemed nothing in the darkness. He waited. Controlled dreaming forever required waiting. Time was immaterial. What passed in the outside world was infinitesimal to the time that passed in dreams.

The water lightened a little. He saw a dark shape move by. A young beaver? A water rat, maybe? It was unconscious of him and it kept on its way. Then he saw his face. An aspen leaf drifted down, twisting, tumbling lazily: it fell into his reflection. The reflection broke into tiny ripples, moving outward. It was like the person who reached outward into the physical world, their waves lapping forward to be stranded in the reaches of space. In the water, his face became whole again. How many of us failed at looking inwards? At holding and embracing just ourselves? How many of us allowed fear to creep up like a damp chill, let loathing engulf us? Oh sure, all of us looked in the mirror. What more pragmatic or cynical way was there by which to judge others?

Marc followed the edge of the pond. The rising sun was in his eyes now, but he was still a shadow among the shadows of the trees. Beyond the end of the pond was a small depression scattered with occasional leaning black spruce. The muskeg began here. He sat on a stump and waited, in that wonderful, peaceful air. Some birds began calling. He looked down about him, into the tangle of stems and sedges and sphagnum at the bog's moist edges. Shapes grew out of blurs and into plants. Here was Labrador tea, cloudberry and crowberry, blueberry bushes and various wintergreens. Here was bog laurel, and throughout, the brilliant tiny red coins of swamp birch that clung tenaciously to the delicate branches of the little bush. He looked beyond them. There were dark pools of water, splotches in the heaving, peaty mat.

His eyes drew back again, caught by a flash of whiteish purple. A late-blooming one-leaf orchis, it delicate spike of tiny flowers poked tentatively into the cold air, its base lost in a tangle of browned sedges. He could hear its song, an exotic melody drifting against the vast hostility of the bog. Here was that rare and special side in each of us; here were those hidden delights we refused to recognize or actively suppressed. By denying them in ourselves, in others, we created hostility, fear. And so often when others chose to express those very feelings, to live those delights, we stoned them with hostile envy. How many gems like this orchis, were ground into the mud by deliberate feet?

Marc pushed back into the forest, through lower branches of spruce, springy like whips, through tangled rose and high-bush cranberry. He pushed his way in mind, but he glided through in spirit, his shadow like a defined blur passing through the shapes about him. He put his foot up on a rock, a special rock. He had sat there many times before, in vigil with his father, searching the moose in the forests of their dreams, picking out landmarks, then returning to the real forest to track and hunt. Close by that rock were the blackened stones of an ancient campfire ring.

There was another reason this rock was important. Evil was in this forest. It cowered beneath the roots of trees, in abandoned burrows, beneath fallen snags. It waited for him under this rock. It waited everywhere to snare all hunters, all warriors. To plant its little fears and insecurities, distrusts and deceits, all seeming so reasonable at the time, but growing, multiplying like a fungus until it consumed with an uncontrollable passion. He looked across to the skeleton of a lodgepole pine where an owl had made her nest. In a crevice near the base, something formless shifted. He shuddered and knocked his foot down hard on the stone as a sign of warning.

Could they ever track evil, hunt it down? Snare it like the muskrat or the wolf? Could they ever be free of its deceiving touch? Even his own people, who knew these forests and swamps as their dreams, failed to hold back pain and suffering from ever-lurking evil. The disease of alcohol. Disdainful condemnation doled out like welfare by the white man. The abuses of federal powers, of police powers, the same powers that had carried out the execution of Louis Riel or beat up Indians in Williams Lake. There were too many spores of evil to overcome, to grind it out. There were too many opportunities for evil to expand into the vain, blind structures of power and persecution. All of it disguised in the cloak of good. It was a frightening and cynical world we faced. To be aware of evil, ever-present evil, to be conscious of it, to perhaps avoid or subvert it, those were the best we could do. For the warrior, that was the only way.

The forest faded into a glimmer of gray and the gray to the late afternoon dusk of a San Francisco bedroom. Marc stretched his arms, then his legs, rubbing them gently with his fingertips.

He glanced at the clock. 4:39. He jumped out of bed. He had to get downtown for the rally. And he was going to meet Gregg for a beer.

20 *Spring Valley, Maryland, Friday Afternoon*

She was stunned by Wannamaker's demands. She was stunned all the way back up Connecticut Avenue, along Massachusetts Avenue and back into Spring Valley. She was too stunned to be upset, angry, or frustrated. She was too stunned even to feel betrayed. All these feelings would come later. All she felt was stunned, and very alone.

She came home to a ringing phone and a gaggle of predatory reporters on her doorstep. They demanded to know her secrets. How much had Ed told her? Had she been in on this plot from the beginning? How was their sex life? She pushed through furiously, ignoring their questions. She slammed the door again. On the telephone, another reporter informed Jo-Lyn that she would eventually have to tell all. The people demanded it. She slammed down the phone, only to have it start ringing again. She unplugged it.

The news channel on the television in the family room was still blaring when she came in. The majority of items dealt with what press people now called the AIDS-gate affair.

As Jo-Lyn sat down with Carolyn, who was whimpering just a little, the White House press secretary once again confirmed that the President would not cancel his trip to San Francisco. ''Mr. President has given this matter grave deliberation. He believes his position has been aggravated by irresponsible exaggerations of the press. Once the public knows the full account of this story, there will be total agreement that no wrongdoings occurred. It is the duty of the

President of this great nation to host a meeting of NATO leaders in San Francisco on Monday. He will not shirk that task.''

Jo-Lyn hardly noticed the television. Once, she had thought the press secretary was cute, but they had met at some party and she couldn't stand him as a person. She unbuttoned her blouse, pulled aside her bra, and guided a hungry mouth to her breast. Little Carolyn fed hungrily and with a good deal of appreciative noise. I should have done this an hour ago, Jo-Lyn thought. She looked up and across the room. "Damn it," she muttered. A man's face peered through the family room window, his camera poised. Clutching little Carolyn, Jo-Lyn got up and struggled with the curtains. She felt violated. Whom should she call? Could the police stop this? Was this freedom of the press? She settled back into her chair, barely noticing the TV where the press secretary continued.

"On Sunday the President has been invited to address a gathering of Citizens For Moral Renewal. To the President, the fight against drugs, abortion, so-called sexual freedom, perversions, and pornography has been a priority. If communism could destroy us from without, it would. These criminal activities would destroy us from within. The President will not shirk this important task of giving encouragement to those who would keep America strong. San Francisco is part of the United States and the President will go there as necessary for the fulfillment of his duties."

The press secretary's statement was followed by some brief, pointed inquiries. The item switched to a taped interview with the Mayor of San Francisco. The City's Board of Supervisors (the City Council explained the commentator) had unanimously voted last night to ask the President to cancel his visit and to shift the NATO meetings elsewhere. The Mayor took a more restrained but parallel tack:

"It is an unfortunate day when the City of San

Francisco cannot offer its famous hospitality to the President of the United States. But I cannot encourage him to come here at the present time."

She was a slim woman, with trim blond hair and a usually pleasant smile that today was somber. Jo-Lyn had never heard of her before. With what little attention she paid, Jo-Lyn decided she didn't like the Mayor of San Francisco. They were all devil worshippers anyway.

"What has happened in the past with regards to the AIDS virus is not yet clear. The city of San Francisco is laying no blame, pointing no fingers, until we know the truth behind these complicated matters. A large number of our citizens are, however, understandably hurt and unsettled over the implications. As you know, San Francisco has worked diligently to prevent the spread of AIDS and to assist its victims. This work has been a model for the rest of the country and the world. This work only intensifies our anguish. Mr. President, this is not the time to visit San Francisco. As Mayor, I am unable to guarantee your safety. There are just too many security issues, and your visit will be divisive. Our police force is fully occupied already in the service of our residents and I am unable to direct it adequately to your own protection."

Jo-Lyn shuddered at the edge of her mind. She'd had a sudden thought. It migt be best if the President were shot. But the thought was so radical that from the moment she thought it she wondered how it could have even occurred to her. Jo-Lyn quickly pushed even that consideration from her mind and subconsciously clutched Carolyn just a little more firmly.

The Mayor's statements were followed by a short documentary explaining "Just how a virus is engineered." Schematics of DNA and genes. Lots of flasks and caged laboratory animals and containment facilities. Interviews with several prominent scientists. Blowup photos of the HIV virus. Jo-Lyn wasn't watching intensely enough to make any sense of it. "Go on," she muttered cynically. "Show a picture of Ed."

More news followed. Reports that the two gay CIA agents who were the initial vectors of the disease had died rapidly following their mission. They reputedly died in isolation, confined to a Falls Church safehouse. Was this how America treated its citizens? the commentator wondered. Was this even America? Then there were reports from Africa: conversations with the ambassadors of Zaire and Uganda, among the many called home for urgent consultations. There were rumors of a South African connection. But the African side of the story was still unclear, the commentator pointed out. Mr. Stephen's statements would require substantial corroboration. Did US agents merely discover the virus in Africa, or was it released there to test its virulence? Next week CIA officials would testify before House and Senate committees on the matter. Perhaps the African situation would become clearer then.

Jo-Lyn's husband had unleashed a devastating storm. She thought of him, she wanted to hold him. He must have done the right thing. He must be following orders. They must be protecting him. She needed her little boy, this lover who began his sexual expressions to her as naive and timid, only to rapidly transform them into assertiveness. She searched through all her feelings of goodness, warmth, affection, all her little recriminations towards Ed, her failures and misgivings. She shuffled through memories of her past, through reams of old notes, diary pages, love letters. She searched for a single clue. A clue that would clearly tell Jo-Lyn whether or not he had actually done what he had claimed to have done. Was it a myth, manufactured as a supposed testimonial to his Fellowship and to God? Was it a myth created and released for some CIA purpose? Or did her husband and his colleagues actually engineer this virus and plant it deliberately so that is could kill?

She wanted to know, but doubtless, she never would. No one would. She let the matter drop.

The feeding was at last beginning to calm her, soothe her. There were those gentle contractions between her legs, almost like the moments Ed stroked her. He could do it with his fingers for hours while he kissed her. Jo-Lyn felt warm, relaxed, contented, this little mouth sucking her tenderly, dependently. The world began to swirl about her, not crazily, but in vaguely defined spheres of light. They said motherhood was a blessed time. She must try to focus more on that and she must turn off the damned world on the television.

21 *The Castro, San Francisco, Friday Afternoon*

People from out of town are often surprised that the Castro is a compact neighborhood. They come expecting long sprawling strips with scattered gay establishments, like Philadelphia's Spruce Street or Seattle's Broadway. What they find is a village, close-clustered, full of variety, and intensely lived-in. A walk through the Castro can tell so much of the mood of the particular time. During Freedom Week, for example, buildings, shops, and windows are festooned with rainbow flags and banners and the mood on the sidewalks is up. When the Supreme Court upheld the Georgia sodomy law, the mood on the street was defiant. People were just plain angry. And when the LaRouche quarantine initiative failed, people everywhere showed signs of relief.

As Christine and Allan walked down Castro from Market, Allan stopping to answer questions, to shake the hands of well-wishers, they sensed a brooding uncertainty. That guy leaning with his back against a closed gate, his leg bent so the sole of his boot was up against the metal grid; that guy looked sullen, restless. He turned, kicked the edge of the gate so that the metal rang, and walked away. Close by, another man, very drunk, sat on the sidewalk crying. Every so often he would punctuate his tears with political pronouncements to the passersby. Outside Castro Station, a small crowd engaged in turbulent discussion. "What do they expect us to do, sit back while they murder us?" Allan heard someone comment, "Kill the bastards." Those who talked with Allan said little about his campaign. Nearly everyone raised the issue of the CIA.

Allan and Christine found a small, isolated table towards the back of Elephant Walk. As the waiter took their orders, Christine pulled out a pad of lined paper.

"Begin with the front of the pamphlet," Allan said. "We'll ask Fraggi to do the final layout in big capitals. WALTER HARRISON. LIAR, CHEAT, DOUBLECROSSER AND THIEF."

"Too strong, maybe?" Christine wondered.

"No, we can get him on all counts. We will when the real goods come out."

"Besides," Christine added, "we want to infuriate him, have him publicly rave over what will turn out to be a phony document."

"Exactly. Now inside. We want an introductory paragraph about the sort of qualities a DA should have. It should be sarcastic."

"Right, Allan—I get you. We need a DA who has a known record of personal dishonesty. We need a DA who's slimy enough to make sure the right cases are dealt with

114

in the right ways. We need a DA who is ignorant of the basic principles of justice and fair play. And more than anything, we need a corruptible DA.

"Great. Keep it vague, no backup. Make it sound infuriating. The words'll stick. When I release the real dirt it will only reinforce it."

Christine took a swig of her Dos Equis.

"You know what, Allan? We should title this section: WHAT YOU NEED IN A DISTRICT ATTORNEY. Then, after it, we put in equally big letters: IF YOU WANT THIS TYPE OF DA, VOTE WALTER A. HARRISON."

"Then do a paragraph on how the DA should spread unnecessary fear, promote extreme measures, undermine justice. How he should work to slow down successful programs that are currently under way. How he should set various community and minority groups against one another through accusation and the unfair application of the law."

Christine took notes on this, making a few changes. She and Allan conferred on them.

"Finally," Allan told her, "we need a paragraph that says something about Harrison's real goals. We need a DA whose secret aim is to selectively enforce laws against those with whom he happens to disagree personally. These laws will be applied first to homosexuals. But single parents, unmarried couples, watch out!"

"Again, lots of stinging headers for each paragraph."

"Finally, something like: the so-called live and let live attitude of this city was never healthy. Now its death is ensured. Support Walter A. Harrison on November 8."

"Great going," said Christine. "We've got half an hour until the meeting. I'll go upstairs now and draft a better copy. You can pass it on to Michael in front of everyone. Warn him of the need for complete secrecy."

"That's wonderful news about the poll."

A survey hired by their campaign office now showed a 50:30 split in favor of Allan Bennett; 20 percent were undecided. A *Chronicle* poll, to be published the next day showed somewhat the same, although the proportion of undecided rose to 30 percent.

"We'll do it yet," Christine told him. "I'm sure of it. Just wait till your bombshell comes out tomorrow at the Chamber of Commerce. That'll do it."

Allan touched his inside pocket, just to confirm that the final tabulations of Christine's survey were really there. He must remember to keep it separate from the material going to Fraggi.

"I got to get upstairs," Christine told him. "See you soon."

Success in San Francisco politics not only requires balancing between interest groups, but demands general support from at least three of five ethnic factions, all about equal in size. Harrison, a black man, thought he had the black vote. He hoped to appeal to Hispanics (through their Catholicism and fear of AIDS). His tactics, however, were in disarray. Some black leaders refused to endorse either candidate in the race, while others endorsed Bennett. The Asian and Hispanic communities, each used to teaming up with the Gay/Lesbian faction in getting their share of city programs, officially supported Allan. (This didn't mean individuals in their communities would necessarily vote the way of their leaders, but there was at least some chance of it.) Harrison's strategy of trying to split off the Gay/Lesbian faction while conquering with the rest, was not working.

Allan had gained support of three of the five factions, at least in name. The fifth faction was still up for grabs as far as both sides were concerned. Its predominant characteristic was that it was white. But beyond this is varied widely from single and married professionals with their newfound tastes for luxury to the aristocrats of Pacific

Heights. From the established Irish families of the Excelsior to the established Italian ones of North Beach. From the Vietnamese veterans who lived side-by-side with the city's Vietnamese refugees to the Americans that had opposed the war. It was a 20 percent faction that voted in all directions. In all likelihood, it was a faction that would neatly (some would say ironically) cancel itself out.

22 *The Eagle, San Francisco, Late Friday Afternoon*

Damn it, Gregg, what do you mean you're not going to the rally?''

The bartender at the Eagle was astounded.

"Terry's even closing the bar from seven to nine so that staff can be there."

''I'm tired, Gary. In my condition I've got to take it easy."

"Come on, Gregg. You know that I don't often go to demonstrations, but this one is important. We need as many moderates as possible there to make sure nothing violent happens."

Gregg took another sip of his Miller. He liked this bartender-biker, this fun-loving bear, his brown beard just touched with red, his eyes doing the pleading for him. He loved this guy all the more because he was not just a pleasant bartender, he was committed to his community.

"Okay," Gregg agreed, knowing he had other plans for the night. "I'll try real hard to get there."

Gregg felt a hand on his shoulder. It was Marc, and he gripped him affectionately.

"Long time no see," Gregg commented.

"Yeah, long time," Marc affirmed.

"We live in the same house," he explained to Gary. "And Allan and I rarely see this guy."

Marc leaned over and kissed him, letting his slightly open mouth rub into Gregg's. Since the onset of AIDS, many gay men has resorted to dry pecks. But others had deliberately used slightly wetter, more involved kisses, as a sign of commitment, even to those with the disease.

Gary went down to the other end of the bar.

"So how're you doing, Gregg?" Marc asked. "You look okay."

"A bit tired. Come on, sit down and I'll buy you a beer."

"You and Allan getting any better?"

"No."

"He loves you, Gregg."

"Fuck, I love him too. You know that. But he almost ignores me. Ever since I came down with pneumocystis he can't bring himself to get close to me in any way, even to talk. Oh sure, he came to the hospital. But it's as if he's frightened of death in his own life."

Gregg moved his beer bottle in little circles over the surface of the bar.

"Listen, guy," Marc told him, putting his arm about Gregg's shoulders. "Allan's also running a brutal campaign. Which he's going to win. You don't think he's doing that just to avoid you?"

"Of course not," Gregg answered unconvincingly. "But it's a pretty rotten way to treat a lover who's got a terminal disease."

"Just wait until after the campaign. You'll come back together."

I wish I could believe that, Gregg thought.

"I know he's busy," Gregg commented. "I admire him for his work. But there's a coldness between us and I get chills real easily."

They were silent for a while. Gary brought Marc a beer, at the same time carrying on a conversation with someone down the bar. Marc shrugged. He'd been through this business again and again with both Gregg and Allan and his moderating never seemed to do any good. Marc turned and looked at Gregg who stared intently at his beer. He perceived that Gregg had other things on his mind, but didn't ask about them.

For just a second, Marc's mind slipped out into the shadows of the bar. The walls became dim and cavelike; boles of trees rose between clustered boulders. Everywhere there was a strong disquiet. He heard sharp, nervously angry voices, nervous because they were dealing with newly experienced rage. He couldn't distinguish the words but he could sense their warning. In the distance the forest was gashed with red, he could see the orange-gold of flame. Marc let go and came back to the bar. Gregg was talking to him.

"So you're doing okay?"

"Yeah. Real well. I slept most of today. Met a real hot guy last night."

"Where?"

"At the Ambush. I was working."

"Oh come on, Marc, when are you going to give up this Ambush nonsense?"

Gregg had criticized Marc for some time about this. Both he and Allan regarded Marc as a sort of relic hippy. They knew he paid his rent. He must earn it somewhere. But these crazy stories about working at a bar that was long closed, that could only be entered through the mind. Both of them had concluded independently that Marc was cracking under the strain. Marc's attempted explanations of dreaming got him nowhere. Gregg and Allan had little time for the weird magic of old Indian tales. At least you're in the right city for mysticism, Allan had told Marc skeptically.

"Listen buddy, I'm not the only one," Marc told him. "See that guy up there by the pool table? That hunk with the blond-brown beard? His name's Bill. Ask him where he met me."

"He was probably drunk."

"No he wasn't, Gregg. And he found his way into the Ambush and he found me. He was amazed. He went back today and all he saw was a closed building."

"Okay. Okay." Gregg had had enough. He changed the subject.

"I've got a date with Tony tonight."

23 *Vacaville, California, Early Evening*

Barely able to keep their eyes open, Sam and Brian had reached Vacaville by early afternoon. They checked into a motel on the strip just west of the Nut Tree, asking for a room with a single, king-sized bed. Until she saw the "DR" on Sam's Mastercard, the manager was ambivalent to their request. She said nothing, but raised her eyebrows.

About six in the evening, Sam awoke. He was tired, but felt much better. Besides, they didn't need to get going until tomorrow morning. A nice relaxed breakfast and then the ride to the city would take about an hour and a half. He must remember to call Jim tonight. He felt relaxed for the first time in days. Brian appeared to have settled down and was accepting things. He hadn't asked any more questions and he'd spent much of their long drive through the Sacramento Valley looking happy, his head on Sam's shoulder.

Sam rolled away from Brian and onto his back. He had a raging hard-on. His dick wasn't long, but it was thick and he had big balls. He was hairy all over, nice golden fuzz that Brian liked to keep well-trimmed in his crotch, since it made a great highlight. Brian also liked to shave Sam's balls and ass crack so that their sweet vulnerability stood out. The shaving was a holdover from their ancient, piggy days of fisting. Not that they still didn't do that occasionally, using surgical gloves.

Sam began stroking his cock, rubbing the head between his palm and fingers. God, I'm horny, he told himself. It's been a week since I've come. Last night, he'd thought about coming in the truck, talking dirty with Brian, and jacking off during their drive down from Shasta. He'd done that once before, in a pickup with a buddy from Tacoma, late at night in the fog-bound valleys of southern Oregon. Now, Sam was ready for Brian.

Brian was snoring lightly, on his side, in a sort of fetal position, knees bent and legs pulled up. Sam reached over and pulled him onto his back. This is sure the best way to get woken up, he chuckled, as he put his head into Brian's crotch, full of rangy hair. Sam fondled the sleeping cock, circumcised like his own. Damn, barbaric custom, he thought. He ran his lips along the cock and moistened its head with some spit. Brian grunted.

Sam loved dicks in this semiturgid state before they got superhard. Sam put the head in his mouth, running his tongue about it, slipping the tip of his tongue through the Prince Albert, and tugging at it. God, how he loved pierced men. He'd done all of Brian's piercings for him. Piercing was a statement of belief in zany, pleasurable sex;

it was a gift to the partner. It sensitized and it extended. Sam felt a hand run through his hair and take control of the motion of his head. Brian was awake.

"Come on, fucker. Get that man-meat down your throat," Brian instructed him. "I want to hear you gag on it."

And with that Sam began to eat with passion.

About five minutes later Sam moved up beside Brian. They kissed long and tenderly. Brian's fingers were working Sam's nipples.

"Hi there, gorgeous," Sam told him, smiling.

Brian was working the tits hard now, pinching them tightly so that each jab of sensation made Sam even harder.

"You're not too shoddy yourself," Brian told him.

They kissed.

"I want you to fuck me," Brian told Sam.

"Could be arranged," Sam said. "Think you can take it all?"

They loved to kid each other about their capacities.

"There's a pack of condoms in the side pocket of the brown traveling bag," Brian instructed him. "And some Lube. Go get them."

"Pushy bottom," commented Sam as he pulled himself away and went for the rubbers.

God, how he'd missed playing with Sam! he thought. How could he have let these differences come between them? Brian still might not agree with all of Sam's plans but the man was too dear to let things come between them.

24 *The Castro, San Francisco, Late Friday Afternoon*

In a room on the floor above Elephant Walk, Allan's campaign committee was meeting. People sat in chairs arranged in a rough circle. Christine, who chaired the group, sat with her back to the window. Allan pulled his chair a little out of the circle so he could carefully study the participants.

Gerry Reynolds, not often at these meetings, waved a copy of the *Examiner.* He was campaign treasurer.

"Anyone seen this?" he commented. "Lots of interesting stuff today."

"Maybe you should brief us before we start the meeting," Christine told him. "It helps all the more if we can keep up. Besides, Michael isn't here yet."

Gerry Reynolds, Allan wondered. Been involved in the Golden Gate Business Association and the Alice B. Toklas Lesbian/Gay Democratic Club for years. An appointee to the Mayor's Small Business Commission. Out of the closet for twenty-five years. That's right, lost his job in New York investment counseling because he was found to be a faggot. Came here. Has fought hard for the community ever since. No. He's no turncoat.

"Well, first, as we all know, the President refuses to cancel his trip, even after the Mayor said she can't guarantee his protection. He's called on the military and protective forces will be in place in the city by tomorrow night."

"Yeah, protective forces," put in Kim White sarcastically. "I can see it now. Tanks in the Castro. They've been just waiting for this excuse."

Kim White. Could it be her? Long-time dyke activist? Had a real sweet lover who was a therapist or counselor or something like that. Allan had met her at Alice some years ago and she'd been persuaded by her old friend Christine to take the thankless task of office manager. She was sitting in the chair next to Christine now. Allan searched for a motive. No, it wasn't likely to be her.

"Don't laugh," Gerry told them. "Be damn sure the administration will take this chance to show they intend business."

"And so will we," someone commented defiantly.

It was Steven Smith, tall and lanky with a bushy tan mustache. Steven coordinated the volunteers, the canvasers, the phone banks. He always seemed to be critical of Allan for not taking a more radical stand. He often lacked in political saavy, Allan thought. He was unable to see the subtleties that had to be perceived and played on in any election. But he was also a good worker and volunteers took fast to him. Could Steven be trying to subvert him? Trying to push him into a more radical position by setting up Harrison? Or even disguising his secret dealings with phony criticism? Maybe, but Allan doubted it. Steven had worked hard in gay campaigns for too long.

"Some international news," Gerry continued. "The world's reacting to this thing. The Netherlands have officially withdrawn from the NATO meeting as long as it's held in the USA. They've offered the Hague. Canada suggests moving the meeting to Calgary."

The seat beside Kim was empty, waiting for Fraggi. In the next seat, and sitting beside Gerry, was Denton Yip. It couldn't be Denton, Allan told himself. Denton was gay and Chinese and an influential member of both Alice and the Chinese American Democratic Club. He was the campaign liaison with other groups and politicians and he had been instrumental in seeking a long list of prominent endorsements for Allen that included all eleven members of the Board of Supervisors. His involvement in politics went back to before the Harvey Milk days. Nearly everyone respected Denton for his careful work, his quiet candor. Could he have motives Allan hadn't perceived? Unlikely, but he couldn't say for sure.

"There were also demonstrations today in Chicago and New York," Gerry continued. "In New York things got nasty. My ex called me about an hour ago. Some cops started letting loose with their nightsticks when some of the crowd pushed over police lines. There were also some brutal arrests outside St. Patrick's Cathedral. A cop car was turned over and burned."

"We can do better than that," Steven quipped. "We've got the White Riots to outdo."

Allan could not restrain himself: "God damn it, Steven," he interjected. "We can't afford any form of violence right now!"

"Can you blame people, Allan? This government tried to exterminate us. They may even succeed. Initiatives have been passed against us. Registries of our names have been compiled. Rights have been wiped off the books. I'm surprised people have been so restrained. I'm surprised there hasn't been some real violence across this country."

It was Mike Stavriakos speaking. He was a friend of Steven. Mike worked for KQED and handled media for the campaign.

"What have we got to lose? What's someone with AIDS got to lose?" Steven Smith interjected. "We've already been fired upon by God's magic bullets. I can name a bunch of people who should be assassinated and I might even welcome the violence."

"Yeah, Mike is right," Gerry interjected. "The mood in the city, in the Castro is ugly. The bitterness of hundreds

of lingering deaths is rapidly surfacing. They'd better watch
out tonight."

"Okay," Allan told his campaign team. "I know we're
sore. The man who's my lover is dying of the disease. But
we're dealing with an election, with someone like Harrison,
with liberal voters who are scared, who could easily be
swayed the other way. I know how you feel, Steven. When
the White Night riots happened, lots of responsible gay
leaders condemned them. I applauded. It was at the end of
the road and our only recourse. We showed our guts. The
case is different now."

"Oh yeah?" Steven questioned with no small hint of
rebellion in his voice.

"Yeah, Steven," Allan answered him. "I predict this
country's going to see some big changes as a result. I predict
the President will be impeached. Half of the CIA will be put
behind bars."

"For doing God's work? For killing queers?" Steven
taunted again.

"They also said that with Watergate and the Iran-
Contra affair," Mike commented drily. "A few faces changed.
A lot of pardons were given. Nothing else."

Allan let the matter drop. He looked towards
Stavriakos. Short, curly black hair, thick bushy mustache.
Greek origin and hot as hell. If these were other times and
not a campaign Allan wouldn't have minded negotiating him
into the sack. Nice basket the way he crossed his legs like
that. They say Greek men have big cocks, Allan thought,
and the smaller the man the larger the meat.

The door opened and Michael Fraggi entered the
room. He appeared harried. "Sorry I'm late," he muttered
and took the one empty chair.

"Go on, Gerry," Allan said. "Anything more we
should know?"

Allan looked at Stavriakos again. Mike did an effective

job. He didn't blame Mike, or Steve for that matter, for being pissed. Allan didn't know much about Mike personally except he'd been around the community for years and was on the Board of MCC. Allan's friend Greg Day, with several past forays into politics, had recommended him with high praise.

"Only one thing and that's the emergency Board of Supervisors meeting called for tonight. And we know about that."

Allan checked his watch. "Yes," he said. "I've got to be there. It'll be right before the rally. Christine, do you want to start the meeting?"

"Sure, Allan. Let me start by telling everyone the results of our latest poll. Then Allen can tell us about our strategy for these last days of the campaign. Then we'll talk about what has to be done."

Allan turned his gaze towards Michael Fraggi. The man looked sullen; he was studying some notes on his clipboard and taking some new ones. Was it really he who was making the leaks? People had too much on him if the truth were known. Fraggi sure as hell wouldn't want his sexual proclivities spread through the wrong circles. Unlike Allan, he wasn't open and proud about them. And unlike Allan, he wasn't running for election. There's some weird perversity in the man, Allan conjectured, some self-hurting guilt-ridden trip. Maybe it comes from the way he was indoctrinated as a kid. Until he died, Fraggi's father was a Mormon bishop, a crony of that notorious liberal Orrin Hatch.

Allan looked away from Michael. The only other candidate in the room was that English woman, Hilary Montford. She was a general go-getter for the campaign and she helped with speech writing and publicity. She'd studied political economy at the London School of Economics before she came here to be with her lover. (Immigration was no problem, Hilary's father was a former ambassador to the US) She'd worked with various gay and radical causes in

London. No, Allan thought. She's too left-wing, she's too careful. Sometimes he had to tone down her draft speeches a bit, whatever her sincerity. Besides, she'd been in San Francisco for less than a year. She didn't have the contacts to dig out information on Allan's past or to pass it on. What about her lover? Could be, Allan thought, but he suspected no.

"What all this means," Christine told them, "is that we're ahead and we're gaining. What happens at the Board of Supervisors and rally tonight, as well as during the Presidential visit Sunday and Monday, could cause big changes in the final vote. I want Allan to tell us his thoughts on this."

Michael Fraggi was writing furiously. Did this mean he handed over meeting notes as well? Why did someone in charge of layout and printing campaign releases need to take so many notes? But then at any business meeting there were people who took irrelevant notes for want of something better to do.

"We are," Allan told them, "at a crucial turning point on which the whole campaign rests. Harrison's position has been so extreme that people don't trust him. The liberals have come to us and many of the ethnic groups, Asians, even the Hispanics are starting to lean our way. Harrison's tactics of sowing fear and division have backfired. Most major community organizations, special interest groups, and city politicians have endorsed me. Yet Harrison is still attempting his tactics of fear. And some people are still listening to them. Not all voters will automatically follow their community leaders. Many voters are uncertain.

"To this, we've also got to add the external events. The revelations of the past twenty-four hours have shocked nearly every voter in the city. As a community we've gained considerable support and sympathy by showing restraint, by not overreacting. A peaceful rally tonight, and a press conference on Sunday at the Mayor's office during the President's speech will reinforce that perception. People see us as suffering injustices and as underdogs. There is, as you know, a tradition of support among San Francisco voters for the underdog.

"All of you can understand the delicacy of our predicament. If we make it calmly through the next few days, Harrison is finished. I can't emphasize enough how much this could change if there is violence tonight, or if some crazy tries to assassinate the President. Please, all of you, tell your friends to keep cool. I'll be one of the speakers and I'm going to push that theme. Once we've made this election, things are going to be different. I promise that my first task as DA will be to pursue applicable indictments of federal officials in this County."

Allan paused for a moment, deliberately looking at each person around the room. He continued:

"There's one other thing I want to say, to all of you. From the bottom of my heart, thank you for getting us this far."

The room broke into applause, even Michael Fraggi clapping vigorously. Was it a phony show? Allan wondered.

Christine McIntyre took the floor again:

"Over the next few days we've also got some important moves to make that will tie things down completely. As some of you know, we've been investigating Harrison's background. (Christine deliberately avoided any mention of campaign funds.) We've come up with a lot of dirt. Allan's going to release it officially at the Chamber of Commerce luncheon tomorrow. It'll barely make the Saturday papers. The Sunday edition is already printed. Monday, the day before the election, the papers will be full of it."

Michael Fraggi spoke up: "That means we've got to get copy ready. I've got to have it now to get it to an overnight printer. Besides, I plan to be at the rally."

"We have the copy here," Allan told him, pulling a sealed envelope from the inside pocket of his jacket.

"Good," Fraggi told them. "I can get going right away."

The campaign team watched as Allan handed over the envelope.

"Michael, I want you to be extremely careful with this," Allan warned. "Only a couple of us know its contents. It must be kept as secret as possible."

"It will," Fraggi assured him. "You can trust me. Let me know how many copies we'll need."

Christine showed no reaction but went on with the meeting. Only she and Allan knew that the real pamphlet was being laid out by a trusted friend and graphics artist and would be printed by midnight.

About a quarter of an hour later, the meeting adjourned. Allan checked his watch. 4:35. I've got to get down to City Hall, he told himself. Michael Fraggi was preparing to leave. Allan walked over and intercepted him as he moved towards the door.

"Listen Michael, I want you to know how sensitive this matter is, how important that it be kept secret."

"You can trust me," Michael said again. "Listen, who should I take the copy to for checking before it goes to press? It'll probably be late tonight."

"Christine. Call her at home if necessary."

Allan was looking over Michael's shoulder and towards Christine. She caught his eye and he winked. Christine's colleagues would be trailing Michael for the next twenty-four hours.

Michael caught the wink and swung around to look at Christine.

"What was that about?" he asked.

"For a man, she thinks you've got cute buns!"

25 *South of Market, San Francisco, Early Friday Morning*

About 6:30 Marc began his walk towards the Civic Center.

He wasn't certain about this. The community's mood was angry, fulminating. He sensed trouble. A lot of people in the bar, men who had been simmering for weeks, were boiling over. The President was sure a belligerent fool to insist on coming. He might even get what he deserved.

Marc passed the building that had housed the Ambush. The doors were closed; he would not be finding his way in there tonight. He turned up Ninth Street and noticed new graffiti sprayed onto walls. One repeatedly proclaimed: U.S OUT OF SAN FRANCISCO. Another screamed: KILL AIDS, KILL FAGS. As he read them, Marc shivered in the gloom of early evening and zippered up his leather jacket. He kept walking.

He had this foreboding. He had seen fire in the woods. He sensed trouble and he would rather not be present, but this was a cause that had to be supported. The community had to make a statement of strength.

Marc wondered what Gregg was really doing that evening. Did he really have a date with Eight-ball? Or was he going off to plot with his friend Jim? Gregg and Jim had been scheming about something for months now. Marc had picked up the nuances, caught the end of telephone calls, observed the tone in Gregg's eyes. But Marc would rather not ask Gregg about it. The response would only have been evasive anyway. Whatever their plans, Marc was certain Allan would disagree with them.

Yeah, and what about Allan? About now he was supposed to be speaking to the Board of Supervisors. Would they believe him when he said the gay community was under control, that violence was unlikely to occur? Bullshit! There was going to be trouble for a good while over this. Too many had suffered too much.

As he reached Howard Street, Marc noticed that the sidewalks were exceptionally busy with men and women walking alone or in couples or in groups towards Market Street. The South of Market gay population was on the march.

When Marc arrived there, a substantial crowd already milled about United Nations Plaza: it was being steadily augmented by a candlelight march from the Castro. Gay marches from Market and Castro were an established custom in San Francisco. They had begun with demonstrations against the Brigg's initiative and then spontaneously after the assasinations of Milk and Moscone. In the years following that event, candlelight processions continued as memorials, Lincoln's statue in front of City Hall becoming a shrine of hope. Then, as AIDS began to take its toll, Memorial Day marches were initiated, again in candlelight, and again in remembrance. San Francisco's Gay community is spirited and peace-loving. While nearly all of these marches and rallies had been characterized by grief and quiet outrage, anger was controlled. Only once, following the Dan White verdict, did a march to City Hall erupt in violence.

Marc guessed the numbers already present totaled eighty thousand. He moved through the crowd, looking for familiar faces. He moved towards City Hall where a makeshift speakers platform and sound system were set up on the front steps. A row of about twenty police cars had been neatly lined up along Larkin Street to the south of Grove. Grove and Larkin had been closed off. Sitting ducks,

Marc pondered, remembering the burning cars at the White Riots. But it wouldn't be them, Marc thought. The police were not the object of this rage.

Marc found himself in front of Brooks Hall. On the sidewalk were Bruce and Paul, two old Ambush buddies. He'd wait here with them.

26 *Civic Center Plaza, Friday Evening*

The crowd that milled uncertainly about United Nations (or Civic Center) Plaza was mixed. It was uncertain, because it barely knew or even dared to think what could occur. Nothing of this magnitude had happened to the community before. In the past, individuals had died, the arm of justice had fallen short, or bigots had pushed their schemes to persecute. All of these had been clearly definable wrongs. But tonight, a people who had suffered collectively for nearly a decade (the years numbering those of the Nazi Holocaust) the deaths of hundreds of friends had come to realize that their own country had committed those murders, and if Ed Stevens was correct, deliberately. Just how are the grief-stricken expected to react in such a predicament? No one was certain.

The crowd was mixed, incredibly mixed, because every element of the community from the A-gays on Pacific Heights to the punk gays of the Haight to the mustachioed queens of the Castro had been touched by this tragedy. There were men in leather and men in guerrilla boots and there were men in Lacoste shirts and baggy pants and shiny shoes.

There were SFGDIs and Constantines and California Eagles. There were men in bomber jackets and men in Forty-Niner jackets and high tech runners with sad looks on their tear-stained faces. Tonight, no one was ashamed of tears. There were people from the Marching Band and the Chorus. There were older queens, aunties to some, from their Victoriana-cluttered apartments in Cow Hollow and Polk Gulch and the Tenderloin and there were gay men who rarely left their Russian Hill apartments except for the ballet and the symphony. There were empresses and dowager empresses and emperors after Norton. A few were in drag, but most had left their regal personas behind and were here to show grief unmasked by makeup. Here and there were groups of men in suits and ties, stopping on their way home from the financial district. In the crowds were thousands of women, mostly Lesbian, but many straight. These women, who as friends, Shanti counselors, AIDS Foundation workers and medical professionals, had been the greatest allies of gay men in the years of sorrow, lovers and mothers in times of true need. Women whose generous actions had reunited a formerly divided community. They were all there, the women bikers, the antinuke and whole-earth women, the wimmim warriors, the professional Lesbians and the lipstick Lesbians, the leather dykes; even the Lesbian separatists were represented there. For the women, like the men, smelled betrayal. They had shared in the grief. And they knew, every one of them, that what had been done to their gay brothers, could well have been done to them.

But gays and Lesbians were not alone. The crowd was full of friends and supporters, from places as far away as Belmont and Kentfield. The crowd was full of all types of Americans who may or may not have been directly touched by an AIDS death, but who now felt the stiletto of this injustice slice their hearts. These were Americans who sensed betrayal by a system in which they had believed since birth and had sworn allegiance to almost daily. These people also milled uncertainly.

The platform party was aware of the volatility of this crowd. The whole Board of Supervisors was present, not only as a sign of support, but also as an indication of the seriousness with which they held this event. Nothing must be allowed to happen. Everyone suspected it would.

Certainly, some people had come to mourn, to shed grief. All had come to show shock and outrage. Many waved placards that carried the names of the dead. Others brandished messages that were more pointed. CIA KILLS FAGGOTS. CIA MURDERERS. Many had come to show their solidarity and to demand strong actions. Rainbow flags waved everywhere. Several placards proclaimed: U.S. OUT OF SAN FRANCISCO. Still others had come to show support for the city, for the society they believed in here. While grief and solidarity are one thing, rage and bitterness are another. Many sought justice, even retaliation. Placards everywhere: WE WILL BE AVENGED. Across the top of the Library (City Officials are still unaware as to who put it there and how) a huge banner screamed BLOOD REVENGE. Many elements of this large crowd had been stung beyond the limits of peaceful endurance.

Even the presence of Joan Baez as MC did little to soothe the hurt. She received the silence and respect and even applause due her long history of tough yet gentle activism. But her presence was not enough to placate the hurt and the belligerent. Five years ago her nonviolent approaches were almost universally applauded by those present here today. Now, to many of the crowd, faced with the current circumstances, these approaches hardly seemed relevant. When Baez called for our finest front, in this, our darkest and most solemn hour, hundreds screamed, "Revenge! We want revenge!"

An invocation, in the form of a rambling sort of prayer

was given by the Minister of the Golden Gate Metropolitan Community Church. It brought a little calm. The minister begged people to remember those who had died, their love, and their love of peace. She asked that they remember their gentleness, their smiles and the beauty of their love. She asked that the crowd act in a way respectful of our dead. She prayed for courage and calm to bear the burden of betrayal. She prayed for strength to fight the battles needed to bring this evil to justice.

During her talk, the crowd remained calm, perhaps out of feelings for the dead, perhaps from the meditation and inward solace some found in prayer. But following her prayer, the calm was continually punctuated by angry screams.

Brian Smith, a PWA spoke. While he called for justice, elements of the assembly shouted for revenge. There were some yells of "Remember Dan White." Smith was shaken. He called on people to work peacefully, carefully, towards full justice. "We mustn't fall into the same trap as the CIA and the government." Applause, in many elements of the crowd, was interrupted by simultaneous cries for revenge. "Don't get me wrong," he told them. "We will be avenged. It's a matter of how." To which someone screamed: "Was the Holocaust ever avenged?"

When Allan Bennett came to the microphone, there was thundering applause. Of course they would vote for this man. Yet as he talked, reminding them of the election, affirming that if elected he would take strong actions from his office against the Federal Government, this was not enough. Many people didn't want a political speech, and although Allan didn't give one, his call for restraint was taken as such. It was even booed. The crowd was now divided. Large groups applauded Allan, trying to drown out the hecklers, the vociferous who waved clenched fists and bandied phrases like "Sell out!" and "Kill them!" Some people in the crowd tried to restrain this scattered dissension. But they had little effect, only creating some scuffles and angry exchanges. "I don't want to hear about justice that never works," one bearded man in a plaid shirt and jeans screamed to a group of women beside him. "I lost three former lovers and my best friend is almost dead. I want fucking CIA blood! I want government blood! I want their bodies on the streets." He didn't tell them that he was an ex-air force pilot, that he'd fought in Vietnam, and that he was honored for service.

The platform party looked uneasy. Some of them conferred. It was time for their biggest gun, the President of the Board of Supervisors. And the tactic seemed to work, at least for a while.

The President of the Board was a politician, but she was one of the most admired in the city. She had created a strong public image as compassionate, as someone who was willing occasionally to sacrifice political advantage to principle. Her outreach and support of the gay/lesbian community had been deep-rooted and sustained. When she spoke, people believed her.

She did not downplay the rage that was present and mounting. "I have cried myself, many times over the last few days with the awareness of our betrayal," she told them. "I understand. I feel your rage. I too am angry. My heart cries for revenge. These murderers have wreaked death upon a whole generation of our citizens. Men who gave with their hearts to San Francisco, men who worked to build the renaissance this city knows today. I will see these murderers brought to justice. I guarantee that this city, this San Francisco, will never let go in its battle against the United States until the evil minds that planned this program are put away forever and retribution is paid for every one of our dead."

The crowd was stunned. Tears streamed down faces. Men and women applauded, shook fists in agreement, waved their rainbow flags and their placards. No city politician had made such a deliberately strong statement. Even the hecklers gave pause.

This was only the beginning. She went on to announce city actions, a resolution that had just been unanimously passed by the supervisors and which the Mayor had agreed to sign.

First, the city would provide full support for its citizens in the pursuit of justice. There was mild applause for this, it merely backed up what she had said earlier.

Second, the city would use all its resources, including the courts, to demand federal compensation for the surviving lovers and kin of the AIDS dead. This statement brought tumultuous applause.

Third, the city would declare a week of mourning for the dead. A cenotaph to the dead would be erected, here in United Nations Plaza, inscribed with their names. Applause for this item was polite. A public monument was long due.

Fourth, the DA's department was preparing at this very moment a warrant for the arrest of the United States President on his Sunday morning arrival in the city and county. The charge would be first-degree murder. The President, she argued, should be tried by the courts here in California, where even if she didn't believe in it herself, there was a death penalty.

This final announcement sent the crowd wild, cynics included. It seemed unlikely that the President, surrounded by military and CIA goons, would ever allow himself to be arrested by San Francisco politicians. But the intent was clear, and the city had the guts to state it.

Perhaps the rally would have closed at that point, peacefully, if Joan Baez, accompanied by the Vocal Minority, had led the singing of "We Shall Overcome." That was what had been intended. But in bringing forward when they did the President of the Supervisors, the platform committee had pushed aside one of those scheduled to speak.

Diane Rossi, President of the Harvey Milk Lesbian/Gay Democratic Club, demanded her right to be heard. There were some questioning looks among the platform delegates, but she was already at the microphone. The bomb was about to be set off.

Diane began unprovocatively enough. She talked about the depths of our sorrow, of our betrayal. She demanded catharsis for the audience. "Remember those who have died. Call out their names. Everyone!" And the crowd responded, some waving placards, as thousands of names were screamed out, the cacophany echoing off the walls of the grand stone facades about the plaza, the sound surging in waves, rebounding on itself, the crowd repeating name after name, louder and yet louder, the shouting suffused with grief and with creeping rage.

Diane's speech may have been intended as a buildup, a prelude towards the President of the Board's address, but there was nothing planned to follow it in its present timing, and large numbers of those assembled were becoming highly agitated.

Diane's voice became difficult to perceive. Words and phrases audible between the waves of noise like the counterpoint to a stormy basso. Principles of the American heritage. Betrayal. This is no longer our country. We need more than purges. We need a new revolution that will shake America to its roots.

The crowd was ignoring her. Names of the dead were still echoing through the air. These were counterposed against loud, threatening cries. Someone had made it to the second floor flagpoles over the portico of City Hall. Screams of approval filled the air as Old Glory was ripped down, torn into pieces and thrown to the crowd. Part of the crowd began pushing towards the steps of City Hall and the speakers' platform. The police attempted to move in. The plaza broke into chaos, with many people trying to leave the area, while others surged forward to cross the police barriers and storm City Hall. Already the platform party had retreated behind City Hall doors.

But the real explosion took place at the north end of the plaza. The police, remembering the White Night riots, moved in fast to protect City Hall, and the crowd, not really angry with the city, pulled back quickly. Rather, it was the Federal Building to the west edge of the plaza that should have been protected.

With little notice, four men took primitive gasoline bombs from rucksacks on their backs. Who the men were and who saw them was never ascertained. Those surrounding them cheered as the wicks were lit. There was the tinkle of breaking glass: two second floor and two third floor windows along the length of the Federal Building. There were dull explosions as the gasoline roared into flame. The crowd cheered again. People let loose with a fusillade of stones and bottles that broke yet further windows. Within five minutes, large parts of the Federal Building were wreathed in flame. Fanned and fed by drafts from broken windows, the blaze spread rapidly.

27 *U.C.S.F. Medical Center, Late Friday Evening*

Peter Steinman worked hard and played hard. Graduate students, in most laboratory sciences, are devoted to their work, monitoring equipment, taking spectrophotometer readings, running columns and assays, often through weekends and late into evenings. Med students go home or study in libraries; graduate students in the arts pore over their obscure texts in remote library carrals. But science graduate students hang about their lab benches.

It was about nine P.M. in a fourteenth floor microbiology lab at UC San Francisco. Peter had wanted to go to the rally at City Hall, but he had another mission. Tonight, he was monitoring the progress of the culture by doing tests for the reverse transcriptase activity typical of retroviruses. Tomorrow morning he would harvest the virus.

His research work was full of ironies. Peter had come here as a Ph.D. student following his graduation from Berkeley in 1984. As a gay man, he had wanted to do his Ph.D. research in an area that would help his own community. Some exciting work on the reaction of immune systems to the human immunodeficiency virus was being done at UCSF. Work that could lead to important new therapies. He'd had a sense that here in San Francisco, where most everyone knew people who had died of the disease, there was a somewhat larger concern about developing treatments for those with the disease. Elsewhere, the emphasis seemed to be on vaccines, agents to protect the uninfected.

So Peter had come to this lab where they routinely grew HIV to be used in sophisticated cell-culture experiments. The techniques for growing the virus became routine to Peter's research. It was a rather straightforward procedure, done under conditions of special containment to prevent its accidental release. However, when working alone, Peter didn't completely comply with safety procedures. Daily, he turned the round-bottomed tissue culture tubes in the incubator to mix their contents, and when he added new medium, he dispensed with rubber gloves. He always washed his hands to prevent possible contamination of other workers. Even when he made the measured initial addition of peripheral lymphocytes, taken from seropositive blood, he rarely used a safety device. There was no need any more. Six months earlier, with the appearance of several KS lesions, Peter knew he had the disease.

It seemed ironic to hold these little culture flasks, to swirl their contents full of things like fetal calf serum, sheep antiserum to one type of interferon and goat antiserum to another. These little flasks full of burgeoning T-cell lymphocytes that were bursting with the very virus that would kill him.

Peter put the flasks back. In a few minutes he would micropipette samples for the assay. He walked over to the corner of the lab and into his research supervisor's office. The lights were off and the city was spread out below. It was a strangely clear night; the fog that usually shrouded Mount Parnassus was absent. Peter loved this view of the city. He could see the Marin Headlands, the tips of the towers of the Golden State Bridge, and the wonderful spires of Saint Ignatius over by USF. He could see the city like liquid light as it poured along the Panhandle and the Haight towards Pacific Heights. Somewhere towards downtown the sky glowed red, but with Buena Vista Park in the way, Peter couldn't tell exactly where. A major fire? He remembered now how he had heard earlier and faintly through hermetically sealed plate glass the screams of fire trucks pouring out of the avenues. He wondered for an instant whether it could have anything to do with the rally, but he dismissed that thought. Joan Baez was chairing it. Nothing would happen with her present.

God, how he loved this city, its views, its people. Peter had come from the east; his father was an academic at Princeton. Both his parents were terribly concerned that Peters had AIDS, terribly sympathetic, but somehow they couldn't understand why he had the disease. It was as if there was something terribly confusing to them about Peter's being gay. In Berekely and here, there had been no questions. Being gay was like being Chinese, Jewish. Sure, Peter had the finest academic records. His supervisor was more than happy to have another gay scientist on his team. Indeed, when Peter had let him know about the KS, his supervisor's reaction had never been stronger. "Don't give up now. You've only got eight months to go until you start writing your dissertation. If I can give you advice, you'll want to keep having some goals to live for."

Peter looked to the northwest. In the distance, lights twinkled on the Headlands. He'd had so much to live for. Committed to this research, meaningful research. Being part of a community in which he felt himself a real member. He had learned to let himself go, in a way that balanced the intensity of his work. Was it 1980 or 1981 he discovered places like the Trock, and Dreamland, and Leather Beach? He was barely twenty-one then, and full of energy. A short man with lots of electricity, a cute face and a bushy mustache that was always smiling, and a bod that could dance for hours, maybe with a little acid or MDA, but more often without. Sometimes he went from those places to the Slot, but not often, because he wasn't into sex palaces. One night at the Slot, Peter met Gregg and Jim, sharing a room, and suddenly a new world opened up. Here were some beautiful, mature men, who knew how to make his body do some special things Peter had never believed possible. Here were some buddies who saw him not as a kid with a lot of growing, but as a young man seeking within himself. Had he become addicted by it all? No, Peter had found balance. Even when he died from this damned disease, he could be content in having tasted a sweetness so few others found.

Peter turned from the window. The assays would take about an hour; then he would head home. Tomorrow morning, he would conduct the harvest.

28 *The Castro, San Francisco, Late Friday*

It took place about midnight and so suddenly that few of the survivors recollected what happened. The Castro was largely deserted. Most leaving the rally at City Hall had gone directly home. Nearly all of the city's police and fire detachments were on duty at the Civic Center.

A ragged 1973 Chevy Impala, stripped of license plates, descended Market and swerved right onto Castro. The car mowed down a solitary pedestrian in the crosswalk, running over him and pulling into the empty northbound lane. The car stopped in the bus zone just long enough to hurl a Molotov cocktail through the plate glass windows of the Twin Peaks bar. From the seat adjacent to the driver someone waved an American flag.

The Chevy screeched off, swerved back into the right hand lane, and headed south down Castro Street. Several gun shots rang out. The car ran the red light at Eighteenth, then disappeared up Nineteenth. Next day, the car was found deserted on Cortland Street under the southbound 101 overpass. It had been stolen from a junked car lot somewhere east of Portrero Hill.

In the Castro, Twin Peaks with its beautiful carved oak bar as well as the buildings immediately adjacent, burned to the ground. The bartender and two patrons were dead. The man mowed down in the crosswalk suffered multiple fractures in both legs, but survived. Further down Castro Street, five other people lay dead: a late-night businessmen, having just emerged from the instant teller of Empire of America; two street gays, lingering on the pavement outside Castro Station; an old woman, instrument box open to contributions who played her keyboard on the sidewalk in front of Castro Super; and, in the crosswalk to Hibernia Beach, a Lesbian lay dead. She had just said good night to a former lover, visiting from Boston, and was on her way from Francine's to her car parked near the Moby Dick. She had wanted to go to the rally, but it was also her only chance in five years to see Barbara. It had been a gorgeous evening.

29 *Noe Valley, San Francisco, Friday Evening*

Gregg kept the radio and television off and played Klaus Schulze while he douched. He'd done a joint to relax a bit and he'd marveled at just how good his butthole felt each time the warm water filled it. Gregg wanted to be spotlessly clean. This was to be his final time, and he was determined to give and to get in a way God had always meant him to use this sweet ass. Finally, he greased a stainless steel egg and slipped it up his butt, pulled on his leather pants, and began to get dressed.

Gregg left for Tony's about nine, a short ride down through the Castro then over the hill to Noe Valley. He could see the glow over City Hall, but, as he had the earlier wail of sirens, he ignored it. He knew that it had to do with the rally. What else did they expect? That afternoon at the office, he had caught Ed Steven's now classic lines on magic bullets, once again replayed on the radio: "I believe that I've been called by the Lord, and I've done proud on just that." Once again Gregg was sure he recognized the voice, even the name, but he didn't linger on the matter. He was thinking almost constantly about Tony. Yeah, what else did they expect? This city was fucking mad.

His body was feeling good, ready. His butt felt wonderful. He loved the way his bike glided up Diamond, over the hill and down toward Twenty-fifth Street. He loved the way the warm steel ball shifted inside and massaged him when riding a bike.

That afternoon, in a call to Gregg's office, Eight-ball had almost backed down. Gregg had used his utmost in persuasiveness. Now, as Tony opened the door, Gregg sensed uncertainty.

Each time Gregg and Tony played they ended up having a wonderful time. But each time they did so, they had to overcome a reluctance, a sort of fear. For Tony that fear had grown thicker with each dead friend, most particularly now with Gary. Underlying this uncertainty was the question of whether or not Gregg, a man with AIDS, should have supposedly unsafe sex with another so far free of signs of the disease. They had talked about it, lots of times. They could switch to activities that were perfectly safe, as Allan had done. But neither Tony nor Gregg were content with that strategy. Fisting each other was a statement of belief, of spiritual union in this crazy time, of a special trust and love. Yet while they took precautions, each time they played, some of the initial doubts were there.

Gregg took Tony into his arms. Tony was short and Italian, with curly, wiry hair and a black beard tight against his face. Gregg hugged him, rubbing his hands over his back. He could feel the body hair through his tank top. They kissed for a few minutes, beards rubbing together, while Gregg stroked his rounded butt.

"You douche?" Gregg asked him.

"Yeah," Tony told him.

So it was going to work out all right, Gregg considered. If Eight-ball had gone this far, his reluctance would be overcome.

"Your housemates?"

"All gone to the rally. Said I could have the playroom for myself if I cleaned up afterwards. Want a beer?"

"Sure," Gregg told him, and Tony pulled a six-pack from the refrigerator. They descended the stairs from the kitchen to the garage and walked back into the playroom. Tony put the beer into a styrofoam cooler already filled with ice, but not before handing one to Gregg. The room was warm and votive candles were lit in its alcoves. As Tony closed the door and locked it, Gregg caught a glimpse of another playroom, of names on a wall. The thought passed. Tony turned to Gregg; he looked uncertain again.

Gregg leaned against a leather-padded sawhorse. "Come here Eight-ball," he said.

Tony leaned against the black-painted wall.

"Wanna start with some video?" he asked. "Get us more in the mood? I put your favorite, *Erotic Hands*, in the player."

"No video," Gregg told him. "Come on over here."

Tony stayed where he was. "What about some music?" he asked.

"Okay," Gregg told him, playing along a little. "Our regular."

Their regular was Bach, hours of piano music that was hypnotic in the intimacy of its counterpoint: the Goldberg Variations, the Italian Suites, the German Suites. The music was unobtrusive, but when the ear picked up on it in the middle of play, the delicate counterpoint of several songs being sung at the same time, one song now dominant, now subordinate, was a wonderful metaphor.

Tony turned on the tape deck, his tight buns staring at Gregg. The playroom was suddenly full of gentle sounds.

"So come over here, Eight-ball."

Gregg was now sitting astride the sawhorse. His shirt was open to the navel so the dark hair pushed out and the chain between his tit rings was draped across it. Tony walked over and leaned against Gregg, tentatively.

"I know, buddy. You're scared. You're hurt."

Gregg put his arms about Tony's shoulders and held him close. A tear ran from Tony's eye. He didn't bother brushing it away.

"Thanks," Tony answered; then: "I sure need that, Sir."

They kissed again, this time for a long stretch.

"Then why don't you get out of those clothes," Gregg instructed him.

And Tony stripped off his guerrilla boots, his jeans, his T-shirt. His nipples showed nicely through his chest hair; they bulged with signs of heavy working. Tony lifted weights and had nice pecs; they pushed his nipples out yet further. "Nipples and pecs, Nipples and pecs"; James Broughton could have composed a wonderful ditty on their exquisite joys. Some even said that it was those nipples and pecs that had got Eight-ball his job as bartender at Castro Station. After stripping off his clothes, Tony pulled his guerrilla boots back over his thick wool socks, lacing them carefully. Like many horny guys, he loved getting his butt worked with those wonderful boots in the stirrups of the sling. Besides, he knew how much Gregg loved to lick boot while he worked butt.

Tony felt more confident now; he walked across to Gregg directly, straddled one of his leather-clad legs, and put his arm about him. Gregg had stripped off his shirt, replacing it with the leather vest. Black arm bands wrapped his biceps.

Tony reached for Gregg's lips with his own, and for Gregg's nipple with his right hand. He slipped his left hand between Gregg's vest and his back. They began kissing, Tony's fingers rubbing the ring in Gregg's nipple, drinking one another, affection poured like wine, each rub of hot flesh sending thrills through the other. Despite more than a year with AIDS, Gregg's body was still muscular, full of sexual vitality. It had the same lankiness, the same thick tangle of hair, heavily touched with gray.

"Tony. I want you to record this evening. I want you to put a clean tape in the video and turn it on before we start playing. Then I want you to forget it's there, taking a special message to the future."

With his right arm, Gregg circled Tony's waist, slipping his fingertips into the moist crack of Eight-ball's butt. Gregg stroked it with his index finger. He knew how much Eight-ball needed this special form of loving from the most special of buddies. Tony shivered as Gregg stroked him, and the shiver broke their kissing for just an instant, then set it going again with even more passion.

"I want your hole, buddy." Gregg told him. "I want to spread your legs and work that hole open and slide my fist in there and work it slow and gentle and then hard all at the same time. I want to work your butt so your gut and mind scream for more."

"Oh, do it to me, Sir. God, how I want you in me again Sir."

Gregg guided Tony backwards into the sling, lifting his butt a little, ensuring it was pushed out just the right distance over the edge of the sling, making sure the stirrups for his feet were at just the right height, making certain neck and head were comfortable. Gregg stroked the hairy, muscular legs, Then, he unrolled skin-tight latex gloves over his hands and halfway up his forearms. With Tony watching him intently, Gregg greased them carefully with one of the water-soluble lubes that was loaded with viricide. He smeared the lube up and down the gloves until they glistened. He formed a fist and then showed it to Tony. Tony stroked it, then leaned forward and kissed it. "When I do you, Eight-ball," Gregg told him, "I want you to not just think of me. I want you to remember that man who initiated you in a Chicago bar with that eight-ball up your hole. I want you to remember how he loved you."

As Gregg made love with Tony, the tears stopped, and the tears started again. He was full of memories of the many men he had played with, times before; dozens of beautiful men from across the world. Many of those men were dead or dying. He held back the sorrow and smiled and allowed the joy of it to take him over. Gregg thought of their many different characters and emotions. He used the happiness of his memories to set himself free, translating it into this love for the cosmic Eight-Ball. And as that transformation happened, Gregg rediscovered in himself that despite AIDS, he was still whole, and that his death, whatever it brought, would never shatter that wholeness. His bitterness towards Allan shifted to a sadness, even to a sympathy. He thought of a lonely lover who found it so very hard to deal with the terrible fragility of life.

Meanwhile, Tony drifted in and out of a wonderful eternity, a sort of fetal basket, wrapped in loving, sensual vibrations, and reaching out about him to a cosmos where stars, alone and in clusters, twinkled on distant velvet horizons. When he looked up from the sling towards Gregg, he saw this tall, sexy man with a rebel cap pulled down and shading his eyes and the lines of a beard across his face. He sensed this compassionate top, full of strength through sadness. He saw a man to whom he wanted to give himself completely. And Gregg's devotion of Tony's boots only made Tony want to yield even more.

He closed his eyes and thought of the first time Gary had fisted him, a basement playroom in Chicago. He hadn't believed it would have been possible. Tony had already been Gary's slave for six months. He had spent many willing weekends stripped and shackled, awaiting Gary's commands or pleasures. He had learned how beautiful it can be to step out from under his own ego and hand himself over to another man's complete instruction. He trusted Gary. He would never had done it if he had not believed in, respected Gary. Gary had honored that trust. At the end of every weekend, when he set him free, Gary always reminded Tony: "Go and be your own man again. I love you as my slave but I also respect your free will. A true man learns to respect that will and knows its limits." Oh how he learned from that man to give. Oh God, how much he owed to that man who had passed on only two nights ago. Tony began to cry again, and let his sadness be swept into and blended with the warmth of Gregg.

30 *City Hall, Saturday Morning*

The Mayor convened her press conference at ten A.M.
Saturday morning in a state of quiet fury.

"What took place last evening in this city," she said,
"Is totally inexcusable."

Unlike a famous predecessor, this Mayor rarely
sported large bows from the neck of her blouse. Today,
perhaps, to deliberately remind her audience of that no-
nonsense attitude, perhaps because it made her look sterner,
she wore a large black bow.

"I wish to make it very clear from the outset that
behavior of this sort in this city, and I refer to deliberate
arson of government and private buildings and murder of
citizens, will not be tolerated."

Behind her, in single file, shoulder to shoulder
were over a dozen community leaders, hands folded
over their chests or at their sides. They watched gravely
into the cameras. Behind them, on standards, were the
Bear Flag of California and the rising phoenix of the
city flag. Discretely, someone had removed the Stars
and Stripes.

"I want to begin by making it very clear that all of
us are fully aware of the grave injustices that appear to have
been committed against citizens of this nation. These
have not been fully proven, and we await their investigation by Congress and in courts of law. The very
suggestion that these injustices occurred has hurt and
embittered us. There is little doubt on that matter. But

bitterness is no excuse for the destructive and criminal activities that occurred in San Francisco last night."

She paused for effect. Several cameras switched to the lineup behind her. They included the President of the Board of Supervisors, and Asian supervisor Tom Leong, the black community leader, the Reverend Lincoln Benjamin and the Latino Supervisor Jesus Arguello. Allan Bennett, in pinstripe suit and maroon silk tie, stood second from the left. The Mayor had long ago endorsed his candidacy for DA. She wanted Harrison's defeat as strongly as he did.

"Let me say once again," the Mayor continued, "that this city believes grave injustices may have taken place. Yesterday evening, the President of the Board of Supervisors announced some extremely strong stands this city has agreed to undertake on behalf of the wronged. We remain committed to our stand. San Francisco has repeatedly warned the President not to visit at this time. If he continues to insist on doing so, and this is a free country, on his arrival in this county he will be arrested by city authorities. We have already warned the President of this, but we have yet to receive a reply.

"Official actions taken by the city and county of San Francisco under its charter, and the laws and Constitution of the State of California, are one thing. They are measures of appropriate response. Vigilante actions, taken by citizens with firebombs and shotguns are quite a different matter. They will *not* be tolerated. I must make this very clear.

"No doubt you have observed the group of men and women lined up behind me. They represent many of the city's communities. Some are elected officials. Others are running for office. Still others are community leaders. These individuals have agreed to be here to show their support for the concerns I have expressed. They have read my statement and they have signed it as a public endorsement of my intentions to maintain law and order."

Meanwhile, the cameras were scanning the lineup, from right to left, halting on each face. Captions appeared on the screen stating names and affiliations.

"I also want to make it clear to the people of this city that we shall track down and prosecute those responsible for last night's actions."

The cameras focused on Allan. He looked grave, serious. He would be responsible for the prosecutions. He must show complete solidarity with her honor.

"When I refer to last night," the Mayor clarified, "I speak both of those that firebombed the Federal Building, and those who massacred people on Castro Street. We shall be relentless in our pursuit of these criminals and justice will be brought to bear. I want to emphasize that Mr. Bennett, a candidate for the public office of DA, agrees with me 100 percent on this matter."

The cameras finally moved off Allan and back to the Mayor. She raised her hands a little to indicate she had only a small amount more to say.

"These are not," she commented, "the easiest of times. Over the next few days we must stick together. San Franciscans must put their faith in their city government as we officially attempt to embark on the road to justice. I know the city will not find this easy. Our citizens will not react kindly to the imposition of military police as the President appears to be planning, for the security of his visit. But we must remain cool and come through with honor. There must on no account be further extremist or vigilante actions of the type we observed last night."

Behind the Mayor, her supporters broke into strong applause.

31 *Spring Valley, Maryland, Saturday Afternoon*

Seamless webs are wonderful creations. The universe can become a series of concentric spheres, each enclosing the other so that the soul lies at the very center. Projected on the outermost spheres are God's universal expectations and revelations, clear to the devoted. Every action in one of the more inner spheres, actions by governments and peoples, by organizations and churches and by individuals, actions by each person at the center of their own concentric universe, are reflections of the larger enclosing purposes of God. Of course these actions differ in their nature. Some are statements, affirmations of the universal truths. They underlie the justice and righteousness of God's holy patterns, whether they be the actions of a congregation, a child or a president. Other actions also reverberate through these heavenly spheres. They warn us of evil that forever lurks, like the serpent, ready to tempt with its betraying fruit. But while actions of evil and immorality, statements against God's righteousness, while these may shake the spheres, they do not shatter them. Indeed, they strongly reinforce God's truths. That is why the web remains seamless.

For years, Jo-Lyn's web had been the source of her deepest security. There was nothing that had ever happened, from the little injustices to Ed's occasional mistreatment of her, from the untimely death of her parents to her brother's fall to the devil, there was nothing that could not be rationalized into Jo-Lyn's worldview. Even Ed's mistreatment by the church and their betrayal in his run for bishop, these too were part of God's plans.

But there are dangers in a seamless web, when it shifts or breaks. When a web cracks, it can drive the soul, caught in the innermost circle, towards insanity.

It was early afternoon in Washington and Jo-Lyn was near breaking. She had never felt so humiliated. She had plugged in the phone to make a call, only to have it ring in her hands. He claimed to be an agent from *Playboy*. Would she tell all in an exclusive interview? She presumed they wanted her to bare all. Shaking, she had slammed down the phone and pulled out the plug.

Once again, Jo-Lyn wired herself to the television screen. She never really liked or watched the game shows and people like Donahue and Oprah Winfrey were dangerous radicals. Since Ed's arrest, the news channel had offered some kind of hope. Of course the announcers never stopped harping like carrion birds at supposed injustices and wrongdoings. They talked as if they wanted to pick away at the flesh of the President and his supporters, to pull this flesh off live, to consume it in his face.

Hourly, the news brought grimmer reactions. Allied nations withdrawing ambassadors. Proposed trade embargos. The fall of the dollar. Hourly, there were snapshots from across America. The burned out Federal Building in San Francisco. Evidence the CIA had run a supersecret genetic engineering lab near Port-au-Prince. The name of a retired biologist, USO, who had supervised the Zaire experiments known now by their official name: OPERATION MACACQUE. Short interviews with the presidents of NOW and the NAACP, (where the heck was the Eagle Forum or the Christian Voice?). Jo-Lyn waited patiently through all this for the slightest shred of hope.

Could there be a report on Ed's whereabouts? Perhaps his impending release? Would they find it had been a Russky plot? Would some brave, righteous, God-fearing preacher come forth to finally defend the whole program as moral and necessary, as it certainly had been? Would even the President come forth and finally say that? Jo-Lyn waited, each shift of the television frame hinting at new hope. In ten minutes, Mr. President would make a nationwide address.

The first tiny cracks in Jo-Lyn's seamless universe had come with Carolyn's birth. All of them in the Fellowship profoundly believed in the immediacy of the Day of Judgment. To members of the Fellowship, world affairs were now those of Armageddon: responsible political actions should account for that. The inevitable nuclear holocaust would mark the Opening of the Seven Seals. Jo-Lyn could accept that for herself and for Ed; it was all God's great plan. But somehow she could never really believe the same end for innocent Carolyn. Was she merely being softhearted? Carolyn's purity would undoubtedly pass the Judgment. In His great wisdom, Carolyn's future bliss was most certainly accounted for. Yet Jo-Lyn could still not understand the fairness of bringing down the Holocaust on the meek, whatever they would inherit. In the end, however, she managed to push these doubts aside, and even though they came forward from time to time, she could dismiss them as her own fears, her own natural motherliness towards a child. Thus the impending cracks closed again, and Jo-Lyn's seamless web remained whole.

When the President of the United States appeared on the screen, Jo-Lyn was fondling the hand-gun. She was rarely separated from it now. She could be suspected as an ally of her husband, a possible betrayer of classified secrets (of which she was completely unaware), or the object of harassment by some radical fag group.

Years ago, when Ed had hinted to her about his role in the CIA, he had shown her his several revolvers. He had told her about the sometimes dangerous predicaments CIA men found themselves in. It was not fair to tell her other-wise. Ed showed her where the guns and the ammunition were cached: The standard revolver was kept in the bed-side table. The hard plastic gun, a more recent development to evade metal detectors, was hidden behind a loose ceiling tile, third row from the end in the basement rec room. He showed her how to load each gun and set its catch, should she ever be in danger in his absence. He had even encouraged her to take up target practice, discretely, once a week at a range over in Virginia. After six months, Jo-Lyn was quite good.

Since Ed's arrest she had kept the hard plastic gun and its exploding bullets with her at all times. The CIA had already, in her absence, searched the house several times. They had taken the other revolver from the bedside table. Or was it press people who had plundered their private lives? She held the gun in her lap, stroking the shaft. It was reassuring.

The President, flanked by the Stars and Stripes, was also backed by a contingent of conservative leaders. There was the head of the Eagle Forum, and beside her, the octongenerian senator from North Carolina whose proposed legislation would root out all homosexuals and put them in camps. To the far right was the tele-vision evangelist who had already masterminded two takeover coups against his competitors, and rumor had it, was out for a third. He sat side by side with an Idaho senator, a Mormon bishop who agreed politically but not religiously with him. Jo-Lyn wondered whether this lineup was an attempt to counter the rumor that some moderate Republican had thrown out on *Night Line* the previous evening: the whole business of this AIDS plot was a fabrication of the extreme right and the CIA to discredit the President, even to have him murdered in San Francisco. Yes, Jo-Lyn decided the lineup was impressive.

She was glad to see them all there. Finally, something positive was going to be said.

Following Ed's arrest, much larger cracks had appeared in Jo-Lyn's web. There were times she could barely bring herself to believe that the CIA was really protecting their own. Yet these little delusions kept collapsing. Ed was being rebuked, and as his wife, she knew it. What had been good, noble, honorable actions, carried out in the service of God, actions in which they all supposedly believed, were being put down and rebuked. And the most incredible thing was that put-downs, expected from the liberals, the anti-Christs and the Satan worshipers, also came from those individuals who constituted the pillers of her own seamless web, those uprights that had until now linked her personal convictions to those of God's purposes.

Why just listen to the President at this very moment! She tapped the shaft of the revolver against the palm of her hand, several times, impatiently.

"Citizens of America," he told them. "You know just how much I believe in the moral and Christian renewal of our great nation. Citizens of America. You know how strongly I fought, and successfully, to put God and prayer back into our schools."

At this point, the platform party applauded.

"Thank you," he told them graciously, as if the people of America had applauded. "Citizens of America, I want you to understand that these great men and women who are on the platform with me today are here to lend support for what I have to say. I want you to know how much I appreciate that."

It seemed everything that Jo-Lyn could have hoped for; it wanted to send her universe soaring again. But she knew, in the pit of her gut, that she couldn't hope so easily.

"Citizens, you know how strongly I've fought perversion, sexual license, abortion, drug abuse, and pornography, all crimes that attempt to destroy America from within. You also know how strongly we've fought together against the evils of communism by attacking their beachheads in Southern Africa, Central America, Afghanistan, even some of our Pacific isles. Ladies and gentlemen, all of you know how committed I am to what is decent, wholesome and American.''

He paused. There was applause from the platform party, growing to a standing ovation.

Asshole, Jo-Lyn told herself. Here it comes. He supports it all, but not Ed.

The President continued. ''We will continue to fight for goodness and justice and God's will. We will fight at home and abroad. America must be seen as God's faithful missionary, as His Angel Moroni, so to speak.''

At this point he turned to acknowledge the senator from Idaho.

''Yet there are certain actions that we Americans will not undertake, however strong our beliefs. Here and now, I categorically swear before God, we would not and we will not undertake the systematic murder of our own citizens. We may disagree with them. We may pass laws to criminalize their activities or to restrict their movement. But the final judgment on their lives is not the responsibility of Congress and this administration, but the task of God. I want to make it absolutely clear that a vicious and evil plot has been perpetrated against this administration and the people of the United States of America. It is a plot that almost succeeded.''

He paused again giving the impression of being under incredible pressure. Directly behind him sat his good friend, a famous Hollywood actor, with a face like a tombstone. Next to the actor, the Secretary of State appeared slightly more relaxed, but still tense.

''Who connived this plot to attempt to destabilize the

United States?'' the President asked. ''Fortunately we have the notorious Ed Stevens in secret custody, and his questioning by the CIA has revealed some answers. About an hour ago, the Director of the CIA informed me that we now have confidential but reliable evidence on the matter. At least part of that evidence indicates that Ed Stevens was a double agent for the Soviet Union.''

Jo-Lyn almost collapsed. It was a shameless allegation that Ed, her husband, a loyal American, could have worked for the commies. Those creeps in the White House were just trying to protect their own butts.

Her seamless web had started to crack when her friends and church community had pulled away their support. Gaping cracks were now opening with these accusations against her husband. Accusations she knew were ludicrous, were totally fabricated. (They could torture anything out of anybody.) And they were accusations by people that had long been pillars of her philosophical universe. Her world seemed very shaky, at best.

Jo-Lyn fondled the gun. She ignored the President's condemnation of the San Francisco riot the previous evening. She barely acknowledged his refusal to be intimidated by a city with a known commie government; the military would protect him as was proper and required. No, Jo-Lyn just fondled the gun and sat dumbfounded. She thought of putting the weapon to her head—a trigger pulled, a blinding end. Then she thought of little Carolyn. God would never forgive Jo-Lyn if she abandoned her child to the vipers of this world.

32 *Guerrero Street, San Francisco, Saturday Morning*

The meeting room was tense. Sure, as always, there was a certain otherworldliness to it, the votive candles flickering along the floor under the ever-growing list of names, the shadows in the corners of the windowless room, the rituals of passage through locked doors. It was easy in a way to come here and believe that one was part of a hypothetical conspiracy. But today, there were less than twenty-four hours to zero hour. Nervous anticipation gripped each one of them. Would their plot work? Would the Secret Service outfox them? Had their planning been discovered? Was it adequate to achieve their ends? In several days, world events had spun relentlessly beyond their every conception. It was as if some larger purpose were playing into their hands. The CIA plot and the facilities used to carry it out had been revealed. Foreign governments had withdrawn ambassadors. San Francisco had erupted in an unprecedented explosion. The President was under siege and trying to blame it on the Soviets. They had every reason to continue with their plans. But had their planning been good enough?

Gregg watched silently as Jim made the final review of their efforts. Jim looked wasted this morning, haggard, as if he hadn't been eating or sleeping. Eating was evidently very difficult for him, he had sarcoma lesions and heavy thrush down the inside of his esophagus. His voice had dropped from its normal pitch to a sort of faint, raspy whine. In other circumstances he would probably have been hospitalized. Gregg wondered if Jim would even make it through to tomorrow. But he was a tough character and he had to: it was his plot and there was only another day. Jim deserved to see success.

Jim talked about the phone relays. Calls to other numbers who would then call here. He reviewed code words and phrases. Observers, placed in key locations, including press vehicles, would apprise them of the President's progress. The team core, he and Sam, would be upstairs, watching, waiting. Most of this, Jim explained, was merely monitoring. There was little they could do to change things. All they could do was wait and watch. The real task lay in the aim of the two marksmen. There would be warning rings to them, depending on which entrance the President's party would use. They were warned to keep telephones muffled. Neither Gregg nor his fellow accomplice were to make or answer any phone calls.

"Sam spent last night in Vacaville," Jim told them. "The trucks and weapons are here. You should be down there about one o' clock to help unload."

Tom, the ex-cop, reviewed the final news on curfews. It was mostly information already released to the press. At five P.M. today, the army would seal off the area between the Embarcadero and Fifth Street and between Market and Bryant. (That's why it's important we get down there early, and out, Jim had told them.) After that, all residents will be required to produce ID and all traffic will be diverted. A curfew of six P.M. will apply to the rest of South of Market. And a general curfew of eleven o'clock will apply to the whole city.

"What about San Francisco police?"

Tom laughed. "You think the White House is going to allow us near the Presidential party? After the Mayor announced she'll arrest him? He'll be protected by army people all the way. There won't be any DA or sheriff waiting at the Embarcadero when his helicopter sets down from

Alameda. The army won't allow it. As for the SFPD, they're
scheduled for normal duty elsewhere in the city.

God damn it, Gregg thought. Talk about setting up
a city for outright rebellion. It was like rubbing the noses
of hurt people in yet further shit. This morning, on the way
to Jim's, he had once more had some doubts. The doubts
grew out of last night with Eight-ball, an experience so
invigorating, so full of the intensity that Gregg had cherished
in his life. Tony, after crying with passion and joy and the
tragedy of it all mixed together, had fisted Gregg for nearly
two hours. Gregg had gone up and over the wall and into
a different land where there was a new dawn rising among
the shiny leaves and the morning birds sang to fading stars
in a velvet sky. When he had come down and hugged Tony,
long and hard, when he had finally tried to sleep, he found
himself remarkably relaxed. Gregg wasn't afraid of what he
had to do. Rather, his doubts rested on the reasons he had
devised to justify it.

His attention slipped again to the names on the wall.
He saw Tony Perles, Chuck Solomon, and Michael Palladino.
There were Karl Stewart and Phil Benefield and Ricardo
Souza. He saw Carl Lind and Dan Jeansone. Every name
stung. He thought of Mark Joplin and Mac Mackinnon,
dedicated, wonderful men. God knows, he himself could
be on that list in less than forty-eight hours. That was the
way this damned disease worked. God's damned magic
bullet. The wall dissolved into a blur of names. Lost brothers.
Murdered by an agency that regarded them as un-American.
No, the spite towards Allan had only been a small spark in
his motives. It was these dead brothers and sisters that
counted. He had to do it for them. There were so many
reasons to do it. Just the way they dared to come here, all
the President's men, to come and grind this city under their
heels.

In his mind he could see the burned-out shell of the

Federal Building. It should never be rebuilt. Its walls should be carved with names, cut into the charred stone. Ivy should be planted. Inside the shell, walkways and gardens should be laid out. It would become San Francisco's Wailing Wall. He thought of the city's indignation. Just earlier that morning, he and Tony had watched the Mayor on television. Allan was there in the middle of it. Christ, just what did they expect the crowd to do, swear the bloody Oath of Allegiance? The city had no intention of prosecuting anyone for burning the Federal Building, he knew that. It was all election hype.

About 11:45, after appropriate signals, the door to the basement room was unlocked and Peter Steinman entered. He passed two small vials to Jim.

"Harvested barely an hour ago," he told them. "Excellent titer of virus activity. As far as possible the vials should be kept near body temperature."

"Yeah," someone joked. "Up Gregg's butt."

33 *The Fairmont Hotel, San Francisco, Late Morning*

Christine was giving him a rough time and Allan was pleased. He needed some waking from these snits into which he occasionally allowed himself to fall.

"Damn it, Bennett. We all know he's going to bring up last night's riot. But it's not going to mean much."

Allan had caught himself in a sort of self-deprecating rut, as if it had been his failure to control the crowd at the rally. As if every swing voter in the city would vote Harrison instead of Bennett because of Allan's failure.

"Things haven't changed one bit," Christine told him. "They wouldn't have changed if you had never gone to the Mayor's press conference this morning."

"Law and order," Allan reiterated. "That's the first thing Harrison's going to hit. We need city officials who can maintain control. This guy Bennett will never be able to effect the needed control."

Christine put her cup down. They were in the back corner of the coffee shop at the Fairmont Hotel. In about twenty minutes they would cross the lobby for a special luncheon meeting of the Chamber of Commerce.

"Listen, buster! They blame this whole damn thing on you. The burned-out Federal Building. The coming imposition of martial law. What the hell do you expect, Bennett? You're too close to your vote getting. People in this city can't believe things went off as lightly as they did! People are reasonable. The anger is justifiable. And it's a federal issue, not a local one. It doesn't change your standing here."

"How do you know? We don't have any polls."

"Listen, Allan! I follow the press. I have lots of people watching, listening. The issue is hardly law and order, although I know Harrison will push that. The issue is justice. Oh sure, tell them you believe in law and order. Applied with fairness. The Chamber will go for that. But what we've got to do is hit home with the injustice that Harrison would bring. And now we've got that evidence, haven't we?"

Yeah, there was the positive emphasis he had to make: a diverse city working together, drawing tourists. A peaceful, stable, business-first community. We had always been able to prove that San Francisco could survive in the modern business world while maintaining quality of life.

"I want to make sure you're up on this release you're going to make." Christine was persistant, and it helped.

Harrison would probably start by attacking him on some of the chickenshit items. WALTER HARRISON. CHEAT. DOUBLECROSSER. DIRTY TRICKS. The arrangement was that Harrison would speak first. Would he be belligerent enough to jump ahead and condemn this literature that hadn't even come out? (Christine had secretly intervened last night to ensure that Fraggi's layout never reached the printer.) Should Allan admit it at all, pointing to Harrison red-handed with stolen goods? No, the phony condemnations were enough. Let them linger while the audience concentrated on the true dirt.

"Start out subtly, carefully," Christine told him. "This is a full-front attack. Like SPUR, the Chamber isn't thrilled by attacks. But if you make it reasonable, believable, if you make it seem like it's such a perversion to their everyday, working conception of the world, then you're ahead."

Good. Let Harrison do the screaming that Allan Bennett had called him liar! Cheat! Thief! Who said what? Where? Prove it! A scrap of paper with no official connection to the Bennett campaign unless he wants to admit to the press that it was an early draft produced by some junior campaign worker and quickly vetoed. This is almost enjoyable, Allan conjectured, this setting up of the morally righteous just to see their outrage.

"Emphasize how important it is to know just who backs who," Christine continued to brief him. "Just who pulls the strings and expects the payoffs."

"Point one," she said, checking about her for potential spies. "Point one is that over 80 percent of Harrison's campaign donations come from groups on the far right and mostly from out-of-state, if not out of the city. You might point out the amount of money

Harrison's been spending with his 'Return to Decency' television commercials, for example.

"Some of the groups we've traced among the contributors. The Christian Voice Moral Government Fund in Pacific Grove. The Eagle Forum in Illinois. The Committee for Freedom in Virginia Beach. The Moral Majority in Lynchburg, Virginia did a fund-raising direct-mail drive that netted thirty-five thousand dollars for Harrison's campaign."

Emphasize the fairness issue, Allan thought. This is the city and county of San Francisco. These groups may have member's here, but are the politics and issues of these groups those of San Francisco? Just where do Mr. Harrison's loyalties lie? Was Harrison to be a pawn of powers elsewhere?

"Point two," Christine continued. "After the fairness issue. San Franciscans participating in San Francisco politics. Mention some of the groups and causes these supporters represent. Don't seem too strident. Remember, this is the Chamber of Commerce. Besides, your best part is still to come. These groups. They're anti-ERA. Anti-civil liberties for anyone except those who believe in exactly what they do. They want a Christian society based on their interpretations of their beliefs. Here are some quotes from people like Pat Robertson and Tim LaHaye that you might want to work in."

She handed Allan a couple of Xeroxed pages, their texts marked up with yellow highlighter.

Yeah, Allan thought. Emphasize the divisiveness this would bring San Francisco. The further turmoil. How we've worked hard and long to build tolerance and respect between communities. How productive this had been to the city.

"Point three. This is the real clincher. Connections and contradictions between the donors."

At the door to the coffee shop she could see Al Leong from the Chamber searching for them. It must be almost time.

"Begin with the simple. The Unification Church and its donations. Insinuate the Jim Jones affair. Connections between the Moonies and Christian Voice and the World Anti-Communist League. Then the connections with the American Values Forum. And their ties to the John Birch Society and to neo-Nazi, pro-Aryan groups in Idaho and Montana. Then the connections with the Klan."

Leong had seen them. He was halfway across the room.

"That's the big card for you to play. Imagine, a black man, receiving money from groups like the Klan. Just what sort of hypocrite is this man? Just who has control over him?"

Yeah, Allan thought, he would push that. Just what sort of hidden agenda *did* Harrison have? He shivered at the thought.

Al Leong was virtually at the table as Christine passed Allan some final sheets.

"We'll be right there, Al," she told him. "Ready in a second."

Allan turned and shook hands with Leong.

"Read over these sheets while you're waiting, Allan. The underlined sections are crucial. You may want to quote them. The president of the American Values Forum had had some interesting things to say from time to time, including what should be done to this country's blacks, Hispanics and Asians, let alone homosexuals."

Al Leong's interest appeared to perk up, but he didn't say anything. He continued his joviality towards Allan, then shook Christine's hand.

"We're ready!" Christine announced. "Let's go!"

34 *South of Market, San Francisco, Saturday Noon*

Gregg knew that this would be his last motorcycle ride; he sensed it and was sad.

If he had really been doing it right he would have made the trip in full leather, his lace-up knee-high black boots and chaps, a leather shirt; even a chain on his jacket. Proper attire for the significance of this last odyssey through what they had once called the Valley of the Knights. Last night, he loved one final time and with every bit of the essence that leather meant to him. There had been titwork and assplay and slapping and loving that were intense and inescapable. Today he had to be inconspicuous.

He pulled the bike into northbound Guerrero Street, ran up the hill and waited behind a van for the light to change at Duboce. A beat-up Lincoln pulled up beside him, teenagers gawking. Him or his bike? Someone mouthed the word faggot, and they sped on, even before the light had changed. He ignored them. They were irrelevant.

Gregg turned right into Duboce, then down the hill and under the freeway. He felt stoned. How many times had he made this trip? Mission to South Van Ness. South Van Ness to Folsom, Left on Folsom. Now it was like all his life was spinning in front of him, in the way people talk about it unreeling in the throes of death. Maybe it was just that he was tired. Maybe it was some of the coke from the night before. No, there was something unreal about all this. Something real and unreal. The posts were plastered with painted decals. CIAIDS. US OUT OF SAN FRANCISCO. KILL

FAGGOTS. He didn't need to move to feel the lump in his shirt pocket, buried under his black motorcycle jacket, that was the vial of cultivated HIV. Unreal. The virus that was killing him and half the joy of California, one by one. The virus that would finally hit home in the target it so richly deserved.

The light changed before he reached Folsom and there was no oncoming traffic. He took the curve in a continuous sweep; it was what he best loved about this motorcycle as an extension of his body. The slightest shift in muscle or limb and his machine responded in continuous, sweeping motions as it did on Sierra highways, coming down the great curves from Miwok to Sonora, or the descent from Tollhouse to Prather, or the long, winding rides through the oak woodlands below, where in little hollows, cottonwoods are tucked into stream crossings, and lacelike gray pine break the monotony of the oaks. Those had been trips to runs, many of them: Satyrs and Barbary Coasters and SFGDIs and Constantines. All these trips came back to this street and to its memories, this street from all worlds and to all destinations, the Leather Mile.

Here was the Oasis, a straight, yuppy hangout that had been in its lifetime so many places. The Covered Wagon and the Leatherneck and the Drummer Key Club and even for a while the Gold Coast. They had laughed at the Leatherneck, some of them. Stand and Stare, they had called it. One of those places where the Castro queens who supposedly got dressed up in leather came down to pose. But Gregg doubted whether this was really so much the case, whether it was more a sort of South-of-Market put-down. He'd met lots of hot men there, men who were still friends (if they were alive). He'd met some of them on the crowded sidewalk after closing.

And there across the street, its venerable old sign desecrated in pink graffiti, the bar that had been Febes, one of the oldest on the Mile, with such a rich history of club meetings and friendships that even the television news touched on its closing, and those that always remember, those at the Ambush, held a retrospective in honor of that warp in time, that bar that reached back into the days of the first gay bike clubs, those days of awakening hopes among forebrothers that were to explode in the Empress Jose's run for Supervisor in the west, and Stonewall in the east. Paradise Garage, the hot pink letters screamed now like an obscenity; the bar was no more than a cheap overflow to the Oasis. Oh Christ, how many times in riding past what had been Febes had Gregg felt so cheated that he could have firebombed the place.

Was it really a conspiracy, these yuppy straights, taking over this sacred turf? He had to remind himself that they could be friends, that they often were. Was it opportunism, the shifting economic conditions? One couldn't run small, low-key bars in an area with increasing rents and absurd insurance rates. Or without heavy tourism. AIDS had helped to cut that support. Sure, yuppy straights could at times be tacky, but he had a sense that they were more bewildered. Some of them had secretly admired the gay community. Some of them actually had gay friends and shared in gay hopes and enthusiasms for new ways of life. Some of them had learned how to let go, to indulge. Others had even tried to emulate the gay community's free and easy life-style. Now they were frightened, aghast at the course AIDS had taken. But many were too frightened to feel anything else. The South of Market straight club scene had taken off with a bang and fizzled; it showed little sign of taking off again.

Gregg stopped at Tenth.

Down there had been the Arena and the Stud and Chaps and the Ambush. He could never forget the Ambush and the dreams it held between its walls. He had met Tony

there. Not Eight-ball, but that other Tony who long ago
introduced him to the club scene back in the days of places
like Folsom Prison and the Boot Camp. Back when those
sleazy parties like the Warlock's Witches Christmas or CMC
Carnival in the basement of (how appropriate) Seamens
Hall down on Fremont Street, parties that drew brothers
from all over North America, flying in, riding in, to be here
along the Leather Mile. Tony was dead now, but he had
given Gregg one of his greatest gifts: how to ride a bike as
part of one's self.

That was the era Gregg had come out into leather.
Leather was not a rebirth of his Vietnam psychoses. He hated
those memories. They were as cold and as unappealing
sexually as he could ever have believed. Maybe he had gone
into the marines with some yearnings for brotherhood. But
he had felt above that, he had disdained it. He was a leader,
whether or not they made him one. He was a hero to himself.
He had never expressed his latent homosexuality, least of
all his leather desires in Vietnam although he sure fucked
the Oriental women. But coming with an uptight ass is like
having tea and cakes, possibly meaningful in other contexts.

When people like his now-dead friend Tony introduced him to leather in places like Folsom Prison and the
Bolt, Gregg was discovering a new world of companionship
that had strength. Men gave themselves and took possession
of others and exchanged their souls because they respected
each other, as far as that was humanly possible. It was not
becuase they were in the same fucking war together that
demanded brutality and might tolerate affections as
something to make conditions more bearable. It was like
boots. Boots in the leather world were a sign of hard work,
of the hard top, of the submission linked to self-respect.
Boots in Vietnam were shit and slime-covered devices of torture and feet screaming with the confinement of heat and
rot. In Vietnam boots were not to worship. Today they were

made to be adored. When Gregg fucked today he tried not to think of Vietnam and its images. Sure, deep underneath he may have longed for leather experience, but the war was not his motivation. He discovered his drive for it on streets like this one.

A block away is the Powerhouse. Gregg remembered it as the Bolt and the Brig, its predecessors. A Wednesday night TAIL party. The first fist in his butt given by that incredible Catholic priest who just glowed with magic fire and Gregg wanting it but scared, and knowing he could take it, but scared, and this man finally going that last tiny inch, smoothing those muscles open, so that Gregg would never go back, so that he came alive to part of himself that had long been buried. There he was, real and whole and feeling as wonderful as ever, a happy spirit as he could never have allowed himself to be.

That was what had been so important about this Leather Mile, that it had sustained a more intense fraternity, men with new joy in their lives and new dreams in their hands. It was undeniably gay, yes, and as an experience it would never fail to support the larger transitions happening in the city. But there was something separate, special about the being that came to be associated with the Mile. It was a seeing: if gay was stepping out beyond western society, then leather was a stepping stone out beyond the self.

It wasn't just the leather for Gregg, it was all the things it changed in him. The self-realization he had never had before. The caring, loving men he had interacted with. Oh sure, there had been those strained lonely nights, the times he'd drunk too much or played cruising games he was now ashamed of, but leather was so much more. Every way of life has its ups and downs and excesses and rough edges. It was that proud feeling of being out in leather, of riding in the Eagle contingent in the Freedom Day Parade, proud as hell that he could love in the way in which he believed and make a better world of it for himself and everybody else.

He stopped again at Ninth.

All of the traffic lights were uncoordinated today. Somewhere up there was where the Black and Blue had been. And Robert Opel's Fey-Way Gallery and 544 Natoma where Peter Hartman had his performance space. That was another important thing about this experience: people saw it not only as living but as art and the Leather Mile had throbbed with persistant people who were damn well going to write and paint and dance and play about the glories and sorrows of their living.

Over there were Ringold Alley and sites of the Trench and the Round Up and the Ramrod. And way back the Handball and the Barracks and the Red Star before the great Folsom Street fire. Memories and faces, souls touching bodies that lingered in the semidarkness. One year, after the Freedom Day Parade, he remembered how the Black and Blue put out their dishes of luscious strawberries on the bar, because it was our celebration and we deserved the best. That was a year Harvey Milk was still alive.

He looked up and down Ninth, waiting for the light to change. He was riding down the runways of his life, and the ghosts were coming back up them towards him. Those songs the drag queens belt out: in Tenderloin bars, South of Market, at the big bike-club shows: Minsky's and Casualty Capers and Folsom Follies. Those songs, full of double entendres for every faggot, leather or otherwise. They were singing them now, coming towards him along the Folsom sidewalks, their gorgeous gowns and grand airs, their arms expostulating the music. "What I did for love." "If you could see me now." (They all knew that song, the theme of the Slot.) "Je ne regrette rien." "Memories." And that most special of songs that had brought them all here: Gregg could swear that Bobbie Wong was standing there on the street corner, singing "Somewhere Over the Rainbow," singing it directly, just to Gregg, so that his eyes filled with tears and the dream of all they had believed in and lived for was alive once more. He, Gregg, might not go on but the dream would not die. Maybe he'd forgotten that for just a little too long. It was like the songs. Were they popular just because they gave the opportunity to create or adulate divas, as if that were all gay people were capable of doing?

Gregg went on with the traffic again, the years catching him at every corner, the memories pinning him down. The Folsom Street Hotel. That German, Rolf, who had almost broken Gregg's relationship with Marc and Allan, a tall wiry man. A top who was so heavy, so demanding, that other times Gregg would have wondered whether or not to trust him. He had never believed he wanted to be a total slave. Yet from the moment they met, at the Catacombs, from those very first slaps across the face that Rolf used as tokens of his affections, to the hours on Rolf's boots, Gregg knew that he would give fully and unquestioningly and he spent most the week of Rolf's vacation collared and serving. He even took a trip to Munich to see Rolf, six months later, but whatever the impassioned letter writing, circumstances were different and it didn't work.

Gregg had come back from Germany to California a little disappointed until he realized that he was whole already.

At that point he had taken Marc and they went hiking in Sierra wilderness. How many knew of Gregg's other passions, of his photography, of his careful work for the Audubon applying his experiences as Forest Service biologist to the battle for the spotted owl? (Christ, how parsimonious they could be about protecting some of nature's most spectacular gifts.) His photography actually wasn't bad; Allan had a few pieces framed and in his office. Yet did it matter that others knew or didn't know of Gregg's different sides. They all had their own. What was important was that he could create them and balance them. It was like that ride back, across the expanses of the Valley, over Altamont, and then across the bridge to this foggy little peninsula. It was a coming home that so clearly condensed and focused the pieces of his life.

At Sixth Street the light was red again. Had the military already taken control of street signals? Across the street was the Slot, barely recognizable now as a repainted Victorian. They were all unrecognizable, the Boot Camp a Chinese restaurant, the Sutro Baths an eratz German nightclub, the Arena a punk nouveau-hideous hangout. Yeah, the grimy, sleazy Slot, almost the heart of the Mile, named for the groove in which the ancient cable cars would turn (South of Market, South of the Slot). The Slot, its vaguely identifiable peace sign suggesting making love, nor war. (What the hell were they fighting now?) For many perhaps, as for Gregg, the Slot was one of those places where he had gone in repeatedly but never came out. Years before his meeting with Allan, he'd had his first tentative leather experiences there. He was a little timid, but he was drawn towards it and determined. Three A.M. with a visiting topman who loved to teach. They'd played until noon. Memories of bondage and teased senses that screamed intolerably for release. Gregg saw the man last year in LA. Two weeks before he died.

By the time he'd reached the Moscone Center, Gregg realized that he was tired, very tired. He felt stretched, and his muscles ached. Had he pushed himself too much last night? His chest hurt a little, felt tight. Gregg ignored it. He could feel the vial against his shirt. It was tension. Whatever the outcome, he'd be glad when this whole thing was finished.

The building Sam and Brian were moving into was on Fourth. To get there, he'd have to go around the block containing the Moscone Center: left on Third and back on Howard and left again on Fourth. On most days a lineup of flags in rainbow colors graced the front of the Center. Today they were all gone, replaced with Stars and Stripes. Several army trucks were pulled into the entrance bay, along with a cluster of delivery vehicles.

How ironic, Gregg noted. The Center that in its earliest incarnations had turned city planning and government on end and that had changed forever the course of politics. The Center, named for the slain mayor who represented that very change in politics. There was an eternal glimmer of candlelight along Market Street; Allan and he and Marc, arm in arm, tears in their faces. There were the intense, screaming flames of the burning police cars, the retort of exploding gas tanks, the crashing of glass in bar windows. Fire and despair burned their ways into and out of their hurting lives, sometimes only flickering, threatening in the distance, othertimes stinging with urgency.

Gregg pullled off Fourth and into the private parking lot. A U-Haul van was waiting, with a bunch of guys standing close by, talking. Gregg again felt the pressure of the vial. He was here at last. And he was determined. Getting off the bike seemed like such a natural thing. It seemed only justice that his last great act would take place here, at the end of the Leather Mile.

35 *Vulcan's Stairway, San Francisco, Saturday Afternoon*

Marc had tried to sleep. That hadn't worked, so he had turned to dreaming, taking himself up and over and into the forest. Even that was unsettling. The woods seemed to be burning in all directions. Not a mass of flames, but little bursts of flame, firebrands waved by shadow spirits, coming towards him. He felt uncertain, even threatened. He knew he could hold his own. They could only threaten and that was their power. This was the way evil multiplied, creeping out of the hidden corners, nurtured on little seeds of insufficiency or personal fear. He knew how these forces fed on shadows, slowly intensifying, with every seeming reason at their outset. They only appeared strong by congregation. History never stopped itself, it told the same hard tales over and over. The forests were always busy.

As a small boy, he'd heard the tales told so many times that they were part of his fiber. He'd understood the stories then as persecution, as an exercise in tyranny. He was taught to perpetuate the resentment, even by Pere Goulet, his first teacher in that single year at Hay River before they moved to Kahntah. The English teacher at Prophet River may have told them differently. But her monarchical leanings made no difference to his father's histories, and the past injustices continued to burn into his heart. That ancient photograph, that yellowed icon of the martyred Riel, still lit Marc's existence with an unreal light. The photograph of the Metis who dared lead active rebellion against the British-Canadians.

Then, as he went into the forest, Marc was brushing away the fire, passing through it. No sounds of Wagner, just the crackle of buckshot in the late March aspens, a month away from leaf. A minority starts with small hopes; it fuels the fears of a majority or of other minorities that hold power. The famous battles on the Saskatchewan were but part of a chain of acts of minority self-definition; the Metis crying for their own land and lives based on the buffalo hunt that was tied to that land. People calling for their own government. At Duck Lake they fought a handful of mounted police, a few impressed volunteers from Prince Albert. The Metis may have won, but their claims were unacceptable and the larger blow waited for them as inevitably as spring. What good were contented and self-proclaimed little republics to an Ottawa with grander plans for their land? Canada was rolling west with its own sense of manifest destiny and its wheels would crush as they rolled. Loyalist Upper Canada was not sympathetic to the right of a ragtag people to determine their own future, unless it was of course, the Loyalist future. Toronto youth were already enlisting to fight the Metis Republic (or rebellion) of St.-Laurent.

So flames burn in the heart, flames of passion that coat the soul, that congeal it. In between, in the cracks the fears grow, nurturing the passions. Some people ignore the fears, grow beyond them. In other people fears rumble ominiously, waiting greater ignition. Still other people disguise the fears, and thus use them. And thus evil grows, from genuine desires, from justified hopes. Men seek power to do good until that power, based on little fears, explodes and consumes them.

The woods shift suddenly; a slightly different place. The weather is different. A solitary man, rifle in his hands, comes through the trees towards Marc. Was it at Duck Lake? The final defeat at Batoche? Marc knew the man instantly:

the icon from above his childhood pallet, the photograph found in every Metis home.

The man looked tired, said nothing. He looked almost crazy, consumed by a dream. They embraced. They kissed, Riel's thick grimy mustache in Marc's beard, the century between them totally irrelevant. They held tight, power shifting nervously between their limbs, feeding, drinking the mutual support both needed in these times of isolation.

Riel said nothing. If there were words spoken in the sprouting trees, in the wind singing in the prairie grasses, Marc doubted they were Riel's words. They had nothing to do with Riel's feelings at the time. This man was confused. Tired. Something of a religious crazy. He could never have accepted what they, here in San Francisco, were trying to build. Riel held the dreams of a people against the relentless intransigence of British tyranny to the only cross they could make for him, the noose awaited at Regina. Marc knew, as he clutched Riel, that this man had seen the end of his road. The wind in the trees, rustling, whispered the elusive dreams, the quickly forgotten dreams of all peoples. The year was 1885.

Marc didn't know whether he yet believed in those causes, any causes. He saw burning police cars. He saw a building wrapped in flame. He heard the anguished screams at Kent State. He heard the wailing of Palestinian refugees. He could taste the gas at Treblinka. He could smell tear gas in Berkeley. The wind, in violent little gusts, flipped over the bleak stones, and the evil beneath each of them flickered awake, the wind fanning the little flames. The little flames grew to meet the big ones already established. To believe in dreams, to want to dream them, that in itself was good enough, it was in the human spirit. But the dreamer, the hunter had to be perpetually on guard.

The tales, the small histories, came and went. Most were forgotten, but little flames still flickered. Some big banks of flames flickered longer, but whether majority or minority, whatever the convoluted social structure, the flames in the cracks were always ready to ignite.

Marc's parting embrace with Riel transformed into new space. The world darkened and he stepped through and out into sunlight and oak woods, hills all about him. Somewhere down the valley mission bells were ringing alarm. His mind followed the shape of the hills. Somewhere in Marin? Sonoma? A few of the peaks were strangely familiar. He felt for their roots but they were so deep that his will slipped and he felt very small. Down there were hot rocks, slipping, grinding, one against the other. Up here this hardness was softened by the illusion of grassland and chaparral over old wounds. Rock faces, occasionally scree, sometimes serpentine, spoke of the millenia of their making. But mostly the cover extolled the here and now, as if the hills were created yesterday and would be gone tomorrow. Only the long eye sensed the deep unyielding beneath these hills, the shadows of a history so deep, that rebellions and causes, big or small, seemed inconsequential. Evil, fanning its little flames, might flicker into blaze in the oak woods and on the hillsides. But in the long run would come to nothing.

If evil was always there, always trying to let itself free, latching onto any cause, petty or big, finding its way into grievances real or illusory, could the hunter ever know what goodness was, other than to be live, to dream? Did good send out its own matching flames, grow its own bonfires, plant its avenues of oaks? When evil finally died, would goodness cloak the hills? The hunter could not know, he could only watch the dark spaces beneath each pebble, each tree stump, each overthrown snag, for the lurking of evil. Otherwise he could look at the hills and feel their strength. He could find humility.

In the valley bells rang out again. Gunshot crackled

in celebration. In Sonoma, the Bear Republic had been declared. Another group of potential oppressors turning against oppression. The year was 1846.

Marc pulled himself out of his dreaming and into the bedroom. It was about three. He felt bewildered, unanswered. He had wanted direction. All he had got was uncertainty and even stranger encounters. He let it all go for another time. He was filled with a sense of urgency. He was needed. He had to get to the Ambush. He didn't know why but he had to get there.

36 *South of Market, San Francisco, Saturday Afternoon*

Gregg hugged Sam. They'd met several times before. He was introduced to Brian who seemed detached. It was as if, on finally seeing the building he and Sam were moving into, Brian wasn't so certain.

"Let's all get going," Sam announced decisively. "If we back the truck in there we can use the service elevator. The manager said the door's unlocked for us."

Sam got into the truck, and with a good deal of guidance, backed it up the narrow laneway. The group of them set to work, full of a sort of giddy tension, knowing they had to do it, knowing the final steps were in place, but saying nothing about personal feelings on the matter.

"What time is it?" Mike asked them as a way of underlining the sense of urgency. He had organized this team of workers.

The building manager, almost apologetically, had

warned Sam of the impending curfew. Sam had told her they were spending the night at friends elsewhere in the city. They'd wait until this whole thing was over to unpack and really move in. But that was where his confidence ended.

While the unloading went well, and quickly, Sam felt a growing uncertainty. They had driven a long road, and now near the end of it, he was having questions. Where would they go tomorrow when the military had broken down the front door and Gregg was under arrest or had been shot? Were these really the best actions for them to take given the recent revelations? What about Brian? He still wasn't certain about Brian's feelings. Brian shouldn't even know about this. He might have been all right last night, but this morning in the truck, all the way from Vallejo, he had been brooding and silent.

Sam's feelings were mixed with the uncertainty both he and Brian had felt many times over the past year. Living with the vagaries of a disease that could shift even in the course of hours, at times things seeming okay, just regular life, then suddenly the grimness of knowing that a consuming hole had opened up about you. But there was something even more threatening about this current anxiety, about its dreadful inevitability, about its vulnerability. Sam wasn't sure why he was so afraid. Was it the chance for hope, a dream of freedom?

He was glad when most of the unloading was done in record time and most of the guys had left. It was only three o'clock. Boxes and empty bookcases clambered towards the ceiling. It was that moment in moving when it seemed doubtful that the apartment could accommodate its new contents. Mike was resting in an arm chair with a cold beer bought at the downstairs store. Gregg and Tom, over in a far corner of the bedroom, were carefully opening the long box shipped by UPS from Boise. Another man, name unknown to Sam, was watching them. Brian had been sent off to clean up the stuff in the cab of the truck. Then, in the scheme of things, Mike was to take Brian to Jim's while Sam returned the truck.

Gregg and Tom had got the box open and Gregg slid out one of the long cylindrical weapons, like guns, but different. He inspected the loading mechanism. He withdrew a small package of darts from the box and inspected several of them. It had been several years since he had used one of these gadgets; they had been streamlined since then, but they basically worked in the same way. Gregg would have liked the luxury of some target practice. It had been over a decade: last time he'd used a dart gun was on a recalcitrant grizzly sow on the Absaroka-Beartooth Wilderness. His aim had always been good, even from a shifting helicopter. Fired at rest, the loaded dart could be effective over more substantial distances.

God damn it, Sam wondered. Where the hell is Brian? He presumed he was waiting in the truck. He wanted to get over to Jim's and relax with a beer. Being here, with these weapons, with the bag of supplies the others had brought for Gregg, with the marksmen handling the weapons, all this was too close to the action for Sam.

Tom had already closed the box and was on the phone. Gregg was carefully explaining the operation of the unboxed weapon to the unnamed man. How to load the dart with the virus solution. How to set the dart in the gun channel. How to set the catch, cock the release. How to prepare standbys in case the first missed.

Mike was in the living room shifting boxes and furniture to create a cleared area about the bay window. Outside, additional army vehicles had arrived at Moscone Center. Some sort of command post was being established.

"I'm on my way," Tom told them, the resealed box under his arm. "It'll be waiting when you get there," he told the unnamed man. "Don't leave getting over there too late."

"I'll begin walking over in ten minutes," the unnamed man told them.

Tom left the apartment. None of them watched his departure. Security at Moscone Center may have seen him leave the building, an oblong package under his arm. He came out of the lobby, stepped into a waiting SFPD cruiser and was taken for a short ride. What the two cops discussed in the police cruiser was uncertain. They may have driven over to Bryant and traveled a number of blocks out of their way. But when Tom was finally let off, under the cover of the tenants' driveway at St. Francis Place, he had only traveled a block from where he had started.

By the time the others set out to leave, locking Gregg behind them into the apartment, Sam was worried. Brian had still to reappear.

"Where the hell has he gone?"

The truck was empty. The contents of the cab had been collected into a cardboard box placed on the seat.

"Does he have a key to the apartment?"

"No," Sam said. "Brian doesn't have a key."

"He's left already. Probably gone over to Jim's," Mike told him. "The others could have taken him. He looked tired."

"Damn it, I'm worried," Sam said.

"He's okay. We're all stressed-out today."

"I'm still worried," Sam said. "Maybe I should wait here for him."

"Listen! We can't stop now. There's too much at stake. You drive the truck to the dealer and I'll follow. You know where you're going?"

"Yeah, Potrero Avenue."

"Okay. Then I'll take you over to Jim's. Brian will be there. Trust me."

Mike was right. There was nothing for them to do but follow through with the plans. Yet Sam was worried. Brian knew where Jim lived, it wasn't that. Something else was going on in that crazy mind of his.

37 *Spring Valley, Maryland, Late Saturday Afternoon*

Jo-Lyn had been tempted to borrow some of Ed's valium, but the reminder that she was feeding Carolyn pulled herself back from the bottle. Television would have to be her tranquilizer. She walked back to the sofa and picked up the gun. She still held it reverently. It was awe-inspiring to hold a thing that could kill. (She could say the same of a knife, but it was not designed to kill.) She shuddered a little, put the gun down, and sat beside it. She forced herself to pick it up again, to hold it. These were difficult times and it would be foolish to let silly fears detract her from what could be her own self-defense.

She looked at her watch. It was 5:37. In about three-quarters of an hour the Christian station would be doing an evening prayer service. That would be uplifting. Then there would be Carolyn to feed. A light supper for herself and then an early night was in order. She would make it through.

God, how she felt alone. All those times Ed had been away, she'd never felt so alone as now, cut off from everybody. There were Jo-Lyn, Carolyn, and God in this world, and that was all. Her parents were dead. Her so-called friends in the Fellowship didn't want to converse. She'd tried calling several this past afternoon but was rejected

icily. "No time to talk now," Ella had snipped. "Got to run."
As if Ella had ever had any lack of time to gossip. She had
considered making a desperate call to Pastor Wannamaker,
but somehow she didn't think of him as a friend, she
didn't trust him. No, Jo-Lyn was truly alone in this vast
capital. And her Ed would never come back.

She stopped herself from crying. She mustn't allow
herself to fall back into that state again. She must be strong.
Have faith. Silly fears and emotional excess were the devil
playing with her being. She must hold onto her life as she
held on to this gun. She was not alone. Little Carolyn
depended on her now. Together they had battles to fight;
evils to vanquish; wrongs to right.

Jo-Lyn let her mind drift to the California of her
youth. What was it they had taught in that little church
Sunday school, in that little rectangular building by the
levee along the Feather River? To know God, to know
Christ Jesus, you had to find him reflected in yourself.
(Today, it sounded so Californian.) But it was ture. You
had to use the things God gave you in his service and in
the way they were meant to be used. Then you were
happy. As a young girl she had sometimes been difficult
by asking questions. "Does that mean you're not free?"
she urgently asked their Sunday school teacher Mrs. Harris
who lived over by Wyandotte. "The thing is that God
gives you freedom," she was told. The very presence of
the devil attested to the choice everyone had. You might
seem happy when you followed an evil choice, but because
you were made by God you really couldn't be happy.
Deep underneath, if you honestly looked, you knew
something was wrong. At the time, Jo-Lyn wasn't sure
she really believed in what Mrs. Harris had said. But then,
that was only a phase her young mind was going through.
It would end when she truly came to understand how things
fell into place.

It was all very much like these worries she faced now. If she let them go free, they would take over and terrorize her; Jo-Lyn would be letting Satan take control. But if she stayed calm, prayed to God (a capacity He gave her), fed little Carolyn (another capacity that was good and Christian), then she would be able to relax and find peace and new strength.

She wondered whether that was happening to Ed under the terrible pressures of his actions—the load that must have sat on his shoulders for accepting God's thankless work. Why hadn't God given him the support he really needed? But God had his larger purposes, and she must accept that. No, Ed was always in control. Cool. Calm. Knowing. Nearly always. That was one of the things about him that had attracted her in the first place. She thought about the accusations against him. Commie spy. It would be easy to get angry again, to let the anger seep up and take control. She must keep calm. She thought of California.

Jo-Lyn went back to the incident that had changed her life, that had finally made her see into God's eye in the center of the universe. It was not that rainy February night when twelve hours of congregational prayer had slowed and then turned back the rising Feather River. Ironically, it was candy. Young Jo-Lyn had an uncontrollable passion for candy and Satan had taken control of her with it. She continually badgered her parents and Gregg for it. If she caught Gregg with a candy bar and he hadn't offered the larger part to her she would whine mercilessly. But that was only the unpleasant beginning. Her passion was so great that she learned to steal for it. By the time she was fourteen, Jo-Lyn had established a reputation of being shifty. No one had been able to pin her down. She could charm the proprietor into giving her, at a discount, more of what she'd already stolen from his shelves. She'd even roped several school friends into her stealing activities, holding them in place by various forms of blackmail. Jo-Lyn knew she was bad and she was confused about it, but she was convinced her stealing had gone too far to change.

It was glorious how fast God could make things clear. One day she was caught stealing candy. And while a slap on the wrist was all she had got from the old storekeeper, her parents had been something else. She knew they were right. Her father had beaten her with his belt, ignoring her screams of confession, her anguished protests that she'd never do it again. Then, it was a month in her room, except for meals and church. It was a sacrifice on her parents' part, they could have used her on the farm. For several weeks her mother would hardly speak to her. Her father, when he spoke, was stern and angry, as if the family reputation were irreparably damaged. Gregg, afraid for his own reputation, disdained her.

Until now, those had been her most difficult moments. Jo-Lyn had prayed constantly to God and He reached out on occasion to look her in the face. She discovered prayer could work. Through tears she confessed daily, sought forgiveness for ignoring His warnings. She began to feel better, her body full of His pulse. She could understand her parents' hurt. Her father was a strong, upstanding Christian citizen. He lived and fought the Lord's battle. Neighbors had wanted him to run for county court judge. Her brother Gregg, however much she'd felt uneasy with him, was a respected senior at Oroville High and was set for service to his country. All that could have been ruined, changed, by Jo-Lyn's absurd cravings for candy. She had let the devil into her life and he had almost won.

Yes, it was glorious how God could demonstrate what was right, how Jo-Lyn could contribute to it, how parents and church fit together so neatly with the state. (She'd always known there had to be a good reason for pledging allegiance in school to God, country and flag.) It was to God's credit how quickly the young Jo-Lyn had changed from a conniving, tempermental girl to a devout young woman. She had renounced candy for good.

Jo-Lyn was still holding the handgun, unconsciously stroking the shaft. She felt strong again. Things might seem difficult, tangled. Yet she knew she had chosen the right path. She refused to let herself dwaddle over the recent contradictions. How would they put it in pop terms? It was the devil trying once again to rattle her cage. She must believe. She could believe. Why even those moments when Ed had forced himself upon her; when she was tired, or just not up to sex, God was telling her something. The women's libbers would have labeled it rape. Once when she had refused to yield, Ed had slapped her hard, then forced his hard cock into her. The more she resisted, the more he had slapped. Underneath she knew he had been right. She was refusing her God-given capacity to love him and she knew God was testing her. Afterwards she cried a little, although she knew she had passed the test. Little Carolyn was proof of that.

Jo-Lyn put the gun down and reached for the television remote control. The Prayer Hour would be starting soon. There would be gentle, reassuring music and many chances for prayer. There would also, no doubt, be commentaries on their current predicament. Last night, the TV evangelist had preached for fifteen minutes on the turmoil in San Francisco and the fate of homosexuals. ''This is their Last Judgment,'' he had told his television audience. ''There will be no calling back to the throne of God, no opening of the graves for these people. They will suffer no hope as their souls find torment in hell.'' Jo-Lyn had shuddered. But she liked his final statement on the matter. ''Whether or not the Soviets had anything to do with AIDS, we know one thing. It was ultimately the work of God. It was God's statement to the despicable. And it was to the greatness of this country.''

Yes, Jo-Lyn would watch the Prayer Hour. First, she would go and get little Carolyn.

38 *San Francisco, Late Saturday Afternoon*

Allan was tired but exhuberant. He was also a little peeved. Following his Chamber of Commerce speech, he'd had most of the afternoon and evening off, for once, and he'd been looking forward to taking it for himself. But in the wake of his well-received speech, a group of business people had inveigled him to go with them to Perry's and all eye signals from Christine said this was not a time to decline.

No, there hadn't been ulterior motives. Just the need on the part of his hosts to hand hold a little. They knew who they wanted to vote for but they just wanted to be certain they could vote for someone who might, on the surface, seem far out. (Harrison made every effort to emphasize Allan's perversity.) They wanted confirmation that Allan knew and understood what business was really about.

Allan had mustered all of his political instincts. While he wanted to go home, to be alone, he suppressed his personal desires. He charmed his supporters and they schmoozed him. He allowed himself a glass of good Sonoma chardonnay. They skirted the serious issues of the day, talking instead of San Francisco and its needs. Issues of small versus large business. It became apparent for every one of them, business or activist, that they all regarded the city as a special place with special rules. It was not merely a matter of simple growth or business as usual. A politician must understand the needs of business, respond to them, but they acknowledged there were other factors that made San Francisco special.

Allan probed them with questions, tried to bring out their concerns. It was an honest discussion. They had obviously pushed aside misgivings of his alleged sexual practices. He could be seen as clean, bright, youthful, and responsive. He presented a good image. And more important, although the never talked about it directly, Allan knew they looked at him with the hope for someone who could bring stability.

Allan even had a chance to display appropriate humor. When Herb Caen ambled over, he asked him whether he though national security curfews might be a brand of chastity underwear for horny secret service men.

When Allan finally did get away it was late afternoon and dark and he'd had to backtrack to get his car. Traffic was awful. It was those damn curfews. What were they, five, six, and eleven? He should be over to Bill's by then, safely secured in a Russian Hill playroom. This campaign had been very different from his previous, unsuccessful race for school board. It was much more focused: he had a single major opponent instead of several and only one of them would win. In this campaign he'd felt much more exposed, much more a representative of his community. It was much more life and death. Less going to fun events and hobnobbing with empresses and high society in fancy ballrooms. More attention to the hard political realities and to *dirt*. He knew it was worth his effort.

He left the parking structure, moving down into the unusually congested Tenderloin. On Van Ness he ran into his first real delay. It took four signal changes just to turn right into Market. Traffic seemed better for several blocks, then it was stop-go again. Were people evacuating the city?

He was suddenly very tired. He realized what a strain this day had been. It seemed they had won. Both papers had endorsed him. Harrison had been exposed. God, how they'd got Harrison! He'd come raging to the Chamber about dirty politics and clutching the chickenshit Fraggi had stolen. He even showed them a printed version, as if it were already distributed. He then tried to link cheating and dishonesty with innuendo on Allan's sex life. He let loose at liberals in general, claiming they were all corruptible and had created the city's problems. If the whole thing hadn't been so serious it would almost have been amusing to listen to tirades on commie-liberal-faggot conspiracies from a black man who received funding from the Klan.

Yes, it was spectacular how they had exposed Harrison; how even that staid audience at the Fairmont had gobbled it up. Chris at the back of the room was all serious smiles. Denton Yip and Steve Smith were handing out material to the press. Allan hadn't focused on the issue for long; the press would do that work for them. Instead, Allan had emphasized the need to work together, the need for stability. He knew the audience was thinking of the next few days. If innuendo out of Washington could detonate yesterday's riot, what could a Presidential visit trigger? The business community wanted to trust Allan. He knew that. But could he prove it to them? Could he keep his community in order? He assuaged their fears and he downplayed the uncertainty. Yesterday had released the anger, he suggested. Over the next few days things would be quieter. People knew that there was an orderly process for achieving justice. Deep inside himself, Allan couldn't be certain. But he couldn't let this audience know that. The uncertainty had to be kept buried. And he would hope like hell.

Allan had lots of time to think on the way home. It

took him nearly an hour to get the five blocks from Laguna to Castro Street. He'd already decided to take the bike tonight. All the cross streets: Dolores, Church, Sanchez seemed backed up. He listened to KKHI play its classical repertoire and give news reports as if nothing had happened in the city. He was too tired to switch stations, and he didn't want to hear about the world outside, even if it meant the army had stationed a tank at Castro and Eighteenth.

Allan was tired with everything that had happened. He was tired with anticipation, even fears of what could or would happen over the next few days. And through the political aspects of this turmoil, Allan was bothered by something else. What would all this cost him personally? What had he done to Gregg?

He had reached that stretch of Market Street near the heart of the Castro, with its wide boulevard, and its large almost European buildings. The traffic sat, crawled six inches, and sat again. The sidewalks seemed unusually quiet. Street people were conspicuously absent. Cafe Flore looked dead. Usually he loved to take his time here, roll down the window and people-watch. But tonight he wanted to get home. Damn it, he thought. I hope Gregg's at home. I've got to talk with him.

He recalled the Sunday they'd met and the following weeks when Gregg was certain he was meant to share Allan's life. After an impassioned forty-eight hours, with sex-dazed eyes, Allan hadn't been so sure. He'd built a wall of excuses: time, career, commitments. Gregg was a little too wild. He did too many drugs. (They all did.) At the time Allan wasn't sure that Marc really wanted Gregg as much as Gregg wanted to stay with them (Marc loved him). For Allan all of it had meant making a further commitment to another man through himself. Allan hadn't been too strong at doing that. Commitment to work, friends, life's purposes, and causes, yes. But to another man? The relationship between Marc and Allan, despite their love, their occasional closeness, had really only survived by keeping at arm's length. Marc had held it together through a respect for Allan. Allan was almost certain now that he'd used Marc as a sort of convenience. Allan didn't want to explore that idea. In all likelihood he was being too negative.

His thoughts returned to Gregg. How those former doubts had eventually melted. How the two of them grew close, almost preoccupied with sex, but finding other things that went well beyond. How Gregg had coaxed Allan into appreciating his own self and what he could give. By the early eighties, when the AIDS statistics had begun to explode, the two of them were almost, by way of their intimacy, monogamous. Marc was beginning to drift out in his own directions, never showing a hint of animosity. Allan had found himself making an unprecedented commitment to Gregg.

In the waiting traffic, Allan felt the jab of Gregg's hurt. He felt guilty. Why did I do it? he asked. It was worse than murder. And a new reality crept over him. He had been so afraid of that damned disease, so afraid of death, that he had distanced himself from one of the few men he could really communicate with. God, how they had been able to talk. That had been one of the things that had attracted him to Gregg, their open, unguarded conversations. Lots of discussion, on themselves, on politics, on friends. Lots of emotional give-and-take, Allan letting his calm, politically manipulative side loose, Gregg able to kid him about it, indulge him, cry at his own fears. Now Allan couldn't even hold Gregg the way he used to.

Allan was almost prepared to blame himself for undertaking this campaign to avoid Gregg's condition. No, the campaign had to be fought. God knows what would happen if Harrison had run unopposed, or against a liberal who couldn't handle the issues! Yet Allan knew he had hurt Gregg. Every morning, when the hurt bounced back to haunt him, he'd deflected it off his newspaper and drowned it in his coffee. Allan knew he did just that. And then, from time to time during the day, often when he reminisced about Gregg, pangs of hurt would come through. Again, life had been too involved, too busy to let those feelings really bother him. Marc had warned him about the situation. Yes, sweet, caring Marc who seemed to be so perceptive of feelings between others. It had been one of those few times Allan had shouted at Marc. Marc hadn't reacted; he knew Allan was afraid and he withdrew.

The worst times for Allan were at night. He and Gregg never slept together any more, even to cuddle. God, how they used to enjoy that touching. Allan's excuse was that work and political commitments were too important to have his sleep disturbed. He claimed to sleep fitfully. He told Gregg that more than ever before, Gregg needed quiet undisturbed sleep.

Allan finally pulled his car through the Castro-Market intersection and onto Corbett. Traffic looked clearer. It was then the thought hit him with a slap. Had Gregg overreacted to this mistreatment by Allan? Was Gregg involved in some form of counterdemonstration against tomorrow's Presidential visit? An act that could embarrass Allan? Allan thought he could smell conspiracy.

"Damn it," he muttered. "I've got to talk with him. I want to talk with him. I want to hold him."

As Allan turned off Temple and walked down Vulcan's Stairway, he could see the house was dark.

39 *San Francisco, Late Saturday Afternoon*

Late afternoon glowered with dark clouds and a threat of further rain. Another surge of tropical storms from the southwest was forecast.

Precisely at five P.M. army trucks near the Moscone Center went into action, closing off street traffic in an area between Mission and Harrison and between Second and Fifth. Some might say it was overkill. Others claimed it was a statement, deliberately overstated. But who knows what is really necessary for the protection of a President? Whatever, the costs were borne by the American people.

Each of the intersections into the area were blocked with barricades. At major points about the quadrant, field stations were set up. Headquarters, including a camp kitchen, a tangle of radio aerials and satellite dishes, and numerous portapotties (lined up like sentry boxes), was established in the vacant parking lot across from Moscone Center.

Almost immediately, military vehicles and men on foot began a patrol of all streets in the area, directing all traffic or pedestrians out. Residents were directed home. After six P.M., anyone still present on the streets was detained. Several highly dangerous characters were picked up and held for questioning at army headquarters. Included were an elderly Filipino man with partial Alzheimer's dementia and strongly unionist leanings, two punks from Columbus, Ohio, looking for trendy night spots, and a feisty octogenarian trying to reach a corner store. This latter person had little difficulty expressing her disdain for the President. One of the sergeants thought she resembled an older Sara Jane Moore. Memories and associations with San Francisco are strongly held and difficult to alter. A helicopter-based squadron of six vehicles had put itself in place on the gravel roof of the convention center. For all they knew, the Zodiac killer was also loose.

Early evening found a foot patrol knocking door to door on all units facing the Center and its entrance-ways. Gregg heard them as they began at the end of the hall. The building manager was with them, opening absentee premises. Damn it, Gregg thought, he hadn't counted on this, although it was only logical, especially given the measures the army was taking. He grabbed the gun and supplies and holed up in a bedroom closet. He could at least hope.

He seemed to wait an eternity. He almost risked rushing about the apartment once more to check that there were no signs. He pulled a blanket over himself and the closet door shut.

Gregg heard the front door of the apartment open, then the manager's voice. "No one here. . . . Just moved their stuff in . . . Saw them all leave earlier."

The light flicked on and the two soldiers began to stroll through the maze of boxes.

"Nothing here," one of them said.

"Check the closets?" asked the other, pulling open a broom closet in the hallway.

"Nah. Put down nothing here and time. Eighteen forty-two."

"Yes Sir."

There was silence. Gregg hardly dared breathe. With a click the light switch went off and the door closed.

Christ, he thought. That was close. Thank God they weren't doing the job properly. He sure as hell wouldn't want to face their superiors tomorrow.

Across from the Moscone Center at St. Francis Place the army patrol happened on a very elegant dinner party hosted by one of Jim's oldest friends. The guest of honor was a visitor from New York (the unnamed man who actually lived in Bernal Heights). They had been joined for dinner by Linda, another friend who lived in the same building. They were elegantly dressed, and when the soldiers appeared at the door in fatigues, they offered them wine. It was refused, and the inspection was a quick one.

About the same time that the Moscone Center area was sealed off, the military placed a few outposts in *strategic* parts of the city. Having received little to no cooperation from San Francisco Police, the army had sort of guessed where the trouble spots could be. They identified the Haight, with its unsavory, un-American reputation of several decades past. Polk Street at California was selected not because the cable cars stopped here, but because of the types that were rumored to hang out there. And at about five-fifteen, a tank rumbled up Market Street in the midst of the late afternoon traffic, turned left on Castro, and with no regard for vehicles or signals, planted itself at the middle of the intersection with Eighteenth Street.

Comments in the Castro combined cynicism and humor. Bars and stores rapidly emptied as people came to view this incongruous phenomenon. A crowd accumulated about the motionless tank. It sat there, like some alien vehicle, showing no signs of life. A waiting crowd began to gather amidst the stalled traffic, as if expecting aliens to descend. No one appeared. Nothing moved. "The boys are out tonight," someone yelled. "We know what you want, you're all the same," someone else yelled. "Remember Pendleton." Again, nothing happened.

There was a crude disbelief in the crowd. This wasn't

Prague, but it could be. Several people waved fists and shouted obscenities. Half an hour later, little had changed except the crowd had coalesced into a spontaneous sit-in that continued to grow so that the intersection became crowded with bodies, sitting and standing. Some headed off for food, blankets, and rain gear. Makeshift shelters appeared. Still, the tank remained motionless and silent. If the tank had got there, it sure wasn't going anywhere now. And prospects of an oncoming storm did nothing to deter the crowd. People who had come shopping seemed to forget their other purposes and camped themselves out. By nightfall, candles flickered all over the intersection and up Castro Street, candles guarded by hands and coffee cups against the increasingly gusty weather. In every candle was the glimmer of starlight, and in that starlight, the glimpse of hope. Dreams and memories of the loved and the dead flickered a thousand times. Tonight, in the Castro, there would be no curfew.

40 *South of Market, San Francisco, Saturday Afternoon*

Brian began drinking at the Watering Hole, about three large blocks up Folsom Street from Moscone Center. He had made up his mind. He would have nothing to do with this evil plot. He gulped down his first Bud at an unsettled pace. His stomach felt awful. He would drink his second beer more slowly.

How had he got himself into this? That was a stupid question. There had been few opportunities at which he could turn away; he had just been swept along. Could he have pushed Sam earlier, back in Portland to find out what the hell was going on? Could he have confronted him there and made demands? No, that wouldn't have worked. Sam wouldn't have told him anything; he was too commited to the goals of their plot. The only thing that had made Sam finally feel free to talk had been that interview on the radio with Stevens. It was as if the revelation of that evil was enough to justify openly what they had planned. What could Brian have really done? Sabotaged their arrival? Slashed tires? Sam would never have forgiven him. What could be worse?

Brian looked around him. The bar was moderately busy. Some chronic drinkers. Some street people. Some raunchy-looking men with big baskets and dirty jeans whom a decade earlier Brian would have gladly taken for a fuck or a blow-job in the back alley. Most everyone in the bar looked tired from trying to forget about grief. He felt for these people. He wanted to put out great arms and hug and hold them all. Somehow, Brian knew that the man over there in the corner—behind the pool tables and onto his fourth rum and coke—had been struggling against AIDS. The man was desperate about himself in a way that could only find expression through drink.

Brian felt the waters swirling, rushing about him, carrying him over rapids, down chutes. Again, there was that sense of things being out of control and he didn't like it. He wanted out of this. He wanted back on those placid, careful waters where they had started out. The whole plot was mad. A bunch of men caught in the terror of disease and death and trying to retaliate. Oh sure, Sam had said it was only a form of pressure, to push the authorities and the CIA into revealing the cure. But no, there was too much bitterness in their actions, too much hurt and fear. They weren't just acting to create pressure, they were after a form of revenge. To Brian, rightly or wrongly, seeking revenge was evil.

Suddenly Brian got impatient and stood up. What would these people in the bar think if they knew what had been planned? He wouldn't let himself answer that one. He put down an almost finished beer and went out onto Folsom Street.

The block-and-a-half walk to the Powerhouse calmed him a little. The bar was almost empty. Brian retreated into one of the dark corners. He didn't want to sit at the bar where the bartender was engaged in vigorous conversation with a patron on trying and locking up the administration. Brian overhead one of them say: "The death penalty's too good for what I'd do."

He thought of Sam. Of those incredible eyes. He could feel Sam's body, the warm mat of its hair, the blond beard. His mind drifted back to easier times, the lazy comfortable moments of their being together. The first time they held hands in the Broadway Mall, a Saturday afternoon in the seventies when gay liberation was sweeping Portland. The way they cuddled at night, Sam rubbing close, and then after half an hour or so, pulling away to sleep by himself. (Just the way he lived his life!) Those Sunday dinners that they had always made an event. Sam's sister Diane always came with her five-year-old daughter. They'd lived together for nearly a year, the four of them, after he'd married Diane. God, he'd loved her for the way she supported Sam and their community. He'd loved her sunlit sense of being a mother. She'd had only trouble from her first husband. Life with two gay men had been more caring and sensible than with a pushy kid from The Dalles whose real signature was written in abusive drunkenness.

God, those were wonderful times. He remembered the picnics, the Portland Forum picnics at Rooster Rock, out there on the Columbia, those great gay outings, hundreds of people spread over the lawns and beaches, a hugh truck dispensing beer. How the joys of those moments came back, men and women together in the sunlight, Diane and her daughter Amy resting in their midst, the perpetual wanderers and merrymakers going from group to group, stopping, chatting, women making statements with their bare tits, men with big pecs, worked up in the gym just for displays like this one, some of them proudly flaunting the arcane secrets of piercings, still other men, satyrs, in and out of the bushes like bees about lilacs, all of their words spoken out of joy, in celebration, like sunlight and shadow dancing over green leaves.

Brian was more relaxed now. He thought of the time Sam and he had made love in a tent on a rafting trip down the Deschutes, the two of them off from the main party in a little pine grove, the incessant roar of the river a short distance away, the brush of their beards, the warm gentle touch of bodies that love with a sense of familiarity, of determination. Out of all they had done together, all the kinky and exotic scenes, that instant in the tent stood forward, two warm bodies in a cocoon of togetherness. How Brian had wished that if there was anything in the universe that could last forever, then this prolonged loving before climax would turn out to be what infinity was really all about. It was like music, Brian thought, music that built you up to the most exquisite heights, then abandoned you, left you mercilessly alone. That was the inevitability of music, a beginning and an end, tied to the inexorable beat of time, an illusion, a wisp of a dream. All of Brian's years, all of his dreams, were trapped in those single, gentle moments. Those moments would never come back and the reality that seemed to unfold from them today was like some disfigured insect emerging from its chyrsalis.

And then, in his mind, Brian heard Ed Stevens talking as he had two nights ago from that Baltimore hotel room.

Some comments that both he and Sam had missed in their shock. "We developed several forms of the virus, some of them highly contagious. The one we most wanted to release on the queers could be transmitted by rubbing and kissing. You know, God's got some great things up there in his arsenal. But using that virus got nixed," Stevens had commented with disappointment. "Some of my superiors thought it a tad too dangerous."

Brian shuddered and put down an empty beer bottle. Time to get going, he decided.

Brian's next stop was the Eagle, several blocks south on Harrison. By now reality was getting hard to shut out. Chuck, the bartender, warned him of early closing and the South of Market curfew. Brian tried to ignore the whole idea. He had several mixed drinks and was visibly tipsy. He sat by himself again, watching the patrons leave, one by one or in groups. Once upon a time Brian would have come out unconditionally against this plot in which Sam was involved. People, whatever the wrongs against them, should never presume to take justice into their own hands. They could right their wronged conditions, they could demand, defy, resist, but to attempt to exercise justice, that was to fall into the same evil as men like Stevens. And yet the cruelty of men like Stevens, their assaults upon Brians' own life, these things raised doubts. Brian couldn't be certain anymore. He was hurt and confused by both Steven's and Sam's revelations. At times he just didn't care. Other moments he was furious. And all the time he felt alone, fearful. And very tired. But more aggravating than any of these emotions was the fact that despite running away from Sam Brian felt that *he* was the one who had been deserted.

He ordered another scotch and soda. Five minutes to closing. Where would he go? What would happen to him? He could go back to Sam, but he didn't want to, yet. What was going to happen tomorrow? Sam would be arrested as an accomplice. Their personal goods would be confiscated. Would they search out Brian as an accomplice? Did he really care? Did it really matter anyway? This virus had already killed so many of them. For all he knew it would get him.

"Time's up," Chuck told him. "We got to clear out of here."

Brian gulped down the rest of his scotch.

"Need a ride anywhere?" the bartender asked. "You know we've got to get out of this area."

"No thanks, I'll be all right," Brian told him, and stumbled out onto Harrison.

With dusk and a heavily clouded sky it was quite dark. The streets were deserted. Brian, still confused, crossed the street and started walking eastwards up Harrison. Occasionally, he would stop. He was crying, blaming himself for leaving Sam, blaming Sam for deserting him. In the final call it hadn't been Brian and his love that counted in Sam's life; it was justice and revenge.

At Tenth Street Brian sat down on the sidewalk, leaning against some construction boarding. He didn't want to go on. Five minutes later he did. He got up and stumbled across Tenth. He could see three pairs of headlights coming down Harrison towards him. They were several blocks away and moving slowly, deliberately, side by side, as if sweeping the street. Brian leaned against a lamppost and watched them. As they came closer he recognized the vehicles as jeeps. They were on patrol. He also realized they had seen him, and had slightly quickened their pace.

Something made him look around. Another convoy had turned from Twelfth onto Harrison several blocks behind, and was coming in the other direction.

Brian decided to run for it. Where? There was a side street close by. Dore. A one-way little street full of those ancient cramped residences so typical of South of Market.

As he fled into Dore, he noticed an open door to his right, hung with a black leather curtain that parted in the middle. He could hear music and voices inside. There was the reassuring aroma of grass. The convoy was almost here. He would never make it up Dore. Brian grappled at the leather curtain and threw himself inside.

41 *South of Market, Late Saturday Evening*

Being holed up, waiting under dangerous conditions, was a familiar experience to Gregg. He hadn't done it for years. He hadn't expected to do it again. But in the war it had been the work of his special unit. How many times had they gone ahead in front of the lines or stayed behind following a retreat, waiting, machine guns ready, waiting to carry out some special action of provocation or defense?

Gregg had waited nearly an hour after the military inspection to come out of his hiding place. The apartment and the hall outside were both unusually quiet. He moved about by flashlight, keeping the light low and bringing the blanket with him. Earlier he had noted those pathways to and from his post that provided least exposure to the windows. Even with the drapes pulled, Gregg couldn't be sure he went undetected. They could be scanning the buildings with infrared cameras. That, in combination with a floor plan showing the building's occupants at the time of visit. The sooner he got fixed in his post, the better.

The window ran from the ceiling to about two feet above the floor. It had five panels, a large continuous one in the center, and to either side, two smaller ones. The lower of these sidepanels opened for ventilation. He would have to open it carefully without exposing his body to the glass. The curtains were already pulled open. Boxes and furniture had been piled about the area so they left a clear path to the window and protected the path from behind. Gregg was glad now he hadn't come straight here when the others had left.

From a position of resting on hands and knees, he threw the blanket across the space in front of the window. He was about to crawl onto the blanket and lie down, when he changed his mind. He felt tired, but he should rest elsewhere. He should spend his first hours in the most protected corner of the apartment. Gregg pulled the blanket back and crawled into the bedroom. He still had doubts. Maybe he should stay near the window, establish his signature on the landscape so that it would be there every time they scanned it. What did he know? Things had changed since Vietnam, the technology for viewing was even finer. Gregg found a corner between an inside wall and some stacked boxes, pulled the blanket around him, and settled in against the angle of the walls. He was suddenly very tired, but thoughts on his mind kept him from dozing. His chest ached a bit more than it had an hour ago, and he was almost out of breath. Again he decided it was nerves.

There was that black night in a village north of Da Nang where he and two other men had been tricked by a small group of refugees into an ambush behind enemy lines. He had known something was going to happen about five seconds before it did. The group of them had been stupid and believed they were following a hot lead. Things were going badly in the war at that point, and his detachment tried every desperate thing it could. His companions were shot but Gregg managed to escape. He'd had to kill to escape. Some of his killings were brutal. He resented that. Twenty hours later he got back to camp.

It was the betrayal that hurt Gregg most. All the way back, sensing his position only with compass, Gregg had burned for revenge. As he fought through impenetrable brush, hacking, pulling at vines, sneaking about rice paddies, his fury rose. He had trusted those informants. He had come to this god-awful country and given them his life. At one point his anger had overriden his rational judgment and threatened his security. Every one of the five physical senses had to be used to survive behind enemy lines. He holed himself up for an hour to allow himself to cool down. A thousand feet later he came face-to-face with an enemy encampment. The Cong were moving south. He managed to bypass them.

As he pushed further south towards Da Nang, Gregg's rage diminished. But he was still determined to see those bastards who had tricked him lined up and shot. Fifteen years later he could see it in a different light. They were probably not Viet Cong or their allies who had sent them into that brush with death. They were refugees who were sick of this god-forsaken war and the abuses it brought to their people. All they had wanted was an end, any end. When he got back to his camp, it was under siege and preparing to retreat. Gregg told his tale, took his orders and forgot about revenge.

He shuddered when he recalled it. That escapade might have proved his abilities as a scout, but how the hell he managed to make his way backwards and through enemy lines during a siege, even today Gregg didn't understand. All chances had been against his survival. It was the same today.

When Gregg had been first hit with pneumocystis and knew he had AIDS, he'd been determined to make it through as well as he had in the war. But seeing friends die, watching friends consumed by foreboding, watching yet others weaken and shrivel, hope seemed to evaporate, An end, Gregg's own end, was inevitable.

Gregg's mind went blank. He hoped that he was tired, that he could doze. His shoulders shook involuntarily for a few seconds; then he saw Tony looking at him from the sling, matted hair of his legs pressed against the chains, his face smiling and content with peaceful exhaustion. He looked only as one can look after being fisted. Tony. Goddamn you Tony, Gregg muttered. Gregg was driven by men like Tony. Tony's warmth swept through him and Gregg shook some more. When men like Tony faced this fear they fought against being themselves, against their basic instincts. Gregg felt a mixture of anger and hurt. Gregg could feel Tony in his arms, comforting, his fingers at the edge of his butt-hole, their lips locked together, God, how he wanted to remember him as that, how he wanted to protect him, soothe those hurts. It was just that. Comfort and shelter in the face of aggression can only do so much. Stronger action had to be taken.

Gregg's shaking became violent; and for a minute he became incoherent, his body moving uncontrollably. Suddenly, he was very cold, sweaty. He pulled the blanket tight about himself, but it didn't do much good: he was too damp. He didn't dare turn the heating on.

Yeah, revenge. Gregg could say he was doing this for revenge. What the hell was wrong with revenge? But this was not some form of petty revenge. There were killers out there who had killed without regret, who would continue to kill. There were the names on the wall, Rick Grasso among them, a friend, a lover, back in Vietnam a member of his own unit. No, it was not just for revenge, this was for friends and brothers, dead, dying, and living. There were killers out there who had to be stopped. They had planted the fucking virus. They had brought in the troops. There had to be justice. The city and its people cried for it. The riot last night had not been for revenge, it had been in helplessness. The dead screamed in his ears for justice. All of them needed this thing done. They depended on him.

Gregg shuddered. He was very cold and damp but his shivering had stopped. He relaxed for a few seconds into blackness. He yearned for sleep, but his mind spun out in another direction.

Two months spent in a sweltering fly-ridden hut. Captured near the Laotian border. He and another man, out from camp on a reconnaissance. Got what they deserved. Half an hour earlier the two of them had knocked up a husband in front of his family to get the information they thought they needed. Then they shot him. Women wailing, kids hiding in the houses, they'd left him face down in the dirt, his jaws oozing with blood. There the dead man was, abused to get his information, then shot as a reward. How wonderfully fair this world was! There were times Gregg might have believed he deserved this disease. Later, in the jungle, they were intercepted by an NVA patrol, obviously too busy to deal with them. They should have been shot. Instead, they were handed over to comrades for special treatment.

The two of them were split up. He never saw Henderson again. No one American did. Never accounted for when the war ended. Gregg was roughed up and chained to the wall of that hut and left in the stench and the flies to try to remember. He was lucky. He could have faced a tiger cage. Why they didn't, he never knew. Even a bowl of rice left for him daily and maybe some liquid like cold soup and a bucket to shit in that they emptied every week. There was a guard posted outside, but never a single word. Gregg lived with his dreams, his memories, and with the growing nightmare of the war hovering like birds of carrion, getting closer.

Every week or so the interrogators came. He never broke. Name, rank, serial number. Nothing more. The first time they kicked him around, slugged him. Another time they went at his balls with lit cigarettes. Everything they did made him want to resist more. They showed no emotion, they seemed like they would never care if he told them anything anyway. Their faces were crisp and cold. It was as if they were his personal torturers sent to punish his acts as a soldier, and this was his personal hell. Any intelligence they could have got from him would have been stale. His unit had likely moved a dozen places since his capture. They didn't care and he didn't give. They fought for a cause as he did. And they fought for revenge.

The last time they stripped Gregg to his briefs and lashed his body with a split fan belt. He was determined as ever not to give them the pleasure of hearing his whimpers. He ate them, as best he could. If he had any gold on him he would die first. They left him in his rags of shorts, chained in the filth of the hut.

He existed in virtual silence. The guard said nothing, even when Gregg spoke to him. The jungle about the clearing was unusually silent. Occasional bird calls, trees creaking, but rare. Every few days the sky would explode into violence, the welcome din of rain on the sheet metal roof, the welcome cool. The rain was usually over as fast as it came. Then the silence again. In that silence he alternately wanted to escape and to scream. He heard B-52s wail on their battle missions. He was alone. No one knew where he was. He wanted to shout for recognition from the aircraft. He was going mad.

Yet Gregg didn't scream. He'd discovered a sharp edge on one of the links in his chain. For days and nights he tried to cut his way through the bamboo strut to which he was chained. Some moments he thought he was going to make it. Others he felt like screaming in frustration at the ferocious strength of the bamboo. He kept his cool and fingered his dog tag. He dreamed of America. Of California. He wanted to go home. He kept working steadily, gnawing with the chain link at the incision in the pole. In the night the noise sounded so loud he was surprised the guard couldn't hear. He concluded the guard spent most of his time in an opium stupor. Gregg obviously wasn't worth anything more to them, even as a plaything.

In the past, thoughts of this confinement had brought Gregg to tears. Tonight, in his South of Market hole, it only brought bitterness. He was captured by disease and circumstances he would never change. His will was captured by emotions that he could never control. He couldn't allow himself to be silent this time.

The end in that hut had been sudden. And sheer luck. A chance incursion by a Yankee patrol came on the clearing in the jungle. The surprised guard fled without torching the hut. He was gunned down as he ran into the trees. The patrol found Gregg. He had cut his way through nearly three-quarters of the four-inch-diameter pole.

Flashlight shielded, Gregg looked at his watch. It was only 9:47. Christ, time was going slowly. Too slowly. Another twelve hours to sit through. Sure, he'd done that before. Hours that had seemed painful, every one of them filled with trepidation. But never before had he been in such anguish. And never before had he felt so rotten, physically, as if the acid was etching a pit in his stomach. He found a candy bar in his bag of supplies and gnawed at it. The sugar tempted him but he wasn't hungry. The caffeine in the chocolate would probably keep him awake.

His mind went off on another tangent. Stateside, fall 1971. The military sent Gregg home almost immediately following his rescue. He was discharged with highest honors. By then he wasn't so certain about the honorability of his condition. Nightmares plagued him. He dreamed he was chained in a house in Oroville. California was in a secessional war, the north wanting to go free. The front lines had formed in an arc across the Central Valley and the Mother Lode. Troops made incursions north and south, terrorized people. In soldiers' faces Gregg saw men he had known in Vietnam. Farms burned. Yuba City was shelled. Napalm fell like magic fireworks on schoolchildren fleeing down a country road. All his time in that hut, Gregg had never broken. He had kept a silent vigil. Now it came, like the spring that is expected but never seems to happen. He woke up screaming nightly. His parents wanted psychiatric help, but there was nothing that could be done. These symptoms were all too common among men back from the war.

In the middle of it, a call from Washington. Gregg went to be decorated. Purple Heart. The President gave it. The President didn't normally hand out Purple Hearts but this was some special ceremony to demonstrate the President really cared. P.R. His parents went with him. Smiles everywhere. No one would think the country was in a desperate, draining war, No one seemed to notice the scandals poking up about the administration. The first he'd heard about Kent State was some joke Pa had cracked. And when Gregg shook Nixon's hand it was all bunting and America, jovial and patriotic. Pa was beaming proud. Nixon shook their hands again, first his parents, then Gregg's. It was good old America all right. But somehow Gregg didn't trust it. Already he had secretly sworn never again to wield a gun.

Gregg had liked his dad. He was genuinely sorry that Pa was dead, despite the fact that it had changed his own life. Despite the fact that Pa would never have accepted him today, on any condition. Gregg best remembered those early Sunday mornings, fishing on Oroville Reservoir. Long talks, and long silences. Even as a boy he knew Pa was proud, damn proud of him. Maybe that was why Jo-Lyn harbored a perpetual discontent, feeling she never got the attention from Pa that Gregg did. Yeah, he used to love going fishing with Pa. There was that quiet peace that is almost religious between two men, the gentle lap of little waves against the boat, the air over the water still cool before the sun's onslaught. It was a meditative calm, a gentle one, in which father and son talked almost circumspectly about his life to be. Not that Gregg questioned much, even those deep unknown feelings within himself. He was receptive and vulnerable and he wanted to grow up to be hard. He was learning the American way and he learned good. Later, Gregg had never figured out whether his father had liked him genuinely for himself or as a vessel for his own ambitions. Gregg tended to believe the latter, although he still liked Pa, held a warmth for him that reached across the chasm. Mother was nice, yeah, a swell woman. But Pa was something else.

Yet Gregg was too restrained as a boy to show his emotions, to react in anything but a perfunctory manner. He was supposed to be restrained. He acknowledged affections, praises, yes, let them bounce off his clean-cut image, but he was too busy doing the things that had to be done to really take note: high school football and honors, ROTC training, all inevitably leading to the marines and service to his country. There was trouble brewing for America, inside and out, and young Gregg was determined to deal with it face on. When he went off to Pendleton for starters, voluntary enlistment (no draft for him), Gregg knew what had to be done. Ma and Pa were at the airfield, happy and smiling, not like the other parents who commented in a sort of resigned excuse: "It'll do them good." Pa had just put his arm about Gregg's shoulder. "Look at this boy, Ma. He's my son and your son and he's going places. He's going to go away and do us proud."

It was like a man going into the priesthood, this service in the rites of the country. You did it with stoicism. Gregg had done better than survive their training, he had come into the priesthood believing he was on top of it. They had taken a young mind in one of its most malleable states, and shaped it for the rigors of service, the commitment of faith. Gregg had proudly marched with them, never complaining when they put another layer of hardship on top of the last to test his nerve or stamina. A drill sergeant who beat the shit out of him, deliberately, time and again. Gregg heard the music, and he marched with it. Special commendations. High-level tough endurance training at a Sierra camp. Amphibious training at the SEAL unit in San Diego. Green beret training in South Carolina. Special language training at Harvard. He wanted the front, the war. Swept along by the melody he ignored the rest of the music behind him. Later, he often wondered why he never questioned them, why he allowed his thoughts to become so directed. But such is the nature of faith.

And when faith breaks, betrayal is all the more painful. Gregg came back to his hole, to his blanket, wetter than ever. He could hear military trucks in the street below. He heard shouting that quickly died, the barking of male voices. He couldn't know that a pensioner, out to buy milk at a corner store, had been apprehended on the suspicion of being gay.

Gregg pulled his blanket tighter. God, he wished this sweating would stop. He was dead cold and the blanket was wet. Oh God, couldn't he turn the heat up? He shook violently some more, this time with anger as well as his condition. He would have them for it. Under his skin little cold shivers ran back and forth as if the skin itself were coming alive. Could one feel the working of the maggots in the flesh after death? He shuddered and tried to ignore the feelings. His mind flooded with images.

The face of his Vietnamese guard, emotionless. He saw it explode, brain and blood in all directions as the bullet hit it.

His father grinning as they pulled in a two-foot

rainbow. Water, glistening on his father's face from the flashing tail of the fish, a fighter.

Refugees streaming down the road from Hue, fear and sorrow in their faces, smoke draped across the horizon behind them like curtains pulled across the future.

A man, barely twenty, in Ward 5B. Gregg had stopped to talk with him on his way to see Tom, before Tom had died. The kid hadn't the energy to move, barely to talk. The promise of his life and dreams reduced to the drip of the intravenous.

Tom's face, matted beard streaked with gray. Lesions showing through the hair. Gregg held one of his hands. A Shanti counselor, years his younger, unaware of the scope of Tom's life, sat beside him. Tom was ready to let go. He'd lived a great life, he said, he'd been lucky with things. The counselor was bewildered.

Gunfire, crackling through the green gloom like firecrackers at a Chinese New Year's parade. Funny how the same sounds take on different meanings. The gunfire retreated. They moved on, pushing the vegetation aside, expecting treachery at every step.

The terror in the eyes of an old woman they had interrogated. They were pushing north. She stood in their way, she supported the enemy. Gunfire had just taken a buddy, with them since early in the war. They slapped her viciously, put a gun to her head. Some of them would have used it. They tied her to the house. Shellfire later turned it to an instant pyre. They had already gone.

Nixon's face. Gregg had wanted to punch him out when he had been given that medal. Was that a serpent twisting in the darkness? In his own darkness? A scared man in a big world? A country whose Presidents were eaten alive by the theory of its greatness. Gregg did nothing; he accepted the award. He even smiled.

The bamboo crosspoles, one eaten half through. He

could smell shit and piss cooking in the midday sun. He was almost too weak to continue filing with the rough edge of his chain.

An LA hospital room. Rick's face, a week before he died. The life and fire gone from it, his body swollen with consumption. Oh, how Rick had wanted to shuck this final mask of living as he had so many others. Oh, the painful searching for reason, for anything that would explain. Oh, the tyranny of friends driven to these ends.

A voice, raspy. Ed Stevens affirmed his role as executioner. Why did that voice, that face, seem so familiar? Gregg imagined he saw a face with the voice. It faded before recognition.

The order given in urgency, in defense. The order, blindly followed. Was war ever free from revenge? Was war merely a cold, rational argument that never accounted for its dead and the desires of the living? The western priest, like the soldier, is trained to follow his superiors' commands. Did Stevens merely follow?

The shuddering had stopped. Exhausted, Gregg leaned against his corner. His body was consumed in fever. He had served this damned country. With luck he had come back to America, almost an invalid. And they had turned him around and stabbed him in the back.

He saw his sister's face, round-cheeked, squat nose. As a girl she had complained without cease about her nose. She whined about it. He saw her as he had last seen her, outside the courthouse. Trying to look pious. She tried too hard. The piousness oozed out of her naturally, like some form of disdain. When she tried to appear pious she looked phony, as if it was put on. Maybe that was the reason the court had ruled against her, in favor of Gregg. He saw the blond curls arranged across her forehead. God knows how she looked today: her hair was probably swept back in something semichic. A definitive look.

On the way out onto Mission Street Jo-Lyn had hissed at him like a snake and called him evil. It was that attitude that had made him fight to the end. Otherwise, out of sympathy, he might have given her, straight off, twenty or thirty thousand from the estate. But he could never forgive the way she had manipulated his so-called perversity in the courtroom for her own greedy ends.

Evil and sin! She was always talking of evil and sin! Could the love, the care he shared with Tony be considered evil because someone couldn't understand it? Could Allan's efforts for the humanity of a people, long oppressed, be called evil? Could liberty of association, talk, and affection — could these be the terrible things Jo-Lyn termed evil? No, that was her religious mumbo-jumbo. A categorization meant to intimidate. Meant to isolate and victimize. Gregg had always believed in good and bad, but not in evil. Good things, often meant to help, could go wrong. They could turn bad. People everywhere intended good, believed they were acting for good. Even in circumstances where the intentions had gone sour. But evil? The way Jo-Lyn talked about evil, as if it were some sort of malignancy ready to consume them all, some sort of faceless horror lurking in the dark. Marc had talked the same way, although he didn't preach about it. It was a product of his Catholic background, Gregg concluded.

Evil! His life had been labeled evil. Gregg thought of the AIDS plot, the minds that conceived and worked it. Could those actions merely be bad, good turned sour? Or was there more there, was there something in their tendency to snicker and gloat about their intentions and actions? And then their own conspiracy. Was it not just for vengeance or desire for justice, not just desire to truly prevent wrong doings, but rather from a smouldering, uncontrolled passion that was evil in itself? Were Sam and Jim and all their partners, dying like himself, just as infected with evil? Was he a prisoner of these emotions, these times, driven along by the sweep of music to present arms, as they had been in Vietnam? God damn it, after that war all he had wanted to do was love, to live in love. And what was so dishonest or evil about that?

And then two realizations came over Gregg that made the whole argument seem inconsequential.

The first was that he was dying, now. This was not exhaustion, anguish, or anxiety. He was losing to this disease. All his worries about soldiers out there on the street, men who in an earlier era would have fought in his unit. Men who would have rescued him from the Khmer Rouge. These men would shoot him today. No, he was no sicky Rambo, holed up against avenging fire. He had a mission, and with or without those men outside, he would accomplish it only to die. This was no time for morality tales. This was time for commitment to action, all the more difficult against the race of this disease, but perhaps all the easier for it.

The second realization came with another thought of Ed Stevens. Gregg could see his face now, and he understood just who he was. It was as if, in some crudely awful game, Stevens had set out to hunt a million Greggs and repossess the fortunes lost to him and Jo-Lyn. His sister's fucking husband! How Gregg had hated the look of Ed at their first meeting that strange Oroville Christmas. The circle seemed to have closed, and it stung hard.

He looked at his watch. 11:47. An ominous smell of thunder flowered like jasmine in the night.

42 *Spring Valley, Maryland, Late Saturday Evening*

Jo-Lyn sat on the edge of their bed, dressed in her whitest and laciest of nighties (a present from Ed on their wedding night; the Fellowship didn't disapprove of loving sex in the right way). The noise of the television had been turned off, although disjointed images of manufactured intrigue flickered obscenely across the screen. A Bible, open to the passion of I Corinthians on faith, hope, and charity, lay on the night table. On the bed beside her, the gun rested, its gleaming plastic hard against the deep red comforter.

With her right index finger, Jo-Lyn tentatively began to stroke herself, catching, teasing the warm edge of her flesh. She was relaxed and somewhat sensual from feeding little Carolyn, just recently put to bed. As if transfixed by her mother's devotion, Carolyn had gently gurgled off to a contented sleep. No howls, no cries from a dark crib. Jo-Lyn knew she was a good, Christian mother. Now was the time to pursue her own sense of peace.

Her fingers moved a little less cautiously now, probing her opening, rubbing about her clitoris. It seemed amazing how good this felt. Jo-Lyn wanted to feel, as she did when she fed little Carolyn, the tiny warm mouth fondling her nipple (more sensually then Ed ever could), the waves of release sweeping over and carrying her adrift. Why, when she fed Carolyn heaven seemed to be sweeping over and through her. Feeding, loving a child in what was proper naturalness, that was something that was all goodness. But Jo-Lyn had too many concerns about sex to feel the same way.

Oh yes, it was all part of God, it was not just a necessary evil in the having of children. (Jo-Lyn was convinced that Susan MacKillop thought of sex that way.) It must be God that made it feel so good. But its voluptuousness, its carnality, those were God's warnings of the dangers that lurked.

She felt herself getting wet; her finger slid in and out much more freely now. for a moment she let herself fall back into the sensation of the feeling. Her reverie lasted about a minute before conscious reality instructed her once more and Jo-Lyn shifted guiltily. On the television screen, a bloodied, blindfolded woman was being led across a dark rooftop by her captors.

Jo-Lyn moaned in anguish as she recalled the sting of a belt furiously slapping her bare ass. Pain screamed through her limbs. "This is nothing to what hellfire will feel like if you don't change your ways." Jo-Lyn had discovered her own sex soon after her conflict with candy. She knew it was nothing like the one she would have got if her little play with herself had been discovered. She had given up candy all right, but she continued for years with this guilt-ridden manipulation of herself. Her play was always particularly intense when Ed was away. Sometimes she found relaxation. More often, she didn't. Her fingers were more easily distracted by her thoughts now, and she massaged herself with less enthusiasm.

Feeding Carolyn had taught Jo-Lyn she could relax and feel good about herself and her body. She began to resent the fact that she couldn't feel this way about other things. No, she was not doubting the Calvanist admonitions she had been brought up with, the strict self-control on matters of food and the antithetical irony of unlimited commitment to faith. No, these warnings were a good thing, because they helped counter evil. But Jo-Lyn knew somehow that they applied mostly to others, not herself. She couldn't think of herself as susceptible to evil (that little crime was so far away). But then could she deny there wasn't the chance for evil within her? Oh how much she wanted to relax, to feel good in herself.

Lifting her legs up onto the bed and opening them wide (so that the television flickered between them) Jo-Lyn leaned back against the pillows. Beneath her right knee she could see the muzzle of the gun. On the screen the captive woman cowered behind a rooftop ventilator, a revolver at her head, while one of the men exchanged gunfire with off-screen police. The story broke to flaunt a pair of female buns in tight jeans attempting to sell a Toyota four-by-four. Jo-Lyn began playing with herself again. She sort of pretended Ed was there. He had been so good (most of the time), he knew how she liked it. How to feed her and just when and how to stroke her. Just as she knew how to make sounds that drove him over the edge. Her desire rose, but this was good, natural desire for her husband.

And then she could hear herself screaming, not with the belt this time, but at Ed: "No, no, please Ed, leave me just this time," as his brutality overrode her. As a woman should, she had wanted to service his needs, but she had been sick and full of grief (Aunt Rosa, her only close relative had just died) and she begged Ed to hold off. "Please, not this time." But Ed, enmeshed in the depths of his desire, had no time for her feelings. He accused her of game playing. He dictated her obligations. And then he raped her.

It was at moments like this that she resented, even hated, Gregg.

Why? Because he had been given so much more than she had (and blew it)? Because he had been the attention of her father's devotion while she had felt little or none? Because his life had assumed a great message to carry forward against communism and for America, while she had been given only smallness, and within herself only certain things she could appreciate? Because Gregg had attained a degree of self-confidence, or self-acceptance (even of things she could never accept) that always seemed to be beyond her own achievement? Or was it because the devil had taken him and denied her every hope the Lord might have proffered?

Jo-Lyn pulled her nighty down over her thighs, smoothing it gently over her knees, as if nothing had ever happened, as if perhaps it had been inadvertently blown up by the wind. She was determined to remain calm. She refolded her hands over her stomach and leaning back against the pillow, allowed her eyes to close.

Jo-Lyn saw her father's face. Not the quiet, reserved face she looked at every night across the dinner table. Not the tired face of a farm owner after a day of harvest. It was an angry face, hard-edged with indignation, with amazed fury. She had seen that face twice. Once, only once, it had been directed at her. And once, it had been directed at Gregg. Oh, how Father's face had been full with God's wrath!

The incident happened almost three years after she had married Ed; they were back in California for the week before Christmas. Aunt Rosa was coming from Monterey and Aunt Christine from Redding. It was their first trip back home together since their marriage in the little chapel down by the river. Gregg had come up from San Francisco.

She had known the minute she saw her brother that something had happened. He was different. He looked older, almost cocky, as if he thought he knew better. He wore jeans and a plaid flannel shirt. He placed his lanky body into a chair as if it had been made for him. Oh, he used to do that before. But this time it was as if he was possessed. Jo-Lyn felt trouble coming.

The trouble came after dinner. Jo-Lyn had no understanding of the agony Gregg was going through, of his heartfelt need to make his statement about being gay.

She knew only that it was a terrible, sinful thing he had done and that it was such a wrong time. Their father was so unprepared, she remembered, he could hardly speak.

Pa had wanted to hit Gregg, he had wanted to flail out at this death blow to his life's dreams. (She even wondered for a moment if Gregg was doing it not because he was really gay but to assert a false sense of independence. Father had certainly given him undue attention.) But Father didn't hit Gregg. He sat restrained, looking very tired, then ordered the devil out of his home. Gregg took his bag, still unpacked, and left.

Father continued to sit there, staring blankly, as if transfixed by the fire. Perhaps he saw hellfire signaling in the flames. He ignored the muted whispers around them, the quiet weeping of his wife. He stared forward (or was it backwards, at the memories of his son, the war hero?) and said nothing.

Twenty minutes later, Ed (at Jo-Lyn's behest) tried to comfort him. She knew Father wouldn't speak with her. Father pushed Ed away, summarily. It was as if Ed had tried to intercede himself as the loyal, righteous son. Father would have none of it. No comfort, no solace for this loss.

The next morning, he and Mother left for Sacramento. They were off, she told Jo-Lyn privately, to the lawyer to change the will. Above the fifteen feet of dense tule fog, it was a clear, blue day. Father was a determinedly careful driver. "Please call when you get to Sacramento," Jo-Lyn had told her mother. And Jo-Lyn had said a prayer for their safe passage.

Four hours later the news reached them via the Sutter County Sheriff. The car had been totaled by a semi down near East Nicolaus. State Route 99 was still blocked in both directions with the wreckage. Both her parents were dead.

43 *The Ambush, San Francisco, Saturday Evening*

In the pre-seventies, when gay men were exiles in their own cities, where few institutions existed beyond the bar, and community groups were either brave outposts or not there at all, the bar took on a special role. Bars were living rooms and community centers, places beyond home where people could to some degree relax with their own. Places where friendship and bitching and counseling occured. Others had their churches and community halls and neighborhood services. Gays had their bars. Despite all the changes of the post-Stonewall era, the bars held their own as community places. No one bar served the needs of all groups (whatever the dreams of a thousand bar owners to do so!) and many bars shifted over time in the clientele they served. Gay bars became straight, and some went back to being gay again. Straight bars became gay or women's bars. Leather joints made the transition to punk and country hangouts and then became disco. Some of then even went back to leather again. But in all this posturing, the Ambush never changed.

The Ambush is a club. Its patrons make it a club, the sort of relaxed, comfortable atmosphere where it was all right to talk, to be friends, to let go. Sure, you could be detached if you wanted, just sitting there in the crowd and absorbing inwards all of the good vibrations, just wallowing in the sort of warm sunshine that drifted through the bar whatever the time of day or season. The word mellow has become dated, perhaps, but it still accurately describes the Ambush. Oh you could come into the Ambush and pose, crackerjack in your new leathers, basket for days (stuffed with socks). No one would object. Some people might even smile with amusement or grapple at you. But that's the Ambush, the sort of rare institution where people can genuinely feel and express who they really are.

It was a busy, lazy, late afternoon that Saturday at the Ambush. It was almost like the old days, as if people were trying to forget that times had changed. The Ambush was more impenetrable than ever, a solid structure of minds that have discovered the quiet certainty of some of life's truths, a meshing of souls that bask together in each other's auras. Near the bar, Bruce, Paul, and Peter were into their usual ruckus with Wayne who sported a headpiece decorated with green and red twinkling lights in honor of Peter's birthday. Wow, that grass was good. In the back corner, Chesley the playwright carried out a somewhat convoluted discussion with Chester the photographer about the real death of Dan White. A good deal of pungent cynicism was expressed. But nothing was said of the curfew or the troops or tomorrow's presidential visit. As in the rest of the bar, memories flocked thick over the reefs that were dreams. In the stronghold that is the Ambush, lack of discussion did not imply lack of awareness.

From behind the bar, Marc enjoyed a sense of detached calm. Something, some need drew him here today, but he still wasn't certain what. He was glad to escape the brooding tension, the screaming media, the raging community, the horror that had shaped itself into a reality. He was glad to leave his own disquiet, to laugh out at Paul's bad jokes about the long-disgraced Reagan and to share a joint with Joe Fratianni, come downstairs from bridge to have a beer. He was glad to go out from behind the bar to collect empties and grab a few moments' conversation with Bert and Jim over by the pinball machines. There was something safe and secure about this place that was stronger than metal because it was not made of any real material (although the beer was real and real piss flowed over real ice in the backroom urinal). They could kill people, they could gut buildings and burn art. They could censor talk and motivate killer microbes. But they could never kill the strength of this space of mind.

When Brian burst through the doorway, almost as if thrown, they were not surprised. Our world offers little refuge to those in greatest need. Marc especially was not surprised. Brian's coming was a sort of confirmation of something he'd felt a while earlier, a sort of disquiet, a yearning of someone in great need.

"They're after me," Brian shouted. "Watch out, they'll be in here in a second."

It was a long second. No one followed Brian through the leather door. The soldiers marching the street outside found a locked door on a vacant unlit building plastered with FOR SALE signs. Everyone in the bar knew the troops were there, like the blackest of dreams, on the streets of their San Francisco. But no one could hear their pounding, shouting at the locked door. No one heard as they kicked it open to find the dark shell of a room, some stairs up into more darkness, and some empty rooms farther up.

"Fuck!" one of the patrolmen said. He was a good Christian and it was a word he had learned at training camp.

Another dangerous, criminal pervert had escaped them.

Brian had been in this bar years ago, before he had met Sam. This had been one of Sam's favorite places. Back in '86, even in Portland, they had mourned its closing. But it took a minute for Brian to realize where he was, to gain his cool. He was frightened and he was drunk and he was near tears. He was incredulous that he had escaped. God knows what he would have told the soliders, what betrayals might have been forced out of him despite his reluctance to the whole damn plot in the first place. But where the hell was he?

Someone had put an arm about him and brought him to a seat by the bar.

"Marc," the man said. "Get him a coffee."

And then Brian realized where he was and he was incredulous again and he started to cry. Had they shot him? Was this heaven, not behind some pearly gates, but behind the black leather curtains? It could only be the Ambush with a spectacular fire of red and orange gladiolus in front of the mirror behind the bar. It could only be the Ambush with the rough-hewn wood of its walls, the protectiveness of its far corners.

Brian felt himself. He was real. He could feel the warm air of the bar and the bar stool under his butt. The coffee had an inviting smell that tickled at his nose. This must be something he didn't know about. He must act cool.

The man who had escorted Brian to the bar still had his arm about him. Brian became aware of him. A burly man with big pecs, and nipples that stood out through a black T-shirt. He had bushy eyebrows and a thick beard streaked with lots of silver. A veritable bear, Brian thought, although this place had always been full of bears. The man gripped Brian's shoulders (was this to show he was real?) and his very blue eyes danced as he spoke.

"Marc, this is Brian. Brian, this is Marc." The bear was introducing him to the lean angular man behind the bar.

Brian, still unbelieving, went through with the formalities of introduction. Who was this man who knew his name? He thought he saw something vaguely familiar in Marc, the bartender, but this bear who held tight his shoulder?

He wanted to relax, he wanted to let go. And he was in a place that wanted him to relax and let go. He could feel that.

"Don't worry," Marc told him. "It's crazy out there, but you're safe here."

Marc's hand touched Brian's wrist as he spoke, a long sustained touch that reinforced his words and said more: I know your lover, brother, man-friend. The touch said: I expected you tonight and I won't desert you. Then Marc turned and drew the hand away and went along the bar to serve another customer, leaving Brian with the bear.

"You don't remember me, do you?" the bear asked.

"No, I don't," Brian answered looking into his eyes, searching for some familiarity. Brian might be a little drunk, yes, but he should recognize this man. He was glad his incredulity had been challenged. And then, as the man spoke, it flashed simultaneously on Brian.

"Portland, 1982," the man told him. "I was staying the night. Driving my way back to the city, from Seattle."

And then he added as if an afterthought, as if the mystery hadn't been fully explained:

"I only had a mustache then."

Right, Brian recalled. Sam was in New Orleans at a medical convention. We met at CC Slaughters. I didn't usually go there but JR's Cell was dead, especially week nights. Yeah, we met and we fucked.

"I remember now," Brian told him. "But I'm sorry, I've forgotten your name."

"That's okay. It's Bill. Bill Smith."

Brian hugged him. He hadn't forgotten how good he smelled. How wonderful those armpits and tits and crotch had tasted. How long and hard and gently this man had fucked him. That's right, they had even used a condom. Few in Portland seemed to use condoms back then although SF men had started. It felt wonderful embracing this man, his muscle and bone and fat (he had a small beer paunch; Brian could imagine the line of curly hair up its middle).

"We had a good time together," Brian told him. "I remember that."

"Yes, I do remember," Bill told him, and purposely gripped Brian's shoulder a little harder.

Yeah, Brian thought, it was one of the few times I ever slept away from Sam. Not that he would have bitched about it; we're very open with one another. We sure went to lots of parties together. Sam was going to stay with that New Orleans leather boy.

Thinking of Sam momentarily broke the spell of the bar. The overwhelming frustration of reality came back, the passion of his love, the horror of AIDS, the inescapable labyrinth of the plot, the troops on his own heels.

"I didn't mean to," Brian blurted out painfully, as if responding to inquisition. "I didn't mean to be part of it. It was their idea, they planned it, I was only caught. . . ."

Yet the reality of the Ambush didn't fade and Bill moved closer to comfort him, pulling Brian's head and shoulders into his arms and working his legs about Brians' knee so that his own crotch just rested there on Brian's thigh and Brian could slip his arms about Bill's waist to grip the love handles.

"I didn't mean to get involved," Brian agonized, once more stopping short of the whole story. Bill stroked the back of his neck.

How he wanted to relax, to forget it all, every moment of this damned agony, every inch of this march to the cross. Yet each time he looked into the warm darkness of the bar, Brian was afraid. He couldn't let go, the fears were still there, like troops, their guns cocked, coming over the edge of a hill and into his mind. Those were real troops, with real guns that had been on his footsteps out there. Nothing like this had ever happened to him. And he had never believed, in his wildest ravings, that it could. God, how he wanted to let these fears go.

Brian opened his eyes and looked forward at Bill's broad, sloping pec, stretched with T-shirt. He threw his head against it and sobbed.

Across the bar, posed beneath Marc Chester's photographic icon of the hanged man, two men were speculating on the consequences of community violence, should it break out the following day.

"I want to see it," one of them said. "They deserve it, those bastards. We can't sit back and take it. And yet I'm afraid of what it would do to the election. Bennett's got a good chance—"

"Just watch," the second man interrupted. "Nothing will happen to the President tomorrow except some picketers. And Harrison will be elected on Tuesday."

44 *Spring Valley, Maryland, Early Sunday Morning*

For Jo-Lyn, one of the nicest things about their Spring Valley home was the second-floor bay window that was Carolyn's, a little alcove with glass on three sides and sloping glass above. It was a private alcove, sheltered from below by magnolias and lilac bushes. Ed and she had placed Carolyn's crib close to it so that she could hear the birds sing and look up through rustling leaves to the stars.

It was about three A.M., and Jo-Lyn, unable to sleep, stood over the crib, clutching the gun and looking into a richly dark and starry sky. Truly she felt God's glorious firmament lifting upwards and outwards from her being, the grandness of creation overwhelming just to look at. Stars and constellations and beyond them galaxies, climbing to infinity. Why, satellites and moon trips only gazed the surface of God's greatness. She looked at Carolyn, then up into the vastness. For a moment, she felt truly privileged.

Dear God, she murmured, clutching the revolver against her breasts. Dear God, that she could feel so close to Him and feel peace once more. Over the past days she had longed to reach out to his blessing and receive his peace. But the turbulence of her life had interceded. Or was it, Jo-Lyn dared to wonder, that turbulence had nothing to do with it? Was it that God now refused to communicate with her?

She shuddered at that possibility.

She reached into her mind to push back all the cascading thoughts, coming down layer on layer like a snow pack, building towards an avalance.

No, she told herself looking upwards to the diagonal studded belt of Orion. She lived and professed His fatih. He was her God. He would not abandon her.

And then, beginning almost subconsciously, she began recklessly to examine the pillars on which her universe was built: not a creed formulated and recited weekly (I believe in the holy, apostolic church . . .) but as tenets so closely held, so integral in holding together the concentric spheres of her seamless web.

God, how I've always believed, supported your church, she pleaded. It's always been part of my life. Never something on the side, never superficial like a new coat, but something bound to everything I do. Since I mended my ways as a girl, I've never avoided you, God. I've trusted you, done right by you, and spread your word. You would never desert me, God, as they have.

They might attempt to deny Jo-Lyn the support of church, of group prayer, of working with the Fellowship for God's glory. And that was a big denial, because the church meant so much to her. But Wannamaker, Ellen Shreiber, Susan MacKillop—who were they to pretend to stand between Jo-Lyn and God? What did those people really know of God? That creep, MacKillop's husband, climbing his way over anyone to get at the helm. Besides, as religious as she was, as terrible as the world was today, she could not agree with a pastor who proclaimed the coming Holocaust. Little Carolyn was too good for that. Yet what could she really do, all by her little self and without the help of the Fellowship?

The inky edge of a cloud obscured the stars on the edge of her horizon. Was bad weather on the way, she wondered? She'd had her television on nearly full-time but had absorbed nothing of the weather reports.

Yes, she could live without the Fellowship, but it would be difficult. For the church helped give her a sense of what was right and wrong, good and bad. The Bible could give her that, but the Bible was so complicated. Was it not so much easier to be part of a congregation that helped her to read it, to have a pastor, who through careful study, knew the answers? Yet did he?

Damn them, she thought. She believed in the bravery of her husband's acts. She believed that homosexuals were evil and deserved to die. Yet the church had failed to support either her or Ed. They claimed to know righteousness, to be so concerned about evil, yet how quickly had they backed away. How did these people know what was good or evil? Would God really condone the killing of queers? Suppose someone disagreed with her own beliefs? Suppose they came to take her away or kill her, or to infect little Carolyn with a fatal disease?

Jo-Lyn gripped tightly at the edge of the crib, letting the revolver drop with a thud on the mattress inside. She tried to disentangle herself from these difficult thoughts. She succeeded, although she knew they would be back.

She looked out now, into the grotesquely inter-twining branches of magnolias, gnarled ends that rapped against the glass on a windy night. They could be so beautiful when they bloomed.

Then there was Ed. How she had believed in mar-riage as an institution of God! Of course she still believed in it. They could never accuse her of heresy. Yet marriage just hadn't been fair. Ed had a difficult job, but he had left her unprepared. She still didn't know what it all meant. She still didn't really know whether he had set out to kill the queers (and her brother) as God's missionary or whether it was all talk. The more Jo-Lyn thought about it, the more it seemed that it could be just talk. Maybe just CIA talk. She couldn't be sure. She didn't care to be sure. She just felt alone, left in the middle of a mess. Oh God, didn't I do right by Ed? she wondered. How many times did I suffer his desires? How many times did he hurt me and I let him because I knew he needed it? And now she had been deserted, left to be gawked at and poked at by those bastards out there. Oh God, why did you let him do this to me?

But there was no answer. Her husband's life and his motives were a sort of black mystery.

Jo-Lyn stood there, very tired and shaking a little with the coldness of the night. The stars seemed to shudder, but it was only Jo-Lyn's shivers that made them move.

The greatest reward of her faith had always been that sense of solace that now seemed unreachable. Before, Jo-Lyn Fellowship had helped her to understand why there was pain and suffering in the world and the reasons why she had to suffer it. None of that seemed reassuring now.

The sky seemed to be falling in places. She was tired and should go back to bed. She should at least get herself a shawl. But instead, she stood there, distraught. It was as if somebody had knocked away some of her pillars. For a moment, she had a vision of her brother beside her at their little family church. It must have been one of those Sundays before he went to Vietnam. He looked so stern, so devout to the commitments of faith. He had appeared so strong, so pure, that even she had been envious. His deception had been so cruel. She brought her mind back to the hard reality of this strange November night.

Had God really meant her to suffer for quietly making her body feel good? Had Jo-Lyn really driven her husband to hurt her as punishment for her own lusts? God would not abandon her like that, to be a vessel for Ed's brutality. Jo-Lyn reached for the gun again. No, she never minded being a safe place for Ed's frightened ego, she had wanted to protect him, succor him, that was a woman's role. But the punishment she had received, did God really mean to punish someone so devout and caring? She could believe in hurt when she was one of God's fighters, a member of God's church, married to one of God's husbands, set on God's purpose. But now? The sky seemed very dark and the stars pale and very close. The room seemed very small. Jo-Lyn was frightened. Why couldn't she see and think straight?

Somewhere out there in the west, high above the Great Plains, the President was on his way to the Coast. God damn the man, she thought. Going to make a big stand. So brave, that man who turned yellow on Ed. Going to address the faithful, that man who attributed God's acts to the commies. A year ago she could have believed they were winning against the devil. Now, there was blackness everywhere.

She felt very dizzy. Jo-Lyn let herself collapse onto the little rug beside the crib. Still clutching the gun, she sat for a moment, then fell over, the gun falling free and onto the wooden floor.

She found herself staring into two fiery eyes. They sneered at her. She pulled her hands over her face but they were still there, locked in the darkness behind her lids. She wanted to scream, but she felt fingers on her throat, cold clammy fingers that took her almost to the point of choking but would not take her over the edge. Her body moved with contortions of pain as the eyes burned into her consciousness. Then, abruptly, as quickly as they had come, they were gone. There was blackness and there was a jumble of voices in the blackness.

"How can I believe anymore?" she heard herself wail.

In the crib, Carolyn shifted and began to cry.

"Why do you desert me?" Jo-Lyn called out.

"God never deserted you Jo-Lyn, you deserted yourself."

"I want to serve you God," she pleaded.

"What do you know of service, Jo-Lyn?"

"I've always served you, God."

"I am a good, just, and righteous God, Jo-Lyn."

"I know that, God."

And then there was silence.

"Would you hurt me, God?" she screamed. "Would you kill to be a just God? Would you take away little Carolyn from me, God?"

In the crib, little Carolyn bawled louder now. In her blackness, Jo-Lyn heard neither the bawling nor answers to her questions. Then, as if rising on the crest of a dark wave, Jo-Lyn lashed out, swearing at God and the world.

45 *The Mission, San Francisco, Late Saturday*

It was a dark gusty night in the Mission. A fitful wind chased scraps of paper up and down the sidewalks like cat and mouse. There were no stars. In the west, a dark hostile horizon rumbled occasionally with the warning of thunder. For a Saturday night, the neighborhood was strangely quiet. Most police detachments were out in the Castro or down at City Hall. Many people had chosen to stay home.

The crowd in the small bar was sparse but jovial and ignoring the curfew. Mostly gay men and women and mostly Latino. A few of their straight friends were with them (which goes to prove not all Latino straights dislike gays). There had been a little discussion about the following day's big visit, but a lot of beer had squelched the anger and fear. No one in the bar noticed the battered black Dodge circling the block like a panther, waiting for a clear moment on Mission Street. Someone coming out of the washroom at the back of the bar might have noticed a dull thud outside as the rear entrance was jammed immovable with a two-by-four. If they did hear a noise, it was unreported.

At 11:37, a youth with a stocking mask pushed open the door of the bar, threw an object into the crowd, and closed the door to protect himself from the blast. Then he was gone, the door held shut by another piece of two-by-four pushed through the handles.

The gasoline exploded into thousands of painful flames. Frightened, desperate screams filled the night, only to be buried in the roar of burning wood. Across the city the sky exploded into terrible thunder and a searing flash of light. Rain began pelting the roadways of Twin Peaks, but as it drew down across the Mission, it did little to quell the flames.

The devil takes his own, it has been said. And some people just can't wait to see their own future.

46 *Russian Hill, San Francisco, Late Saturday*

It felt wonderful to let himself go. To let this man kiss him so deeply that their mustaches crackled together, his tongue deep into his mouth. To let him hold his face between his warm hands before he buckled it into a leather head harness with its bit placed firmly into his mouth so that all the talking of the last four weeks became irrelevant.

Allan needed this. Others had their immersion tanks and meditation chambers, their rolfing and primal screaming and their Mill Valley gurus. Allan looked to these prolonged moments when he could hand himself over to a buddy, to be tied down, to be immobilized in a quiet metaphor of the stranglehold of existence.

Even the trip over here had been an escape, a ride through the streets of the Haight and the Western Addition on a blustery night. He hadn't ridden his bike for nearly three weeks now, and he missed it. He parked the Harley on a somewhat level stretch where Bill's driveway intercepted the steep sidewalk. Bill greeted him at the door. It was like old times, Allan's arrival out of the unsettled night, this greeting by a hot, dark man. Bill was no stranger of course, they had been friends and played on and off together for nearly a decade. But his reserve in greeting Allan was a sort of foil for the commitment that would come, a reflection of the seriousness. For Allan, the detachment was liberating and it made Bill seem all the hotter, the dark busy mustache under grave reasoned eyes, the thick hair curling up and over the straps of his harness as seen through the unbuttoned leather shirt.

No, he had not come to this remodeled Russian Hill townhouse with its postcard views of Sausilito and the Golden Gate Bridge and its ample playroom tucked into the basement to discuss politics. Sure, Bill had contributed generously to his campaign. But they spoke not a word of politics, of the riot, of the campaign, even of the Presidential visit. They drank a beer in the living room in front of a fire. Allan stripped off his clothes in the bedroom and was led downstairs to inspect the ropes and restraints laid out on the playroom table. Allan already knew the hooks in the corners and he could recall the countless possibilities of their pull. But it was not his role to decide, even mentally. That would distract from it. No, he was here to let go.

He liked the sort of formality with which Bill started: it was almost like an airport departure. Bill hugged Allan, stroked his arms and back, pulled gently as his nipples, ran his gloved hands over his crotch. Perhaps a little more than what they would have done in an airport departure lounge, but the intent was the same. Then Bill guided Allan over to the large wooden frame in the center of the room and pulled himself back, dropping the affection, leaving Allan to walk down the ramp to the plane himself, while Bill prepared for the ordering of the flight. There was all the trust of passenger for pilot. When the plane landed, Bill would be there to greet him as he stepped down.

As Bill set out, Allan made every effort to calm

himself, to detach the strings of reality. He told himself that he must relax.

Bill attached leather restraints about Allan's ankles and wrists. He fixed these to the uprights and crossbars of the frame. He stood back a moment to watch Allan, his thickset body vulnerable in the candlelight.

Allan closed his eyes and began to let go mentally, dropping off his packages into the pit that had opened below him. First, he dropped the turmoils of campaigning. He dropped Christine's welcome naggings, Harrison's diatribe, and the ceaseless demands of the campaign team. Victory may be almost certain, but he dropped even thought of that.

Bill began his craft now, enmeshing Allan's body in an artistry of rope so that an intricate web of macrame gripped Allan's butt and thighs and enclosed his chest.

Allan was letting further things drop. The moment Harrison had tried to explain fist-fucking to an audience at Grace Cathedral. Fraggi's betrayal and the exposure of Fraggi's betrayal. Christine's warnings, pleadings of what and what not to say to the Chamber. The quiet, often tense, meetings with campaign contributors and political allies who provided expensive support. (Oh, the joys of the idealist volunteers who worked for the campaign out of clear belief and nothing else.) His meeting with the mayor two days ago and the telephone conversation with her early this morning. Allan allowed all those to fall: he could hear her voice fading into the void.

Bill pulled the strands of rope through the crack of his ass and up and around his balls. Allan was hard and Bill slapped the cockhead a couple of times before fashioning the rope into a tight, knotted cockring.

Allan rolled his eyes behind their lids and wallowed in the feeling of the rope, in the warm stillness of his muscles. He disengaged some more bags, so that his soul climbing like a balloon over Napa, rose another hundred feet.

He dropped the burning Federal Building. He dropped the firebombed shell of a Castro bar and the dead in the ruins and on the sidewalk. He thought he heard screaming as those bags fell. He glimpsed at contorted, agonized faces.

Already he had relaxed the muscles in his arms and shoulders, even those little ones in the small of his back that could cramp the wrong way under tension so that the pain could nearly kill him. Bill had begun to tie out each set of limbs to the frame and to the walls with connecting ropes. The ropes counteracted each other so that the effect was total immobilization. God, Allan loved this, the gentle caress of the taut rope, the feel of freedom. He still had a raging hard-on.

He disposed of some more baggage. The law practice for which he rarely had time anymore and the pressures of his partners who, while supporting his political cause, still thought mostly of business. The President's visit. Worries that something would happen during that visit. Fears Allan held about developing AIDS. He let them all fall. He knew they would be back, but it was good therapy to pretend they were gone. He thought he saw Michael Fraggi's face staring at him out of the void. He slapped it back, mentally, and it disappeared. Was it Michael Fraggi's face, or was it little Jimmy Wilson, that man he had met five years ago at the Slot? Jimmy and Allan had shared a three year on-and-off affair. Last year Jimmy had died on the fifth floor of the Kaiser Medical Center, a hearbroken child of the seventies. Allan had only had time to visit him once more before he died. He had told himself he was too busy.

Now that Bill had Allan restrained, he turned to address the audacity of a hard cock. He tied it and the balls with a slip knot and pulled the rope outwards and taut through a loop in the opposing wall. But thinking of Jimmy, Allan had lost his hard-on and Bill tightened the rope some more so that it would hurt just a little when Allan regained it, a reminder of who was in charge. When it got sore Allan would have to bite some into the leather that poked between his lips, but that was why it was there.

Allan seemed relaxed. He opened his eyes to a room of flickering candlelight and the grotesque shadows of ropes and limbs. He felt cleared, to some degree peaceful. Bill had gone, leaving Allan alone with himself in the warm darkness. Allan thought he heard thunder, but he wasn't certain and he didn't care. He felt a sort of glow about him, and he determined to settle into its embrace. Just for a moment he tensed his muscles to reaffirm that the ropes were actually there. Then he let himself go, dropping his own being into the void.

In this state Allan drifted for about an hour. There were moments of calm. There were sensual, almost tense moments in which his eroticism surged up and his cock went hard and he longed for someone to grip his flesh through the rope or for a free hand so he could beat himself off. There were moments in which fear wallowed up around him, like an omen, and figments of his discarded baggage taunted him across the void. But he refused to respond. He told himself he deserved, he needed this detachment. Why, about six months ago he had spent eight full hours in the glorious freedom of suspension bondage in this very playroom! And yet now, after the initial calm, Allan was finding it increasingly difficult to relax. Below his mind's surface, there was a good deal of heaving.

It began, innocently enough, as reminiscence. Allan let his mind wander away from relaxation. The subject seemed innocuous enough.

He saw his parents. His mother, her once regal attitude crippled with arthritis. His father, elderly and frail. That they came to mind surprised Allan; he rarely thought of his parents. They were both alive and less than twenty miles away. He talked with them maybe once a month.

Sometimes he let it slip to two. They were there and he was in the city and that was that.

Why did they come to mind? He closed his eyes and saw the grand entrance to their Tiburon home. He had grown up there. He rarely went back. Was there animosity between them? No, it was more a diffidence. He had a sister with children in Napa and a married brother with children in Pasadena. Allan might see their families once a year, his parents saw them every month. No, his parents were never hostile or critical. He would occasionally see them at the Symphony across the lobby of Davies Hall, although they could as well be a thousand miles away. On one such occasion Allan had introduced them to Gregg, but they had only been politely interested. No—if anything, they were cooly diffident. They knew their son was running for District Attorney, but they hadn't contributed anything to his campaign. They hadn't even wished him luck, although doubtless there would be a formal note of congratulations when he won. They might even be mildly proud, although Allan's life-style was certainly not part of their scheme of things.

Did he think of them because they were a start of all this? Allan felt vulnerable and he shook at his bonds. He tried to call, but the gag prevented him. He wanted to end the scene, to go upstairs and sit down with Bill and just talk over a beer. But no one came, and Allan heard the slap of storm-whipped leaves against a window.

It was his parents who represented his style of doing things.

Allan saw his life as a pattern of wanting to control. Everything he did was part of wanting that control. Why? Was he afraid? He didn't think so. It was just that he felt more confident when he knew things were under his own direction—not necessarily going his own way, but under his own direction. A logical outcome maybe of a childhood in a wealthy, established family. Old railroad and legal money. His father was cronies with them all from the Gettys to the Chickerings. It was expected plainly that Allan had been born to control and that as he grew older, he would control. Little was said of it directly. A lot was presumed for all the children, but especially for Allan, the eldest.

Presumption had somehow failed to account for several things. Young Allan, at Cal in the sixties, despised the very concept of Governor Reagan and he was diametrically opposed to the war in Asia. He was going for law (quite a respectable choice according to family traditions; they presumed he would outgrow his radicalism). Allan was going for law and was determined to set the world to rights. No sooner had he completed his undergraduate years than Allan was drafted.

The draft confronted Allan with several choices.

The first was to accept it, to go. He would lose the control of himself that he valued. Besides, he would never fight their illegal war. The second choice was to rely on his father. They discussed it, one summer weekend, on a trail near The Cedars. He rarely went to The Cedars anymore, it was too establishment. His father was prepared to seek actions in high places. It seemed insane to him that a man the quality of his son and from the stature of his family should be sent off to be butchered. His father knew senators and high administration people. He would do his damndest. Allan said no. He could not allow another man, even his father, to exercise this level of control over his own life. It was the only time his father had made a commitment to Allan of this magnitude. But Allan was determined to make his own statement and his father never recovered from the refusal.

To remain in the United States would mean a loss of Allan's self-control, so he fled to Canada, at first Toronto. There he exerted his own control as a prominent figure in the antiwar movement, working with draft resisters in exile. He finished law school at Osgoode Hall. A different system maybe, but valuable experience. As with most things, Allan did well. He was in the control seat. He came out in Toronto, and he took control of that. Later, he went to Vancouver where he met Marc. He continued to work with the resistance. He trimmed his beard to a fashionable length. And he gained widespread public recognition. Before his commitments had fully taken control, amnesty was declared. Allan went home to work out his public service, to study some more and to do his exams for the California Bar. He went home to regain control.

Control. Was that the motivator of his life? Did involvement, masked as a need to control, substitute for closeness? Sure, Allan liked emotions such as tenderness, eroticism, he allowed himself to fall into them. But intimacy never lasted for long. Marc had shared a special closeness in him, but despite being good friends, they drifted apart. Was it that Allan could never return the closeness, instead substitued other excuses? Let's face it, he told himself. I'm a power-hungry bitch.

He wrenched at his bonds. He pushed hard against the ropes—backwards, forwards. They cut into him and the pain felt good. He told himself he was being too hard. All he was doing was for good causes. He was only human. Everyone had limitations.

But then he slapped himself mentally. He was covering up his own excuses for Gregg. He loved Gregg. Not just the control, the man who could give himself to Allan's ropes and razor, who opened himself to Allan as if he were giving to God, who had been faithful and kind as a lover, who had overlooked Allan's shortcomings. And it wasn't just the sense of this man loving him, giving to him, but what this man had taught him. Gregg was the first man that Allan had let tie him up, top him. He had appreciated that. Allan's emotions had long wanted a respite from their own subtle arrogance. Gregg had given him just a little of that.

Now, as he strained against his ropes, pushing backwards as hard as he could so that his tied-up balls ached with fiery pain, he saw Gregg. He saw him in the corner of their own playroom, damp with sweat and sobbing, the lashmarks hard across his back, his face intense and pleading for the contract of Allan's warm embrace, Allan's soft words that would turn his lover's pain into thickened desire before Allan made love to him, before Allan fucked him. There was Gregg, at his most vulnerable, hurting and wanting in that sensitization of pain-pleasure, and there was Allan, wanting to reach out and to give.

"Christ, don't do this to me," Allan screamed inside his gag. "I deserted you. I was afraid of death when you needed me most."

There was no response. There were sounds of distant thunder. Down in the Mission, like a modern day *auto-da-fé*, flames licked at the flesh of heretics. The Spanish Conquistadors and their accompanying Fathers would have felt proudly done by. The Pope would beatify the saintly.

Allan flailed some more at his ropes.

"God damn you, Bill, get down here."

But there was no Bill, there was only thunder. There was no man to paddle his flesh through the bonds, to put clamps on his tits, to distract Allan from this mental agony. There was only Allan facing himself.

Was it really death he had been afraid of in Gregg's illness? Or was it again the loss of control in his own life, the demands of love and loyalty in difficult times? Allan had failed, he was certain. This damned campaign, for all its good reasons, was a fraud. Allan was doing it to avoid Gregg. To try and reassert his own control.

Allan struggled again. How phony could he get?

Still, there was no Bill. He longed for the door to

open, for that quiet leatherman stripped to his harness to enter, to take control again, to slap him silly, to torture his balls to the point of screaming pleasure, to hold him and kiss him as he did so often following these periods of isolation. But there was no Bill. Just Allan. Yet it was only fair. If Allan wanted self-control so much, then he should damn well face his predicament on his own. This bondage served him well. He must stay here and he must accept it.

He saw a face, the gray beard, the words now ominous. They were spoken in a Guerrero Street playroom in 1980. Rumors of the "gay plague" had just begun to emerge from New York. Jim was outraged. "I have this sneaky feeling," he had told Gregg and Allan as they chatted in between play, "that the CIA has had something to do with this. And if they did . . . ."

Allan had dismissed Jim's speculation as idle thought and buried it under a blanket of more timely concerns. Allan remembered now how he had watched Gregg's response. How much Gregg admired Jim. How gullible Allan had judged Gregg.

It all came home, and Allan found himself peering directly into the void. He shook in his bonds, afraid. He wanted to scream as he realized it. He did scream, biting at the gag. Gregg had been spending a lot of time at Jim's lately. He had been secretive about it, but Allan presumed it was some sort of sharing between two dying men. Allan had kept his distance. Now he knew better. Tomorrow was the Presidential visit. They had planned something. Not a word had been said, but he knew it, instinctively.

If there was one thing that could cost him this election, it was violence tomorrow that harmed the President (God damn the evil fucker!) and his party. All of Allan's efforts would be in vain. The liberals could support him, wanted to support him, but they couldn't support violence.

Allan was very afraid. Outside, thunder boomed, and

rain pelted against the side of the house. Gregg had every reason to be upset with Allan. Every reason to want to hurt his campaign. He was also one of the finest marksmen in the city.

How could Allan have been so naive? He shook violently at his restraints and the thunder answered him.

47 *South of Market, San Francisco, Saturday Night*

Imagine a viewer from the roof of the Slot. Night had fallen across the cityscape. Over there are the great blocks of office towers, dozens of Ginsberg's Molochs spelt out in the checkerboards of their windows. Through them, one can catch the shape of the Transamerica pyramid, paeon to the symbol of the dollar bill. Coit Tower, blocked by downtown high rises, is no longer visible from this vantage point.

Men fucked on this roof, on the stairs to the roof, in the wells under the stairs. Can you hear their grunts, the squeals of ecstasy, the screams of passion, the sound of the whipmaster? Men came here in ritual to this dream spot on the Mile, to take and give and share in acts that say "I belong." Can you hear them still, the echoes of years imprinted layer on layer into the frame of this building where an army of ghosts still walk the halls? Can they still smell the Crisco through the new paint, the residents of this refurbished Hotel Shiva of the many hands and arms, painted a fresh blue and white to suggest spring? Can they still sense the black, looming magic impregnated into these walls under the new paint?

Over there, the lights of Folsom Street run towards
the Mission and the lights of Market Street climb to the
Castro nestled in Eureka Valley. Over there a bank of fog
obscures the lights of Upper Market and Twin peaks and Diamond Heights, but above the fog the night sky is thick with
heavy clouds pushing in from the west. Thunder peals out
across the city, and then there is silence again, an unusual
silence.

Men fucked on this roof, snorted poppers, drank each
others' piss and cum; at least one man and probably many
more loaded his paws with Crisco and moved in on a hungry
butt in the early hours before dawn touched the Berkeley
Hills. Men fucked here with the passion they brought to this
city to give to their brothers (and to themselves) in sight of
the dome of this only true republic.

Thunder and lightning splits open the sky. Rain breaks
over Pacific Heights in a furious downpour. Somewhere out
in the Mission firetrucks are responding to a five-alarm blaze.
Down below, an army truck, on patrol, moves quietly up
the street.

Can the soldiers hear the sirens that drew men to this
city from the days of the Gold Rush? Can these soldiers on
patrol fell the dreams of comraderie, the logical extension
of hand to butt to cock, the firm embrace about the shoulder,
the soft determined kiss of lips on lips that only men who
have been denied their emotions for so long can understand or know? Were San Francisco's sailors so deluded in
their rainbow dreams? Were they stranded brutally on the
reefs of desire, their souls left to be washed adrift in the
rising waters?

What madness is this that the army patrols the streets
of San Francisco? The storm explodes over Mount Sutro now
and jolt after screaming jolt of lightening strikes out at the
radio towers. The storm sweeps on, across the spine of
Diamond Heights, and down the hills from the Haight to

the Fillmore, down Noe Valley to the Mission. Somewhere out there, despite the rain, a fire glows on.

Is this madness, the breakdown of order? The collapse of kingdom upon kingdom, the last throes of the republic falling in decadence? Lear pelted with the sharp ravings of the storm and his fool? Are we wanderers, lost in our strange fantasies, on the heath by night? Have our dreams exploded into vitriole and nightmare?

Imagine this viewer from the old days, this ghost of hot passions, this soul that marched Market Street against Bryant and Briggs, that mourned Milk and Moscone, that marched to mark the White Riots, and then marched on each May in Memorial and each June in celebration. Imagine this soul who loved and fucked with a commitment because commitment was sharing and the dream was worth dreaming. He turns around. Behind him, the squat buildings, offices and warehouses and artists studios and autoshops, hidden gardens among them, march towards the Bay. The lonely streets that reverberated at night with sounds of motorcycles and dance palaces and dream halls, the same streets that roar by day like their overhead freeways with commuters' ambitions. Imagine this viewer: here San Francisco meets the Bay and beyond it looms the Bridge that connects the city with America and its strange yet somehow familiar dreams. Men fucked on this roof, men fucked and dreamed in sight of this causeway that so many followed to exile and to dreams of freedom. Was it all madness, like the lemmings rushing to the sacrifice?

Most of the city's lights are obscured now by the driving rain. Sheets of lightning let loose in rapid sequence capturing the tumult in still-life shots. Up in the Castro, the tank sits silently in the intersection beside Hibernia Beach. About the tank sit the huddled masses of thousands, enduring the rain in brave protest. Men, women, even children clutch one another under coats or bits of plastic.

Here and there they protect their candle flames, still burning despite rain, unobscured by sudden lightning. A rising wind blows a bouquet of flowers off the tank's gun, placed there earlier in a sort of nostalgic statement of the sixties. The carnations fall into the crowd. They are taken up by an eight-year-old girl who runs with them to her mother and her mother's lover. The women hug her and the flowers closely. Their tears are indistinguishable from the wetness of the rain.

48 *Vulcan's Stairway, San Francisco, Early Sunday*

Outside, the trees were fighting with the storm, screaming their defiance at the wind. Inside, Brian fitfully slept off his drunkenness. Marc, sitting cross-legged on the bed beside him, had gone elsewhere.

Back in the woods, Marc searched for signs of advice. This man he had struggled to bring home was deeply troubled. Marc wanted to help. But the woods were confusing, buzzing with uncertainty. Thick underbrush, fallen logs plugged his way. There were no answers in the unsettled gloom beneath the boughs, and time and again he found himself brought back to this third-floor room where sudden punctuations of light broke through the square of the window.

He heard a mumbling beside him. Brian was wakening.

"Where am I?" he asked.

"In a house in San Francisco. Safe," Marc told him, putting a hand on his shoulder.

Another question. Brian was trying to pinpoint things.

"South of Market?" he asked.

"No. Upper Market."

"Oh", said Brian, with what could be disappointment. "I dreamed we were at the Ambush."

"We were," Marc told him. "You were very drunk."

"I know," Brian responded, as if that answered all uncertainties.

Brian dozed off again.

Marc leaned over and kissed him. This man was still scared of something. Marc could wait; Brian would tell it in his own time. He went back into the woods to wait.

About fifteen minutes later he heard a branch crack. Brian rolled over, grunted, and started talking. This time he was agitated.

"You've got to stop them," he demanded.

"Stop who?" Marc asked.

"They'll ruin us," Brian pleaded.

Did he really mean *us*, Marc wondered? Or did he mean it would ruin him. It had something to do with Brian's earlier pursuit by soldiers, he knew that.

"They're going to try to shoot the President. It's true. They want to shoot him full of AIDS virus," Brian blurted. "I saw the gun," he whispered as if the whole world was trying to listen.

Marc took Brian's head in his hands, gently, pulling it over so that it rested on his thigh, stroking the hair with his fingers.

"Who?" Marc asked quietly. "Who wants to do this?"

Brian hesitated, and then the story came out: his lover, the Portland physician dying of AIDS, the conspiracy, Jim's name, (Marc knew now that Gregg was involved), the tortuous conspiring to occupy apartments near Moscone Center, the burglary and fire in Missoula, the long ride from

Portland, Brian's own doubts and anxieties. He spilled them all, tears streaming from his eyes, fear in his voice, as if his emotions would save the world.

"You've got to stop them," Brian demanded. "We've got to stop them."

Marc said nothing, just stroked Brian's hair reassuringly. He was not surprised. He had heard and known the anger and fear in the community. Bar talk had been full of it, the streets of the Castro had rumbled with it. "It's too long since cop cars burned at City Hall." "Shoot the bastards." "Find the most painful way to kill the President and the CIA Director and do it!" "California should get out of the Union." "We want revenge. We want blood." Rebellion was in the blood of Marc's ancestry but he was no longer certain that it was his answer. He could see how the flames of injustice flickered. But he had no answers, only the warrior's path.

Brian was still pleading: "We've got to do something."

"Would you call the police?" Marc asked. "The army? Would you turn your lover in?"

There was silence.

"That's not what I meant," Brian said.

Marc knew what Brian meant. He wanted them—him and Brian—to go out and find Jim and intercept the whole thing themselves, throw themselves in front of Gregg and his weapon if that was necessary. But Marc knew Gregg too well, Green Beret and skilled soldier that he was. There would be no getting through to either Gregg or his dart gun. Marc had long suspected something like this, and he knew the uncertainties of emotion that were involved. No, Marc could never bring himself to interfere. He changed the direction of conversation. There was something familiar about this man.

"Tell me," Marc asked. "Where are you from? Before Portland? You're not American."

"No, I'm Canadian," Brian told him, almost defensively.

"So am I," Marc confided. He heard his ancestors groan with disbelief at this blasphemy.

Brian had sat up now, and was looking at Marc with a new curiosity.

"So what's that to do with it?" he said. "They're still trying to shoot the President. We've got to do something."

"Listen kid, it has everything to do with it. Law and order. Canadians, and especially the WASP ones, whatever injustices they suffer, believe in law, order, and good government."

"And Americans?"

"It's a strange sort of opposite," Marc told him. "A contradiction. They're taught to defend the system. But they're also taught the glory of the revolution. That under totally unfair and unyielding injustice, where all other means have failed, rebellion, acts of organized violence are justified. That belief lies huddled in the hearts of every true-blue American man and woman. Sometimes it lets loose, as the blacks did in Watts. Sometimes it finds expression in a deranged gunman whose life has become a closed box and who pursues the symbolic rebellion of a supermarket massacre as the only way out. That's the difference. Nearly every one in the community sees violence as a last, justifiable way out. You only see law and order."

Brian was impatient.

"But you're Canadian. Why aren't you opposed to it? Have they corrupted you, these Americans?"

"I might be Canadian," Marc told him, "but I'm also Metis. Remember Louis Riel? How he hung from the gallows following an attempt to lead the Metis to freedom? Your people, the people of Sir John A. MacDonald, cherished law and order to their own advantage. My people embraced rebellion for a just cause, and lost."

There was silence. Lightning flashed once more, then a sudden gust of rain, then silence. The storm was waning.

"But it's evil," Brian pleaded. "People taking justice into their own hands. God, I know we've been hurt. But it's not right, it's evil."

"What is evil?" Marc asked him. "Who are we to judge?"

"Fuck off," Brian told him, getting up from the bed and walking over to the window to look out, to check that this really was San Francisco. "Don't lecture me on the philosophy of evil."

Marc persisted.

"Put it in perspective," he said. "Are we to be the loyal citizens watching silently as the Nazis march off their victims before coming back for us? Are Jim and Gregg men set out to persecute others for their own insecurities, Klansmen burning black homes and bombing black churches?"

"That's not the question," Brian almost yelled at him from across the room.

"It *is* the question," Marc told him quietly. "We are people who have suffered repeated injustice. We have fought long and hard within a system that has used part of its apparatus to manufacture a virus. To attempt to exterminate us. What are we to do?"

"Then why aren't you out there, rebellious half-breed! Why aren't you fighting the battles that Riel taught you?"

Brian turned to face him, his dark shape visible against the window. Marc ignored his insult. Brian immediately regretted it.

"Because for all this, I'm not sure, Brian. I'm not sure that's meant to be my path of action."

What sort of crazy remark is that? Brian asked himself, but remained silent.

"Come here," Marc told him quietly.

Marc stood up and Brian came towards him. Marc threw his arms about him, pulling their naked bodies together. Marc hugged him and through the grip of the flesh he could feel Brian's tentative, frightened hugs in return.

"Come on brother, warrior," Marc told him. "Let yourself go. As Canadians we should value we've a part in this history, but we know when it's best to stand back and give it space."

Brian pulled himself away and climbed onto the bed, pulling the blankets around him. Mentally he was still fighting. Physically and emotionally he had given in. Lying down beside Brian atop the blanket, Marc put his arms and legs about his buddy, holding him in an embrace that Brian did not resist.

"You know what really gets me?" he confessed to Marc. "It's Sam. I love him. I gave up so much for him. My country, even. And now he's going to die. Alone in some fucking prison. I'll be tried as a coconspirator, jailed, and then deported. I'll hardly see him again, and probably never sleep with him. Is that the way for a sick brother to die?"

"Hang in there," Marc told him. But Brian was already asleep.

49 *South of Market, San Francisco, Early Sunday*

Gregg chose the breaking storm as his opportunity to visit the can and take up position. Even though the rain, slamming against the window, could have obscured surveillance, he took full precautions, moving on hands and knees to the edge of the stacked boxes, then crawling crablike into the area in front of the window. As he crawled, he pulled the dart gun and the blanket with him.

By the time he had reached his station, Gregg was out of breath and exhausted. He was drenched in sweat. He realized now that he was on his last roll. He would make it through this morning. He would fire his shot and hit. But it would be a dead man they found on the floor of this room. Gregg was not afraid of that death now, and he was certain he would accomplish his mission.

He dozed fitfully. Between his little sleeps, lightning split apart the sky. Faces and thoughts exploded in his mind. Many of them were reassuring thoughts. His life was going, transforming into an irretreivable past. In less than a dozen hours, this last great statement would be an irretrievable fact as well. It mattered not that it was avenge or revenge, seeking justice or atonement. They had suffered enough, every person who had died, every person who was dying from this disease. He wanted to do this thing now. He had to do it, one last statement of love for his community. One last statement for the honor of this country that had hurt, cheated, and deceived. He wanted to do it for Jim, for Sam, for Bill, for Tom, for all of his colleagues. More so, he wanted to do it for himself. He kept thinking of Ed Stevens. He kept thinking of the President's face, a pious laconic face of a bombastic leader who might not have had anything to do with setting up this plot but whose very self-serving attitudes made him all the more guilty. The President was a symbol, and Gregg wanted to reach out and hold that body by the neck and brutally dismember it with his own hands while the face screamed for mercy. He wanted to put the dismembered head on a fence post as they had years ago with dead gophers, and use it for target practice. He wanted to totally obliterate it.

The intensity of the rain helped Gregg to sleep. It cooled, assuaged his feverish temperament. He relaxed into the sounds, the incessant splattering, the rushing fury of water as if the whole world were coming to an end and the rising ocean were pouring through the Golden Gate and up into the streets of San Francisco, drowning the plazas and the underground transit lines, creeping ever upwards, until the hills and peaks, Nob Hill and Mount Sutro and Mount Davidson, were receding islands, slipping into the engulfing darkness that would inevitably drown them all.

In his mind Gregg sobbed softly, with a sort of sweet sadness that knows the end is near, that at the same time can touch upon a wealth of beautiful moments from a life that has just been lived and that should never be forgotten. Sometimes, at these moments, bitterness and failure can well up. All that was not accomplished. All that was done badly. All that hurt others. But Gregg's mind was embraced by different, gentle thoughts.

There was that wonderful richness of people he had known, so many people—each one different, each earnest in his own way. He had known so many. Some shared and confided in him; others opened only selective sides of themselves. Some passed at a distance, pulling the covers back from their lanterns only just long enough to glimpse at their radiance. Life was this gift of wealth, measured in people. No, he didn't want to think of those he detested, those he was hurt by. He wanted to touch the souls of the wonderful people he had known, the satyrs and the nymphs, the dancers on the hills, the men in the woods, the workers on the railway lines. They were his first joy of living.

And then, out of all these individuals he knew, were those he had touched and loved. Others might label it promiscuous, anonymous, cheap. Those were insults. To Gregg, his loving and touching created a sweet, tender warmth, a blanket of feeling that he was part of. Each time he had made love he had added to the collective unconscious so that every island became part of the main and every death was a loss to each. This was the greatest feeling of Gregg's life, this camraderie, this sense of being together. He called on it now, and while the rain came down on the army encampment across the street and on the gravel roof of the Moscone Center and on the chic, sculpted edges of modern high rises, Gregg slept in the arms of his dreams.

After the evil of the war, after the torment of his return, Gregg had joined a different army, an army that could move without destroying, that thought it brought hope. He knew just how the feminists felt, the women who believed that in matriarchy the human race would find a sort of careful, productive nurturing and not a constant rattling of sabers. They had felt that too, Gregg and his brothers, they were to be armies of dreamers and lovers and once they grew through the initial, indulgent ramblings of self-discovery and its joys, they would change the world. Oh, how sweet had been that dream. An army for humanity, not one against it. An army anchored in the sea of caring, touching brotherhood, of men who would rather love one another than kill.

* * *

About three-thirty Gregg awoke. The storm had mostly passed; somewhere in the east, flickers of lightning occasionally colored the sky.

About him he could see the dark shapes of the items of his trade. He had taken advantage of the storm to lay them out. The inch-high vial containing some clear, frothy liquid. The cartridge for the dart gun. A watch. And alongside Gregg, the gun itself.

About five-thirty he intended to open the window slowly, sliding the panel aside. He had another six hours until zero hour and he wanted to sleep again. But he was afraid that if he did sleep he would either miss his cue or fail to open the window.

He was feverish again, and the sweat poured off him as if his body was air-conditioning an already cold room. Gregg wrapped himself in his blanket, but it was already damp. He wished he could find another blanket. He thought of getting up and searching through the boxes. In his mind he was already unpacking boxes, lifting them down off each other, opening the cardboard flaps. Oh, for an electric blanket. He pulled out kitchenware. He unwrapped wine glasses for days (Oh, how queens, even butch ones, love their stemware!) He was sorting through boxes of tools and wires and bits of hardware. There were records and books, all his favorite titles, and *Drummer* magazines full of his fantasies. He found himself mentally pausing at each item and staring. Even reading a few lines, then continuing in his frenetic, mental search. Oh, if there was only an electric blanket tucked in between the china and the dildos, or between the aspirin bottle and the blender and his set of hand-tooled cowboy boots—bought in Wyoming on a trip to the Grand Tetons, oh how life got so complicated in times of need: how much baggage we seemed to collect.

Gregg stopped suddenly in his search; he could swear the door had opened. Someone coughed: he knew that cough, it was Allan's cough. It was exactly the sort of cough Allan made when he discovered Gregg at something unexpected. Had Allan come to see why all this stuff was boxed and ready to go? Gregg still had to say good-bye to Allan. But when his mind looked up from a box of canned goods—everything from tiny peas to smoked oysters that he was sorting through—he saw no one, only a sort of black delirium. Out of the blackness he heard Allan moan in frustration. Then he saw him, his body straightened against rope bonds that held each limb immobilized, the sweat dripping from his chest, the candlelight flickering in splotches off the dampness. Gregg saw an agonized face, he saw each moan, each sob, each furious lunge that Allan took as if trying to free himself. What was his lover saying? What was he in such torment about? It looked as if he was on a bad acid trip. But Gregg could hear no words from his lover, and his questioning brought no answer.

The vision vanished into a frustrating blackness. Where had Allan been? When? Was he remembering some bad trip from the Hot House or the Slot? Was it last week? Was it tonight? Gregg had to know, he was agitated about what he had seen. He was in a library, taking book after book from the shelves, opening their bindings in maroon or green or amber leather, flipping dusty pages. He saw old bindings with recent names. He opened the books to frontispieces that showed his friends. The answer must be here. He saw strange equations and baroque engravings. Some of the texts he couldn't read. The answer had to be here on these universal shelves. His searching became frantic. His mind became desperate. And then it collapsed and books came tumbling down on him by the hundreds. He saw wisps of type and fragments of paper swirling like cigarette butts down a giant toilet bowl.

The books vanished and Gregg was climbing through a landscape of exposed granite, wrapped in cloud. He had to find Allan. He had to know what Allan wanted. He had to say good-bye. Gregg was holding onto the bare rock now, lifting himself forward slowly and with great effort. Was the air thin up here where John Muir had met the heavenly messengers? Was this the road upwards? It was cold, and Gregg shivered in these vast Sierra rocklands with their giant fields of eroded gruss, tilled only by wind, snow, and rain like the raked stones of a Japanese temple garden. Vegetation was scarce: a stunted manzanita clinging to a rock edge, a patch of chaparral buckthorn or the scattered lonely Jeffrey pine rising into the mist. It was a landscape of gray stone and gray mist. It was incredibly peaceful and it was freezing cold.

Gregg woke again at five thirty-five. A pale sickly light was creeping across the cityscape. He managed slowly, oh so slowly, to raise his hand to the bottom of the window panel and slide the small left-hand square open. How Gregg wished the sun would come up and the room fill with warm light so that he could lie there, basking in its glory. Oh, how desperate are these last little hopes.

Gregg had been dreaming hard for an answer about Allan. When he awoke, he found one. Allan was screaming over his own vulnerability, as if he had never discovered it before. Maybe that was because he kept himself so busy doing things. Allan's inability to come to grips with Gregg's condition was an everyday statement of it. Gregg wanted to reach through the barrier between them to say good-bye in a way that showed he really felt for Allan. At the same time, Gregg felt hurt, isolated, and he didn't want to do anything. Just keep on flipping through the pages of the books, just keep hoping it would all solve itself.

How much was he, Gregg, to blame in this mess? He remembered moments following his diagnosis when he withdrew himself, soaked in his own fears, and avoided any undue contact or affection that might point out his condition. Had he encouraged Allan to keep his distance, to magnify Gregg's own vulnerability? Gregg wondered about that. Could he even say that his own isolation, and Allan's detachment towards him, had helped to justify the actions Gregg was about to take? That in loading this gun, he was taking a potshot at his lover's campaign? In his delirium Gregg knew that Allan wasn't guiltless. But he also had more doubts about his own motives. Was this really the way to say good-bye.

50 *Spring Valley, Maryland, Sunday Morning*

The Reverend Bill Anckenburg (Jo-Lyn thought he was cute) had just handed over the Christian Network to the White House News Service. The President was due to arrive at any moment at Alameda Naval Air Station.

Jo-Lyn, who had wakened on the floor at four A.M., then pulled herself into bed, was remarkably calm. Her mind seemed clear of agitation, and she sensed a new, important purpose. She would watch the outcome, the arrangement of today's events, with great care. Jo-Lyn was, one could say, hardened. God had spoken with her and put the events of the last few days into perspective. The time for tears and wailing and self-reproach had passed. She could live with the betrayals she had been dealt, by her husband, her minister and her President. She would live with the betrayals and she would step beyond them.

She still clutched the gun as she watched television, but with a more natural, relaxed feeling. It was needed for defense, and Jo-Lyn was determined she would protect herself and her feelings. She held the gun now with the ease she might have held little Carolyn. Indeed as the television switched to California, she picked up Carolyn from her bassinet and cradled her and the gun.

"Fellow Americans," Jimmy Johnson told them. "Welcome to this historic broadcast of the White House News Network. We're here in California for the President's arrival. After last night's storm, it looks like it should be a fine day."

When several years ago, the White House had created their own news reporting service to cover the President's activities, Jo-Lyn was not surprised. It was not that the nation's press were being denied access to the President. But it was felt to be much more efficient and accurate to provide the networks with tapes of policy statements and question-and-answer sessions as supervised by the Oval Office itself. Over the past decade it had become quite clear that the press was largely incapable of nonjudgmental, non-biased reporting. The real facts were not getting out. Besides, times were becoming increasingly dangerous. The few public opportunities, like those with a hostile press, for the President to be exposed to assassins and the like, the better would be chances for his safety. There had, of course, been public debate over the issues involved. At the time, Jo-Lyn had disagreed with most of them. This wasn't censorship, the President was capable of speaking for himself and for what was right. It was just that the press never gave him a proper chance. Times were also getting to be unsafe; the public just couldn't expect the same degree of contact with the man. Now, however, on both of these counts, Jo-Lyn wasn't sure.

"According to controllers here on the base," Jimmy Johnson was telling the world, *"Air Force One"* is about ten minutes out. It's just coming into position for descent and landing."

He smiled copiously behind a cutesy little mustache meant to signal that the Presidential staff had just the right touch of hip. He generally smiled a lot anyway; it had been recently decided that there had been too much gravity emerging from the White House.

"I am sure there are few Americans who don't appreciate the historic proportions of the President's visit to California."

He went on to describe "difficult times" and "uncertainties" and the need for clear insight, which the President would bring. The President's coming was a statement to America of renewal, of what was good and right and Christian. It was a statement to America's allies that we would not back down in difficult times. It was a statement to the world that the President was not afraid.

Jo-Lyn listened, without emotion, as Jimmy Johnson went on about the "grave dangers" likely to confront the President on this particular visit. Assassination threats. Armed crazies in the streets of the city. Lunatics and sick men who would try anything. Why, two days ago, the San Francisco lunatic fringe had burned a large part of the downtown.

It irked Jo-Lyn deep inside that Jimmy Johnson could so laud the President's bravery. That maybe, just maybe, he was the special sort of hero that this country needed. No, Jo-Lyn could not accept that. Any man who would turn his back on a loyal patriotic American who had served his country as had her husband, was no hero. It irked her no end that Jimmy Johnson could pontificate about communists lurking in the government. That was all rumor. The President's word. They sure didn't have anything on Ed and she knew it. Jimmy Johnson was a creep and the President was a wimp.

But Jo-Lyn wasn't going to let this emotional outrage take control. She was amazed at how calm she could remain, almost accepting of the facts and her predicament while she listened to this horrid man presume he could destroy their life. She was amazed how tranquilly she listened, her mind almost elsewhere in its resolve, but at the same time perfectly conscious of all going on, her hand gently clutching the shaft of the revolver, her face almost beatific with joy as she smiled sweetly at little Carolyn.

In between his chatter about the President's bravery, Jimmy Johnson was plugging the security system. "No measure has been overlooked, every point in the President's travel plans has been made secure." In between these claims, Jimmy Johnson was pushing the real purpose of the San Francisco visit. The meeting of NATO Defense Ministers. But Jimmy Johnson did not report (as had the *Washington Post* this very morning) that only two of the other NATO members were still coming to the conference and that those two nations were only sending lower-echelon staff as observers. Jo-Lyn knew the situation all right. America's allies sure as hell didn't want to support a coward. How shameful could the state of this country become? How long would it have to suffer while wimps like Johnson mutilated the truth and the rest of the world laughed? Jo-Lyn was ashamed.

When Jimmy Johnson talked of the other conference, this rally of Citizens for Moral Renewal, it provoked the same reaction. Jo-Lyn knew all about it: for months it had been the talk of the Fellowship. Then it had been decided that Susan MacKillop and her husband would represent the Fellowship at the San Francisco rally. Why them again? And what did they or the President know about moral renewal? This man had deserted her own Ed! And the Fellowship had also deserted them. Here were these people going to San

Francisco to show the world what they thought of perverts and commies. Where was the respect, the loyalty that was owed them by these brave Christians? Her husband and she had already demonstrated to the world what was good and necessary.

Air Force One had landed and Jimmy Johnson was preparing to greet the President. The door would open and the ramp would be put in place. The President would descend, waving at the cameras of the White House News Network, in perfect safety. Jo-Lyn knew the routine well, several times she and other well-wishers had seen him arrive at Andrews Air Force Base just outside Washington. She could visualize it now.

51 *Vulcan's Stairway, San Francisco, Sunday Morning*

At six A.M. the kitchen was in a confused state. From opposite sides of the room radio and television struggled with the hype of the presidential visit. On the table, the *Chronicle* had been ripped into its sections and distributed across chairs and floor. The first section was open on page A6, where under the headline "Army," reporting continued of the front-page article. It was Sunday's paper, and there was little in the way of recent news in it, but Allan had devoured it frenetically.

Adding to the confusion, Allan, already dressed in dark suit and tie, was making coffee. He translated his agitation into slammed cupboard doors and heavy-handed actions. Confrontation with troops in the streets of the

Castro was one thing. But he was convinced that was only a smoke screen. Just where the fuck was Gregg? Damn it! He'd added water to the coffee maker without putting the pot underneath. Liquid hissed on the hotplate and dribbled onto the counter. Allan grabbed the pot and shoved it in. Damn it, why did things have to go like this? Why couldn't he just come home and find Gregg asleep in his room? He knew something was up. There were footsteps at the kitchen door and Allan swung around in anticipation. It was Marc, wrapped in a terry-cloth robe.

"Where the fuck is Gregg?" Allan demanded.

"Boy, we're testy this morning, aren't we?"

Allan ignored the comment. "Where is Gregg?" he repeated, this time a little more evenly.

"No idea," Marc answered. "Maybe out with that little Italian number he's been having an affair with. You know, the bartender — "

"Bullshit," Allan said. "He doesn't expect me to believe that crap!"

"Gregg saw him the night before last. Probably saw him last night."

Allan grabbed a coffee cup and pulled the half-filled pot from the machine. Coffee dribbled onto the hotplate. He ignored it, poured himself a cup, and put the pot back. He turned to Marc again.

"Listen Marc, where the hell is he?"

"I told you Allan, I don't know."

"He's up to something. I know it. That friend of ours, Jim, he's been hanging around with him a lot. Their circle. They've got something planned for today or my name isn't Allan Bennett. I don't trust them."

So that was what it was all about, Marc concluded. Allan was worried that Gregg and his friends just might be out to do something to the President. And why was

Allan so concerned, damn him? Allan—who was so tied up in this fucking campaign that he'd almost ignored Gregg.

On the radio a commentator reported the latest in ambassadorial withdrawals. A number of African nations had already severed diplomatic ties with the United States. The Soviet ambassador had been called home for urgent consultations. Neither Marc nor Allan paid any attention.

"I know the feelings that are running around among Jim and his friends," Allan continued. "They're hurt. They want revenge. They're going to try something."

"Come on Allan, Jim's been sick. Gregg's been over there giving support. It's more than you've given him."

"Don't try to cover up for them. You're involved too, aren't you?"

"I don't know anything."

"Bullshit, Marc, you don't expect me to believe that. All your crazy meetings in secret places using the code names of defunct bars. You know what I'm talking about."

Marc remained silent. He poured himself some coffee, then, getting a sponge, wiped up the slop on the counter and the coffee maker.

"Listen Marc, we've got to stop them. Do you realize what it'll do to Tuesday's elections if a bunch of irate faggots go out and shoot the President?"

"Allan, I don't know what you're talking about.

Strictly speaking, it was true. He'd heard Brian's ravings about a plot, but they were only rumors. As for Gregg's involvement, Gregg hadn't volunteered anything to Marc directly. As for reading truths between the lines, he'd let Allan be the expert at that. And anyway, why the hell should he keep Allan informed on things that were none of his business? He thought of Brian upstairs and hoped he wouldn't come down. When Marc had left the bedroom, Brian was still gently snoring.

Allan tried another approach.

"Marc. We've been friends and lovers for years. We've always trusted each other. You've got to trust me now."

Yeah, Marc thought. Now your campaign's on the line. Well you can just screw it. Everybody's had to bow to your ambitions for too long. I was expected to do everything just to make you happy. Sure, I wanted to, but I wasn't given a chance. You wanted to be in control.

Footsteps sounded upstairs. A bedroom door opened, than a door down the hall closed. Please, Marc thought. Please don't let him come down.

"Allan, I have no answers. Take your campaign and run with it. You'll do okay. But don't come to me for gossip."

"Who's that upstairs?"

"A friend of mine. I met him last night."

"Damn you, Marc. This city's in chaos. The army's in the streets. Gay people are dying. Bars are getting firebombed. And all you're doing is cruising around as if it's the seventies."

"Is that the way you get elected? By insulting your best friends?"

Allan sat staring grimly at the paper. On the radio Norman Miller, asked his opinion of current American affairs, stated the need for guts. He didn't come out and praise the President's actions. Upstairs the toilet flushed. You could always hear flushing toilets in this old house, the gurgle of passing water and emptied guts as they flowed through the pipes and down beneath Vulcan's Stairway to the city below. Upstairs a door opened and there were uncertain footsteps in the hall.

Allan stood up sharply. On the run again, Marc noted.

He looked briefly at Marc.

"I'm sorry. I didn't mean to insult you and your friends. Really! These are rough times and my thinking's not straight."

He wanted Marc to hug him, first of all tight, then

gently rub his hands down Allan's back. But that would be asking too much. His leaving after that would be like throwing away a paper towel.

Footsteps descended the stairs.

Allan turned to go.

"Three days and it'll all be over. We'll talk then. A nice long talk. I've got to run."

Allan turned and brushed by Brian who was just entering the kitchen. He went out into the hall without saying anything. The front door closed. Marc relaxed several notches.

"Take a seat and have some coffee," he told Brian. "We're just about to watch a replay of *Gotterdammerung*."

52 *Guerrero Street, San Francisco, Sunday Morning*

I'm scared, Jim. I shouldn't have told him. But he forced it out of me in the truck. He suspected something. He kept insisting. It was only because he was my lover."

Sam and Jim were alone at Mission Center, the second-floor living room of Jim's Guerrero Street home.

Jim appeared gaunt and sad and very tired. He looked out at Sam through a grotesque mask created by purple and black lesions that had spread across his cheeks and forehead, even his eyelids, as if they were trying to crowd each other out. He squinted in order to see better; just last week his eyes had been diagnosed with retinitis. Some moments, Sam could see him as a strange creature, a goblin maybe. Then he would see himself in Jim's image,

Sam's own lesions gone mad. And then he remembered the earlier Jim, the ruddy face and its penetrating blue eyes, the gray beard, the devoted expressions of a man who knew how to make love. He remembered Jim's holding, probing, his arm about his shoulders as he cradled you, his eyes full of care, his gentle smile touched with the complex tenderness and delight and wonder of it all.

"Sam, we all swore to tell nobody, to say nothing. Not even lovers."

"I know. I almost didn't. But when that Stevens guy made his announcement to the press, I figured things had changed."

Jim sounded sad in his response.

"Things haven't changed, Sam. You shouldn't have done it. You know you shouldn't have done it."

Jim had a way of lecturing that sometimes made his friends uncomfortable. Sam refused to react.

"It'll be okay," he answered. "I know I've been worrying, but Brian probably just needed some space to think. Nothing's going to happen to ruin things."

Sam said this almost hopefully. Inside, he knew Brian's stubbornness. His set ideas about what was right and wrong. But Sam mustn't get Jim more upset than necessary. Damn it, he wished now he'd resisted those questions in the truck. But damn it, he loved that man. They had so much between them. Couldn't Sam claim the right to maintain one of the few dear things he had left in this life, as short as it would probably be?

Yeah, Sam pondered, there were a lot of people committed to this. Tom, the ex-cop. Bill, the guy who'd chosen the apartment. John, another marksman who had taken up position in St. Francis Place. Gregg. Peter, who'd made the virus. Wayne, up in Seattle, who'd engineered the Missoula break-in. Tony, who'd died last week and used his contacts in the press to get needed information. There were many others, whom Sam had never met. All dying. All counting on their brothers in this one final statement. How could Brian not understand the importance, the need of it all?

The phone rang. From the third floor of the Audiffred Building across the Embarcadero from the Ferry Building, Richard phoned to wish Jim a belated happy birthday. That meant the Presidential helicopter, flying over from Alameda, had just touched down.

Jim hung up, then dialed a number in Bernal Heights. "Just checking," he told Steve. "We're still on for that drive to Santa Cruz tomorrow?"

"Sure am," Steve told him, "Pick you up at nine-thirty."

A chain of phone calls followed. Bernal Heights rang out to the Sunset. The Sunset called Hayes Valley. Hayes Valley called South of Market, and across from the Moscone Center the phone behind Gregg rang. Four rings that went unanswered. The President, this signal announced, was in the city. Outside the Ferry Building, a bullet-proof limousine awaited.

Jim, looking very grim, put down the phone and turned to Sam.

"Nothing," he stated belligerently, "nothing had better fuck up this operation. Your Brian included."

The President and his wife, surrounded by security men, were escorted briskly through the emptied halls of the Ferry Building and passed lines of armed soldiers. At the street entrance to the building, two San Francisco police cars had pulled up, and a small party of city officials waited. The press had not been permitted at this point, although cameramen from the White House News Network were in place to record history. It was a prominent party that was here to greet the President, and they moved to cross the metal barriers as he walked out from under the protective canopy leading to his car and the Embarcadero.

"Mr. President," the Chief of Police called out. He clutched a sheaf of papers.

The President of the United States turned briefly, hesitating just for a moment. An aide spoke quietly in his ear, and the President, holding his wife's arm, strode on to the waiting limousine.

"Mr. President. In the name of the law I demand you stop."

The Police Chief had crossed the barrier and was followed by the rest of the city party. Preinstructed, the White House News Network ignored them, catching with perfect finality the President's determined stride to the car. The limousine door closed and the car sped off.

On the pavement in front of the Ferry Building, army and security officials moved in to detain the members of the city party. Those held were the City Attorney, the District Attorney, the Sheriff, the President of the Board of Supervisors, and a superior court judge. They were led away, the Chief of Police still clutching the county/city warrant for the President's arrest.

53 *City Hall, San Francisco, Sunday Morning*

The morning was grim and clear. The greened bronze of City Hall dome pushed hard edges grimly against a cold blue sky. Out from the facade of the building and below the dome, several flags fluttered briskly at half-mast. Old Glory, ripped down during Friday's rally, had not been replaced.

Inside the building the Mayor prepared to face the press, national and local, displaced from their duties elsewhere in the city by the White House News Network. She was dressed in black, and before the official conference began, she told reporter Wendy Tokuda that "Here in San Francisco we are mourning those who have died of AIDS, not condemning them." Notably, all of her contingent, including Allan, were dressed in black or dark attire.

What the Mayor said was simple, forceful, and elegant. She left her biggest bomb for the last. Her speech was touched with sadness, but that was not its most apparent aspect. Its strongest element was its toughness, a fiber that was not flagrant but subtle: Watch out, this is only a beginning. There's only so much San Francisco will take. If you don't think we've got the strength or resources, watch out!

Throughout the speech Allan was aware of these overtones; he knew of certain contingency decisions that had already been made, but he hardly focused on them or the speech. His mind was elsewhere.

"Members of the press," the Mayor stated. "Fellow Citizens. I want to begin this conference by saying that we still regard as unfortunate the choice of our city for today's rally of Citizens for Moral Renewal. The attitudes expressed by the organizers of this rally do not reflect the feelings of many San Franciscans. Indeed, many people in our city are repulsed by statements such as, and I quote: 'Queers are by nature unnatural and evil and must be stamped out of America.' Unquote. It seems to us here in San Francisco that the rally's nationwide publicity has emphasized things in San Francisco that it dislikes, and that it had deliberately tried to stir up local hostility. It is even more unfortunate that the President of the United States should choose to come and address this group."

Damn it, Allan thought, ignoring the Mayor's remarks and staring outwards formally as befit the tone of the press conference. Damn it, I don't deserve to win. But I've got to win, for the sake of the community. Not for me, *I* don't deserve it. I'm a self-seeking manipulative bastard. I should never have treated Gregg the way I did.

"If San Francisco doesn't reflect their value systems, then why did CMR's organizers insist on coming here unless it was to provoke trouble? When they first approached us, we suggested to CMR that they try Cleveland or Dallas. If they had to come to California, San Jose had convention facilities. The Concord Pavilion was available. Yet no. It had to be here, we were told. There was hope for great conversions. We were told that we underestimated San Francisco's commitment to the values of CMR. Many people here, like Walter Harrison, say enough is enough. As we found out yesterday, Mr. Harrison, a black man, has made history by receiving political donations from the Klan. I do not attribute Mr. Harrison's predicament to a mellowing of attitudes or to a desire for reconciliation."

This speech was not an easy one for the Mayor to give, and she was under considerable political pressure. She had built her support from numerous splinter groups, community organizations and political causes. Some of them did not favor her standing here today to threaten the American government. Others felt she had not gone far enough. Yes, they were all horrified at the CIA's recently revealed plots. But as Allan had been told yesterday, this city needed stability. The Mayor had spent much of the past night on difficult phone calls between conflicting factions. She had pleaded to her critics the need for her statement, a strong statement. It was in their interest. If the city didn't take a stand, certain of its people would. What could happen might be even more threatening. After the Mission firebombing and the deaths by immolation last night, another riot could well become an uprising. Her detractors could also remember how the city had a tradition of posturing on many past issues, the Olympics, Homeporting the *Missouri*, for example. Beneath her calm composure, her forthright presentation, the Mayor was a mass of nerves. Indeed, it was surprising how good a face she was giving the cameras.

"Despite our misgivings about this conference, we believe in free speech and free assembly. Not all groups that come to this great city necessarily believe in everything in it. Few San Franciscans do either! But we find it regrettable that over a year ago we signed an agreement to rent Moscone Center to a group that promotes bigotry in the name of values."

Values, Allan thought. Where the fuck are my values the way I treated Gregg? That man who put out so much for me, who shared so much of his life. Damn it, where was I when he needed me? Me, the creep, playing my political games. Arguing that getting the edge was more important than compassion. A cheap excuse on my part because I was supposedly afraid. Shit! Afraid! After all, I put up with Harrison and Fraggi, and I was afraid to take hold and stroke the man who has given me so much. Where are you, Gregg? I need you, Gregg.

A tear showed in the corner of Allan's eye, on an otherwise grim, determined face. He didn't care what the press thought.

"Values," the Mayor continued. She paused, creating anticipation. "If CMR thinks that they have an exclusive right to define what is meant by values, then they are even more dangerous than any of us thought. And if they believe that they hold the prerogative on moral renewal, they had better do some learning. Because we here in San Francisco believe in moral renewal. We here in San Francisco believe in values."

She was a relatively short woman although the dais raised her roughly to the same height of the other platform guests. Her dais was a small personal demand she always made of her speaking engagements. But today, no one would have noticed. This was national press and this was San Francisco speaking. Indeed, the whole world was watching. Under the lights, a bead of sweat had broken out on her brow. She ignored it and went on. The tension in the air was evident.

"What are those values that San Francisco believes in? What is the moral renewal that we seek? Let me review these, for some of our fellow Americans who may have been confused by the drivel put forth by CMR.

"We believe in the rights of each women and man to honestly make, in accordance with their conscience, their own choice and creed and spiritual belief. Those beliefs may be personal or part of a more organized network, but whatever the choice, each individual is due the respect for making it. Coercion by the state must have no role in any of these choices. And moral renewal will only come when citizens know they have this freedom of choice."

And then there was Marc. Allan was upset at how he'd treated him this morning. How many times had Marc warned Allan about Gregg's hurt? How many times had he pushed Allan to reach out and overcome his fears and give Gregg support?

Allan shuddered at himself. Marc had so much to say, but he'd laughed at him and passed him off as an aging hippy. Marc never pushed his native roots, but Allan refused to listen or inquire where he could have learned. I was too busy pretending I had to stay in control, he told himself. I claimed that people out there needed me. I don't deserve to win. How many other friends have I treated like this? How many of the dying did I avoid, even in their final days, because I thought it was so necessary that I succeed? Time has gone by on them. They've crossed the river. But this creep who claimed to love them, never said good-bye.

A tear broke loose and ran down Allan's cheek. It was

joined by a second one. Well, he thought, her honor was certainly giving an impassioned speech.

"We also believe," the Mayor continued, "in the morality of helping others, particularly the oppressed, the hurt and the sick. We believe in doing so without questioning or condemning personal beliefs or lifestyles. This city has a strong, compassionate record of the helping hand. In the AIDS crisis for example, we have demonstrated to America some of our finest abilities. We have shown how our communities can work together in respect for one another. With moral renewal, sickness is not overcome by fear and loathing or by the spreading of hatred. Moral renewal comes with compassion and respect for one another."

Yes, thought Allan. This was San Francisco at its finest. But do I deserve to represent it?

"Here in San Francisco, we believe not only in freedom of choice of spiritual belief, and in compassion, but we also believe in the right to chose one's style of life according to one's conscience. This is something that America is supposedly famous for, but we have become so preoccupied with what is right and American, we have tended to forget about the minorities who came here seeking freedom and now exercise it. For it is not enough to merely have this freedom. Moral renewal means respect for freedom and the rights of others to exercise it. Moral renewal does not mean snickering or prejudice for those freely exercising their rights as citizens. We can not have moral renewal when one group, however widespread, sets out to impose on others a morally right way to live.

"We also believe in a fourth element of moral renewal. And that is justice. We in San Francisco believe in the fair and equal application of all laws to all people. We do not believe in laws designed to intimidate any group that is living in its self-chosen way. We do not believe in laws for the rich that are different from those for the poor. We do not believe in separate justice for blacks, for Asians, or for the physically constrained. And we do not believe in one set of laws for elected officials and another for those who elected them.''

Allan watched the Mayor pause. This, he knew, was the most difficult part of her statement. She appeared visibly tense. She was waiting to make her conclusion. He had a vision of Gregg with a gun. He was in a room near the Moscone Center. The gun was pointed towards the President. One side of Allan's brain screamed: No! No! It wanted to rush out of the press conference and call up the army. Stop him! There's a Vietnam vet out there and he's holed up with a gun. The other side of Allan's brain said simply: Shoot!

"I want to conclude my little homily on moral renewal by showing you just what I mean by equal justice for all. As all of you are no doubt aware, this city committed itself to the arrest of the President of the United States on his arrival. He was to be charged with various felonies related to the alleged virus plot of the CIA. The President would, of course, be released on his own recognizance.

"At nine forty-five this morning, on his arrival at the Embarcadero, the President was met by the City Sheriff, District Attorney, City Attorney, President of the Board of Supervisors, and Chief of Police. Our Police Chief carried the warrant for the President's arrest. None of these officials were allowed to speak with the President. All have been detained indefinitely by the army. This is America. Is this equal justice? Is this what we mean by moral renewal?''

Shoot! Shoot the fucker. Allan's mind was screaming. It was provoked by thoughts of Harrison's insults, aimed not at Allan but at his community. It was provoked by the deaths, brought about by the CIA machine, the lingering, horrible ends that he had so often avoided in his push to get ahead.

Those made it worse. Shoot, his mind screamed at Gregg. Shoot! Fuck my campaign. Kill the bastard and all he represents.

Allan was openly crying now, tears falling down a resolute face.

The press was asking questions of the Mayor. How long would those arrested be detained? Would another attempt be made to arrest the President? What other actions had the city planned?

"The city will not stand for this blatant injustice. We shall do everything within our powers to rectify the situation. We will resort to stronger actions as necessary."

"Just what does the city mean by stronger actions?" asked television reporter Crystal Yee.

"For example," her honor replied, "the city intends to petition Congress to begin impeachment procedings."

Allan thought it sounded a bit hollow. He noted that nothing was said regarding the move towards secession some of them had discussed earlier.

54 *South of Market, San Francisco, Sunday Morning*

The phone rings and Gregg awakes. Four short rings. The call comes via Bernal Heights and Twin Peaks. In an office tower on New Montgomery where the chain of calls began, an observer has noted the presidential motorcade en route down Howard Street. After getting no response from Gregg's number (and no response expected) the caller will start a new chain via the Marina to St. Francis Place.

The big moment. Three minutes approximately, and the President will be here. The car door will open. Already his greeters, a busload (Vallejo Unified School District) of Lesbian and gay demonstrators, disguised in polyester and clutching Bibles, has passed the checkpoint and is moving towards Moscone Center.

Gregg moves to pull himself into position. About three quarters of an hour ago he has loaded the dart with the virus and set it into the gun. Yes, he can do it. He damn well can do it. His body will do it. This will be the best shot he's ever made. His aim will be perfect. In his mind he can imagine his hands along the shaft of the gun, he can feel it balanced along his arm.

His mind moves into the intricacies of holding and aiming the weapon. His body remains supine on the carpet. He can do it. Yes, he can muster the energy required for this one focused instance, he can find the concentration needed to aim, to freeze, to shoot. He can do it, even if this is his last moment alive.

Gregg lies there, his mind yearning for Allan. What does this all mean? This getting even? Avenge? Revenge? Hadn't he been through all this before? Should this be anyone's last act? He remembers the post-Vietnam oath he made. Never. Never. Never to fire a gun at another person again. I love you Allan, he murmurs.

For the last hour, buses have disgorged thousands of CMR supporters at the doors of the Moscone Center. The disembarkment has been orderly and without incident. Most passengers clutch Bibles and American flags. The flags draped across the front of the Center indicate this will be a grand day.

Gregg's body struggles once more to get ready, but his mind resists. He hears Marc talking of evil, of little flames, spirits hidden under every stone, waiting to infiltrate any action if given the chance. How he chuckled at Marc's mysticism. Gregg has enough of good and evil, sin and grace in his Fundamentalist past. But Marc's words keep coming back. "What is justice against the immeasurable forces with which evil has to play in this universe? Can justice, countering a single little act, ever stem the tide, ever overcome the relentless subversion of evil?" And then the words, "We can only try, but in all our efforts we must beware. When is an act good, or just, or simply evil speaking in another flame?"

Gregg makes one last struggle, pulling his body half way off the floor. No, he consciously tells himself. I could but I won't. Those people never learn anything from situations likes this. Gregg collapses onto the floor.

Outside, the Vallejo Unified School District bus had pulled up under the portico and its passengers are dismounting. The passengers do not go directly into the Center but mill around waving unfurled placards. At almost the same moment, the President's car arrives. The door opens and he steps out.

The view from Gregg's open window, if recorded on tape, would have shown how perfect the setup was. The President was clearly visible. There were about five yards of pavement across which he and his wife would walk. The line of sight would have been fully unobstructed. The President even paused, midway in this walk, to gesture at the chanting demonstrators. The demonstrators, along with their bus, had effectively blocked access to the northernmost part of the Center. It could have been a perfect shot.

Gregg, on the floor, has a fleeting glimpse of the whole scene. Somewhere across the city, Jim, Sam, and various others would be watching on television. Watching. Waiting. Gregg hears Marc again, talking of dream maps: the landmarks of the voyage to the world across the river. He feels himself drifting almost effortlessly through forests, over mountains. The forked tree, split by lightning: beware of the spirits that linger like serpents in its cracks. Will he travel alone? Will he need the map? He hears words coming to him, the metaphors spoken with meaning in all tongues and by all peoples. He had laughed at the idea of dream maps. When one died, one was dead. It was ridiculous to think of maps to help the dead find their way, to help the living live. Maps so precious that the native peoples rarely disclose them. Maps so secret, so culturally essential, so spiritually important, that to reveal them was like self-exposure and was done only to loved ones. In the past, Gregg had disdained those ideas.

Now they seemed incredibly sweet thoughts. Marc's words, spoken softly, fell into Gregg's mind like a spring shower, each drop blossoming into sense and emotion like the words of a poem. Gregg is swept with a delicious feeling of relief, of wanting to cry, over and over again in a happy sort of ecstasy that mingles with the words that carry him away. He wants to struggle to write down the words, to record them. But there's no need: he will know them forever. They are his words and his dream map. Gregg wants to hold Marc as he drifts into peace. Somewhere out there he can hear birdsong.

55 *Guerrero Street, San Francisco, Sunday Morning*

In the end, the television stations had refused to cooperate. The networks had been annoyed when the White House News Network had been given exclusive coverage of the Presidential visit. Security risks were too great, the White House had said. WHNN coverage would be more than adequate. After some last-minute wrangling the networks had stood firm: they refused to carry WHNN reporting.

For Jim, with a row of televisions lined up, his hope of watching the steps of his plan fall into place from different vantage points was clearly frustrated. All local networks of the major affiliates largely ignored the Presidential event, and played up the Mayor's press conference now under way at City Hall. PBS was showing Sesame Street reruns. Only one station, a conservative Christian operation in San Jose, directly broadcast WHNN coverage. A roomful of glibly smiling Jimmy Johnsons was too much in the way of good company, and Sam, at Jim's behest, shut off all but two of the screens, one showing City Hall and the other playing the WHNN. A few minutes later, they toned down City Hall.

"So this is freedom of the press," Sam commented.

"Yeah," Jim said bluntly.

It was as if Jim's inability to watch the precise details, the President's arrival, the movement of the motor-cade down Howard Street (another phone call from Bernal Heights, again on the Santa Cruz trip: the motor-cade had crossed by Howard and New Montgomery Streets), the car turning into the entrance of the Moscone Center, the President stepping out—it was as if their inability to monitor all of this had imperiled the success of the mission. Jim was finding it difficult to contend with this cheerful dialogue of Jimmy Johnson on just how important to the rest of America this Presidential visit to San Francisco was. He almost retched when Jimmy spoke of the coura-geous presidential statement we could expect on the CMR rally.

"Where the hell do they get this slime?" Sam asked.

"Drawn automatically to the White House," Jim answered him cynically. "Like attracts like. Flies drawn to shit. This is America, you know."

Suddenly, they were there. The WHNN cameras showed the President and the First Lady stepping out. The polyester-clad, Bible-clutching protesters had spread out to the north and however much the WHNN cameras tried, they couldn't avoid just a glimpse of them. The President paused for a second; he raised his hands in quiet defiance as if enough was enough.

"Now!" Jim exclaimed. "Now, Gregg. It's perfect. You must be able to see clearly. Come on Gregg. Shoot! Get the bastard!"

But it was too late. The Presidential party entered the building with no sign of harm. There was no reaction to any sort of shot.

"Sam, we could have got him."

There were tears in Jim's eyes.

"There's still the second chance," Sam assured him. "When he comes out. John's over in St. Francis Place."

Secretly Sam wondered whether Brian could have had anything to do with this. No, he told himself. Brian would flee from all of this, but he wouldn't talk.

WHNN cameras panned the inside of the Center now, draped in bunting and jammed with CMR supporters from all over the country. There were religious groups from Oroville and Visalia and Garden Grove. There were Moral Majority members from Phoenix, Arizona, and Elko, Nevada. There were Mormons from Provo and Ogden and Pocatello. From Boise, Idaho, and Birmingham, Alabama, there were staunch members of General Singlaub's World Anti-Communist League. There were people from Liberty Lobby and the Eagle Forum and from Christian Voice. All of God-fearing, drumbeating America was crammed into this center to affirm to the world just what was intended for this great country (and once restored to greatness, for the rest of the world). Legions of them were there, beaming, respectfully waiting, like the mannikins in the dioramas in the Mormon

Visitor's Center in Salt Lake, where the chosen multitudes, faces full of radiant joy, climb the steps through the clouds to heaven.

Here were book burners and record smashers and those who would cleanse the airways of the voice of the devil masking itself as filth and free speech. Here were anti-abortionists and creationists and those who had ripped *The Wizard of Oz* and *The Diary of Anne Frank* from school shelves as subversive and un-Christian. Here were white supremacists sitting in the same room as black ones. The people who supported prayer in school were here, as were those who opposed sex education. There were those who would snatch the children away from gay and Lesbian parents. And everywhere were those who believed the time had come for America to get really tough, to fulfill at last its moral destiny. By the time the President had been introduced by Walter Harrison, the crowd had worked itself into top form.

Jim got up, struggled to the television, and switched off the sound.

"Why did we even try?" he asked Sam, not expecting an answer. "Why did I try?"

It was to have been his last statement to the world. Jim, former professor at Cal, former Rhodes Scholar, hauled off to jail as he died from this disease. Now it would never happen. Good. Evil. Who was to say what it would have meant?

But whatever, it would have been a symbol.

"A symbol, Sam, of the strength of our camaraderie, of our brotherhood, that, even if smashed by AIDS, was strong enough to carry out this great action, to let the world know once and for all that we would be avenged."

Sam was silent. On the screen, the President pontificated silently. There was no need to hear his words, his expression said it all: self-congratulation, adulating praise, and pious judgment from a confined mind. He seemed to speak from the shadows and to them, whatever the spotlights, however perfectly focused the WHNN cameras (that deliberately avoided the tiny mole on the left side of the presidential neck). And as he spoke, his words, even these silent ones in this Guerrero Street living room, created even deeper shadows that seemed to loom about and over him.

"Remember Sam. October 1987. The March on Washington. You and I and Gregg were there. How strong we were."

Jim looked visibly weaker. Fatigue from anxiety had clearly set in. He had started to cry, the tears glistening on the violet-black lesions of his cheeks. He broke into a prolonged session of coughs, hacking, bitter, desperate.

"You know, Sam," he said when he had finished coughing. He was exhausted by the coughing and he spoke faintly and with difficulty.

Sam had tears in his own eyes now.

"You know, Sam," he repeated. "I don't believe Brian really did anything. His heart's too good."

Sam got up from the armchair and walked over to the couch. He put his arm about Jim and pulled him close.

"There could be other things that went wrong, Sam. Suppose the army checked out all the apartments about Moscone Center and found Gregg? We had little contingency against that. Suppose the gun broke? Suppose Gregg—"

He stopped in midsentence. Sam pulled him closer and stroked his hand reassuringly.

"We had to try!" Jim continued. "They laughed at us all, even under their supposed sympathy. They said we deserved it. They said all we cared about was sex and fun. They said we had no bonds between us, we just fucked and forgot. We had to show them. We're together and we're as strong as we ever were."

Sam said nothing, he just held Jim firmly to show that he shared his convictions.

"Oh, you can say there's another chance," Jim continued. "John will get him when he leaves from the north-side or the back-side exit. But it won't happen, you'll see."

"We tried, buddy, we love each other and we tried," Sam said.

There was no answer. Only the President on the screen proudly mouthing hollow judgments. Jim's mind had settled into quietness. He could glimpse dark waters, flowing slowly. Somewhere out there was the sound of a boat. He would step out of this shell and into the boat perhaps.

And Jim was right. The Presidential party left as it came, unexpectedly, by way of the front door. The motorcade retraced its route up Howard Street, and by two o'clock the President had arrived by helicopter at a friend's ranch outside Fresno. Here, he would share barbecue and prepare for tomorrow's meetings of NATO representatives, whether or not they were reduced in number.

56 *Civic Center Plaza, San Francisco, Sunday Morning*

Allan, standing outside City Hall, was feeling alone. There was a gap in his life. He wasn't certain how that gap had got there, but it had. Over the past half hour that vacant feeling had expanded. There was something lonely about it, an isolated, regretful feeling that comes from losing a chance that will never come back. Allan had been there with the Mayor. He supported her. They all had to stand together, especially now. But as the Mayor had spoken, and the gap within him had grown, full of consuming emptiness, Allan had wondered whether he could ever support another cause again. It was as if his will to fight had dried up.

Was it simply the news from the Deputy Chief of Police that the President had come and gone from the city unscathed? Outwardly, he had told the Deputy Chief that he was pleased. Inwardly, he was even more disconcerted.

More than anything, he wanted to be with Gregg, to kiss him deeply. Something told Allan that would never happen. This thought upset him. Or was it just that whatever Gregg's plans, they had obviously failed. Was Allan upset that something hadn't happened? Maybe it was all paranoid imagination that Gregg had been up to something in the first place.

Allan looked across the scattered debris from Friday's rally and riot. He could just see the charred walls of the Federal Building, like the ruins of some oversized mansion. They probably wouldn't need the building by the end of the next few months anyway. Still, he couldn't get excited.

He was standing alone. No Christine. No press. Just Allan, facing reality. He would win his election, but that was no consolation. He wanted Gregg. Gregg would never believe him anymore. He wanted to hold Gregg. Gregg would reject him. And it was Allan's fault. The air was still and empty. Somewhere uphill bells rang solemnly. In celebration of the President's safe visit? No, of course not. It was Sunday, and people were still going to church. CMR would have lots of prayers as well. Allan felt bitter and empty and tired. There had to be a way. Gregg couldn't reject Allan's love. But he would.

Causes. What the hell were causes worth in this world? He'd given over big chunks of his life to them. He had embraced them as passionately as he had pushed away

Gregg. They needed him, the causes and their people, more than anything else now, just as he needed Gregg.

The bells stopped. Disturbed pigeons rose from the plaza where a solitary civic worker attacked the litter.

A week from now, the new proposal would be made public. A special ballot measure for the secession of San Francisco along with whatever parts of California wanted to follow. It would pass here. They would leave the United States and form a new republic. Berkeley would join them for sure. Maybe even Marin and Oakland. It was the dream child of a coalition of liberals, minorities, and environmentalists. Allan had been among them. It might lead to bloodshed, reoccupation by the army. But he couldn't get excited about any of it. There was this gap in his life, and it was growing.

57 *Spring Valley, Maryland, Sunday Morning*

Jo-Lyn watched the whole affair. She saw the President arrive and caught a glimpse of the demonstrators. She saw him being introduced to a tumultuous CMR audience. She saw him speak to CMR but address himself to the nation. She saw him leave, safely. She saw Jimmy Johnson as he seemed to breathe a sigh of relief and praised the fine security. (Everyone seemed to have presumed that if something crazy were to happen in San Francisco, it would happen in connection with CMR.)

In better times, Jo-Lyn's spirit would have soared. So many of her heros were present at that rally and they spoke her deepest-held beliefs. But things were not right. Today, it all seemed phony.

She put down the revolver and went to pick up Carolyn from her bassinet. She brought Carolyn back to the couch and sat down with determination. She seemed to make up her mind. Jo-Lyn picked up the revolver and slipped it into Carolyn's swaddling robes. Yes, that was how they would do it.

It seemed almost certain now, that little Carolyn had been sent for this special purpose. He would get what he deserved.

Oh, how difficult is the battle one must fight, the good battle, the Lord's battle. She saw the face of Lieutenant-Colonel Oliver North. Oh how she had admired him, his bravery for God and country. But for all her admiration, she had never believed that she, Jo-Lyn, would suffer similar stings of betrayal from the men who had set this thing up, encouraged it, but now refused to support their players. She must give her husband and the men about him the necessary support. There were principles involved. There was the honor of America. There were God's higher laws. The traitor must not be allowed to continue his acts. To allow him to do so would only perpetuate a chain of future betrayals.

Secretly, Jo-Lyn had hoped it would all happen in California, but that was fear for herself. Now she realized that if it had, it would have been done by the wrong people making the wrong statement. Perhaps even her brother would have been involved. Everyone knew that the commies and liberal queers foamed at their mouths and were in it together. What else was new? But the world also had to know that God was angry. Yes, Jo-Lyn thought, the gun tucked into little Carolyn's robes. Perhaps she should sew a pocket in there so that it was held firmly in place. Then, on Tuesday, as she so often did, she and Carolyn would join the welcoming contingent at Andrews Air Base, one of the few places where a screened public was yet allowed to see the President.

Jo-Lyn clutched little Carolyn tightly, so tightly that she whimpered. Oh God, she pleaded, at first in thought, and then verbally. "Oh God, that this thing would not have to happen as it must. Oh God, that we could live in a kinder, gentler world. Oh God, that our world could be based not on fear and vengeance but on goodness, love, and trust."

These are such simple desires, she thought, and hardly unreasonable. Truth. Goodness. Love. Could she ever be at peace with herself and the world at peace with her? Could she ever heal the hurts she had suffered? Was the only peace to be found in Heaven?

"Oh Carolyn," she murmured. "It's a difficult world, but we must do what God wills. I'm so glad you're here to help me."

58 *Guerrero Street, San Francisco, Late Sunday Morning*

Sam sat with Jim's head in his lap, his dead body stretched out along the couch. Beneath his scarred face, Jim finally looked relaxed — that sort of relaxation that commonly happened, long ago, after a session in the playroom. Sam was happy that Jim had found his release, but he was sad that Jim had departed. For how long, and in what intricate detail, had the two known each other? Those were things beyond measure. Jim had never really been an outdoorsman, but years ago he had come north to Oregon and Sam and he had rafted the Rogue together, camping nights under the redwoods and Sitka spruce, talking of old times, listening to the rushing waters. They had even discovered they were from the same state, born within thirty miles of one another. It would be even closer when they died.

Sam wondered if having Brian here would help. No, it wouldn't, he told himself. Brian, as the living, would only distract. Jim and he were alone, together, the two of them. Buddies who had shared dreams of love and friendship and God. He and his buddy Jim. All the things they had shared together, cared for together, hoped for. God's gentle warriors. They were as much that as any of the Christians wanted to tell them otherwise. They too believed in justice and peace. But would justice ever be done? Sam looked at Jim, and despite a conscious revulsion, leaned over and kissed his disfigured lips.

In a sweet black void, Gregg was drifting, listening to birdsong. Dawn was near. There was that creaking again, like the strain of rigging in the wind, like the heavy passage of the hours, like the back and forth of a weighted sling.

He saw an abrupt flash of light. There was gunshot. He saw faces, women and children screaming. Bone-faced men looked on, unbelieving. People were rushing to break through security, to help. There was a woman's face. She clutched a child in swaddling robes and with dazed eyes she looked aghast at herself. She had dropped the gun.

Gregg saw the dismay grow in her face. He knew her, instantly, but it didn't matter anymore.

The visions faded into blackness and gentle birdsong. The strange creaking sound came nearer. He was feeling comfortable with himself. He was feeling good.

59 *Vulcan's Stairway, San Francisco, Sunday Noon*

In the city where buses go to Persia, a man of dreams stands at the window looking across Eureka Valley.

Outside, the November sky is crisp and implacably blue. Another lull between these waves of tropical storms and there is no sign of fog. Behind him, a man dozes peacefully in the bed.

Somewhere nearby an owl hoots at the full daylight: short, rich tones that seem to echo on themselves. The owl is a good omen.

The dreamer gazes out the window, and up, and through. Tears of passage crowd the corners of his eyes. Across the city his brother is dying and moving on. Someday they will all move on. Nonetheless, it hurts.

Brian, asleep in the bed, hardly knows Gregg. It had been Sam and Gregg who had been the close ones. Brian smiles in his sleep. As far as he knews the ordeal is over. An hour ago, they had watched as the President left the Moscone Center unscathed. Then they had made love. A strangely symbolic sort of love in which Marc was Sam and Brian was Gregg and neither was neither. They affirmed old bonds and they made new statements. Lots of empty space seemed to be filled by that lovemaking, and Brian found himself curiously satisfied.

Now, while Brian sleeps, relaxed, Marc looks out across the city. Marc's mind shifts between the forest and the city, between views of Castro Street and tamarack swamp, between the leaning black spruce and the rollerina, who in cape and mask, his silent music feeding him from a walkman, whirls for an eternity at Sanchez and Market. The slowed traffic stops. The mind stalls. The owl calls again.

Marc's brother is dying and moving on. Tears roll down Marc's face, measured tears, one by one. His mind reaches out, touches, grasps for words that will cross time and space. Marc finds a word, then some more, makes a sentence from them. Wings. Dark waters. Flickering shadows. The poetry moves out silently. He knows Gregg can hear it. More words form, more lines, like the vague tracery of a road on a map. A grove here. A clump of oaks there. The shape of hills. The sound of warning in a bird-call. The scent of a strange flower. The danger lurking beneath roots. Slowly, as the words and the lines form, the map takes shape across the clear expanse of the horizon. More tears fall from Marc's eyes. He has made his map this man of dreams, and he has passed on.

In a city where a street called Java and another called Saturn run up the opposite sides of a hill, gasp breathless at the views, and just plain stop, a man stands at the window, smiling beneath his tears.

Marc laughs, Good-bye, little Blanche, he thinks. Years ago, under protest, a group of them had given Gregg that nickname. Gregg vociferously opposed feminine labels for men. Marc wasn't sure why. A fear in himself of losing something, maybe? A reaction against the public supposition that to be gay was to be femme? A refusal, when it came to himself, to be categorized? What did it matter now? Marc wasn't even certain where the nickname had come from, although he had an image of a jesting black trick Gregg had come home with late in the seventies.

The more Gregg opposed the name, the more he rejected it, the more it had stuck, especially when Allan had got wind. Reluctantly, Gregg had relented and the name had held.

Good-bye, little Blanche. Another sister on this terrible guillotine of life, this machine that kills so coldly, that slices with presumptuous accuracy, so disdainful of charity. Good-bye Gregg, Marc thinks once again. You lived life with zeal. You shared love and caring. From out of difficult times, you chose a good track. It took you back into difficult times. But you succeeded.

At a window in the city where one can watch the Sun God climb Mount Parnassus, lifting his train of fog up the hills as he goes, a man wipes the tears from his face and smiles in remembrance. The owl hoots one final time and sinks into silence. The passage has been made and the message given. It's time to go on.

Gentle Warriors

With a Ph.D. in Biochemistry, Geoff Mains works in Environmental Management in the U.S.A. and Canada. He has published many scientific and environmental articles for professional journals.

As a writer, he has contributed short stories for leading gay magazines, as well as written two books, *Urban Aboriginals* and *The Oxygen Revolution.* He presently lives in San Francisco.